Josephine Cox was born in Blackburn, one of ten children. At the age of sixteen, Josephine met and married her husband Ken, and had two sons. When the boys started school, she decided to go to college and eventually gained a place at Cambridge University. She was unable to take this up as it would have meant living away from home, but she went into teaching – and started to write her first full-length novel. She won the 'Superwoman of Great Britain' Award, for which her family had secretly entered her, at the same time as her novel was accepted for publication.

Josephine says, 'I love writing, both recreating scenes and characters from my past, together with new storylines which mingle naturally with the old. I could never imagine a single day without writing, and it's been that way since as far back as I can remember.'

For information about the Josephine Cox newsletter, please see page 453.

For automatic updates on Josephine Cox, visit HarperCollins.co.uk and register for Author-Tracker.

Also by Josephine Cox

QUEENIE'S STORY
Her Father's Sins
Let Loose the Tigers

THE EMMA GRADY TRILOGY
Outcast
Alley Urchin
Vagabonds

Angels Cry Sometimes
Take This Woman
Whistledown Woman
Don't Cry Alone
Jessica's Girl
Nobody's Darling
Born to Serve
More than Riches
A Little Badness
Living a Lie
The Devil You Know
A Time for Us
Cradle of Thorns
Miss You Forever
Love Me or Leave Me
Tomorrow the World
The Gilded Cage
Somewhere, Someday
Rainbow Days
Looking Back
Let It Shine

The Woman Who Left
Jinnie

Bad Boy Jack
The Beachcomber
Lovers and Liars
Live the Dream

JOSEPHINE COX

~

The Journey

HARPER

HarperCollins*Publishers*
77–85 Fulham Palace Road,
Hammersmith, London W6 8JB

www.harpercollins.co.uk

This paperback edition 2005
1

First published in Great Britain by
HarperCollins*Publishers* 2005

A catalogue record for this book
is available from the British Library

ISBN-13: 978-0-00-779670-0

Typeset in New Baskerville by
Rowland Phototypesetting Ltd, Bury St Edmunds, Suffolk

Printed in the UK by CPI Bookmarque, Croydon, CR0 4TD

For my darling Ken, as ever

In September 2004, I was honoured to be asked if I would officially open a meadow in memory of all the many generations of Brogborough families. It was so wonderful to see all the familiar faces who came along for the occasion.

This small, estate in Brogborough, where I first came when my parents split up, was a haven for me as a young girl. My husband Ken grew up there, as did many of our friends and members of our families.

For me, Brogborough will always be special. Memories of that magical place will stay with me forever, not least because of the people who have moved on or moved away, and are always remembered in my heart. Brogborough was where I met my Ken; it's where I grew and flourished; and it's where every member of every household was family.

I still have family there, and part of my heart will always be there.

I hope the meadow gives the children and families great joy over the coming years.

A big 'well done' to everyone involved, and a

heartfelt thank you to Tracey, Claire and Madge, for making me part of that very special day.

God bless. Love you loads,

Josephine

CONTENTS

PART ONE
January, 1952
The Woman
1

∿

PART TWO
Summer, 1930
Lucy's Story
95

∿

PART THREE
Onset of Winter, 1930
A Choice for Barney
273

∿

PART FOUR
Back to January, 1952
Mary and Ben
423

PART ONE

∼

January, 1952

The Woman

CHAPTER ONE

Salford, Bedfordshire

HE HAD SEEN them twice before, and each time his curiosity was aroused. Arm-in-arm, the two women would come softly into the churchyard, place their flowers, and linger awhile before leaving in the same discreet manner in which they had arrived.

Today, as his bumbling black Labrador Chuck tugged on the lead, the dog's nostrils twitching at the secret scent of rabbits in the churchyard, the women came again. He tried not to seem interested, but the moment they walked through the gate and passed him by, he could not stop himself from sneaking a glance. They acknowledged him with a polite nod of the head, then moved on, intent about their business. It was almost as if he was not there.

In her own way, each of the women was beautiful. The taller of the two, who looked about fifty, had long chestnut-brown hair, grey in places, tied back with a ribbon, and lovely golden-brown eyes, a smart though ample figure and softly rounded features. Today, the bouquet of evergreens cradled in her arm seemed to accentuate her beauty; though it was not a virgin beauty, for the crippling seasons of time and emotion were deeply etched in her face.

She walked with a stick, long and slender with bone handle and silver-capped toe. It was obvious that she was crippled in some slight way, though this did not detract from her air of dignity and sense of purpose. With her sombre bearing and her carefully-measured steps, she made a striking figure.

He knew they were headed for the same headstone, where he himself had paused many times. In the shape of a cross, the headstone was small and nondescript, yet the words written there were so powerful, they raised that humble stone above all others. The words, carved deep, read:

BARNEY DAVIDSON

1890–1933

A MAN OF COURAGE.
HE MADE THE GREATEST
SACRIFICE OF ALL.

Having read the inscription and been intrigued by it, Ben knew it off by heart. It had set his thoughts alight with all manner of questions. What had this man done to deserve such an accolade? What did the words mean? And who had ordered them to be inscribed? Somehow, he didn't think it had anything to do with the heroism of war. This Barney Davidson would have been twenty-four when World War One broke out – and no doubt the young man had played his part – but he had died well before the second lot.

His attention was drawn to the two women.

With such tenderness that it took him aback, the older one stroked the tips of her fingers over the dead man's name. Her voice broke with pride as she murmured, 'Oh, my dearest Barney.' In that moment when she lifted her gaze to the heavens, her brown eyes glittered with tears. So much pain, he thought. So much emotion.

He sensed that, somewhere deep inside, she carried a terrible burden. What was that old saying? 'The eyes are the mirror of the soul.' He wondered what sorrowful secrets were hers.

The man's discreet gaze went now to the younger woman. Smaller, with a neat, if slightly plump figure, her fair hair was bobbed to the shoulders, and even from where he stood, he could see that her pretty eyes were the deepest shade of blue lavender. He imagined that normally, those eyes were quick to smile – but not today. Today her concerned gaze was trained on the older woman.

The two visitors were sensibly dressed. Like himself, each wore a long coat and sturdy shoes, for the weather had been foul of late, and in places the ground underfoot was treacherous.

In the early hours of this January Sunday in 1952, ditches and paths had run high with the melting remnants of a heavy snowfall. By midday the wind had heightened and now, judging by the darkening skies, it seemed a new storm was gathering.

'Here, Chuck. Here, boy!' he said in a harsh whisper, and tugged on the leash, quickly bringing the dog to heel. In a burst of affection, the animal jumped up and licked him, nearly sending him flying. Recovering, he patted the dog, then set off for the lych-gate and home.

He was only a few strides away from Barney Davidson's tomb when the women left it and began walking on, merely an arm's reach in front of him. Slowing his step, he continued to follow, the dog plodding obediently at his side.

They were almost at the gate when the older woman's stick slipped in the mud and she fell heavily, seeming to twist her leg as she did so.

When her young companion cried out and immediately began struggling to bring her upright, he ran forward. 'Please ... let me help?' Sliding his two hands under the older one's arms, he gently hoisted her up. When she seemed steady, he let go, recovered her walking stick and handed

6

it to her. 'No real harm done, I hope?' he said politely.

'Thank you.' Her dark eyes appraised him. 'As you can see, I'm not as agile as I once was.'

A softer voice interrupted. 'Yes, thank you, Mr . . . ?' The young woman frowned. 'How can we thank you properly, when we don't know your name?'

His warm gaze enveloped her pretty face. 'The name's Ben,' he revealed. 'Benjamin Morris.' Holding out his hand in greeting, he was pleasantly surprised and thrilled when she put her small hand in his. Surprised, because he found her grip firm and strong, as though she worked with her hands in some way. Thrilled because she seemed to hold on just that moment longer than necessary.

Having witnessed his reaction, the older woman gave a pleasant laugh. 'My daughter Mary has a strong grip for a little one, don't you think?'

Mary tried to explain. 'It comes from gardening,' she said shyly. 'A few years ago our old gardener retired, and rather than take on someone new, I persuaded Mother to let me have a go at the job.' Her face flushed with pleasure. 'It's hard work, mind, but I love every minute of it.'

'Mary is a worker, all right,' her mother declared. 'When she's not up to her eyes in the garden, she works five days a week in her flower-shop in Leighton Buzzard, and whenever the chance arises, she's out and about delivering the flowers herself, driving the shop-van.' Tutting, she finished quietly, 'I don't know where she finds the energy!'

'A busy lady then?' Ben looked down into that bright lively face and wondered why she was not married. 'And may I ask what you do in this garden of yours?'

It was the mother who answered. 'She spends every spare minute she's got in it, that's what she does!' From the reproachful glance she gave Mary, it was apparent that she thought her daughter should be enjoying her life and doing other things while she was still young. 'She grows all our own produce,' she said proudly, 'and she's completely redesigned the garden, made it into a little paradise with delightful walkways and colourful blossom round every corner, except,' she glanced at the ominous skies, 'of course, on days like this.'

'Then it sounds like time well spent,' Ben commented. He wondered why it was that Mary spent every spare minute in the garden. Did she never go out? Was she never approached by men who would like to enjoy her company? She was such a fetching little thing, *he* certainly wouldn't mind the opportunity to get to know her better.

'Oh, but the garden is so lovely!' That was the mother talking again. 'She's even managed to carve out a number of little nooky holes – quiet places where you can escape the weather and enjoy your own company.'

The younger woman's soft voice intervened. 'I just thought it would be nice to have a quiet place where you could hide from the rest of the world.' Blushing under her mother's lavish praise, Mary made an effort to divert attention from herself. 'Do you like gardening, Mr Morris?'

For a long moment he gazed down on her, his heart turning over like never before. 'Why would you want to hide from the rest of the world?' he asked, ignoring her question.

Mary had not expected him to answer with a question of his own. 'Isn't that what we all some-times need?' she asked cagily.

He wasn't sure how to respond to that, so he didn't. Instead he went back to her original ques-tion. 'I farm,' he answered lamely. 'I'm afraid there isn't a great deal of leisurely time left for gardening, or much else.'

Her smile was appreciative. 'In a way, farming could be called gardening, only on a larger scale . . . don't you think?'

'If you say so.' When those lavender-blue eyes beamed as they did now, her whole face seemed to light up.

'Well, I never!' With a quick, mischievous smile on her face, the older woman reminded them, 'There's me badly injured, and you two exchang-ing pleasantries as if I wasn't even here.'

The pair of them were mortified. 'Whatever am I thinking of!' Ben exclaimed. 'I'm so sorry.' He had been so occupied with the daughter, he had neglected the mother, and he was ashamed.

'I must get Mother home.' With her eyes still on Ben, Mary shifted closer to the older lady. 'I don't know what I would have done if you hadn't been here just now.'

She had seen this stranger before, striding down the streets of Salford with his faithful dog in tow as she drove past in her van. Discreetly taking stock of him now that he was here, close beside her, she liked what she saw. Handsome, of manly build, with dark, expressive eyes, he seemed to be taken with her, and it was strange, but she felt oddly drawn to him.

'I'm glad to have been of help.' He wondered how he could sound so calm with his heart thumping fifteen to the dozen.

He glanced at the older woman and caught the glint in her smiling eyes; he realised she was taking everything in. He gestured at her ankle. 'From the look of it, I don't think you've broken anything.'

She nodded. 'It's probably just a sprain. Once I get home and put my feet up, I'll be right as rain.'

'It's best you don't put too much weight on that foot.' Pointing across the fields, to the rambling, white-washed house in the distance, he informed them, 'Far Crest Farm, that's where I live. I'll help you up there, shall I, to take a look at the ankle and see what can be done.'

Sensing their reluctance, he quickly added, 'Or,

if you'd prefer, I could nip up and get my car and take you home. It's only a few minutes to the farmhouse.'

The older woman thanked him. 'Don't think I'm not grateful.' She had a natural friendliness in her manner that warmed him to her. 'But I'll be well taken care of. Look there?' Gesturing to the long dark car that waited by the kerbside outside the church, she revealed, 'I have a car and driver waiting.'

Flustered, Ben apologised. 'Oh, I'm sorry. I didn't realise . . .'

'How could you?' Her smile deepened. 'I might be a frail old biddy walking with the aid of a stick, but as you see, I'm not short of a bob or two.'

Ben smiled. 'You don't strike me as a frail old biddy,' he remarked, holding open the lych-gate for the two women to pass through it. 'In fact, I imagine if anyone got on the wrong side of you, they might rue the day.'

The girl Mary had to smile at his comment. 'You're absolutely right. What you see is not always what you get.' She gave her mother a curious glance. 'Still waters run deep, isn't that what they say?'

The older woman nodded but said nothing, though her gaze roamed back to the headstone, and the name *Barney*.

He had been a man amongst men, she thought. A man of such bravery it made her humble. Even now after all these years her heart wept for him, and for the unbearable torment he had endured, all in the name of love.

'Oh, look! Here comes Adam now.' As the driver approached to help her down the pavement, she reached out and shook Ben by the hand. 'You've been very kind, Mr Morris. Thank you again.'

Leaning on the arm of her driver, she set off for the comfort of the big car, calling as she went, 'By the way, my name is Lucy.' She had taken a liking to this young fella me lad and, from the look on her daughter's face, she suspected Mary had done the same.

'Goodbye then,' Ben replied. 'Take care of yourself.'

'Not goodbye,' Mary said hopefully. 'I'm sure our paths will cross again.'

He smiled into her eyes. There was so much he would have liked to say, but not now. Maybe not ever, he thought sadly.

In a moment the women were gone, and he felt lonely, as never before. Retracing his footsteps to the simple headstone, he read out the inscription. *'He made the greatest sacrifice of all . . .'*

The words burned in his soul. 'Barney Davidson . . .' he mused aloud. 'Lucy's husband, maybe? Her brother?' Somehow he didn't think so. His curiosity heightened. 'What great sacrifice did you make, Barney?' he wondered.

Deep in thought, he almost leaped out of his

skin when a quiet voice said over his shoulder, 'Barney was Lucy's husband – died soon after they moved here. And as for the inscription . . . I've wondered that myself, many a time.'

Swinging round, Ben came face to face with the new vicar, the Reverend Michael Gray. 'Oh, it's you, Vicar!' He greeted the older man with a sheepish grin. 'I don't usually make a habit of talking to myself,' he explained, 'but I must admit, I *am* curious.'

'You know what they say about a man who talks to himself?' In his late fifties, balding and bespectacled, Mike Gray had the hang-dog look of a man with the weight of the world on his shoulders. And yet his smile was heavenly.

When he began walking towards the gate, Ben went with him. 'As you know, I've only been here a matter of a few months,' the vicar went on to remind him, 'but like you, I'm intrigued by that grave.'

'Maybe you should ask the ladies?' Ben suggested. 'I'm sure they wouldn't mind it coming from you – I mean, you being their vicar here at Saint Andrew's.'

Mike Gray shook his head. 'There have been times when I was sorely tempted to ask,' he confessed, and slid a finger round to loosen his dog-collar. 'Then I felt I might be intruding, so I thought it best to wait, at least until I know them a little better. They've been worshipping here for around twenty years, I believe. But of course, the war has occupied everyone's thoughts, and that tombstone is old history now.'

'You're probably right,' Ben replied. 'All the same, it's a curious thing, an inscription like that.'

'Yes. As you say, a curious thing.' The Reverend paused to stroke Chuck's glossy head. 'Our man obviously did something out of the ordinary.' His features crinkled into a wry little smile. 'It's to be hoped we might all of us aspire to great things before we're called.' Raising his gaze to the skies, he gave a long, deep sigh. 'Sadly, a lot of poor devils had to be heroes in the war, whether they wanted to, or not. The truth of it is, most of us simply do not have greatness in us.'

By the time they reached the gate, the men had covered every possibility. 'Maybe he saved a life by forfeiting his own?' Ben speculated.

'Mmm.' The vicar nodded. 'Or he may have shown true bravery during the Great War. Certainly his age suggests he could well have been called up to serve his country.'

Ben considered that. 'Could be.'

Pausing in his stride, Mike Gray glanced back towards the headstone, now dim in the failing light. 'Whatever that inscription means,' he declared soundly, 'we can assume that our Barney Davidson was a remarkable man.'

Hearing a scuffle behind a great yew that stood near the vestry, Chuck suddenly slipped his lead and raced off. While Ben called him back, the vicar had spotted a dark object lying on the ground. He stooped to pick it up. 'Well, I never!' He wiped off the smears of dirt and dampness with the cuff of his sleeve.

A knowing smile creased his face. 'This must belong to one of our ladies,' he said. 'Maybe, if you were to return this, you might be privileged to discover the true nature of that inscription?'

'Mary's mother must have dropped it when she fell over earlier. I would gladly deliver the handbag.' Ben recalled the young woman and those pretty lavender-blue eyes. It would be good to see her again, he thought. 'Only I don't know where they live.'

'Couldn't be easier. They live at Knudsden House – you must know the place,' the Reverend Gray prompted. 'I recall admiring it when I came into the village for the first time. It's that big Edwardian house, with the large, beautifully kept gardens. You can't miss it.'

Ben *had* seen the place. An architect by training, he took a keen interest in the buildings around him. 'Of course!' he cried. 'It's the one set back from the lane, behind tall iron gates.' He shook his head in disbelief. 'I would never have guessed they lived there.' Somehow, despite the elegant walking stick, and the chauffeur-driven car, he had pictured the women living in a large rambling cottage, with thatched roof and roses growing at the door.

The vicar remarked thoughtfully, 'According to my housekeeper, Knudsden house used to belong to the village squire; he passed on some twenty years ago, and the house was put up for sale.'

Taking a moment to recall his housekeeper's exact words, he went on, 'It was then bought by Mr Davidson and his wife. Their daughter Mary was just an infant at the time. They were a family who preferred to keep themselves very much to themselves.'

There was a silence as Ben digested all of this information.

The vicar added thoughtfully, 'For a long time they rarely ventured out. In recent years though, they have concerned themselves more with the community, and have given generously to any good cause; the daughter with her time and labour, and the mother with cash donations.'

'Hmh! For someone who knows very little about the family, you seem to have gathered a fair amount of information.'

'So I have.' The vicar had surprised himself. 'Don't forget, I have my spies,' he said wryly. 'My housekeeper comes from a long line of gossips who've lived in this village since time began, so it goes without saying that what she doesn't know isn't worth knowing. Mind, the dead are good at keeping secrets – and even she doesn't know the answer to the mystery of that inscription.'

When the Labrador bounded up, Ben grabbed

his lead and wound it around his wrist. He shivered. The temperature had dropped, almost while they were talking.

'And what about the daughter?' Ben asked. 'Did she attend the village school?'

'No. Mary was educated at home. A tutor arrived each morning and departed every afternoon.' The vicar's voice dropped to a whisper. 'It must have been a very lonely life for a little girl.'

Ben was thinking the very same, and his heart went out to her. 'So, as far as you know, she never made friends?'

'From what I'm given to understand, the daughter has no close friends, but she does get on very well with the two women who help them out. Elsie Langton does a bit of housekeeping. Her married daughter Rona works in the flower-shop. Mary is closer to Rona, which is understandable when they're at the shop together most days.'

Ben had heard the name. 'Is that the same Langton who keeps the smithy on the farm adjoining mine?'

'That's the father. He doesn't own the farm, I know that much, but he makes a reasonable living, what with his smithy and the market-gardening. The Langton family are closer to the Davidsons than anyone else in the village.'

'What about the man who drives for them?'

Again, the vicar was able to satisfy his curiosity. 'Adam Chives is an old friend of Mrs Davidson's who comes from Liverpool. He's a quiet, well-liked man who lives in the cottage next to the big house.' He passed the handbag to Ben. 'I really must stop chatting and be on my way. I'll leave this with you, shall I?'

'I won't be able to return it straight away.' Ben took the handbag from him. 'I've got hungry animals to be fed.'

'Of course. I understand.' Having worked all his adult life in rural parishes, the vicar was familiar with the way of things. 'The animals don't know or care what day it is, they still need tending.' He gave a knowing nod. 'Much like my own flock, eh?'

Ben examined the handbag; it was an expensive-looking leather one. 'I wonder we didn't notice this on the ground before,' he remarked. 'I mean, you could hardly miss it, could you?'

The vicar agreed, but just then he spotted a small, round person calling his attention from the lane. 'That's Betty . . . my housekeeper,' he groaned. 'No doubt she's landed herself in another crisis. Last week she broke the new vacuum cleaner; the week before that she let the bathroom sink overflow and nearly flooded the Vicarage.'

He rolled his eyes heavenward. 'The Lord only knows what kind of chaos she's been up to now!'

He waved a hand to let her know he was on his way. 'I'd best go,' he grumbled, 'before the house comes tumbling down round our ears!' His good-natured laugh told Ben he would probably forgive the housekeeper her latest mishap.

'What about the handbag?' Ben called after Mike Gray. 'What if it doesn't belong to them?'

'Then it will belong to someone else, I suppose,' the man turned and answered. 'But we won't know until you ask, will we? Just take the handbag with you. You can return it to Knudsden House, after you've seen to your animals.'

His wink was meaningful. 'Besides, I saw you and young Mary chatting, and if you don't mind me saying, I thought you made a right handsome pair. I'm sure she would be very pleased if you turned up on her front doorstep.'

Then he was away, rushing down the lane with a sense of urgency, following the small round person tripping on in front, shouting over her shoulder and seeming frantic about something or another.

Smiling to himself, Ben went on his way. A vicar's life wasn't as dull as he'd imagined. Then he thought about Mary, and his mood softened. The vicar was right: he and the girl *had* got on very well, though whether she really would be pleased to see him turn up on her doorstep was another matter altogether.

Away from the church-grounds and into open countryside, he set the dog loose. 'And don't go splashing through the brook!' he called after the big animal. 'I haven't got time to give you a bath today.' He had more important things to do. Uppermost in his mind was the proposed visit to Knudsden House.

Striding across the field, he kept a wary eye on the dog; when the Labrador took off after a rabbit, he called him back. 'Here, Chuck! Good boy.'

On his master's call, Chuck came bounding back, but was soon off again at the sight of another dog being set loose across the field. Seeing the reason for his pet's excitement, Ben let him have his head, smiling at the sight of Chuck canoodling with the smaller, prettier animal. 'Casanova! Chase anything in a skirt, so you would,' he said aloud.

Covering the ground at a fast pace, he drew his coat tighter about him; the wind was getting up, the skies were darkening and the smell of storm was strong in the air. He called the dog to heel, but by now he was nowhere in sight. 'Chuck! Here, boy!' He scoured the landscape, and called again, but the dog was gone.

Ben was nearly home now. Quickening his steps, he made for the top of the rise. From there he had the world at his feet, and the dog in his sights. 'C'mon, fella!' But Chuck was too engrossed in dancing after his fancy piece. With a sterner voice Ben caught his attention. 'Here, boy!' he bellowed.

With ears pricked and head bent to the wind, the dog raced up the hill and was soon close to heel. A few minutes later the two of them were hurrying down the path to the farmhouse.

~

'I'm off now, Mr Morris.' The old man came through the field gate and clicked it shut. 'I shan't be sorry to get home,' he told Ben. 'It's turned real chilly all of a sudden.' Taking off his flat cap, he scratched his head and looked up to the skies. 'I reckon it's blowing up a real nasty storm.'

Ben agreed. 'You're right,' he observed. 'Mind how you go and I'll see you tomorrow.'

When Ben bought the farm, old Les had been part and parcel of the place. Ben had never regretted agreeing to keep him on because he was hard-working and reliable, a real treasure; besides which he had a cheery wife to keep, and a lazy good-for-nothing grandson, who showed up from time to time looking for a handout, and though he was more trouble than he was worth, poor old Les never turned him away.

'I've stripped the tree-branches and brought them down,' Les informed him now. 'You'll find them all stood up at the back of the barn, ready for chopping. By the time you've finished, there'll be enough to keep the whole of Salford in firewood. Oh, and I've levelled that back field just as you asked – though you'll need a new axle for the tractor. If you ask me it won't last above another month at best.'

Quick to agree, Ben put a proposition to the old fella. 'I think it's time we had a new tractor altogether. What would you say to that, eh?'

The old man's face lit up. 'I'd say that were a blooming good idea!'

'Right then. We'll make arrangements to go and look at a few. Now get off home, Les, and take a well-earned rest.'

'I could stay and help you with the animals if you like?' From the moment he had shaken Ben's hand, Les had recognised the good in him. His first impressions had proved right, for Ben was fair-minded, caring and generous, and though he had never worked on the land before he bought Far Crest Farm, he had taken to it like a duck to water.

'The missus won't mind,' Les persisted. 'Just say the word and I'll be right behind you. We'll have that lot fed in no time at all.'

Ben shook his head. 'Thanks all the same, but I can manage well enough on my own.'

'I'm not past it yet, I'll have you know,' the old man argued. 'And it weren't my fault that the boar took against me.'

'I know you're not past it. And I also know it wasn't your fault that the boar took against you. But he did, and you were almost killed, and I'm not prepared to take that chance again.'

Ben didn't want to hurt the old man's feelings, but if he hadn't managed to distract the boar that day, Les would have been killed for sure. As it was, he suffered a broken leg and had been left with a slight limp. Ben still felt guilty. 'Look, we've gone over all this time and again, and I won't change my mind,' he said gently, then: 'Besides, don't you think you do enough round here already?'

'I could do more, if only you'd let me.'

'There's no need, Les. The arrangement we have works very well. We do the ploughing and sowing between us. I keep the hedges down, you bring in the old branches, and I chop them up. With the help of casual work when the harvest is got in, this little farm runs like clockwork, so let's not spoil a good thing, eh?'

The old man shrugged. 'If you say so, Mr Morris.'

'I do, but don't think I'm not grateful for the offer. I'll let you into a secret, shall I? I enjoy feeding the animals.' He grinned. 'They've begun to think I'm their mummy.'

The old man laughed. 'You certainly have a way with 'em, I'll say that for yer.' He pulled the neb of his cap down over his forehead. 'If yer sure then, I'd best make tracks. I expect the missus will have the tea on the table and the kettle already singing away.'

Before they parted, Ben assured him quietly, 'Les – you do know I could never manage this place without you?'

That brought a smile to the old farmhand's face,

for he was well aware of how Ben Morris had by-passed younger, stronger men in order to keep him in work. 'You're a good man, Mr Morris, God bless you.' With that he was quickly gone, away down the path, off to the village, and home to his darling woman.

~

For the next couple of hours, Ben was kept busy. He had a tried and tested feeding routine; despite this, it was not only a dirty job but a time-consuming one, too. There were two hundred chickens in the hen-house; twenty fat porkers in the pig-pens; the same number of milking cows in the small barn, and a small flock of thirty sheep in the big barn.

Feeding them all took between two and three hours in the morning and the same at night, and when they were let loose in the fields, all the barns and sheds had to be mucked out, ready for when the weather turned and the animals were brought back in again.

As he went inside the farmhouse, Ben gave a sigh of relief. He had fallen in love with the place the moment he set foot through the door. It was like a calm after the storm, a haven where he could lick his wounds and grow strong again.

The year leading up to the move had been the worst of his life. After leaving the RAF, in which he had served for three years after his training, he had gone back to his career as an architect. When the company went bust through financial mismanagement and shortages of some basic materials, he took out a loan to start up his own business. Sadly, it never really took off. He sold the premises at a loss, and found work with the local council, but hated every minute of it. His wife grew distant because there were no longer the funds to maintain the kind of life she wanted. Then his lively, darling daughter Abbie, by then aged eighteen, moved out of the family home and he had missed her terribly.

He hoped he and his wife Pauline would grow closer, and he believed this was happening – until he caught her in bed with his best friend, Peter. There had been a long and unpleasant period when he didn't know which way to turn. His daughter had been his salvation, but she had already forged a life of her own; she shared a flat with two other girls and had a good job, working for a tea-importer in London. Thankfully, the break-up of her parents' marriage had not seemed to interfere too much with all that.

The divorce had been a messy business, and the only ones to come out of it winning were the lawyers. Still, Ben was determined not to slide into bitterness, because what was done was done, and there was no turning back for either of them.

When it was over, he and his wife were left with enough from the sale of their family home to start again. She had gone to live abroad with her new husband, while Ben chose a completely different way of life. He was happy enough now. Perhaps happier, in a strange way, than he had ever been.

Taking a deep invigorating sigh, he looked around the farmhouse. There was a warm feel of history in this delightful little place. He could not deny it had its disadvantages, though they were small compared to the joy he had found here. The whisper of a smile crossed his features as he recalled the number of times he'd banged his head on the low cross-beams, and the wood-burning stoves caused more dust and dirt than he could ever have envisaged. The small windows were draughty, and when the wind drove the rain, it came right through the framework to soak the walls. The flagstone floors were sunk and broken in places and even in the height of summer there was a dampness in the air that got right into the bones. This was his first winter in the cottage, and once the better weather arrived, he knew he would have to put in many a long hour working on the house in between his other responsibilities.

Yet in spite of all that, he would not have changed one single thing.

As always, he went straight to the kitchen, where he turned on the gas stove, filled the kettle and set it for boiling. 'Now then, Chuck.' Going to the pantry, he took out a lamb chop and dropped it into the dog's bowl. 'You chew on that while I see who's been writing to me.'

Returning to the dresser, he picked up the mail which had lain there since yesterday. There was a bill for animal feed, a card reminding him to return an overdue book to the local library, and a white envelope with a tuppenny stamp and a small pink flower drawn in the corner.

'We know who this is from, don't we, eh?' He cocked an eye at the dog, who was far too busy enjoying his treat to worry about what the postman had brought.

Ben took out the letter and unfolded it, his eyes scanning the words and his heart warming as he read them aloud:

Dear Dad,

I've managed to get time off at last, so if it's OK with you, I plan to visit for a few days. It's been too long since we had a real heart-to-heart, don't you think? I'm not sure which day I'll turn up, but it'll either be next Sunday or Monday. If that doesn't fit in with your plans, you'll have to let me know a suitable date. If I don't hear from you, I'll assume it's all right to arrive sometime on one of those days. I'm really looking forward to seeing you. Meanwhile, take care of yourself,

Your loving daughter,

Abbie xxx

Folding the letter, he slipped it back into the envelope before dropping it onto the dresser.

'You'll need to look to your laurels,' he told the dog with a wag of his finger. 'Abbie's coming to stay, and when she's about, no one gets any peace!' His daughter was noisy, untidy and could be the most irritating creature in the world. More than a week of her company and he would likely be pulling his hair out. But oh, how he was looking forward to seeing her.

He was so excited that he cut his finger when making himself a cheese sandwich, and then found he could only nibble at it, though he swigged down three cups of tea and ravished the jam-tart made especially for him by Les's wife. In fact, she'd made him a whole bagful only the day before yesterday, and this was the last one. 'Sorry, matey,' he told the dog who had demolished his chop and was begging for a crumb. 'You've had your tea. This is mine, and besides, there isn't enough here to share.' Nevertheless, he was still shamed into throwing him a bite.

With the jam-tart all gone and the teapot emptied, Ben put on his work-clothes and with the dog at his heels, made his way to the yard where he unlocked the feed room. Here he laid out three large galvanised buckets; one for the chickens; one for the sheep and another for the pigs. That done, he lifted the lids from three of the drums and scooping out several sizeable helpings of food from each of them in turn, he filled the buckets to brimming.

Taking up the buckets, two in one hand and one in the other, he made his way over to the big barn. Knowing exactly when feed-time was, the sheep were already crowded round the food-troughs. On sight of him, they began pushing and shoving their way forwards. 'Get back! BACK, I SAY!'

Fighting his way through the bleating animals, he partway filled the various troughs, then leaving the sheep to sort themselves out, he climbed the ladder to the hayloft, where he threw down four slices of hay, making certain that they landed far enough apart for everyone to get a fair share without too much argument.

Afterwards, he stood at the barn door for a minute or two. Satisfied that the sheep were all feeding and seeming content, he went outside to the tap, filled the bucket with water, returned inside and emptied it into the two water-troughs. 'That should keep you going for a while,' he told them. 'Come the morning, I might let you loose in the fields.'

It was always a pleasure to set them free, for sheep were not indoor animals. Small-minded and built to eat, it was in their nature to nibble the pastures, get caught up in brambles and go lame at every opportunity.

With the sheep fed and set up for the night, he

tramped off to the undercover pig-pens. Here he went through the same procedure, but with a different and coarser food, for pigs were gluttons and required bulk. Ben was always wary when surrounded by the porkers. Weighing upwards of half a ton each, they were capable of doing a man some considerable damage if he got in their way.

The boars in particular were an angry sort when penned, as old Les was quick to point out to Ben at the first opportunity. 'I once knew a man whose prize boar drove his tusks clean through the poor chap's thighbone; crippled him for life, it did. So don't go messin' with them big buggers, 'cause if they don't get yer with their tusks, they'll have yer over and trample yer underfoot!' Les did not have to tell Ben twice. It was ironic that poor Les himself came a cropper soon after he'd issued that warning.

With the pigs happily burying their snouts in the troughs, Ben attended to the other animals; first the cows, then the chickens.

The cows were housed in the smaller of the two barns. The area had been divided up to provide eight large pens on one side and six on the other, with a birthing pen at the far corner. The beasts had more than enough room and as long as they were fed and watered and clean underfoot, they saw out the winter in comfort; though once the worst of the weather was over they, too, were always happy to be let loose in the fields.

The spacious chicken-house was a vast, open area, which gave the chickens ample room to run. At night they would either roost in the lower beams, or retire to the many small wooden houses set along either side of the walls. Sadly, some of the chickens fell prey to the odd fox who dared to burrow under the wire, which was dug in and around the entire perimeter. Thankfully it had not happened just lately, and Les kept a wary eye out for weak links in the netting.

A long while later, Ben made his weary way back to the farmhouse. At the door he kicked off his boots and overalls before going through to the parlour.

First, he made himself a cup of well-earned tea, then it was off upstairs for a much-needed bath. He'd lit the geyser to heat up the water long since. 'I can't be going to see the ladies smelling of pig manure and chicken-muck,' he told the dog, who simply rolled over, gave a long, shuddering yawn and fell into a deep sleep.

In the bathroom he turned on the taps and let the bath fill while he stripped off. A few moments later he slithered under the water and lay there for awhile, luxuriating in the warmth and thinking of young Mary, with whose pretty lavender-blue eyes and the way her mouth turned up at the corners when she smiled . . .

CHAPTER TWO

At eight o'clock that evening, Ben arrived at the front door of Knudsden House. Standing on the top step of the little flight of stairs, he fidgeted nervously before reaching up and knocking briskly.

The door opened and Mary stood before him. His breath caught. Divested of her heavy winter coat, she was wearing a lilac-coloured twinset and a pretty knee-length skirt. The light from the hall and from her, too, dazzled him.

Fumbling, he brought out the bag from where he'd been hiding it under his coat. 'I found this,' he said jerkily.

'It's my mother's! Thank you.'

The women had discovered the loss of the handbag once they'd arrived home. Fortunately, Mary had her own front-door key and could let them in. Adam had offered to go and look for it, after searching the car and not finding it, but Lucy had said no, not to worry. She felt far too unwell for any fuss, and the bag would turn up somehow. People round here were honest men and women.

'Won't you come in?' Mary asked now. 'I expect Mother will want to thank you herself.'

Accepting her invitation without hesitation, Ben followed her through to the drawing room. 'Is your mother all right? I mean, has she suffered any ill-effects from the fall?'

'She *says* she's all right. With Mother, you're never really sure.'

When Mary turned to smile at him, Ben felt foolish; like a shy young boy on his first date instead of a forty-year-old man of the world.

For what seemed the longest moment, she continued to gaze on him, her quiet smile reaching deep into his senses. Suddenly the smile fell away and, slowing her step, she confided in him.

'The truth is, since she fell in the churchyard, she hasn't seemed well at all,' she whispered. 'I'm worried about her.' Before she inched open the door, she confessed, 'I wanted to call Dr Nolan, but she won't hear of it.' A sigh escaped her lips. 'She's so independent – and stubborn like you wouldn't believe. But I'm half tempted to call the doctor anyway.'

'There's no use you whispering, my girl!' Lucy called out from the inner room. 'I can hear every word, and there'll be no doctor coming into this house!'

On entering the room, Mary was told in no

uncertain terms, 'If I needed a doctor – *which I don't* – there is only one I would agree to seeing, and he's living out his retirement in Liverpool. So we'll have no more talk of doctors. Are you listening to me, Mary?'

Reluctantly, the girl nodded. 'Mr Morris found your bag in the churchyard. He's brought it back. I thought you might want to thank him yourself.'

'Mmm.' Her reproachful gaze rested on her daughter for a second or two before switching to Ben. 'I love my daughter dearly, but she will fuss.'

'Only because she's worried about you, I'm sure.'

While he spoke, Ben was aware of how the room reflected Lucy's personality. There was the solid furniture, reliable and stalwart, and then there was the colour and vibrancy in the curtains and the rugs. On following Mary into the room, he had felt her life all about him, in the lavish bright paintings on the walls, and the many figures, sculpted in china and pewter – some in the throes of embrace, others dancing, with arms in the air and feet atwirl.

They reminded him of Lucy herself; mature in beauty, yet very much alive.

'She's no need to worry,' Lucy snapped. 'I'm fit as a fiddle, thank goodness – always have been.' Her thoughts went back to her youth, to the time she'd gone astray, and the consequences that followed. Good times and bad, when life was lived to the full, when friends helped you through and nothing seemed to matter. *And then there was Barney.*

Her heart grew sore at the thought of that wonderful man.

Mentally shaking herself, she told Ben, 'That's two kindnesses you've shown me in one day. So thank you again, young man.'

'It was the vicar who found it,' Ben explained. 'I simply offered to return it.' He liked being called 'young man', though in truth, he was only about twelve years younger than Lucy, and indeed, had a grown-up daughter of his own. His feelings for Mary, however, were definitely not those of a father.

When he turned to smile at Mary, Lucy was quick to see the spark between them. 'I dare say that's because you wanted to see my Mary again.' Her face crinkled into that same mischievous smile he had seen at the churchyard. 'Taken a liking to her, have you?' When she gave a naughty wink, he couldn't help but grin, despite his bashfulness.

'Mother!' Mary's face went a bright shade of pink. 'What a thing to say! Don't embarrass Mr Morris. I'm sure he was thinking no such thing.'

But Lucy took no notice. Addressing Ben, she put him on the spot. 'Tell the truth and shame the devil, Mr Morris. You volunteered to return my bag because you hoped to catch a glimpse of Mary, isn't that the truth?'

Ben laughed out loud. 'Do you always see through people so easily?' It was strange, he thought, how easy he felt in her presence. 'Yes, you're right. I *was* hoping I might see her again.'

'There! I knew it!' Clapping her hands together with excitement, the older woman said triumphantly, 'I knew he'd taken to you, Mary – didn't I say so? And here you are – you haven't even asked our guest if he'd like to join us for supper. Shame on you, my girl!'

'Shame on *you*, Mother, for embarrassing us both like that.' Even though she was elated by Ben's admission that he had been hoping for a glimpse of her, Mary was so mortified she wanted the floor to open up and swallow her. Whatever would Ben think of her now? She hoped he would refuse the offer of supper and make some excuse to leave straight away.

Lucy's instincts were meanwhile telling her that here was a good man, a fine husband for her daughter, if he were free. She had little doubt but that these two could make a fine, happy life together. Yes! Should anything untoward happen to herself in the near future, Ben Morris was the very man to take good care of Mary, for he reminded her of Barney, in his smile and his manner.

Lately, she had been feeling very low in spirits and health, and Mary's future had come to concern her deeply. Although Ben must be twice her daughter's age, and would have his own story to tell about his life and the reasons for his arrival in Salford, he seemed a kind and honourable man. She had already noted the hint of sadness in his eyes, and his beautiful artistic hands, not yet roughened by farmwork. It was time to find out more about him. She would start with the most important question.

'Are you married?'

'REALLY, MOTHER!' Horrified, Mary sprang forward. 'One minute you invite Mr Morgan to supper, and the next you're quizzing him about his private life. I'm sure he won't stay a minute longer than he has to – and who would blame him?'

Over the past few years, there had been several young chaps who had shown an interest in her; to her dismay, Lucy had systematically sent them all packing. Yet there were good reasons for this: not one of them was good enough for her, Lucy said grimly, and had been proved right when each one had eventually shown his true colours.

'Nonsense! I mean no harm. I'm just being my usual, nosy self,' Lucy replied with a stay of her hand. 'Besides, I should be old enough now to speak my mind without offending anyone. I'm quite sure our Mr Morris won't mind. After all, we need to know the calibre of the man who's crossed our path twice today.'

Addressing Ben she asked pointedly, 'Are you offended by my questions?'

Ben shook his head. 'I was married and now I'm divorced,' he said quietly. 'Not the most pleasant experience of my life, I have to admit.'

'And have you children?'

'A daughter . . . Abbie.'

'And where is she?'

'Abbie lives in London, where she shares a flat with other young working people. I miss her, but she is due to come down to Far Crest Farm next week to spend a few days with me.'

'That's enough, Mother!' Stepping forward as though to protect Ben, Mary told him, 'You're welcome to stay to supper, but you can leave right now if you want to, and I wouldn't blame you. You see, Mother won't stop asking questions until she knows everything about you.' Mary so much wanted him to stay, but it had to be his choice.

'That's OK. I might even ask a few questions of my own, later,' he said.

Lucy laughed out loud. 'Now then, young man. Will you stay or will you run?'

'I'll stay.' His mind was already made up. 'Thank you very much. Should I go home and change for the occasion?' He had an idea that Lucy Davidson might be a stickler for protocol.

He was wrong. 'You look decent enough to me,

so you can put that silly idea out of your head,'
she said. 'It won't take Mary long to rustle up a
meal for the three of us. Meanwhile, just make
yourself at home.'

'If you say so.' It was a strange thing, but her
brisk, authoritative manner was not offputting to
him. His instincts told him it was all an act on her
part. 'I'm grateful to you both.' When he and Mary
exchanged smiles, Lucy was thrilled. The more
she saw of Ben, the more she liked and trusted
him. He was the one for her daughter; she was
sure of it.

So it was settled.

Ben considered himself fortunate to be sharing
an evening with Mary and her mother. He liked
Lucy, she was a rare character. Though it was Mary
at the forefront of his thoughts. For some inexplicable reason, the young woman had captured his
imagination – and possibly his heart, though it was
much too early to tell, he thought warily.

He had been in love before, and it had turned
out to be a heartache.

After that crippling experience with Pauline, he
was not ready to throw himself in at the deep end
with anyone.

CHAPTER THREE

MARY PEERED OUT into the garden from the big bay window. Its light spilled out onto the lawn, where Ben was carefully picking his way along the path, looking at her handiwork.

'You don't need to send for Elsie,' she told her mother. 'I'm a poor thing if I can't organise a simple dinner for three.'

'I know that,' Lucy retorted. 'It's just that I want you and Ben to get to know each other, and you can't do that if you're in the kitchen cooking, can you?'

'Oh Mam, you're a devil, you are!' Mary couldn't help but smile. 'I know what you're up to, and I think you've embarrassed him enough, without trying to throw us together. If he likes me and I like him, then things might happen naturally, and if they don't, they don't.' Though she hoped they would, for she had not met a man like Ben before. He seemed so mature beside her former boyfriends.

'And do you?'

'Do I what?'

Lucy groaned. 'BEN! Do you like him?'

'I'd be a fool to tell you if I did.' Mary shook her head. 'Think whatever you want,' she said casually. 'You will anyway.' Her mother was the rarest and most wonderful of characters. She never missed a trick. When Lucy Davidson was around, there was no use trying to keep secrets.

'Where is he now?' Curious, Lucy stretched her neck to see out of the window. 'He's not escaped, has he? You've not frightened him off, I hope.'

Mary laughed at that. 'No! He wanted to see what I'd been doing to the garden, that's all.'

Lucy tutted. 'Silly girl! Don't you know anything?' Sometimes she despaired of her, and at other times she was proud of Mary – and proud of herself – because it meant that she had raised an intelligent, trusting girl who saw the good in everyone.

'What are you getting at, Mother?'

'It's fairly obvious, isn't it? He wanted *you* to go with him. Oh, dearie me!'

Mary would not admit it to her mother, but she had been sorely tempted to join Ben in the garden. However, there wasn't enough time. If the women had been on their own, a bowl of soup and slice of cold apple-pie would have done them proud for supper, but having invited Ben to join them, they had to do better than that. Mary was planning to cook some pork chops, and serve them with mashed potatoes and homemade pickle.

'You forget, I've a dinner to cook,' she answered. 'There'll be time enough later for us all to get to know each other.'

A familiar tap on the living-room door curtailed their conversation. Hurrying to the door, Mary drew it open. 'Hello, Adam,' she said, and hugged him. These past years, the small man had been like a father to her although, like the gent he was, Adam had always kept his distance.

Lucy's face lit up. 'Adam, come in. *Come in!*' Dismissing Mary with a wave of her hand, she reminded her, 'I thought you were away to start supper?'

'I was ... I am.' Looking from Adam to her mother, the girl couldn't help but wonder what was going on. Whenever her mother wanted her out of the way like this, there was usually something brewing. But then she was always involved in some scheme or another, bless her heart. It was what kept her going.

'Go on then,' Lucy reprimanded her. 'Adam and I have business to discuss, so be off with you.' She had been unable to speak to him privately earlier, when he'd driven her and Mary to the churchyard, and now she wanted a quiet word with him.

'She doesn't change, does she, Adam?' Mary groaned light-heartedly. 'Same old bully as ever.

Adam's fond gaze bathed the older woman. 'She'll never change,' he said softly. 'Thank God.' The same age as Lucy, he had stayed with her through thick and thin, and every inch of the way he had loved and adored her from afar. Lucy knew it, yet she never said. She felt a lot of affection for him too. But it was not the same deep, driving passion she'd had for Barney. That kind of love happened only once in a lifetime.

And yet in her deepest heart, though he had taken good care of her and showed her nothing but kindness, she knew that Barney had *not* loved her back in the same way. How could he, when his own dearest love was thousands of miles away, probably still yearning for her darling Barney and suffering bitter-sweet thoughts of this wonderful man, whom she had adored more than any other, and who for reasons she might never know, had broken her heart and her life.

It had been a tragedy; a cruel and sorry business that only the gods could have prevented – at least, that was what Barney always claimed.

'I'm sorry I had to use the key to let myself in,' Adam explained. 'I did knock a few times, but no one answered. You obviously didn't hear me.'

'No need to apologise,' Lucy chided. 'The key was given so you could use it whenever necessary. It was necessary on this occasion, so we'll hear no more about it.'

'It's no wonder we didn't hear you at the door,'

Mary remarked good-naturedly. 'Mother was too busy having a go at me, laying down the law and trying to fit me up with a man who was kind enough to return her handbag.'

'Dear, dear!' With an aside wink, Adam tutted loudly. 'Interfering again, is she? Mind you, I can't say I blame her.'

With her sound and wary experience of men, Lucy could tell the wheat from the chaff. Mary, on the other hand, was more trusting and less worldly-wise. The lass was not what you might call beautiful, but she was a good-looking young woman all the same, with a heart of gold and a great deal to offer. Adam had no doubt but that she would make some man a loving and loyal wife one of these days.

~

With Mary gone, Lucy bade Adam sit in the chair opposite her. 'Have you done what I asked?' she said in a low voice.

He nodded. 'I have. I drove straight up to Liverpool early yesterday and went to see him at his house.'

Lucy gave a long, deep sigh. 'Thank you. I knew I could rely on you.' Her eyes clouded with tears, she asked next, 'What did he say?'

Adam was reluctant to disappoint her. 'He was surprised to hear from me. I mean, it's been a good few years, hasn't it?'

She nodded. 'Nigh on twenty, plus there's been the war and all. And is he well?'

'None too bad, yes.'

'What was his answer?'

The man had no choice but to relay the truth. 'Sorry, Lucy. Much as he would love to see you again, he can't visit. At least not yet.'

Lucy was dismayed at the news. 'Oh Adam, why not?' Disappointment shook her voice. 'Why can't he come down here?'

Adam explained: 'He's been ill for some time, see – bronchitis and some sort of complication, like pleurisy. He's only now beginning to come through it. He's not as young as he used to be, think on. None of us are.'

Lucy nodded her understanding. 'He can't help being ill, I suppose,' she said.

'But he sends his regards and says you're to take care of yourself, and he promises to come and visit at the first opportunity.' Fishing in his pocket, Adam handed her an envelope. 'He asked me to give you this.'

Taking the envelope, Lucy tore it open and took out the letter, which she read aloud:

My dearest Lucy,

How wonderful to hear from you, after all these long years. I hope you are well, and that you're being your usual self . . . living life to the full, the brave young woman I remember from my days as a doctor.

I don't need to tell you how sorry I was to hear about Barney's death. Like you, I will never forget him, or what he did. When he begged me to keep his secret, I wrestled with my conscience but God help me, I could not refuse him.

Over the years, I have often thought of Barney, and his impossible situation, but I have never regretted doing what I did; nor I imagine did he.

Take care of yourself, Lucy my dear, and when I'm well enough, I promise I will come and visit. It will be just the tonic I need, I'm sure.

May I say, I was most pleased and surprised to see Adam Chives; your dear friend who, as I understand it, is never far from your side . . . as ever.

Best wishes. May God bless you both,
Raymond Lucas

Lying back in the chair, Lucy closed her eyes. For a long moment she remained silent.

'Lucy!' Adam knew she was bitterly disappointed. 'He *will* visit – he said so, and as I recall, he was always a man of his word.'

'I know.' She opened her eyes, which were bright with tears. 'Poor Raymond. I don't doubt he's had his own fair share of problems, but oh, it would have been so good to see him.' She paused, suddenly exhausted. 'Jamie . . .' she whispered.

Concerned, Adam touched her on the hand. 'Are you all right, lass?'

'It's brought everything back, that's all.' Needing to reassure him, she gave her brightest smile, and for the briefest moment he saw her as she had been all those years ago – young and vibrant; hardworking and so generous of heart.

'So tell me, Lucy, what was the real reason behind your need to see him?'

'What d'you mean?' Lucy demanded.

Adam knew she could be wily. 'What I mean is this: are you ill and not telling?'

'If I was ill, you'd soon know about it,' she lied. Carefully choosing her words, she went on, 'You remember how it was all those years ago, don't you?'

'Of course I remember.' Looking away, he saw it all in his mind's eye. He had often wondered whether, if he had been put through the same test as Barney, he could have been as strong. 'I remember it all,' he whispered. 'How could I forget?'

'And you recall what a valued friend Dr Lucas was?' Her voice shook. Oh, the memories! She swallowed hard and went on: 'I just thought it might be nice to renew an old friendship.'

The truth was, Lucy had other reasons for wanting him here, but she didn't want to worry anyone. Not yet. Although the doctors hereabouts were fine, experienced men, she could not bring herself to trust them for something this serious. If there was one man who *would* tell her the truth, it was Raymond Lucas.

'I'm getting older, Adam. As each day passes, the memories become more vivid.' She drew herself up. 'I need to thank Dr Lucas for what he did. I want to see him, that's all . . . before it's too late.'

Alarmed, the little man looked her in the eye. 'Are you sure there's something you're not telling me?'

'Such as what?'

Dismissing her question he asked, 'What exactly did Dr Nolan say to you when he saw you at the surgery last week?'

She tutted. 'I've already told you. He said I needed to slow down. That I was exhausted.'

'And that's all? Nothing else?'

Tutting again, Lucy snapped, 'Stop fretting! I've already told you, I'm fit as a fiddle – for an old 'un anyway.' She chuckled, 'If they want rid of me, they'll have to shoot me first.'

There was a lengthy silence, charged with things unsaid. The bond between them was deep.

Even though the passage of their lives was already well run, there was nothing Adam Chives wanted more than to make Lucy Davidson his wife. He longed to take care of her, spoil her, hold her tight when she was sad and laugh with her when she was happy. To be there when she went to sleep and waiting beside her when she awoke; to share every precious moment of her life. That was all he had wanted for a long, long time.

Lucy knew it had been on the tip of his tongue

to propose to her. She recognised the signs, the twinkle in his eye and the ache in his voice, and she had to disappoint him yet again. 'I don't want you worrying about me, old friend. You just need to remember, I'm no longer a spring chicken – and the same goes for you.' Sometimes her bones ached until she thought they would seize up altogether, and on occasions, when she had walked with her stick too far, her fingers curled round the handle and would not let go.

Reaching out, she took hold of his hand. 'I'm a lucky woman to have such a friend – the very best friend any woman could ever have.' Except for Barney, she thought. But then he had been more than a friend. He had been everything to her: friend, hero, lover, soulmate and confidant. All the men in the world rolled into one could never replace her beloved Barney.

Yet she owed this dear man so much. 'I could never have got through these past years without you.' She squeezed his hand fondly. 'You have to believe that.'

Gazing at her, his heart flooding with all kinds of emotions, he said gruffly, 'You know I'll always be here for you, whenever you need me.'

His heartfelt promise touched her deeply. 'Oh, Adam! So many secrets,' she murmured regretfully, 'so much pain. Whatever I do, I can't bring him back. I can't make it all better. Sometimes, when I'm in my bed with the sleep lying heavy on me, the awful memories come flooding back, and I think about Barney's loved ones.' She lowered her gaze. 'I *should* tell them, shouldn't I?'

Adam sighed deeply. 'You must follow your heart on that one, Lucy, my lass. I can't advise. No one can.'

'If only I knew whether it would make matters better or worse.' Her voice broke. 'God help me, old friend, I don't know what to do.'

'You should ask yourself: if you *were* to tell them, would it be to ease their burden . . . or your own?'

Lucy had already asked herself that same question many times. 'I don't think anything could ease my burden,' she answered thoughtfully, 'but it pains me badly, to think they may never know what sort of man he really was.'

Sometimes the weight of it all was unbearable. 'For the rest of their lives, they'll remember what happened; they'll think of it and the bitterness will rise. They can never see the truth. They'll see it the way Barney wanted them to see it.' She gulped back the threatening tears. 'That's a terrible thing, you know, Adam. It isn't fair to them, and it isn't fair to Barney.'

Weighing it up in his mind, Adam slowly nodded his head. 'You must do what your heart tells you, my darling,' he reiterated kindly. 'Like I say, no one can advise you on that, though once the truth is out, there'll be no going back. You do realise that, don't you?'

'Only too well.' The words sailed out on a long, quiet sigh. 'What would it do to them? Would they blame themselves? Would they blame *me* . . . or Barney? And could they ever find it in their hearts to forgive?'

With both her hands she grabbed him by the arm, as though clinging to him for support. 'God help me, Adam, if I make the wrong decision, they could be hurt beyond belief. And that wouldn't be right, because none of it was their doing.'

'What about Mary?' Having seen her grow up, he had great affection for Lucy's daughter. 'Will you tell *her*?'

'She will have to know at some stage.' Lucy had been giving it some thought for a long time now. 'I've agonised about what it would do to her if she learned the real truth about her daddy, but I've always known there would come a day when I would have to tell her the whole story.'

A look of pride flashed in her eyes. 'Mary is strong. What she learns will come as a shock to her, yes, but I truly believe that in the end, she might just be the one to hold it all together.'

For a moment, the two of them sat and held hands, united. Then, breaking the moment, Lucy let go and looked mischievously at Adam.

'Before I let you go, will you do me another favour?'

'Of course!'

'Knock on Elsie Langton's door and ask her if

51

she wouldn't mind coming back to prepare a meal for three.'

He chuckled. 'You old fox! You've got it all planned, haven't you?'

'Well, the two of them will never get together with him in the garden freezing half to death and her in the kitchen getting all hot and bothered. It's up to us old ones to show them the way.' She gave him a little push. 'Go on then! Fetch yon Elsie back and tell her she'll be paid double time for the pleasure.'

Standing up, he looked down on her with admiration. 'Consider it done,' he said.

She waved her hand impatiently. 'Get a move on, then! Don't stand there until Mary's up to her neck in potato peelings and cabbage. A whiff of that and our Prince Charming will be gone for good!'

Adam laughed out loud. 'Mary's right. You really are all kinds of a bully.' With that he went away at a smart pace, chuckling and jingling the keys to the big car.

Then he wondered once more about the real reason she had wanted to see Dr Lucas, and his heart sank. God forbid that anything should happen to her, for the world would be a darker place without his Lucy.

~

Reaching the smithy, Adam parked the big black car and walked up the footpath to the front door. Knowing how Charlie Langton was a bit deaf, he made a fist and knocked soundly on the door.

'Gawd Almighty!' Having rushed to see who was at his door, Elsie Langton's husband was none too pleased to learn the reason for this late visit.

'Can't you buggers look after yerselves for five minutes!' An old Lancastrian who had moved down south many years back, Charlie had lost none of his accent, and even less of his attitude. But he was harmless enough and there had never been such a dedicated blacksmith; besides which he always gave sweets to the children and was straightforward to deal with. You always knew where you were with Charlie, and after a while, folks had come to respect and like him.

Calling him inside he told Adam, 'The poor lass never stops! She's rushed in from the big 'ouse, got the dinner on the table, gulped hers down, and now she's upstairs changing the bedclothes.'

An ordinary man with ordinary needs, Charlie suffered from a nervous twitch in his left eye whenever things got too much for him. The more agitated he grew, the more his eye twitched, and it was twitching now like never before. 'Bloody folks wi' money . . . think yer can do what yer like wi' such as us!'

Being used to his ways, Adam took no offence. 'I haven't got any money,' he said loudly, 'and you know as well as I do that the Davidsons always do their best by this village.'

Charlie snorted and turning round, he informed Adam, 'Aye well, that's as mebbe, but I might like to 'ave the wife to mesel' now an' then. You buggers up at the 'ouse want to think o' that.' He gave the smaller man a shrivelling glance. 'Besides, I might be a bit deaf, but I've still got one good ear, so there's no need to shout like a damned fishwife.'

To Adam's amusement, Charlie grumbled all the way down the passage. 'She'll not want to come back, and I wouldn't blame 'er neither! If it were up to me, she'd be in the chair warming her feet by the fireside, but she'll not listen to me, so I'll not waste me time.'

Arriving at the bottom of the stairs, he raised his voice. 'ELSIE! It's the man from the big 'ouse to see yer!' Giving Adam a scathing glance with the steady eye, he bawled again, 'WANT BLOOD, THEY DO! YOU'D BEST COME AN' SEE TO 'IM, 'CAUSE I'VE OTHER THINGS TO BE DOING.'

Within minutes there was a flurry of activity from the upper level, swiftly followed by the sound of footsteps coming down the stairs. 'What's to do?' Round and homely, and looking flummoxed, it was Elsie. 'Oh, Adam!' Her first thought was for Lucy. 'She's not fallen over again, has she?'

'No,' he reassured her, 'it's nothing like that.

She just wondered if you might be able to come back with me and help cook a meal and clear it up afterwards.' Raising his eyebrows in intimate fashion, he explained, 'She's got a visitor – yon chappie from Far Crest Farm – and he seems to have taken a real shine to Mary, and —'

Before he could finish, she gave a knowing wink. 'I see. And she wants me in the kitchen, so's the two of them can spend some time together, is that it?'

He smiled with relief. 'You know her almost as well as I do, Elsie, and yes, that's the general idea.'

'And does Mary know what her mother's up to?'

'Well, she doesn't know I've been to fetch you, if that's what you mean. She's in the kitchen as we speak, preparing the evening meal. I tell you what though, Elsie, she does seem to get on very well with the fellow in question.'

Elsie was delighted. 'In that case, how can I say no? Mary is a lovely young woman and deserves a good man to take care of her. Is this man a decent sort? Only I've not met him to speak to. We exchanged pleasantries as we passed in the lane once, but he didn't linger, 'cause he was off on one of his long walks. Every morning come rain or shine, he's away across the fields with that dog of his.'

From his chair by the fireside, Charlie had seen their lips moving but heard not a single word.

'What's he saying?' he asked irritably. 'What's going on now?'

'Nothing for you to worry about,' his wife told him sharply. 'I'm off to do an extra shift for Mrs Davidson, that's all.'

'Oh aye, I gathered that much. An' how long will yer be?'

'A couple of hours at the most, I reckon.'

He sat bolt upright in the chair. 'Don't forget to tell the buggers yer want double time!'

'Lucy will give me that without asking,' Elsie replied. 'She's a good woman.'

'An' what am I supposed to do while yer gone?' The old smith looked like a sulky child.

Elsie chuckled at that. 'You can do what you always do, whether I'm here or not.'

'Oh aye, an' what's that?'

'Hmh! As if you need telling. You can lie back and snore, or listen to the news on the wireless and swear at the bits you don't care for. An' if that fails, there's always your precious crossword.'

He gave her a fond smile. 'Cheeky bugger! Come 'ere an' give us a kiss afore yer go.'

Adam thought this was all wonderful. The Langtons didn't have much in the way of luxuries, but they were content, and obviously still in love after all their years together. It was what he wanted for him and Lucy. But it wouldn't happen, and deep down he had always known that.

With the kiss deposited and her coat on ready

to go, Elsie was almost at the front door when Charlie came after her. 'I'll get yer bike for yer, lass.'

'No need, thank you, pet. I'm sure Adam will run me there, and fetch me back when I'm finished.'

'Oh no, he won't! I'm not 'aving that,' her husband retorted. 'I'm not letting every Tom Dick nor Harry run yer about. For all I know he might be a shocking driver. Like as not he'll get yer killed. *Then* where would I be?'

'Hey! I'm a good driver! I take Mrs Davidson and her daughter all over the place, as well you know.'

Charlie was having none of it. 'I don't give a bugger what yer get up to wi' other folks. Yer not driving my Elsie, an' that's an end to it.'

Climbing down the steps, he hurried to where Elsie had leaned her bike against the wall on her return home earlier. Taking it by the handlebars, he walked it back to Elsie and thrust it at her. 'For me, lass,' he pleaded. 'Do it for me, 'cause it would mek me feel content, to know yer were safe, on yer bike,' he sneered at the black car, ''stead o' being rattled about in that there ve'ickle.'

Put like that, Elsie could not refuse him. 'The trouble with you, Charlie, is that you refuse to catch up with the times. All you know is horses and bicycles.'

'Aye, an' that's all I *need* to know, an' all!' His

parting words were for Adam and his shiny, new car. ''Orses will be 'ere long after then noisy damned things 'ave 'ad their day.'

'All right, I'll go on my bike,' Elsie assured him. 'Now you get back inside and put your feet up by the fire. I'll not be long.'

With that she set off on her treasured steed through the chilly evening air, with Adam following in the car and feeling like a right fool; though he had to smile at what he thought was a comical situation.

CHAPTER FOUR

The first Mary knew about the arrangement was when Elsie marched into the kitchen. 'Right then, miss, you get off and see to your visitor while I crack on with the meal.' She cast an experienced eye over the preparations. 'Well now! You've already done the vegetables and got the meat sizzling away in the oven. There's not all that much left for me to do, is there, bar serve it and clear it all away. I'll make a nice drop of gravy, shall I?'

Caught unawares, Mary asked her, 'This is Mother's doing, isn't it? She sent for you. Poor Elsie, I'm sorry for all the trouble you've been put to. Wouldn't you rather be at home with your Charlie?'

'No. I'd rather be here, cooking for you and earning double time, than listening to my old man snoring his head off.'

'All right then,' Mary conceded, 'but only on one condition.'

'What's that?'

'Put a plateful out for yourself. There'll be more than enough, and if there's any left over, take it home to Charlie.'

'I will, thank you.'

Mary gave her a hug. 'Thank *you*, Elsie. I won't forget this.' Washing her hands and patting her hair, she asked the woman shyly, 'Do I look respectable?'

'You look lovely.' Elsie had always thought Lucy's daughter had something special. Though she wasn't beautiful, she had a spark about her . . . soft, shining eyes of the loveliest shade, and a kind of warmth that endeared you to her. 'Go on, miss . . . go and rescue your young man. I'll have supper on the table in twenty minutes.'

Mary found Ben in the summerhouse. All the lights were on, and he was sitting in one of the easy chairs, deep in thought. 'Hiding from my mother, are you?' Her smile lit up the evening.

Having been miles away, reflecting on his disastrous marriage and the years he'd wasted, Ben was mortified. 'What must you both think of me?' he said. 'I'm invited to supper and here I am, lounging in the summerhouse. I only meant to be a few minutes but lost track of time.' On his feet now, he smiled down on her. 'It's your fault, you know.'

'Oh, and why's that?' It was strange, Mary thought, how she felt as though she'd known him all her life.

He gestured towards the garden. 'Your mother's

right. You've done wonders with the garden ...
it's just beautiful. So many lovely hidden places.'
It wasn't hard to imagine what a feast of life and
colour it would be in the height of summer. 'If you
wanted to, you could lose yourself forever here.'

'And do you want to lose yourself?' Just now
when she came upon him unexpectedly, she had
seen the sadness in his eyes, and it touched her
deeply.

It took a few seconds for him to answer. There
was so much he could have told her, but that was
all gone now, water under the bridge as they say.
Besides, if he didn't let go of the past, how could
he ever have a future? Turning to her, he recalled,
'It was you who said there are times when we all
need to hide from the world.'

Her blue eyes shone with mischief. 'And here
was I, thinking you were hiding from Mother!'

He chuckled heartily. For a moment he studied
her upturned face, the full plumpness of her lips,
the small straight nose and smiling eyes, and he felt
a rush of contentment. If he let himself go, he could
love this woman, he thought. But *if* he let himself
go, he could lose his heart and be hurt, *again.*

He looked towards the house. 'Have you come
to fetch me?'

She nodded her head. 'Dinner will be ready
soon.'

'Do we still have a few minutes?'

She nodded her head again.

Taking her by the hand, he asked light-heartedly, 'Would you care to join me?' Leading her to the bench, he sat her down. 'Welcome to Paradise.'

For a little while they sat and talked and laughed, and when she gave a long, trembling shiver, he dared to put his arm round her shoulders, and like Ben, she was afraid, of her feelings, and of the future.

Suddenly their private idyll was shattered, when a homely figure came rushing round the corner, calling out: 'Supper's ready. Your mammy says you're to come in out of the cold.' Elsie chuckled merrily. 'I'm to tell you, she doesn't mind you canoodling out here, but she doesn't want you catching pneumonia, and if I can't persuade you back into the house, she'll be out here and she'll chase you both inside with her walking stick. What's more, I've made a big jug of creamy custard, and I'd like Mr Morris to enjoy my apple-pie while it's hot. It's a deep-dish pie, stuffed with best cooking apples and covered in pastry that'll melt in your mouth. It's only reheated, mind, but I made it fresh yesterday.'

Ben's stomach rumbled. 'Sounds wonderful.'

'I'm not one for singing my own praises,' Elsie declared self-righteously, 'but I do make the best apple-pie in the whole of Bedfordshire, and woe betide them as says any different.'

~

The evening was a great success.

The pork chops were succulent, and the vegetables done to a turn, and just as she'd promised, Elsie's apple-pie was the best Ben had ever tasted. Lucy had produced a bottle of wine and drank more than the others put together. She also did most of the talking. She told Ben about her hometown of Liverpool and got carried away with the memories – *though there was one particular memory she did not divulge.*

'What did you love most about Liverpool?' Ben asked, intrigued by her stories.

'Oh, the docks, and the Mersey of course!' Taking another sip of her red wine, Lucy savoured it for a moment, rolling it round her tongue and smacking her lips, like a dog after a bone.

Ben was ashamed to admit it, but he'd never seen the Mersey.

'Maybe you'd think she was nothing out of the ordinary – just another river flowing away to the sea,' Lucy speculated, 'but to the ones who've lived and worked alongside her for most of their lives, she's very special. She changes, y'see – from day to day she's never the same. She has moods just like us . . . dark moods, quiet moods . . . and after a while you get to know her, and you can't help but be affected, in a kind of magical way.'

She gave a long, nostalgic sigh. 'If you've never seen the early morning Mersey when she's covered in mist, or stood beside her when the moonlight dances on the water and brings it alive, then your life is sadly lacking.'

'I can see I'll have to take myself up there at the first opportunity,' he said obediently.

'Quite right!' Lucy applauded. 'Make sure you do!'

While Lucy and Ben chatted, Mary thought it amazing how well they got on together. But then, right from the start, she had felt comfortable with him. Maybe it was because he was older than her? Ben was so easy and natural, it would be hard not to feel at home in his company.

'Do you mind if I ask you something?' With her engaging manner and interesting tales, Lucy had commandeered him, though he hoped that he and Mary would make up for lost time together later.

'Go ahead, young man. Ask away.'

'Well, I was just thinking . . . if you were so happy in Liverpool, why would you ever want to leave?'

Suddenly the air was thick with silence, and Ben immediately wished he had never asked. But then his hostess answered and her manner was curiously sombre. 'Life sometimes gives us problems that we aren't equipped to deal with. So we run away . . . like the cowards we are.'

Ben was mortified. 'Oh look, I'm sorry. I seem to have opened up old wounds.' She had that same look about her that he had seen in the churchyard; a look of resignation, a sadness that was almost tangible.

Lucy, too, was mortified, for she had let them both see through her armour, and now she was afraid. 'It's all right,' she assured him hurriedly. 'I did love Liverpool. I still do, but I can't go back.' Her voice stiffened. 'I could never go back.'

Mary had never heard her mother talk in that way, and it worried her. From a child, she had known there was something in her mother's past that played strongly on her mind. Her own memories were unreliable; her early childhood often seemed tantalisingly out of reach. With Ben having opened a door to which she herself had never had access, secrets might come out and at last she would know what it was that haunted her mother so.

Turning to Ben she confessed, 'You're not the only one never to have seen the Mersey. I was born in Liverpool yet I can't recall anything about it.' She glanced at Lucy. 'Time and again, I've offered to go back with Mother, but we never have, and now I'm beginning to think we never will.'

Lucy smiled. 'Oh, you'll see Liverpool,' she promised. 'Maybe not with me, but you'll go down the Mersey and know the wonder that I knew as a young woman. Curiosity will get the better of you and one day, you will go back, I'm sure of it.'

Mary asked her outright. 'And if I really wanted you to come with me, would you?'

Lucy shook her head. 'No.'

'Why not?' In spite of her mother's emphatic

answer, Mary felt she might yet uncover the truth; until her hopes were dashed with Lucy's firm reply.

'Because I'm too old now. Travelling tires me, as you well know.' She laughed as she told Ben, 'We went to London on the train. Dear me! What a trial. All that climbing in and out, up and down. You wouldn't believe the traffic in the streets there, and folks rushing about as though it was the end of the world . . . It was all too much for me.' Sighing, she finished, 'No, my travelling days are well and truly at an end.'

With dinner over, they retired to the cosy sitting room. Here, although the hour was growing late, they chatted on; among other things they talked of the introduction in America of the first colour television. 'The mind boggles!' Lucy declared. 'Colour television, indeed! Whatever next?' She herself thought the wireless was sufficient – why would you need one of those big, ugly television sets?

Mostly they talked about the grave illness of King George. 'He has been a good King,' Ben said. 'He'll be sadly missed.'

Mary had her say and it was this. 'You're right. He will be missed, but his daughter Elizabeth will make a wonderful Queen.' And without hesitation, the other two readily agreed.

'Right!' After tapping on the door, Elsie showed her face. 'I'll be off now. I've washed the dinner things and cleared them away. I'll see you in the morning.'

'Thank you, Elsie.' Lucy was fond of that dear woman. 'Off you go and put your feet up.'

Elsie chuckled. 'Hmh! Chance would be a fine thing.'

Mary excused herself and saw Elsie out. When she returned to the sitting room, she saw how tired her mother seemed. 'I think it's time you went to bed,' she said affectionately.

'Nonsense!' Lucy was bone-tired, though she would never admit it. 'I'm getting to know our new friend,' she said. 'The more I learn about him, the more I like him.'

Ben laughed. 'I'm flattered,' he told her, 'but I have to agree with your daughter, and then there's that business of you falling and hurting yourself in the churchyard. It's been a long, heavy day and no one would blame you if you wanted to rest now.'

He had noticed how every now and then she would close her eyes and relax into the chair, and occasionally she would fitfully rub her hands together, as though fighting some inner demon.

'I see!' Looking from one to the other, Lucy smiled wickedly. 'Trying to get rid of the old biddy so the two of you can be alone – is that it?' Mary smiled, but in fact, she had been concerned about her mother these past months. She seemed to have grown frail, and less mobile, though she would not hear of seeing a specialist.

Changing the subject completely, Lucy told Mary, 'I think I'm ready for a nice cup of tea. What about you, Ben?'

'Sounds good to me, thank you,' he said, swallowing a yawn. It was high time he was in bed, too. The animals would be waiting to be fed at dawn.

'Go on, then! Get the kettle on, Mary, before we all die of thirst, and don't bring the teapot, there's a good girl . . . too much fuss and ceremony. Just pour three cups, that'll do.'

Frustrated at her mother's insistence on referring to her as 'child' or 'girl', Mary groaned. 'All right, Mother, I'm on my way.' Turning to Ben she confirmed, 'One sugar and a little milk, isn't it?' She had remembered when Elsie brought him tea earlier.

'That's it, yes. Thank you.' He was surprised and pleased that she'd remembered.

'There you are!' Lucy chipped in. 'Already she knows how you like your tea. That's the sign of a good wife, wouldn't you say, Ben?'

'I'd say your daughter has a good memory,' he answered, and that was as far as he would go.

No sooner had Mary departed for the kitchen than Lucy was quizzing him again. 'You do like her, don't you?'

He had got used to her directness and thought it refreshing, but now and then she would ask a question that took him off guard. 'I do like her, yes.' What else could he say, when he had been drawn to Mary as to no other woman since his divorce.

Lucy seemed to be reading his thoughts. 'I know I can be impertinent, and I know what you must think of me, but I do worry for my daughter, and when I see how well the two of you get on, I can't help but wonder if she's found her man at last . . .' Her voice trailed away and her eyes slowly closed.

For a moment Ben thought she had fallen asleep, but then she suddenly straightened herself up in the chair and asked him another question. 'Do you think you'll ever get back with your ex-wife?'

Ben shook his head. 'It was a long and messy business, and now it's over, and so is our relationship.'

'And the girl?'

'You mean Abbie, my daughter?'

'Yes. How does she feel about you and her mother splitting up?'

To Ben, the question was like a stab below the belt, but he answered it all the same. 'It was hard for her – hard for all of us. In the end it was all for the best.'

'And is she an only child?'

'She is, yes.'

'Would you like more children?'

Ben smiled, a long, lazy smile. 'You mean, if I ever got married again?'

Lucy nodded. 'Of course! When you and Mary

get married, I want a whole horde of grand-children.' She grew wistful. 'A boy, especially. It would be wonderful to cuddle a little boy.'

At that moment, Mary returned with the tray. 'Here we are!' Setting it on the coffee-table, she handed each of them a mug and pointed to the plate of chocolate slices. 'Help yourselves,' she told them.

Over the next half-hour, the conversation centred on Ben and his farming.

'So you've found a new way of life, is that it?' Lucy was ever inquisitive.

'It's certainly a very different world from the one I knew,' Ben answered. 'As you said yourself, London is busy and demanding. I used to get up at seven, struggle into the office . . .' He had expected her to interrupt, and she did.

'What work did you do?'

'I'm an architect by trade.'

Lucy was impressed. 'And were you good at it?'

'Yes – or so I'm told.'

'And was it your own business?'

'It was, but I eventually went back to work for the local council in my home town.'

'Mmm.' She glanced at Mary, who was trying desperately to bring that particular conversation to a halt. 'So you're not short of a bob or two then?'

'Mother, please! No more questions, or I'm sure Ben will never want to set foot in this house ever again.'

Lucy addressed Ben. '*Have* you had enough of my questions?'

He gave her a half-smile. 'Look, I'll make you a deal. I'll tell you all I think you should know, and then there'll be no more need of questions.'

Lucy agreed. 'So, you were saying . . . you got up at seven and struggled into work.'

'That's right. Then I worked until eight or nine at night and struggled home again.'

'Hmh! It's no wonder your marriage broke up.'

'MOTHER!' Mary gave her a warning glance.

Lucy closed her mouth and listened.

Curiously relieved that he was finding it easier to talk about his troubles, Ben went on, 'One night I got home and found my wife in bed with my ex-partner, Peter. Apparently they'd been having an affair for almost a year.' He gave a sad little smile. 'So, you could be right. Working all those hours probably was the reason for my marriage break-up.'

Lucy couldn't help but make a comment. 'I hope you leathered him good and proper?'

'Oh, I was tempted, but it would have solved nothing. My wife wanted out, and I said yes.' Dropping his gaze to the floor he said in a small voice, 'I think the love had long gone, on both sides. By the way, you were right, Lucy. I am worth a bob or two. But that means little when your whole life has been turned upside down. I didn't want to stay in London, so I packed a few things and set off. I looked far and wide before I found this lovely part of the world, and now I'm settled and content.'

He laughed. 'I'm a farmer and proud of it. These days I'm up in the fields checking my sheep at five in the morning, and often fall into bed just before midnight, but I've never been happier in my whole life.'

He paused to reflect before ending light-heartedly, 'So there you are!' He smiled. 'I hope that's told you enough to be going on with?'

His hostess gave a long, contented sigh. 'Even *I* am satisfied with that,' she said. 'Thank you, lad. It's been a lovely day today, all due to our having met you. And now, I really must go up the wooden hill to Bedfordshire!'

CHAPTER FIVE

IT WAS STRIKING eleven when Lucy announced she was ready for her bed. As she got out of her chair, Mary handed her the walking stick and Ben hurried to open the drawing-room door for her. 'I'll take you up, Mother,' Mary offered.

'No, you won't!' Waving her stick at Mary, she ordered, 'You stay here with Ben. I'm perfectly capable of taking myself up the stairs to bed without your help.'

Knowing how stubborn her mother could be, Mary did not argue, but walked on with her to the bottom of the stairs. 'Leave me be, lass!' Lucy was growing agitated. 'Don't make me out to be a useless old biddy who can't even climb a few stairs.'

In fact, if truth be told, Lucy was beginning to feel the worse for wear. The wine, and the long evening, and her fall in the churchyard, had all caught up with her. Halfway up the stairs, she suddenly took a dizzy spell; aware that the two of them were watching from the foot of the stairs, she clung onto the banister and braved it out. 'Go on, be off with you!' she complained impatiently. 'You're making me nervous.'

Regaining her composure, she set off again, but when the dizziness returned with a vengeance, it seemed as though the treads were moving beneath her feet and the whole flight of stairs was spinning round. As she felt herself falling, she could only think of Barney . . . *and them.*

Mary's voice lifted her senses. 'It's all right, Mother, I'm here.' She had run up the stairs to catch Lucy's crumpling figure. For a moment, she staggered; her mother a dead weight in her arms.

Mary was glad to let Ben take over. Sweeping Lucy into his arms, he followed Mary's directions and took Lucy straight into her bedroom, where he laid her on the bed.

'Please, Ben, run and tell Adam what's happened, will you? He lives in the cottage at the side of the house – you can't miss it.' Mary wondered how she could sound so calm, when her insides were in turmoil.

By this time Lucy was shifting in and out of consciousness.

'Tell him what's happened,' the girl said. 'He'll know what to do.' Lately, she and Adam had been so worried about Lucy that they were ready for any event.

Startling them both, Lucy took hold of Mary's cuff. 'No ambulance . . . no doctor,' she pleaded.

'Promise me!' And she was so agitated, Mary could do no other than promise.

In a quiet voice so her mother would not hear, Mary spoke to Ben. 'Tell Adam . . . no ambulance, but he's to fetch Dr Nolan as quick as he can.'

Ben was already across the room. 'Don't worry.' Though from the pallor of Lucy's skin and the laboured breathing, he knew Mary had cause to be anxious.

Although it was midnight now, and the whole village was asleep, Adam was still up and dressed. On hearing the news, the little man was beside himself with worry. 'I knew something like this would happen,' he said as he bolted out of the door. 'I could see it coming, but like the stubborn devil she is, she would never admit she was ill.'

Climbing into the big black car, he asked of Ben, 'Go back to Mary. Tell her I'll be as quick as I can.'

He was as good as his word. No sooner had Ben returned to the house where Mary had got Lucy into bed and was now bathing her face with cool water than Adam came rushing in with the doctor in tow.

Somewhat revived, Lucy was determined to fight him off. 'I told you, I don't need a doctor. GET AWAY FROM ME!'

Dr Nolan was equally adamant. 'You won't get rid of me so easily this time, Lucy.' Having suffered her temper once or twice before, he had finally learned how to handle her.

Turning to Adam and Mary, he told them, 'She might co-operate more readily if you were to wait downstairs.'

Reluctantly they did as he asked, and as they went they could hear Lucy ordering him out of the house. 'Just leave me be! I'm not ill!'

The pair lingered on the stairs. 'Sounds like she's getting her second wind,' Adam joked, then glanced at Mary, his eyes swimming with tears. 'Do you think she'll be all right?' he asked the dear girl beside him, his voice choked.

The little man had never been afraid of anything, but losing Lucy filled him with terror. For the past twenty years and more, he had seen life through her eyes, laughed with her, cried with her, and through it all, he had loved her from afar.

The ironic thing was, in the same way that he had loved her, Lucy had loved Barney. Yet Adam consoled himself with the belief that she had a different, special kind of love for him. It was that which kept him close to her, and always would.

'I hope so.' Mary's thoughts were on a par with his. She felt sick to her stomach. 'She's fought with poor Dr Nolan before and sent him packing,' she reminded him, crying even as she joked. 'But this time, he's as worried about her as we are.'

Each wondering what the outcome of this night would be, they continued down the stairs in silence.

They were still silent and sombre as they came

into the drawing room. 'How is she?' Ben had not known Lucy long, but already she had won a place in his heart.

'We'll know soon enough,' Mary said quietly. She lingered at the door, her eyes searching the upper levels. *Dear God, let her be all right,* she prayed. *Don't take her from me yet.* Somewhere in the back of her mind she had always known there would come a day when she would lose the light of her life. But not yet, dear Lord. Not for many a year to come.

The waiting seemed to go on forever, until at last the doctor walked briskly into the room. 'She's sleeping now,' he told them all. 'I've given her a sedative.' His long thin face broke into a weary smile. 'She's hard work,' he said, 'but I got the better of her in the end.'

'What's wrong with her?' Mary cared nothing for his smile.

The smile fading, he took a moment to consider his answer. 'I can't be sure . . . I'd like to take a blood sample and have some tests done in the hospital labs.'

'What sort of tests?'

'Well,' he answered cautiously, 'she's unusually tired, and complaining of breathlessness: this could point to anaemia. She seems to have little strength.' The smile crept back again. 'Though she did manage to fight me off once or twice.'

Knowing how all three of them were hanging

on his every word, he continued on a more serious note, 'I'm a little concerned about her heart and blood pressure, but I can't be sure about anything until we do those tests. For that I'll need her to come into hospital overnight.'

At the mention of hospital, Adam turned pale. 'But she will be all right, won't she?'

Careful how he answered, Dr Nolan momentarily lowered his gaze. Lucy Davidson was a legend in this hamlet; despite her reclusive nature, she had made many friends and as far as he knew, no enemies. She was generous, funny, honest and outspoken, and he understood why these good people should be so concerned. However, at the moment, he could only make a guess at her underlying condition. She was ill, though. There was no denying that.

'Had she not worked herself into a state, I would have admitted her to hospital tonight,' he said. 'As it is, and because she's calmer now, there'll be nothing lost if we leave her till morning. She needs plenty of rest. Let her sleep, that's the best medicine for now. I'll be back first thing.'

'But *will* she be all right?' Like Adam, Mary was desperately seeking reassurance.

'We can only wait and see.' He chose his words wisely. 'I would rather not speculate, though I won't deny that your mother is ill,' he said kindly. 'She's very weak and, as you saw for yourself, her breathing was laboured.'

Before they could question him further, he put up a staying hand. 'Once we get her into hospital, we'll know more.'

As he left, he said, 'You may look in on her, of course . . . I would want you to do that. But she must *not* be disturbed. Rest is the best thing for her just now.'

With the doctor gone, the mood was solemn. Ben felt as though he was intruding, but when he suggested leaving, Mary persuaded him to stay awhile. 'I'll go and check on Mother. Adam can put the kettle on, if he doesn't mind?' The little man nodded his agreement and set off for the kitchen. Mary then turned to address Ben. 'We can all keep each other company for a while, unless you really want to leave?'

She thought of how he had come here to Knudsden House in good faith, to return her mother's bag, and had been quizzed relentlessly about his personal life; on top of that he had been made to think he was duty bound to ask her out one evening. Any other man would have been long gone, but she truly hoped he would stay; his presence gave her so much comfort.

'I'll stay as long as you like.' Ben did not hesitate. 'There's nothing urgent waiting at home.' He had only offered to leave out of consideration, and was delighted that she felt need of him.

'I won't be long.' While Ben went to join Adam in the kitchen, Mary ran upstairs and crept into her mother's bedroom. She gazed down on Lucy's sleeping face. In the gentle light from the bedside lamp, her mother looked so much younger; her skin was clear and smooth as alabaster, and her lashes lay like spiders' legs over the slight curve of her cheeks. Her long hair was loose about her shoulders and her wide, pretty mouth was ever so slightly turned up at the corners as in a half-smile.

Reaching down, Mary laid her own hand over that of her mother. She could feel the warm softness of her skin, and beneath the tip of her fingers, the blood running through Lucy's veins. Holding hands was not something she and her mother did all that often, so she felt privileged, and oddly humbled.

Choking back the emotion, she slid her mother's hand beneath the sheets and covered it over. She then stroked her fingers through the long greying strands of hair where they lay nestled on the pillow like silken threads; so soft in her fingers.

She gazed long on Lucy's face, her eyes following every feature, every shadow and shape, and all the while she wondered about her mother, and about her father. What had transpired before she was born? What was the secret that she had always known existed? And why had she never been told of her parents' true past?

Her heart turning with emotion and the questions burning bright in her mind, she kissed the sleeping woman and made her way back down-stairs to the men. Adam had brewed the tea and was busy pouring it out. 'She's sleeping well,' Mary told them, gratefully accepting the cup that was handed to her. 'I don't think I've ever seen her looking so peaceful.'

'Thank God for that.' Adam knew what a restless soul Lucy was, and unlike Mary he knew the reason why. 'It will do her the world of good to sleep through the night.' His voice fell until it was almost inaudible. 'If she's in a deep sleep, maybe she won't be plagued by the bad dreams.'

'What bad dreams?' Mary had heard his quiet words and they bothered her. 'Mother never told me about any dreams.'

Silently cursing himself, the little man tried to dismiss his remark. 'Oh, it's nothing,' he lied. 'I recall how she once told me she'd had a bad dream, that's all.'

Mary wasn't satisfied. 'You said she was plagued. That doesn't sound like one bad dream to me.' She knew Adam had known her parents long before she was born, and now she realised he was part of the secret she had never been privileged to share. 'Is there something you're not telling me?'

Sensing something too deep for his understand-ing, Ben wisely changed the subject. 'The fire's almost out. Shall I put more logs on?'

Relieved that the moment was broken, Adam

turned to him. 'I think it might be a good idea,' he said, and to Mary, 'if that's all right with you?'

Having believed that she was on the verge of a long-awaited peep into the past, Mary now felt cheated. 'Yes,' she answered, 'best keep the fire alive. I for one won't be going to bed tonight.'

Adam was horrified. 'You must get your sleep,' he told her. 'I'll stay here and keep a check on your mother. I promise to wake you if needs be.'

Mary looked at Ben. A man of few words, he had such quiet strength. 'Will you stay?'

He smiled on her, a slow, easy smile that filled her heart and made her feel safe. 'Of course. Adam's right, though. Your mother will need you to be bright and alert tomorrow. You'll sleep better in your bed.'

Mary would not hear of it. 'I'm staying here with you two. Three pairs of ears are better than one, and we can take it in turns to check in on her. Look – there are two big sofas and a deep armchair. We can all snatch a moment's sleep when we grow tired.'

She smiled from one to the other. 'Meanwhile, we'll drink our tea and talk.' She paused. 'The time will soon pass.'

~

While Ben and Mary sipped their tea and chatted about things other than the one which pressed on their minds, Adam became increasingly agitated.

By referring to Lucy's nightmares, he had almost betrayed his long-held loyalty to her. *'Mary must never know . . . promise me you won't ever tell.'* That had been Lucy's request to him, and though he had done everything possible for the woman he cherished, he had managed to avoid making an actual promise not to tell.

Somewhere deep in his soul, he truly believed that one day, Mary would have to know the truth of what had happened; not least because she herself was part of that fascinating, devastating story, for without it, she would never have been born.

Discreetly watching him, Mary saw how Adam was pacing the floor, faster and faster, until it seemed he would go crazy. She saw the panic in his face and the way he was rolling his fists together, much like her own mother did when anxious. And she knew, without a shadow of doubt, that old secrets were tearing Adam and her mother apart.

While she watched him, Ben was watching her. And just as she had seen the anguish and pain in Adam's eyes, he saw the very same in hers. Without a word he took her hand in his and, when she swung her gaze to him, he stroked her face, fleetingly. 'Your mother will be fine,' he whispered. 'You have to believe that.'

Mary acknowledged him with an unsure nod of the head. She wanted him to hold her, and kiss her, and be the safe haven she craved; for in that moment she had never felt so alone in the whole of her life.

Suddenly, Adam was standing before them. 'I thought I heard a noise – I'm sure it came from upstairs. Please, lass . . . will you check on your mother again? See if she's all right?'

Mary didn't need asking twice. She was on her feet and out of the room before he'd finished speaking. While she was running up the stairs, Ben grew concerned for Adam. Taking the little man by the shoulders, he sat him in the armchair. 'Here, sit down . . . before you fall down.' And when Adam was seated, head low in his hands and his whole body trembling, Ben dashed off to the kitchen and brought him back a glass of water. 'Drink this . . . it'll help calm you.'

By the time Adam had swilled down every last drop of the cool water, Mary had returned. 'Mother is fast asleep,' she told them. 'She hasn't moved, except to pull down the covers a little.' Lucy never did like being too warm, even in her sleep.

Adam grabbed her hand. 'Are you sure she's all right?'

'Yes, I'm sure.' Mary squeezed his hand comfortingly. 'Like the doctor said . . . she's sleeping soundly.'

And then Adam was weeping, quietly at first, until the sobs racked his body, and when he looked up at them he was like a man haunted. 'I couldn't bear it if anything happened to your mam,' he said brokenly. 'I love her, d'you see? I have loved her for a long, long time . . . and always will till the day I die, and even after that.'

Mary sat on the edge of the sofa, opposite Adam and next to Ben, but she did not let go of Adam's hand.

'Do you think I don't know how much you love her?' she asked tenderly. 'I've known it since I was very small. I've seen the way you look at her, and I've heard you whisper her name . . . talking to her when you thought she couldn't hear. But *I* heard, and I know how much you adore her.'

She had a question. 'Why did she not love you back in the same way?'

Adam was curiously hurt by her question, though he understood it well enough. 'She *did* love me . . . she still *does!*'

'Yes, I know that, but why did she not love you *in the same way?*'

He smiled painfully at that, a sad, lonely smile that made her feel guilty. 'We can't always choose whom we love,' he answered wisely. 'I didn't choose to fall head over heels in love with Lucy, any more than she chose to fall head over heels in love with your daddy.'

He gave a long, rippling sigh. 'And who could blame her for that? Y'see, Barney Davidson was a very special man. Not because he was handsome or rich, or even because he was exceptional in ways we mere mortals might understand.' His eyes shone with admiration. 'No! He was *more* than that. He was deep, and kind . . .' Hesitating, he gave a shrug. 'Sometimes, words alone can never describe someone.'

'Please, Adam, will you try to describe him for me? No one ever talks about him.'

Adam was shocked to see the tears running down her face and once again, was tempted to tell her everything. 'You never knew him, did you, lass – not really?' he murmured. 'You were only a wee thing when we lost him. He was my dear, dear friend . . . the best pal a man could ever have, and I loved him for it.'

Afraid of losing the moment again, Mary persisted. 'Please, tell me what you know, what you and Mother have always kept from me.' Her voice broke. 'I will never rest until I know what happened, and don't tell me there was nothing untoward in my parents' lives, because in here . . .' she tapped the cradle of her heart '. . . I know there was.'

Deeply moved, he looked into those lovely, tearful eyes. 'Your mother should never have kept it from you,' he conceded gruffly. 'I've always known she was wrong about that. I told her you had every right to know, that you were Barney's child through and through. But she was afraid . . . always afraid.'

'Afraid of what?' Mary gave a sigh of relief. At last she was getting nearer to the truth.

'I can't tell.' He looked from her to Ben. 'I made a promise. NO!' He shook his head. 'I never did make that promise. I thought it would be wrong, d'you see? I told her, "Mary will have to know everything one day" . . .' His words trailed away.

'Adam?' The girl's voice penetrated his deeper thoughts. 'That day is here and now. And you're right: I *have* to know, so tell me . . . please.'

Snatching his hand from her grip, Adam scrambled out of the chair. He paced the floor awhile, then took a moment to stare out of the window at the night, but he said nothing for what seemed an age. Then he walked to the door, opened it and went out, and from the room they could see him standing at the foot of the stairs looking up. His lips were moving, but they could not hear what he was saying.

Mary went to get off the sofa, but Ben reached out and, with a gentle pressure of his hand, held her there. 'Best to leave him,' he whispered. 'Give him time.' And, knowing Ben was right, she remained still until the little fellow came back into the room.

～

Upstairs, Lucy thought she heard something. A voice. *His voice.* Half-asleep, her brain numbed by the sedative, she called out his name. 'Barney!' Her voice, and her heart broke, and she could speak no more.

Restless as always, she turned. Forcing open her

eyes, and summoning every last ounce of strength, she stretched out her hand, and felt the hard edge of the bedside drawer ... Inching it open, she took out a long metal biscuit-box and drew it to her chest, where it lay while she caught her breath and recovered her strength.

A moment later she had opened the lid and dipping her fingers inside, she lifted out a photograph and a long envelope, yellow with age and worn at the corners from where she had opened it many times over the years.

Holding the photograph close to the halo of light from the bedside lamp, Lucy could hardly see it for the tears that stung from her eyes and ran unheeded down her face. 'Oh Barney, dear Barney!' The sobbing was velvet-soft. No one heard. No one knew. No one *ever* knew.

For nearly twenty years, she had kept his face alive in her heart and soul, but now, as her senses swam from the effects of the sedative, when she saw him smiling up at her from the photograph, it was as though he was real: the slight film of moisture on his lips, the pinkness of his tongue, just visible behind those beautiful white teeth, and the eyes, soulfully blue, and so sad beneath the smile; yet the smile, and the eyes, were so alive they twinkled.

It was almost as though Barney was here in the room with her.

The sick woman took a moment to rest, before

in a less emotional state, she studied the familiar and much-loved features: the shock of rich brown hair, those mesmerising blue eyes – not lavender-blue like Mary's, but darkest blue, like the ocean depths. And the mouth, with its full bottom lip. The wonderful smile was a reflection of Barney's naturally joyful soul; through good times and bad, his smile was like a ray of sunshine.

As he smiled at her now, Lucy could hear him singing; Barney loved to sing when he worked. She could hear him so clearly, his voice lifted in song and carried on the breeze from the fields to her kitchen. He never sang any song in particular. And when he wasn't singing, he would whistle.

Barney was one of those rare people who, without realising it, could raise your spirits and make you feel good; even at your lowest ebb.

Lucy's heart grew quiet. Times had come when Barney's song was not so lilting nor his smile quite so convincing, and there had been other times, though they were few, when she had caught him sobbing his heart out. She knew then, that he was thinking of past events. And with every moment of anguish he suffered, she suffered it with him, and her love grew all the stronger.

Over their short time together, Barney became her very life. He was her and she was him. They were one. Together they would see it through, and nothing would ever tear them apart. But it did. Death claimed him much too soon!

And when she lost him, her own life, too, would have been over but for Mary, and Mary was a part of Barney. She saw him every time Mary smiled or sang, or chided her.

And she loved that dear child with the same all-consuming love that she had felt for Barney. It was Mary who had been her saviour; Mary who was like her daddy in so many ways; Mary who had brought her untold joy.

Adam had long believed that Mary should be told about the events which took place before she was born. But Lucy thought differently. The little girl was an innocent and must be protected, and so she was never told.

But what of the other innocents? Dear God above!

WHAT OF THEM?

Weary now, she dropped her hands and the photograph fell onto the eiderdown. Too weak to raise her head, she felt about until it was safe in her grasp again, and then with slow, trembling fingers, she laid it down beside her.

Unfolding the letter from inside the envelope, she held it up where she could see it in the light from the bedside lamp. She remembered receiving this, one dark damp day in her little cottage up north, and knew that only the truth could put things right. She had read the letter so many times, she knew every word by heart. She whispered them now, the sentences etched in her soul for all time:

To Lucy Baker,

It pains us to put pen to paper, but we must. Word has come to us here that you are now living with our father and have a child by him. Because of what you have done, we feel only hatred towards you. Hatred and disgust! Lucy, you betrayed us! We thought you were our friend, our sister. We all trusted you, especially our mother, but you were a viper in our midst.

The day we left, we vowed we would never be back, and that vow remains strong as ever. We just want you to know what you and our father have done to all of us; and to our mother most of all.

You helped to ruin our lives. You are a wicked, evil woman, and if there is any justice in the world, there will come a day when you will both pay for what you did. We pray with all our hearts for that day to come.

We don't need to sign our names. You know them already.

We are Thomas, Ronald and Susan Davidson. We are your conscience.

Lucy shakily folded the letter away. 'Such hatred!' she sighed. Her heart ached for those young people ... for them and their poor mother, because of all their suffering. But they didn't know the truth. THEY DIDN'T KNOW! How could they?

Carefully, she replaced Barney's photograph into the biscuit-box, then the letter into its envelope. 'What am I to do, love?' she whispered. 'You said they must never know, but I feel I *must* tell them, even if it will be too much for them to bear. It is time to put things right, if God will grant me the time I need.'

Then weariness closed in and the sedative claimed her. But the dreams remained. Awake or asleep, the dreams were never far away.

~

Adam went over to the fireplace and stood there for a while, his arms reaching up to each side of the mantelpiece, and his head bowed. 'I'm not sure if it's my place to tell you,' he murmured.

Mary felt instinctively that she ought not to speak. If he was wrestling with his conscience, then she must not influence him either way. So she waited, and hoped, and in a while he turned round, looked at them both, and slowly made his way back to them. 'I think Barney would want you to know,' he told Mary heavily. 'I reckon you're right, lass, the time *is* here.' The haunted look had finally left his eyes.

'So, will you tell me now?' Her mouth had gone dry; she could barely say the words.

He nodded.

'And will you tell me *everything*?'

Mary knew this was it. At long last she was to

cross that threshold which, though it had never affected the deep love between herself and Lucy, had always been present between them. Excitement and fear mingled as she sensed the door opening to her, that secret door which had been too long closed, and she had no doubts that something wondrous waited beyond.

'I don't know if I'm doing right or wrong, but I believe the truth is long overdue,' Adam answered. 'Though I may live to regret it, and Lucy may not thank me for going against her wishes, yes, I'll tell you everything, sweetheart. I promise I won't leave anything out.'

Ben hastily prepared to leave. 'This is private family business,' he said. 'I have no right to be here.'

Neither Adam nor Mary would hear of it. 'Please, Ben, I want you to stay,' Mary told him, and Adam gave a nod of approval. 'I believe you should *both* hear what I have to tell,' he said.

The little man had a deep-down instinct that these two were made for each other. In the same inevitable way that Barney was woven into Mary's past, Ben was destined to be part of her future. He had seen her look at Ben in the same way her mother had looked at Barney, and tonight in Ben, he had caught a glimpse of his dear friend. Something told him he was witnessing the start of another deep and special love, and he knew that Ben truly belonged here.

And so he settled in his chair and cast his mind back over the years. Drawing on his memory, he mentally relived the story; of Lucy and Barney, and of course the others who did not, and could not, see the truth of what was happening before their eyes.

But Adam had seen, and it had scarred him forever. Just as it had scarred Lucy, and the others; though to this day, those others had not learned the truth of what happened, and maybe they never would. *Maybe the hatred and the pain would always be paramount.*

Adam thought that was a sad thing, because the tragedy that had taken place all those years ago had given birth to something glorious.

~

As the night thickened and the story unfolded, Mary and Ben were in turn shocked and uplifted, and the more they heard, the more they began to realise that their lives would never again be the same.

During the telling, Adam was at times joyful, then tearful, and when he recalled the awful sacrifice Barney had made, his eyes filled with pain. But above all, he was proud to be telling Barney's story.

Because, in his deepest heart, he believed it to be one of the most powerful love stories of all time.

PART TWO

~

Summer, 1930

Lucy's Story

CHAPTER SIX

THE SUMMER OF 1930 was proving to be one of the most glorious on record, as if to compensate in some way for the misery of mass unemployment on Merseyside. Today, 25 May, the docklands were almost deserted but the narrow, meandering backstreets were as busy as ever. Young children played; scabby dogs lounged in cool, shadowy corners; floral-pinnied women in turbans busied themselves white-stoning their front doorsteps, pausing only for a snippet of gossip as a neighbour passed by; and having emptied gallons of milk from churn to jug, the milkman was on his lazy way home, the wheels of his cart clattering a tune on the cobbles . . . *clickety-clack, clickety clack, drink your milk and I'll be back* . . . the children made up the song and as he passed by, they ran after him chanting the words, skipping away once he'd turned the corner.

Back down in the docks, sailors disembarked, glad to come ashore after being at sea for many months. Placards everywhere gave out the news: *British Aviator Amy Johnson flies from London to Australia in nineteen and a half days.*

'There you go, boyo.' The tall, bony man with the unkempt beard had been at sea for too long, and now at last, he was done with it. 'While we've been conquering the seven seas, that brave lady's been conquering the skies.'

'Hmh!' The younger man was rough in looks and rough in nature. 'I'd rather her than me, up there all alone. I never have been able to stand my own company.'

The older man laughed. 'That's because you're a miserable bugger, and I should know, being the unfortunate that had the next bunk to you.'

'What d'you mean? We got on all right, didn't we?'

'That's true – but only because when you're on a ship in the middle of the ocean, you've either to get on with your shipmates, or jump off the ship. And I for one didn't fancy being the sharks' next meal.'

'So where are you off to now?'

'Home to South Wales, thank God. What about you? Where might *you* be headed?'

A crafty smile flickered over the younger man's features. 'I've a woman to see.'

'A woman, eh?' The other man knew of Edward Trent's liking for the ladies, because he'd witnessed it many a time in port. 'So, she's *another* one you left behind, is she?'

'Whether I left her behind or not, she'll still be waiting for me.'

'You're an arrogant devil, I'll give you that.'

'I might stay this time ... make an honest woman of her,' Trent boasted.

The older man laughed out loud at the idea. 'Never!'

'Ah, but this one's different. She's full of fun, a real stunner. Moreover, she'll do anything for me.' He preened himself. 'A man could do worse than settle down with a woman like Lucy Baker.'

'Well, good luck to you then, boyo. As for me, I'm away to my beloved Wales. No more sailing the world's oceans for me. I'm finished with all that.'

'So, what will you do? There's mass unemployment, you know. It may not be much of a picnic in your part of the world, matey.'

'That won't bother me.' The older man took a deep, gratifying breath, and when he released it, the answer came with it. 'I've not made up my mind yet, but what I do know is this: I'll spend my days as I please, tending my bit of land and fishing, and not be driven by money and command. I've worked hard and saved my wages, and God willing, you'll not see me again.' With that he threw his kitbag over his shoulder and strode off, with never a look back.

Watching him go, the other man laughed under his breath. 'That's what they all say,' he sneered, 'and you're no different from the rest.' Dark-haired, dark-eyed and with a heart to match, Edward Trent was a regular Jack the Lad who fancied he should please every woman he came across, and he had done just that, in every port across the world.

We're *both* going fishing, he thought as he walked on. I'll leave you to catch the ones with the tails, Taffy Evans, while I settle for the others – the ones that pretend to fight you off when all they really want is for you to catch 'em and show 'em a good time.

As he left the docks and headed towards the nearest lodging-house, he had only one woman on his mind: a young and spritely thing, with long flowing hair and a smile that could melt a man's heart from a mile off. 'You're a lucky girl, Lucy Baker!' he chuckled. He hoped she'd kept her looks and taken care of herself, because Eddie boy was on his way!

He called her up in his mind and smiled. Even after two years away and countless other women, he'd still got a soft spot for her. She'd been a virgin when they'd met, a hardworking shop girl, still living with her parents, and she'd fallen for him hook, line and sinker. Who knows, if she treated him right, he might even consider putting a ring on her finger. Somehow, she had got to him, where the others hadn't. Maybe it was her innocence and loyalty – things in short supply among the women he usually had dealings with.

He squared his shoulders and marched on. That doesn't mean to say I'll be staying for sure, he thought. Oh no! Like the man said, there are plenty of fish in the sea, and half the fun is catching them, then throwing them back for another day.

An hour and a half later, he had drunk a pint, had a strip-down wash and bedded the landlord's daughter, twice. And now he was on a bus, headed for Kitchener Street, a mile or so from the docklands – number 14. He checked his notebook and scanned the many names there. Yes, that was it – Lucy Baker at number 14, Kitchener Street, Liverpool.

'Will that be a return ticket, or one way?' The conductor had his ticket-machine at the ready.

'I might be coming back, or I might not.' Edward liked to hedge his bets, especially as he didn't quite know what awaited him. 'I'll have a return ticket, if you please.'

'Return it is.' Turning the handle on his machine, the conductor ran the ticket off. 'That'll be tuppence ha'penny.'

Twenty minutes later, the arrogant young seaman was strolling down Kitchener Street, checking the door numbers as he went. 'Here we are!' He had remembered the street as being long, with every house looking the same; narrow doors and white-stoned steps, and netted curtains up at the windows. But yes, this was the one – halfway down and looking exactly as he remembered. He rapped hard with the knocker.

After a couple of minutes, a plump, red-faced woman flung open the door. 'What the devil d'you think you're playing at?' she demanded angrily. 'I'm not deaf but I will be if you keep rattling the door like that?'

'I'm looking for Lucy Baker.' He'd forgotten that familiar lilt of the Liverpudlian tongue; it was a comforting sound to a man who had travelled a hostile world.

'The Bakers don't live here no more.' Leaning forward, the red-faced woman looked up and down the street. Content that she would not be overheard, she confided, 'There was a bit of a to-do in the family, if you know what I mean.' And seeing that he did *not* know, she went on, 'Ted Baker – Lucy's father – he took another woman to his bed, d'yer see? Then his poor missus chucked him out, and rightly so if you ask me!'

'I don't need to know all the ins and outs,' he told her irritably. 'I just need to find Lucy.'

'I'm coming to that. When Lucy's dad was thrown out, he moved in with his new woman – went to live on York Street, they did – and good riddance to 'em! This house became vacant, and me an' my Eric moved in. Been here a while now.'

'So Lucy went with her father, is that what you're saying?'

'Did I say that?' She liked to tell her story properly, and wasn't finished yet. 'Well, soon after she gave him the old heave-ho, his missus upped sticks and buggered off and nobody knows where she went.'

'So where is Lucy?' Frustration rose in him. 'What happened to her?'

'Oh, aye, you might well ask!'

'I *am* asking, and I'd be obliged if you'd give me an answer.' Trent had no patience with folks like this, especially after the travelling. He'd come a long way to get here, and no doubt he'd be going a long way back, sooner or later. So, there was no time to be wasting.

'All I can say is, it's a good job Lucy was the only child.' Folding her fat little sausage arms, the woman rattled on: 'Y'see, her mam had such terrible trouble bearing a child. Lost four of 'em over the years, she did, an' as if that isn't enough to be putting up with, 'er scoundrel of a husband ends up in some other woman's bed. Shame on him, that's what I say!'

'That's enough o' the chatter, lady! All I want is the whereabouts of Lucy.' Another minute and he might end up strangling the old biddy.

Not one to be bullied, she declared sharply, 'Hold yer 'orses. I were just getting to that!'

'For Chrissake, woman, get on with it, then! Where the bloody hell is she?' When he now took a step forward, the red-faced woman took a step back.

'She's moved in wi' Bridget.'

'Who the hell's Bridget?'

The fat little woman gave a wicked grin. '*Everybody* knows Bridget!'

'Well, here's one who doesn't.' When he took another step forward, she took another step back. 'I couldn't give a toss about Bridget. Just tell me where my girlfriend is, and I'll trouble you no more.'

'All right! All right! There's no need to get aeryated. I already told you, I were coming to that.'

When he glared at her, she nervously cleared her throat and hurriedly explained, 'Bridget is a woman well-known in these parts . . . particularly by the *men*, do you get my drift? Oh yes, she might be generous with her favours, but she charges well enough, and so do her girls, though o' course we ain't supposed to know about what goes on in that place. The bizzies'll put her away if she's found out, an' none of us would want to be responsible for putting Bridget away, nor any of her girls neither.'

She took a well-deserved breath. 'For all her wrongdoings, she's gorra good heart, has Bridget, and she'll help anybody in trouble. Lives along Viaduct Street, number twenty-three. You'll find Lucy there.'

On seeing the question in his eyes, she quickly assured him, 'No, she's not one of Bridget's girls.

Lucy Baker is a stray lamb. She met up with a no-good fella who promised her the world then cleared off to sea, and then she had nowhere to go when her mam and dad split up, so Bridget took her in. Y'see, as I told you . . . Bridget's gorra soft heart and likes to help such folks.'

As he hurried away, she called after him. 'Hey! There's summat I forgot to tell you!'

Edward was not in the mood for listening, however. 'Silly old fool!' he muttered, and ignoring her, he walked on.

Seeing him march away all the quicker, the woman shrugged her fat little shoulders. 'Don't listen then,' she told his back. 'It won't matter to me. Anyway, I expect you'll find out soon enough.' The thought of him being caught unawares made her smile – until she recalled how he had nearly banged her door down and then stared at her so threateningly. Her hackles were up.

Shaking her fist after him, she yelled, 'And don't come bothering me again, Sonny Jim! I were busy at the wash-tub when you came pounding on my door with your damned questions. It's no fun washing blankets, but you wouldn't know about that, would you, eh? Oh no! You men with your damned questions. Go on! Bugger off and don't come back!'

When he turned to scowl at her, she slammed shut the door and scampered back to her wash-tub, grumbling as she went. 'If Lucy Baker gives that fella so much as the time o' day, she wants her head examining!' she muttered to herself.

~

When Edward Trent reached Bridget's house, he knocked on the door with the same force that he had used in Kitchener Street. 'You don't need to knock.' The woman who opened the door was in her late twenties, tall and slender, with a shock of dark hair and over-painted features. 'We don't stand on ceremony here.' She ushered him inside. 'It's down the passage and first left.'

He went first and she followed at a quickening pace. It wasn't often the younger men came to visit, and this one was handsome into the bargain, if a bit surly.

As she came into the room she quietly closed the door behind her. 'The other girls are out,' she confided. 'Mandy's having her hair done and Sandra's got a day off. So I'm afraid you'll have to make do with me. I'm Lynette.'

His frown became a smile. 'You think I'm a client, is that it?'

The young woman shrugged. 'I hope you are,' she replied. Giving him a knowing wink, she went on in silken tones, 'You make a nice change. We normally get the older men here – the blokes who don't get treated right by their own women . . . at least, that's what they tell us.' She chuckled. 'So, what's your reason for being here? Wifey kicked you out, has she?'

Thinking that here was too good a chance to miss, he led her on. 'And what if she has?'

'Well, I dare say I'd have to cheer you up then, wouldn't I?' As she spoke, she walked over to him and slowly, tantalisingly, began to undo the flies on his trousers.

'Did I say you could do that?' He was enjoying every minute.

'I'm sorry. Was I supposed to ask?'

'Not now.' Taking her blouse by the shoulders he ripped it clean off her back. 'It's too late to turn back now.' Leaning forward he kissed her neck, then wiped his tongue along her throat. 'If you're game, then so am I.'

For the next fifteen minutes they played and touched and he took her without feeling or shame, with an insatiable hunger, and in the same aggressive manner that he might sink his teeth into a fat lamb chop or swill back a tankard of ale.

Afterwards, while she was dressing, he threw a few coins on the bed. 'That's for your trouble.' He threw down another. 'And that's for what you're about to do.'

'And what might that be?' This time, Lynette was not so sure of herself. He had been unexpectedly rough and slightly cruel, and she was right to be wary.

'Fetch Lucy Baker to me.' He wagged a finger

in warning. 'One word to her about what we've just done, though, and your pretty face won't be so pretty any more.'

Astonished that Lucy would know such a man, she told him, 'Lucy isn't here.'

She had hardly finished when he caught her by the throat. 'You'd best not be lying to me!' he hissed.

'I'm not lying.' Fearful, she began to struggle. 'She skivvies at the squire's house, Haskell Hall – all the way over in Comberton village. She's there now. Let me go, please. I'm telling you the truth.'

Throwing her on to the bed, he stood over her. 'What time will she be back?'

'I'm not sure. Five, maybe six o'clock. She likes to work long hours. She needs the money for—'

'Shut your mouth!' Taking hold of her he yanked her up and held her close, kissing her mouth, her hair, her eyelids. 'How do I get there?' His voice resembled the soft, deadly hiss of a snake.

Cringing at his touch, she told him, 'Across the fields at the end of this road towards the water-tower.'

'How far?'

'Take the bridle-path, alongside the brook, towards the village of Comberton-by-Weir. It's sign-posted. Head for the hilltop, and you won't go wrong. Once past Overhill Farm, go down the other side and you'll find the squire's house half a mile on. It's called Haskell Hall. You can't miss it – a big old house with great trees lining the way up to the entrance. It's about a mile and a half in all.'

Throwing her aside he scowled. 'Ah, well. I suppose I've come this far, another mile or two will seem like nothing.'

Before he left he warned her again. 'We had our fun and that's an end to it. But one word to anybody, especially to Lucy, and you'll rue the day. D'you understand me?'

Fearing for her life, Lynette nodded. 'I won't say anything.'

'Good girl.' For an unbearable moment he stared her out. 'I expect I'll see you when we get back.' Grabbing her hair in a bunch between his thick strong fingers, he drew her head back and kissed her throat. 'Oh look, you're starting to bruise.' With a devious grin, he screwed a straightened finger into her forehead until she winced. 'Not a word!' he whispered. Then he went on his way, whistling merrily as he strode briskly down the pavement.

So far it had been a good day, he thought smugly.

Seeing Lucy would be the icing on the cake.

～

Back at Bridget's house, the woman herself had arrived; large-boned, with her mass of fiery hair and eyes green as a cat's in the dark, she was as Irish as the Blarney Stone, filling the front parlour with her presence. She was astonished to find one of her young people in tears. 'Hey now!' She dropped her bag into the nearest chair.

'Aw, will ye look at that!' she exclaimed. 'You'll have eyes like split walnuts if you don't stop the bawling, so ye will.' Sensing a man was involved, she demanded to know, 'Who was he? What did the swine do to you?' She banged her fist on the dresser. 'Sure, I'll have the bloody head off his shoulders if he's messed you up.' And by the ample size of her, she was well capable of carrying out her threat.

'It's got nothing to do with any bloke.' Afraid to reveal the truth, the young woman lied convincingly. 'It's just that I've had this awful toothache all day and it's giving me some gyp.'

Bridget relaxed. 'If that's all, you'd best get yourself a drop of the hard stuff out of the dresser. That should see you through the night, and if you're no better in the morning, you can take yourself off to the dentist. All right?'

'All right.' Lynette gave a sigh of relief. 'Oh, and there *was* a man here . . . not a client or anything like that,' she added quickly.

Bridget was disappointed. 'Pity. So what did he want?'

'He was looking for Lucy.'

'Was he now? And did you tell him where to find her?'

'Yes. I told him she was working over at the squire's house. He's gone there now, to meet up with her.'

'Mmm.' Bridget did not like the sound of it. 'And what did he look like, this fella?'

The young woman shrugged, her bottom lip turning down as she pretended to recall his features; while in truth she would never forget them. 'Rough-looking, I suppose, but handsome all the same.'

'That doesn't tell me much, does it? A description like that could fit anybody.' Bridget threw herself into the chair opposite. 'Come on, Lynette – what else?'

'Well, he had a weathered face as though he'd been in the sun a lot, and he was carrying a kitbag.' As the images burned deeper into her mind, her speech quickened, as though she wanted it all said and done with as swiftly as possible. 'He was dark-haired and he had this look about him – a real mean, peevish kind of look. I tell you what, Bridget, I wouldn't like to be Lucy if she's got deep in with that kinda fella. No, I certainly would not!'

Bridget was curious. 'For someone who's got a bad toothache, you seem to have found enough time to get a real good look at him.'

'Well, o' course I did, because he stood on the doorstep and wouldn't go until I told him where Lucy was.'

'What, you mean he got nasty?'

'No, I don't mean that at all.' She had not for-gotten his parting threat. 'He wanted to know where she was, and at first I wasn't sure whether to tell him, then he stood his ground and I had no choice.'

'So you told him, and he went?'

'That's right. I had to get rid of him. To tell you the truth, I didn't like the look of him.' Involun-tarily, she shuddered.

'I see.' Bridget detected a great deal of fear in Lynette's manner. 'He sounds like a nasty piece of work,' she said quietly. 'You sure that's not why you were crying just now?'

'No!' Leaping out of the chair, Lynette laid the palm of her hand over her mouth. 'It's this damned tooth. It's driving me crazy.'

Bridget got out of her chair and wrapped her arms about the girl. 'You're to fetch a drop of whisky out of the cupboard, then get yourself off to bed. Come down later, when you're feeling better. A good night's sleep, then it's the dentist for you first thing in the morning.'

Before Lynette left the room, Bridget had one more question. 'This man . . . was he a sailor, d'you think?'

'He could well have been a matelot,' the girl said. 'He did have a tattoo – oh, and sailors do have kitbags, don't they?'

Bridget was quiet for a minute, as though she had just remembered who he was. 'Dark, with a mean kind of a look, you say. Mmm.' Then, her tone brisk, she told the young woman, 'All right, darlin', don't worry. Get off and take care of yourself. I'm sure Lucy will tell me all about it when she gets back.'

A few minutes later, with Lynette off to her bed, and the other girls not yet back, Bridget went through to the kitchen, where the young housekeeper, Tillie, having heard her come in earlier, was already pouring Bridget a cup of tea. 'Thought you might be ready for this,' she said, pushing it along the table to where Bridget had pulled up a chair and sat down. 'Had a good shopping trip?'

Having been thrown out of house and home by a violent stepfather these four years past, Tillie Salter had found a welcome at Bridget's house of pleasure. At seventeen, innocent and plain-looking as the day was long, there was never any intention to recruit her into the 'business'; so she was given a roof over her head and paid a wage to cook and clean and generally look after number 23, Viaduct Street, leaving Bridget free to keep a tight rein on her business, count her money, take care of her girls, and shop to her heart's content.

During the four years she had been there, Tillie Salter had loved every minute, and had come to look on Bridget as a surrogate mother. Bridget was her idol – her hero and her friend. She might run a brothel, but she was discreet in her dealings, she looked after her girls well, and had a heart of gold. So those who knew of her business said nothing, and those who thought she was a woman who had come into money legitimately, chatted with her in the street, and saw her as a kind soul, with a happy personality.

Moreover, she seemed ever ready to listen to their problems when others would not.

Bridget thanked her for the tea. She removed her light jacket and fanned her rosy face. 'You've no idea of the crowds,' she groaned. 'Pushing you this way and that . . . treading on your toes and thinking it's your fault and not theirs. Jesus, Mary and Joseph! What is it about shopping that makes martyrs of us poor women?'

Bringing her own tea, Tillie sat at the other side of the table. 'But you love it, don't you?' she said shyly. 'You love the noise and bustle, and spending your money across the counter. And I bet you went down the docks, dreaming of your homeland across the water.'

Bridget squeezed her hand. 'Ah, you know me too well, so ye do.' She gave a deep-down sigh. 'Aw, Tillie, there are times when I really do miss my Ireland.'

Tillie loved to hear the stories of Bridget's upbringing in Kilkenny. 'Tell me again, what do you miss most?' she asked eagerly.

Bridget was pleased to answer. 'I miss the rolling valleys and the way the sun goes down behind the hills of an evening. I miss my folks and I miss other people – like the old fella that used to sit outside the pub of an evening and play his accordion, so the people would throw a generous handful of coins into his cap as they sauntered by.'

'What else, Bridget?' Tillie persisted. 'Tell me what else.'

Bridget laughed. 'How many times must I tell you, before you're satisfied? I shall have to be careful, so I will, or you'll be up and off and across the water one of these foine days, so ye will!'

'Just tell me about the music, and the dancing,' Tillie urged, her grey eyes bright with anticipation in her homely young face.

'Ah, the dancing!' Rolling her eyes, Bridget leaned back in her chair; she could see and hear the festivities in her mind and her heart ached. 'I remember the fair in Appleby, when the horsemen would come from all over Ireland and even across the Atlantic from 'Merica, just to show their horses and traps and watch the goings-on. And if somebody took a liking to one of their best horses, they'd offer a price and when the haggling was done, they'd do the spitting of the handshake and the deal was agreed.'

Tillie cringed. 'Ugh! I don't think I'd want anybody spitting on *my* hand!' She hid her hands behind her back as if to protect them.

Bridget roared with laughter. 'It's the way things are done, so it is,' she said. 'Sure it's been that way for a hundred years and more, and likely it'll be that way for many more years to come!'

Caught up in the housekeeper's excitement, Bridget continued, 'When the deals are all done, the men go down to the pub and celebrate, drinking and singing and dancing, too – and oh, the good crack they have!' She threw out her arms with sheer joy. 'I'm telling you, Tillie me darlin', it is pure magic, so it is.'

'And what about the dancing, Bridget? Tell me about that!'

Bridget leaned forward. 'Sometimes it would be one couple on the floor and everybody watching, and when their feet got a-tapping and their hands got a-clapping and they couldn't watch no longer, they'd all link arms, so they would. Then they would all dance in a line, every one of them in tune with the other – feet crossing and jumping, and going high in the air as though they were one, and the tapping and the rhythm, and the noise against the boards . . .'

Her voice rose higher and higher and soon her own feet were a-tapping and her hands a-clapping, and, 'Sure, there's no magic in the world like an Irish jig!'

Suddenly she was calling for Tillie to clap a tune, and when the girl started, Bridget leaped to her feet and holding her skirt high, she began kicking out to the sound of the clapping. And soon the clapping got faster and faster and Bridget danced and laughed and it wasn't long before she fell into the chair, face bright red and aglow with delight. 'Come on!' she told Tillie. 'Get up and I'll show you how to do it.'

But before Tillie could do so, the sound of a child crying brought the laughter to an end. 'Oh, the poor little divil, we've woke him, so we have!'

Quickly now she ran through to the cot and took the child out – a healthy-looking little chap with a chubby face, startled from his afternoon nap by all the tapping and the clapping and the laughter that rang through the house.

'Ah, sure he's a bonny little fella, so he is,' Bridget cooed, and soon he was quiet on her lap, his mouth open like a fish at feeding time and his small hand stroking her blouse as he woke up properly.

'Will ye look at him,' she laughed tenderly. She handed the child to Tillie. 'Best get his supper ready, me darling,' she suggested. 'Then you might take him upstairs for his bath. It'll soon be his bedtime, so it will.'

Tillie put him in his high chair and there he sat, quiet as a mouse, chewing on his knuckles and watching Bridget as she gazed down on him. 'I can't believe how he's grown,' she declared. 'How old is he exactly?' She was never a one for figures – unless it was a strong man with a gorgeous arse and broad shoulders.

Tillie looked round from buttering his fingers

of freshly-baked bread. She added some little squares of cheese for Jamie to nibble on while she cooked his soft-boiled egg. 'He's a year and six months old,' she enlightened Bridget. 'A real little boy now, no longer a baby.' She chuckled girlishly. 'He walked along the sofa-edge yesterday, and his fat little legs went all bandy.'

Bridget laughed. 'If he keeps on like that, it won't be long before he's off to work with his pack on his back,' she teased.

The women were tender with the little lad, as he had been born with one of his legs shorter than the other, and found it hard to balance. Bridget studied the child's features. Unlike his mammy, whose eyes were golden-brown, he had the darkest eyes; his hair, though, was the same colour as hers – the shiny rich brown of ripe chestnuts.

Like his mammy, the child had that same quick smile and infectious laughter; though these last two years Lucy had not laughed overmuch, because she was lonely and sad, though as with every deep emotion, she tried hard not to show it. But Bridget knew, and she wondered now about the man who had come to her door. 'There was a man here today,' she told Tillie, who had returned with the egg-cup and spoon, and a small beaker of milk for the child.

'I know.' Tillie was as discreet as ever. 'I heard him knocking the door down. He was determined to be heard.'

'Lynette answered the door, didn't she?' Bridget wondered if Tillie knew more than she was saying.

'Yes, I was changing this one's napkin. The others were out. They're still out, as far as I know.' She held the beaker-lip to Jamie's mouth again, cautioning him when he snatched at it and almost sent it flying. 'Why?'

Bridget thought a moment, then in a quiet voice she told Tillie, 'Lynette described him to me.'

'Did she?' The girl wiped the child's mouth and put the beaker to the floor. 'I didn't see him.' But she had heard him. She had heard *them*. Yet she never spoke of what she heard in this house. Bridget had given her a roof over her head and she never questioned or judged what went on here.

Bridget was quiet for a time, then she spoke, again in a quiet voice as though she was deep in thought. 'I've a feeling it's *him*!'

Tillie had spooned a helping of yolk into the child's mouth, but it was now all over his face, so she was wiping him with the flannel she had in her pocket. She looked up at Bridget's statement. 'Who?'

'Edward Trent – the baby's father. I think Lucy told you how things started with him. He followed her home from Wavertree Park one day and was all over her, the bad bugger. Had his way with her, promised the earth then cleared off about three months later. After that, her parents split up and she lost her home. Fat lot of good her so-called boyfriend was then, eh?'

Having finished the feeding, Tillie lifted the child out onto her lap. 'Crikey!' Her eyes grew wide as saucers. 'I thought he'd upped and gone to sea. Got fed up wi' working on the docks, didn't he? An' he ain't never been in touch since.'

'That's right – and good shuts to him. But bad pennies have a way of turning up again. And he was a bad penny if ever there was one – though she never saw it.'

'She loved him, that's why.' Lucy had spoken long and deep to Tillie about her sweetheart, the father of her child. 'He was good to her, wasn't he?'

'Not all the time.' Bridget's expression hardened. 'I reckon he used to hit her – oh, not so's you'd notice from the outside, but he hurt her all the same. Even her mam an' dad warned her against him. She couldn't see what he was truly like, though. She loved him, y'see? She *still* loves him, even after he buggered off and left her with child.'

Bridget was afraid for Lucy. Afraid of why Edward Trent had come back. What was he after? As far as she was concerned, the man was no good, and never would be.

'He never even wrote to her, did he?' Tillie had not forgiven him for doing that to her friend. Poor Lucy had been frantic for a long while, not knowing which way to turn, wanting to tell him about his son once Jamie was born, but with no idea how to contact him.

Bridget didn't answer because her thoughts were miles away. What's he up to? she mused silently. Why is he here after all this time?

It seemed the very same question was crossing young Tillie's mind. 'Why do *you* think he's come back?' she said apprehensively.

Her employer shrugged. 'Who knows?' She recalled what Lynette had told her. 'He came looking for her, that's for sure. And he's gone to find her as we speak.'

She sighed. 'I only hope Lucy has enough sense not to be taken in by him a second time.'

CHAPTER SEVEN

Unaware of developments at home, Lucy drove her energy into the last task of the day. 'Almost done now,' she told the curious magpie who had been watching her for the past ten minutes or so. 'Another few good wallops, and there won't be a speck of dust left.'

Raising the beater, she brought it down against the rug so hard that it danced on the clothes-line; another good hard wallop, and the dust flew in all directions, not as much as when she had first brought the rug out, but enough to give her a coughing fit, and send the startled magpie off to the skies.

'Cowardly creature!' she called after it. 'Mind, if I had wings, I'd be off too.' Oh, and she would an' all! Away above the chimney-tops ever so high, she would raise her head and flap her wings fast and furious until she was across the oceans, then she'd keep going until she reached some tropical paradise. But she wouldn't go alone, oh no. Wherever she went, she would take her darling son with her.

From the office window upstairs, the tall, elegant woman watched Lucy as she worked; the squire's secretary could hear Lucy's voice raised in song, but that wasn't unusual, because during her working day, whether inside or out, Lucy's melodious singing could be heard all over Haskell Hall. 'You're a good soul, Lucy Baker,' Miss McGuire murmured, putting down her fountain-pen. 'Hardworking and happy as the day is long.'

As she watched Lucy hoist the rug from the line and drop it to the ground, she was taken by surprise when the girl suddenly looked up to see her there. 'I won't be long,' she called out. 'I'm finished just now.'

Lucy quickened her steps towards the house, the hot breeze playing with the hem of her skirt, her feet bare as the day she was born; with the rug carried in her arms, like a mother might carry a bairn, she made a fetching sight.

When a moment or two later, Lucy burst into the kitchen, Miss McGuire was waiting for her. 'For the life of me, Lucy, I don't know why you beat the rug when you could use that new vacuum cleaner. It *was* bought to suck up the dirt and dust from the floor, after all, and to save the staff here from heavy work.'

'I *do* use it,' Lucy protested, 'but it's not very good. Sometimes things get stuck in it and it won't work, and then old Jake has to see to it, and while he's doing that I still have to beat the rugs.' She prodded the one in her arms. 'This one is no good at all. It's got long fringes and they go flying up into the workings and then it's the devil's own job to free them. It's much quicker just to give it a sound beating on the clothes-line.'

The squire's secretary tended to agree, but did not say so. Instead she looked down at Lucy's bare feet. Small and neat, they were covered in a film of dust, and there was the tiniest leaf sticking out between the toes. 'Never mind the rug,' she retorted. 'Perhaps you'd like to tell me why you aren't wearing your boots?' Exasperated at the times she had asked the young woman to always wear her boots for fear of hurting herself on the harsh ground, she groaned. 'Just look at your poor feet, Lucy . . . covered in dust and picking up all the debris from the ground. One of these days you're bound to get an injury. I've asked you so many times to wear your work-boots, I'm worn out with it.'

Lucy looked down at her feet. 'I'm a mucky pup, I know,' she conceded, wiggling her toes to be rid of the leaf, 'but I feel so uncomfortable with the boots on. I'm sorry, Miss McGuire. I'll try to wear them, I promise.'

'And how many times have you said that?' The secretary rolled her eyes. 'And how many times have I seen you running about in your bare feet?

It isn't as though you're a child, Lucy. You're a grown woman of nearly thirty, for heaven's sake, and you have a little one to think of. What would happen if something fell on your feet and broke them? How would you go on then, eh?'

'I know, and I'm really sorry,' Lucy repeated. 'I promise I'll try to keep the shoes on.' Lucy hated wearing shoes of any kind, almost as much as she hated cold porridge.

'Mind you do then.' The secretary was a kindly sort. She had little to do with the housekeeper's staff here at the Hall, but she had always had a soft spot for Lucy.

'Anyway, enough of this. It's time you went home,' she told Lucy now. 'There hasn't been a day in the past fortnight when you've left on time.'

'That's 'cause I like to finish all my work before I go,' Lucy explained.

'I know that, all too well,' came the reply. 'But you must leave time for yourself . . . and the child.' The secretary tried hard not to be shocked by the young woman's situation as an unmarried mother. The squire never listened to gossip so he remained ignorant of Jamie's existence; however, some of the other staff were aware of her status and shunned Lucy because of it.

'Oh, I do!' Lucy answered eagerly. 'When I'm not working here, I spend every passing minute with him.' A look of sheer joy lit her face. 'You can't know how much I love him. No one can.'

Dorothy was fond enough of Lucy to tell her, 'I'm sure I *do* know how much you love him. All I'm saying is this: it's no wonder you still haven't found a man to take care of you and the child, what with you working all hours, and here you are already twenty-nine years of age. Most young women are safely married and settled in their own home at that age.' This didn't apply to her either, she acknowledged sadly.

When she saw the downcast look on Lucy's face she was mortified. 'I've spoken out of turn, my dear. I didn't mean to be cruel. It's just that you're such a lovely young woman and I do care what happens to you. I'd hate to think you were destined to spend your life all alone.'

'It's all right, Miss McGuire, I don't mind.' But she did, and now her thoughts were filled with memories of a dark-eyed man who had quickly come into her life and filled her days with fun, and then just as quickly gone out of her life, without so much as a how's your father!

But she had not forgotten him. She never would. Especially when he'd left her with child, and it had caused so much trouble at home that she was made to leave in disgrace – and soon after, her mother and father split up and went their separate ways. And now she had no family at all, save for her little boy, who was everything to her.

'Go on then! Be off with you, before the housekeeper finds you another job to do. And don't worry. I'll let her know you've gone.'

The woman's voice invaded her thoughts, and when she looked up, the kindly secretary was already on her way down the long corridor.

Dragging the rug through the kitchen, Lucy got it to the drawing room, where she rolled it out before the big fireplace. 'All done for another day.' Sometimes Lucy sang, and sometimes like now, she talked to herself, and then there was the time when she got caught dancing on the sofa-table and almost got her marching orders from the housekeeper.

It was the same at home. Often Bridget would say, 'For the love of God, will ye sit still and be quiet!' But she couldn't. There was too much life in her, and it wasn't her fault.

Without wasting any more time, Lucy ran to the cupboard where her two pairs of shoes were lined up: black lace-up boots for work, and daintier shoes with ankle-straps for going home in. Taking out the ankle-strap shoes, she put them on and, flicking her long hair out of her eyes, she hurried out of the back door, her voice raised in song and her feet skipping as she went.

By the kennels at the side of the house, Lucy stopped to pet the hounds. She had a marvellous way with animals; whenever they had the chance, the squire's hounds would follow her everywhere, and while everyone else would stay clear of the bull in its pen, Lucy could often be seen defying instructions to lean over the gate and stroke its nose.

Lucy was halfway down the hill when she stopped to take off her shoes. The grass looked so warm, lush and inviting in the evening heat. Tying the ankle-straps together, she slung the shoes over her shoulder and went on in bare feet.

She was almost at the brook when she saw the figure of a man coming towards her. It wasn't the squire, or he'd have his dogs with him, and it wasn't Barney Davidson from Overhill Farm, because he was smaller-built.

She often spoke with Barney when he was out on the hills with his sheep or doing other work on the land. She liked him; he had a kind, caring manner, and was easy to talk with. In fact, if he wasn't married and she wasn't still completely infatuated with Edward, she could have fallen for him herself.

While Lucy grew increasingly curious about the man approaching from the bottom of the hill, he was also straining his eyes to see if it really was Lucy drawing ever closer, though when he saw that familiar wave of long hair flowing in the breeze and the cheeky swagger of her long limbs, he knew it was her and began to run. 'LUCY!' The wind carried his voice across the valley. 'LUCY BAKER, IT'S ME! IT'S YOUR SWEETHEART COME HOME!'

Hearing the voice, but unable to decipher the words, Lucy stopped and stared. With the sun directly in her face she couldn't see his features. But she saw the long, confident strides as he ran to her, and when he dropped the kitbag from his back, there was something disturbingly familiar about the way he moved. Slowly but surely, realisation dawned. 'Edward? My Edward?' She whispered his name; was it really him? Excitement coursed through her, but she didn't call out or run forward. She didn't dare trust her own judgement.

By the time he got close enough for her to recognise him, she took to her heels and ran to meet him. When he caught her in his arms and swung her high in the air, she laughed and cried with sheer joy. 'Oh Edward, I thought I'd never see you again!' She looked into his dark eyes and thought she would never again be so happy.

'I told you I'd be back.' Breathless, he set her down. 'I've never forgotten you, Lucy. Every day, every minute we've been apart, I've thought of this day.'

Caught up in the excitement of the moment, he kissed her long and hard, and held the kiss until Lucy thought she would suffocate.

'Stop!' Flattening her hands against his chest she remembered how he had walked out on her. 'What makes you think you can waltz back into my life and just pick up where you left off? You signed up and sailed away without a by your leave, and now you're back with the same damned cheek of it!'

Lucy had not forgotten the humiliation, the pain of it all, and then the despair. It had been a bad business for her, and then she found out she was with child and had to suffer in silence until she could hide the secret no longer. Her pregnancy – which caused a great scandal in the neighbourhood – created rows and repercussions between her parents, and in the end she witnessed the break-up of her family, and that was as much Edward's fault as her own.

For a long time things had gone from bad to worse, and still she had hoped he might return. But he never did – until now. And though she was thrilled beyond words to see him, she couldn't help but chide him. 'You let me down good and proper, Edward Trent!'

When he now looked desolate, she instantly forgave him and taking off at the run, shouted, 'If you want me, you'll have to catch me!'

And catch her he did; on the little slope just above the stream. He threw himself bodily at her, and together the two of them went rolling down the hill, until they landed up right next to the brook. She cupped a handful of water and chucked it at him while he lay helpless with laughter.

'You're a bloody lunatic!' he screeched, and she couldn't speak for spluttering. Her heart was leaping about inside her like a crazy thing: after all this time, when she had given up any hope of ever seeing him again, *Edward Trent was back*.

It was too wonderful for words. Her baby's father was home to make a proper life for them. They would be a family at last, and if Lucy could have jumped over the moon right then and there, she would have done.

Wrapping his strong sailor's arms about her slim waist, he inched her towards the soft rich grass that lined the stream's edge, and right there, with the clean, fresh water lapping over their bare feet, he laid her down and took her with a kind of animal hunger; not tenderly, not gently or cruelly, but the only way he knew how, driven by lust and the over-riding greed to be satisfied. This was his third partner of the day, his fourth coupling, and for a little while, his passion subsided.

'That was so good, Lucy,' he said hoarsely. 'You don't know how long I've waited to be with you like that.'

But Lucy had not yet heard the words she yearned to hear. 'Do you love me?' she asked hesitantly. '*Really* love me?' Somehow she couldn't be sure, even now.

He laughed. 'That's a silly question.' And then, as though to dismiss the thought, he kissed her mouth. 'Didn't I just show you how much I love you?'

Lucy drew away. 'But you didn't *say* it. All the

time we were making love, you never once said you loved me.'

'I did! I'm sure I did.' Bloody women, he thought. Are they never satisfied?

'Say it now.' Lucy needed convincing.

'What? Say *what?*' Anger trembled in his voice.

'That you love me . . . say it!'

'Jesus, but you're a persistent bugger.' Suddenly amused, he grinned down on her. 'But then you always were a spirited devil. It's what I liked most about you.'

'Say it then.' Melting to him, Lucy traced his lips with the tip of her finger. 'If you don't say it, I'll know you're not serious about us.'

Twice he opened his mouth to say it, but telling a woman that he loved her did not come easy, mainly because his idea of love and hers were not the same. Where she might think of something precious to them both – a sharing, giving emotion, with a deep-down need to build a life together – he was a cold, selfish man who saw his own needs to be of paramount importance.

Now, as he looked into that small, upturned face with the appealing brown eyes and the sun-light dancing off her long unkempt hair, he had to appease her. 'Silly bitch, o' course I love you!' Snatching her to him, he held her there for what seemed an age; until she drew away, to divulge a secret which shocked him to the core.

'Edward, I've got something to tell you.' She

was so nervous, she could feel herself trembling.

He kissed her again. 'Have you, now. Well then, you'd best tell me, hadn't you?'

She nodded. 'When you were here before . . .' She hesitated, not knowing whether he would be pleased or angry. Yet, if they were to be married and start their own home together, he would have to know, and so she told him in a rush. 'We have a son, Edward. His name is Jamie, and oh, he's so beautiful.' As she gabbled on, intent on getting it off her chest, she did not see how the light in his eyes had dimmed, or the set of his jaw had hardened. 'He has such a look of you, and oh, just now he's beginning to learn to walk . . .'

She was silenced when he suddenly grabbed her by the shoulders. 'What are you saying, Lucy?' His hands dug into her skin, hurting her. 'A son? You're telling me that you have a child?'

'That's right, Edward – *we* have a child. He was born nine months to the day you went away. I had no idea that I was expecting. I wanted so much to let you know about him, but I couldn't, because I didn't know where you were.' Her voice faltered. 'I called him James – Jamie – after your middle name. Jamie Baker, he is – but now we can change it to Trent.'

Only a few minutes ago, her heart had been singing, but now she could see what a shock it was to him, and she was fearful.

'It'll be all right,' she gabbled. 'We'll get

married and rent a little house and I'll work at Haskell Hall like now, and oh, Edward, it will be so wonderful . . .'

She paused, hope smiling in her eyes. 'It *will* be wonderful, won't it?'

The man didn't answer straight away. His mind was feverishly working. A child? A bastard to keep his feet tied to the ground while he broke his back working to keep him, *and her.* He didn't want that. Besides, how could he be sure it was his? He only had her word for it. For all he knew, he could be taking on another man's throwaway.

'Edward?' her small voice persisted. 'It will be all right, won't it?' Lucy had always realised that if he ever came back, the news would be a shock, but she had hoped that, in the end, he would be overjoyed to have a son.

'Of course, and why wouldn't it be?' His quick smile belied the rage inside. If she thought he was staying now, she'd soon find out different.

'And you're not angry?'

'Angry?' He held her close as though he would never let her go. 'How could I be angry? I won't deny it was a shock, but what man wouldn't be pleased to know he had a son waiting for him?'

Lucy was thrilled. 'We'll be a proper family, and I'll make you happy, I promise.' Even though there was still that little voice warning her to be wary, Lucy had to believe him.

'Where is he, this son of mine?'

'Back at Bridget's house. Oh Edward, she's been so good to us. Some people say she's the worst of the worst because she has girls who entertain, but she's a good woman. You'll see when you meet her. She has a helper by the name of Tillie who takes care of our son when I'm working . . .'

'I see.' He stopped her there. 'And you say she has girls who entertain?' He thought of Lynette, and smirked.

Lucy nodded earnestly. 'They're my friends. Bridget looks after them . . . like she looks after me.'

'Took them off the street, did she?'

'Something like that, yes.' Lucy didn't care for the way the conversation was going. 'But they're good girls . . . I mean, they're kind and thoughtful, and they've helped me through a bad time. When my parents found out about the baby, they went crazy. My mam wanted to send me to a woman in the back streets who does away with unwanted pregnancies, and my dad said she was callous, and that we should wait until you came back and he'd make sure it got sorted out.'

The memories had never gone away, though thanks to Bridget she had managed to push a lot of it to the back of her mind. Now though, it all came flooding back; the rows and upsets, and the terrible things that were said. Lucy had always thought her parents were happily married, when all the time they had just been 'rubbing along', as her mother had put it.

When she told them she was pregnant, it was as though she had lifted a lid they had each been struggling to keep shut, and all the venom came to the surface. 'Oh Edward, it was awful. In the end, they split up, and I found myself out on the streets. That was when Bridget took me in. She was at convent school with my mam, but she's as different from her as chalk from cheese.' Tears filled her eyes. 'Mam didn't want anything to do with me, or her grandchild, but Bridget's been both mother to me and granny to the bairn.'

Edward curled his lip at this description of a 'tart with a golden heart'. 'Well, you've no need to worry now,' he lied. 'I'm here and like your father said, it will all be sorted out.'

In reality he was already wondering where he'd dropped his kitbag, so he could go back and collect it and be gone like the wind out of here. If he'd had any feelings for her at all, they'd been suffocated by the news she'd given him. A bastard waiting to claim him for life, women who 'entertained' – and how could he be sure that Lucy herself had not 'entertained' some man or another, and that's how she came to be with child? Oh no! He might be a fool for a good-looking woman, but he was not fool enough to truss himself up like a chicken ready for the oven.

'Edward?' Lucy could see he was deep in

thought. 'What's wrong?' She knew he was think-ing of the news she had just given him.

'Oh, I'm sorry, sweetheart.' Scrambling to his feet, he took hold of her hand and pulled her up to him. 'I'll get my kitbag, then we'll walk back and you can introduce me to my son. Then we'll make plans. It's all going to be fine, Lucy.'

They got up and walked on, and she nestled in the curve of his arm, a spring in her step and a song in her heart. Edward was back. Everything would be fine now.

As they walked, Lucy was full of plans. 'We'll find a little house to rent with a good-sized garden, and we'll sit outside and watch our son playing, then of an evening, we can see the sun going down. Oh, sweetheart . . .' She looked at him and her heart was full. 'I'm so glad you're back.'

The man cared nothing for her dreaming. He had plans of his own, and they certainly didn't include sitting around in a garden and watching somebody else's kid playing. But he didn't want Lucy to know what he was thinking, so he said all the right things and convinced her that if that was what she wanted, then so did he. And Lucy believed him.

'Look!' Drawing his attention to the flock of sheep being driven to the brow of the hill, Lucy told him, 'There's Barney Davidson.'

As he turned to see, Lucy gave him a playful push and ran on. 'Race you to the lane!'

'You little sod!' She had caught him offguard, and he was thrilled. This was what spurred him on, a spirited woman fleeing and himself in full chase: and when he caught her, what fun it would be. 'Come on, Eddie boy,' he said to himself. 'Get after her. Leave her with another mouth to feed and happen she'll find some other poor bugger to take her on!'

For a moment he stood his ground and watched her running, bare-footed, with the pretty shoes dangling from her hand and her hair flowing behind, and the sound of her laughter exciting him – and he had a moment of weakness. For one dangerous, fleeting moment, he actually thought she might be worth staying for. But when fear took over, the moment was quickly gone.

Wickedness surged through him, and a sense of fun. There was no need to commit himself, not when he could have it all and walk away. Right now, Lucy wanted him to chase her and he would, and that was all right, because this was what he believed life was all about. Never mind responsibility. That was for other folks, not for a free-and-easy-living man like himself.

With a shout to let her know he was right behind, he set off at the run.

High on the hill, Barney saw the two of them careering across the field towards the stile; Lucy in front and going like the wind, and the man fast closing in.

He could hear the young woman's merry laughter and he smiled. 'Seems like she's found a bit of happiness,' he told Jess, his red-setter bitch, who trotted beside him, keeping an eye on the sheep. 'Lord knows, she deserves it after what she's been through.'

He knew Lucy because the two of them often chatted as she wended her way to work, and last winter, he had taken her along the lane in his cart because the hills were snow-covered. That was the very first time she had confided in him. After that, they had often walked the hills in the same direction, her going to and from the squire's house and himself to the outlying fields where he would check his flock.

As they got to know each other better, Lucy had confided in him more and more. Then one day when his lovely Vicky was walking with him, Lucy came along and joined them. The two women had got on so well that Vicky invited her up to Overhill Farm for tea, and it had been a very enjoyable evening.

'I don't know if that's the boy's father,' he told Jess as they strolled on, 'but even if it's not, Lucy seems content enough with him.'

Just then he heard a scream and on looking down again, he could see that Lucy had taken a tumble as she climbed the stile; he could see her lying among the big stones there and she didn't appear to be moving. 'Good God! Looks like she's hurt!' As he ran forward the dog bounded in front, ears pricked, sensing danger. Lucy wasn't getting up! What the hell was the bloke playing at? Cupping his hands, Barney called out: 'You there! Is she all right?'

As Barney drew nearer he could see how the man was standing still, looking down on Lucy and not making any move to help her. Suddenly he threw his kitbag over his shoulder and, with a backward glance at Barney, he began walking away, slowly at first then quickening his steps, and now with Barney less than fifty yards away, he bent his head, lengthened his stride and took off at speed. 'I can't help her, I've a ship waiting!' he yelled as he ran. 'I don't even know the woman.'

Barney had a choice; he could either go after the man and teach him a lesson he might never forget, or he could help Lucy, who was lying in a crooked position with her head oozing blood against a boulder.

His choice was no choice at all. He had to help Lucy. By now she was groaning; trying to move but seeming unable to.

Coming nearer, he began talking to her, soothing her as he fell to his knees beside her. 'It's all right, Lucy,' he said softly. 'You've taken a knock to the head, but you'll be fine, don't worry. I'll get you home to my Vicky. She'll know what to do.'

When Lucy gave no answer, he continued talking to her in a quiet voice, at the same time gently sliding his two arms under her slight form and collecting her to his chest. To him, she was but a feather in his arms, for he was a man possessed of strength that came from a lifetime labouring in the fields.

The movement disturbed her. With dazed vision she stared up at him, her shocked eyes looking into his. 'Where's Edward?' she asked brokenly, but her voice remained silent. Try as she might, she could not make her voice be heard. And now she closed her eyes and let herself drift. 'Edward?' Where was he?

'Lie quiet, Lucy.' Sensing her agitation, he guessed she was wondering about the cowardly man. 'I've got you now,' he told her. 'You'll have to trust me.' All the way home, he kept reassuring her, until she was limp and senseless in his arms.

Barney was a fit man who would have normally taken ten or fifteen minutes to reach his home from that particular spot, but Lucy was now a dead weight and with his every footstep she grew heavier in his arms, until home seemed a million miles away. 'Go in front, lass!' he called to the red-setter. 'Let her know I'm on my way.'

Vicky was taking in the washing when the dog came running up to nuzzle her legs. A small, golden-haired woman with soft grey eyes, she greeted the dog with a stroke of the head. 'What's the matter, girl, eh?' she laughed. Jess was a devil for the play and leaping at her now, even though she had an armful of clean clothes. 'No! Get off, you unruly hound.' The setter had run a long way at a fast pace and now her tongue was hanging out and slaver running from her jowls. Vicky feared she might drop the washing, and then: 'You'll slobber on the clothes, and I'll have to wash the blooming things all over again!'

When Jess continued to nuzzle her, Vicky dropped the clothes into the basket. Snatching it up into her arms, she chided the animal. 'What's got into you? Behave yourself!'

Now, as she turned, she caught sight of Barney out of the corner of her eye; a distance from the house and treading every step with care, he was carrying what she at first thought was a dead sheep. 'BARNEY!' Raising her voice, she ran forward. 'WHAT'S HAPPENED?'

Encouraged by the sight of home and his beloved, Barney hurried to her as fast as he could. 'It's Lucy,' he panted. 'She's taken a bad tumble. I reckon she needs a doctor and fast!'

Running before him, Vicky opened all the doors and in no time at all, Lucy was laid on the spare bed, with a blanket over her. 'You fetch the doctor,' Vicky instructed her husband. 'I'll get her out of these clothes and make her comfortable.'

And so, while Vicky set about helping Lucy, Barney rode into the village of Comberton on his bicycle to fetch the doctor.

By the time Vicky had bathed the wound on

Lucy's head, changed her into one of her own nightgowns, and tucked her up in bed, Lucy was more alert, though still dizzy and not yet able to focus properly. 'Jamie!' Her first concern was for her son.

Vicky quietened her. 'He's fine,' she said. 'If you want, I'll ask Barney to go over and bring him to you, but for now, he's safe with Tillie, isn't he? She's taking good care of him.'

Subdued, Lucy cast her mind back to when she fell. 'I was running . . .' she tried to explain. 'Edward . . . he . . .' She raised her head a short distance from the pillow and dropped it again as though it was too heavy for her shoulders. 'He was behind me when I fell.' She tried to look into the room. 'Where is he?'

Vicky had no idea who this Edward was. 'I don't know,' she replied kindly. 'I expect he won't be far away.'

Lucy despaired. 'He's gone, hasn't he?' she whispered sadly. 'He's gone – and he's never coming back.' In her deepest heart she had always known he would be gone at the first opportunity, but she had so much wanted to be wrong. Her heart and her head had been at odds about Edward from the day he had set his sights on her. It was so hard to give up hope, to see things as they really were.

'I can't answer that,' Vicky answered softly. 'We'll find your Edward, I'm sure, the minute Barney comes back.'

However kindly her intention, Vicky's assurances gave Lucy small comfort. Desolate, she closed her eyes and let the sleep roll over her. He was gone. Edward was gone; and it had all been too good to be true. He hadn't even seen their son.

When Dr Lucas arrived he gave Lucy a swift yet thorough examination. 'There doesn't seem to be any lasting damage,' he concluded, 'though I would prefer her not to be too active, for at least a week.'

He handed Vicky a bottle of dark brown liquid. 'Bathe the wound in this morning and night, but it must not be covered . . . fresh air is the best thing. Light food, and a little exercise, but she must rest. A week of that, and I expect her to be good as new.' Having given his diagnosis and delivered the prescription, he bade them goodbye. 'You know where I am if you should need me,' he declared, in that abrupt manner of any good doctor.

Afterwards, while Vicky went downstairs to put the kettle on, Barney told Lucy what the doctor had said. 'It might be best if you stay here with us for the week,' he suggested, and Lucy thanked him. 'If it isn't too much trouble?' she said tearfully.

'No trouble at all,' he promised. With a smile he added, 'With three offspring and yon Jess, I can't deny we're a noisy family at times, but I'll make sure you're not too disturbed. One of us'll nip over to the squire's tomorrow morning and let 'em know you've had a little accident so they won't expect to see you again for a few days, all right?'

Lucy thanked him again, and when he left her to rest, she cried until she thought her heart would break. Edward was gone, and with him, her own chance of a proper family. Her son would never know his father, and she would never experience the true happiness that she had witnessed between Barney and his Vicky.

Those two had something beautiful, a very special belonging that she could never even hope for.

CHAPTER EIGHT

I T WAS ONE of the happiest weeks Lucy had ever known. Having worked at the squire's house for some time now, she had come to know the countryside well, but she had never lived as close to nature as she had done this past week. She loved it all: the sound of the pigeons cooing at early morning, the dew glistening on the grass and the sun coming up over the hill, sending out warmth and light, and making the heart feel good. After a couple of days, her concussion had passed, but the kindly doctor advised her to stay where she was. Bridget and Tillie had brought Jamie up to Overhill Farm and enjoyed some country hospitality. Out here, the shortages and hardships of the townfolk had, to some extent, been kept at bay.

In the evening she could see the lake in the distance, shimmering and twinkling under the moonlight. It was all a new and wonderful experience and she found herself waking earlier than she had ever done. At 5 a.m. she would run to the window where she would see Barney's familiar figure as he went away to check his flock, the dog beside him and his master's merry whistle echoing through the quiet morning air.

Later, when she was pushing Jamie on the old swing in the orchard, it was a pleasure to see Barney and his sons as they worked the fields, always with the dog running behind, and the lovely Vicky, busy all the day long, collecting eggs, tending her washing, cleaning house and baking treats for her large, loving family; ever busy, ever noisy, just as Barney had promised.

Barney and Vicky had three children. Thomas, at seventeen, was a serious and hardworking young man. Like the others he was devoted to his father who, in his eyes, could do no wrong. A handsome fellow, with sincere eyes and dark hair, he burned with ambitions of one day owning his own farm, unlike Barney who managed Overhill Farm for the wealthy local landowner Leonard Maitland, who lived at The Manse, down in the village.

Along with his brother Ronnie, Tom helped Barney run the farm; the two sons did all the basic tasks, like feeding the many animals, collecting food from the supplier, taking produce to market and chopping trees, selling some wood and logging the rest for the home fires. In addition it was their responsibility to generally maintain the house and buildings.

Winter or summer, there was always work to be done, and come harvest it was all hands that could be spared.

At fifteen, Ronnie was two years younger than his brother. With wild fair hair and his father's blue eyes, he was accident-prone, fun-loving, sensitive, sincere and fiercely loyal. When he flirted outrageously, which was often, the girls fell at his feet. Though he loved his mother dearly, he was devoted to Barney, attempting to emulate him in everything he did.

Quiet and thoughtful, Susie was the only girl. Thirteen years of age and looking like a smaller replica of her mother, she adored her parents – especially Barney, who called her his 'little angel'.

Susie loved to do things for her daddy. She would polish his Sunday shoes before they all went to church; make daisy chains for him when they were picnicking, run and meet him when he came home of an evening. She would scold him when she thought he was not looking after himself and, except for when she was learning the art of hat-making under the scrutiny of an old eccentric by the name of Doris Dandy, over in Everton, she was never far from her daddy's side.

'I'd rather farm than make hats,' she told him once, and because he wanted her to acquire a regular skill that would stand her in good stead for the rest of her life, he would hear no more of such talk.

Lately, having become increasingly curious about the deeper things of the heart, Susie would often corner her daddy to discuss the mysteries and meaning of life. Sometimes out of his depth, Barney would talk and listen, and they would each learn from the other.

As for Lucy, in the short week she had lived under their roof, she had come to care deeply for Barney's family. Everyone who knew them had a good word to say for them. The love and support they all gave each other was wonderful to see; even when brothers and sister argued, that bond of togetherness never broke.

Witnessing family life at first hand made her own loss and disappointment all the more poignant. If only Edward had stayed, instead of running away again, she thought, maybe they could have had the same close family life. Yet in all her regrets, she did not hate him, though God knows she had tried hard enough to do so. She was bitter though; bitter and resentful of the fact that he could casually show up after all this time, only to turn her life upside down yet again. Thank goodness that the shock of the accident had brought on her monthly bleeding a week early. To have allowed Edward to make her pregnant *again* would have been a disaster.

Today was Lucy's last day with the Davidsons. While she got herself and her son ready, Vicky and her family were downstairs waiting for her to join them for the evening meal. 'I wish we could stay,' Lucy told the child as she fastened his blue jacket. 'It's been so lovely here. I'll miss it all so much.'

In reply, Jamie ran his little wooden engine over the floor making train sounds. He loved being read to and petted by the older children in Barney's family; in turn, they all adored the little chap and had spent many happy hours showing him all the farm animals. Like his mother, Jamie would miss all of this.

Lucy had been strong with every disappointment that life sent her way; Edward going off to sea; the discovery that she was with child, and having to tell her parents the truth; then her parents splitting up after weeks of rowing and fighting, and afterwards finding herself out on the streets.

And only a week ago, when Edward had come home, her hopes had soared only to be shattered again; and as though to add insult to injury he had run off and left her lying hurt, leaving Barney to take care of her. That was a cowardly thing he had done.

Through all of these events she had been strong. But now, as she prepared to leave Overhill Farm and the Davidsons, she felt so sad. It was one disappointment too many.

Now her stay was over, and when the meal was finished, Barney would take her back to Bridget's and life would resume exactly as it was before. She would rise early, leave her son in the care of little Tillie, and trudge through the fields to the squire's house, where she would work a hard day before trudging back again. She had never been afraid of work, but it was a lonely kind of life, and she missed her son. He was growing fast and she was losing out on his development.

No home of her own, working every hour God sent, and no man to stand by her. Lucy thought it was not much of a life to look forward to. But that was the life she had been given and it was up to her to do the best she could with it. And she would, for what other choice did she have? She knew she should never have given in to Edward's wiles, should have kept herself pure for marriage, but somehow she'd never met the right man when all her schoolfriends did, and in her mid-twenties had felt like an elderly spinster. And oh – how Edward's caresses had thrilled her, and made her lose her head, heart, and virginity too. Oh well. It was true, the old saying that there was no use in crying over spilled milk – that was for sure. And now it was very unlikely that she would ever find a decent man who was willing to take both her and Jamie on . . .

As she walked into the homely kitchen, Lucy was astonished to see the family standing round the table, waiting for her; Ronnie, she noticed, had taken time to tame his unruly hair, Thomas gave her a welcoming wink, and Susie was quietly smiling.

Barney and his wife were standing together, he with his arm round her and she so content beside him. 'Come in, my love!' She ran to greet Lucy, and as she led her and Jamie across the room, she said, 'Look. I've made the table pretty for you.'

Overawed by what they had done, Lucy looked at the table and wiped away a tear. It was laid as if for a banquet. Normally the table was simply laid, with the meals already served on the plates. There was never any fuss or ceremony. Over dinner, everyone would get together, tuck into Vicky's home-cooking and talk about the day's events.

This evening, though, was extra special to all of them. There was an air of excitement which Lucy could not understand; especially when they knew she was unhappy about having to leave.

It was almost as though they were pleased at the prospect of having the house back to themselves. Yet even while the unfortunate thought crossed her mind, Lucy could not believe it. This past week, Barney and his family had done everything they could to make her feel like one of them, so why would they be relieved to see her go? No! She was wrong. All this fuss and excitement was their way of trying to make her feel better about it. That was it. This was their going-away present to her. They wanted her to leave on a good note. And, for their sake, she would smile and laugh, and they would never really know how wretched she felt.

'Well, Lucy?' Vicky nudged her elbow. 'What do you think to my table? They wouldn't let me do it on my own. Everybody helped and even then, we were worried we might not get it all finished before you came down.'

Draped in a long, flowing tablecloth of crimson, the big old table was set like Lucy had never seen it. There were candles in pretty holders; glasses with long stems and a twirl of napkin in each one. In the centre of the table stood platters laid with all manner of meats; there were bowls of steaming vegetables and a long dish of small crisply roasted potatoes – Lucy's favourites; there was also a wicker dish filled with freshly-baked rolls, whose aroma filled the room, and right in the middle, two bottles of Barney's homemade elderberry wine.

For what seemed an age, Lucy was speechless. 'Aw, Vicky. It's just . . . beautiful!' Now, as the tears threatened, she let them fall before discreetly brushing them away. 'You shouldn't have gone to so much trouble.'

'It was no trouble at all.' Vicky slid an arm round her waist. 'It's our present to you,' she said, 'to show how much we love you, *and* this little one.' She tickled young Jamie under the chin, laughing as he gurgled with delight.

The child's response broke the atmosphere.

Rushing forward, Barney took Lucy by the arm. 'Tonight, you've been allocated my very own seat, at the head of the table.' And with no more ado he marched her there and sat her down. 'And as for this little chap . . .' Lifting the child out of her arms, he sat him in the homemade high chair, which had been finished only that afternoon, with sturdy legs and straps to hold the little fella safe.

'He can sit with the rest of us, like a grown-up,' Ronnie declared with pride. 'Father made the structure, Thomas made the legs, and I cut the leather straps to hold him in. We were still working on it up to half an hour since.' He groaned. 'In fact, if you'd come down that much earlier, the babby might be rolling on the floor, because we only had the one leg fixed to it, and that would never have supported the fat little lump!'

Everyone laughed, with Susie protesting that Lucy's Jamie was *not* 'a fat little lump'.

As always before the evening meal, Barney stood before his chair and said Grace. Being farmers and working closely with the land, they all understood how, with one dark mood, Nature could devastate a whole year's crop, and leave them desolate.

In all of Barney's experience that had only ever happened once, soon after he'd taken up the post of Farm Manager here. He had never forgotten. Nor had he forgotten to always give his thanks.

He gave his thanks now, 'For the food and warmth You send us. For bringing Lucy back to health, and keeping us all safe from harm.' Looking down on his wife, he stroked her hair. 'And for this wonderful woman You blessed me with. Thank You, Lord.' His words were spoken with such quiet gratitude that there seemed nothing more natural in the whole world. And in equally quiet voice, everyone echoed his thanks.

When Lucy looked up to see Vicky taking a discreet hold of Barney's hand, Lucy's heart was both sore and joyous. That small significant gesture between husband and wife was unseen by everyone else, but Lucy thought it the most touching thing she had ever been privileged to witness.

It was obvious that, even after more than twenty years wed, and three children into the bargain, Vicky and Barney still adored each other, as much as on the day they first met. Theirs was a deep, everlasting love, and one which Lucy sensed that neither she nor countless others would ever experience in their whole lives.

The meal was wonderful, and so was the company. They chatted and laughed and drank the wine, and when the child fell asleep in his chair, Barney lifted him out and made him comfortable on the sofa. 'Right!' Returning to the table, he told everyone to fill their glasses and raise them for a toast, and when that was done he stood for a moment looking from one to the other, until his gaze rested on Lucy. 'We would have liked you to stay here with us,' he said, and Lucy's heart rose, 'but as you know, your being here meant that Susie had to sleep downstairs on the couch, and though she didn't mind that . . .' he looked at Susie and she nodded in agreement '. . . it isn't a situation that could continue for any length of time.' He hesitated. 'You do understand, don't you, Lucy?'

Lucy understood, and even managed a bright smile. 'Of course I do,' she assured them. 'I never really expected that I could stay here. I'm just grateful for the time and help you all gave me. I'll never be able to thank you enough.'

Barney smiled at her. 'Look under your plate, lass.'

Lucy was confused. 'Under my plate?'

'That's what the man said!' That was Ronnie, being his usual comical self. But there was a certain twinkle in his eye. In fact, as Lucy glanced at each family member in turn, she saw a twinkle in *all* their eyes.

'Go on then, Lucy. Look and see what he's put there.' Susie was excitedly bouncing up and down in her chair.

Gingerly, Lucy lifted her plate and moving it aside, took out an envelope that was folded there. She opened the envelope and dipping her fingers inside, withdrew a large, shiny coin. 'A guinea!' Her eyes widened in astonishment. 'What's this for?'

Barney told her fondly, 'It's your first month's wages. Me and my Vicky have discussed it with the family, and we all agree there's enough work on this farm for all of us. When harvest comes there's no time to catch your breath; then there's the carting and stacking, and any number of other tasks that could do with another pair of hands . . . especially for Vicky, who's always rushed off her feet. This house is too much when she's needed outside. That's where you come in, Lucy. So, the job's yours, if you want it?'

In a minute Lucy was out of her chair; running round the table she threw her arms round Barney's neck. 'Oh Barney . . . all of you! You don't know what this means to me.' Going from one to another, she kissed and hugged them in turn. 'Instead of passing this house every morning, and trudging all the way on to the Hall, I'll be turning in at your gate.' The excitement was all too much. 'I'll be working with you all. Oh, it's wonderful!' She laughed through her tears. 'I can't believe it!' She was sure that no one apart from Dorothy would miss her at Haskell Hall.

At that moment there came a knock on the door. 'All right, matey, come on in.' Barney appeared to know who it was even before the door opened.

The door inched open and a man appeared; small of stature, with a kindly face and smiling eyes, he greeted everyone in turn. 'Hello, Lucy,' he finished. 'I hope you're fighting fit after your accident?'

Lucy was not surprised to see him. 'Hello, Adam,' she answered. 'Yes, I'm well, thank you.' A kindly man in his early thirties, Adam Chives was well-known throughout the village of Comberton-by-Weir. In fact, there wasn't a single house that he had not been into at some time or another, for he was the local handyman, tried, trusted and greatly respected by one and all. Lucy always suspected that he had a soft spot for her, on the quiet. However, he was far too much of a gentleman to say anything.

'Come on then, m'laddo!' Barney held out his hand. 'I trust you've brought it with you?'

'I have,' came the proud reply. 'I've done everything you asked of me, and more besides.' He handed something to Barney, winked at Ronnie, and said, 'I expect there'll be a bonus in there somewhere for me, will there not?'

Barney took up the tease. 'There certainly will be – in the shape of a roast dinner with all the trimmings . . . if you want it, that is?'

Adam didn't need asking twice. 'That'll do me,' he told Vicky, who was chuckling at the pair of them. 'In fact, I could think of nothing else all the way here.'

'Right then! You sit down and fill your plate while I have a quiet word with Lucy.'

'Whatever you say.' In fact, Adam was already privy to the reason for Barney's need to talk with Lucy in private.

Adam had known Barney for many years; in their childhood they had learned the times-table together; ridden side by side across the fields on whatever horse they could borrow; shot rabbits for the pot, and later sat many a while on the porch, exchanging tales of when they were lads. They knew each other as well as any brothers might, and loved each other the same.

Leaving the others to chat, Barney rounded the table and taking Lucy by the hand, led her out to the back porch. They sat on the bench and there, Barney spoke his mind. 'There's summat you need to think about.'

Lucy asked him what he meant. But she could never have imagined in her wildest dreams what he was about to say.

Barney continued, 'I know it's none of our business, but well . . . Me and Vicky have been talking and what we think is this: it's not good to bring a child up in a house of women – if you know what I mean?'

Lucy had no doubts. 'You mean women who entertain?'

Sucking in his lips he took a deep breath. Afraid she might have taken him wrong, he answered sincerely, 'It's not for me to judge other folks. All I'm saying is this: for little Jamie's sake, and yours, it won't be a bad thing when you move out of there.'

Lucy gave a wry little laugh. 'It's easier said than

done.' She shrugged her shoulders. 'For a start, where would I go?'

He smiled. 'So, you would leave if you only had somewhere to go. Is that what you're telling me, Lucy?'

'Oh, yes.' Lucy was aware of her environment and knew as well as did Barney, that it was not a suitable place to raise a child. 'If I had somewhere to go, I'd leave – though I have to say, I would miss Bridget and the girls. They've been such good friends to me.'

'I know that,' he agreed. 'Haven't they visited you time and again since you've been here? And haven't I heard you laughing with them, when only hours before, you were fit for nothing? Believe me, Lucy, after you being so poorly, it did our heart good to hear you. Now then, lass, I want you to take this.' Opening his hand, he revealed a heavy iron key lying in his palm. 'Take it!' he urged. 'There's no rush. Just give it some thought and let me know what you decide.'

Lucy was confused. 'It's a key.'

He chuckled. 'Well, of course it's a key!'

'But where does it belong?'

'It belongs to the little cottage at the other end of the brook. The one where Leonard Maitland's gardener lived afore he threw him out for robbing him.'

Realisation began to dawn. 'What? You mean, the pretty one with the thatched roof and the little

160

garden which runs right down to the brook edge?'

'Aye, that's the one.'

She took the key, which weighed heavy in her hand. 'So, this is the key to that cottage?'

Barney nodded affirmatively. 'That one opens the front door. I've another for the back. If you decide it's what you want, I'll let you have the other key an' all.'

The merest smile trembled on Lucy's mouth. 'But I don't fully understand. Why are you giving me this key?'

Smiling into her inquisitive eyes, he explained, 'The boss, Mr Maitland, and me had a little chat yesterday.'

'About me?'

'Sort of, yes. He was aware of your accident – you know how gossip flies around a village – and being the kindly gent he is, he took the time to ask after you. I told him the way things were, and he said if I thought it would help to offer you the vacant cottage, he wouldn't mind one bit; though he would expect you to give him half a day's work per week in lieu of rent . . . a bit of cleaning, that sort of thing. Besides, the cottage needed living in, that's what he said, or it would fall to rack and ruin. Y'see, his new gardener has his own cottage and has no need of this one. In fact, the boss had a mind to sell it off with a parcel of land, but he never got round to it. Moreover, he mentioned as how it's so tiny it wouldn't fetch much in the way of cash.'

He took a breath. 'To tell you the truth, Lucy, the cottage is of small interest to Mr Maitland, so it's yours if you want it.'

Lucy gasped. 'I can't believe this is happening!' Thrilled to her roots, she was astounded for the second time that evening. 'The cottage is mine? Really? Are you sure?'

Laughing out loud, Barney squeezed her hand. 'Well, aren't you the cloth ears,' he teased. 'Isn't that what I've just been saying?'

Lucy was speechless. And now the tears she had managed to hold back all day ran down her cheeks and all at once she was laughing and crying, and telling Barney, 'I haven't got a stick of furniture, but yes, oh, yes!' She was beside herself. 'We'll move in as soon as possible. Never mind a bed. We'll sleep on the floor if we have to.'

'There'll be no need of that. The cottage comes with its own furniture and such. Yon Adam has cleaned and aired the place all ready for you and young Jamie. All you'll want is new bedding and certain silly bits and pieces a woman needs to keep her happy. And you needn't worry about the bairn when you work the half-day for Mr Maitland, because Vicky's already said she'll be more than happy to keep an eye on him. And it goes without saying that when you're working here for the rest of the week, the bairn is welcome as the day is long.'

And so it was settled. Lucy would move in within

the next few days, and while she was getting organised, Barney would make sure the garden was cleared and all was spick and span for her and the child.

~

A few days later, Lucy was saying her goodbyes in Viaduct Street. 'I'll never be able to thank you enough for what you've done for me.' Emotion thickened her voice as she threw her arms round Bridget and hugged her so hard, the poor woman had to wrench her off.

'Be Jaysus, will ye get offa me! Are ye trying to strangle me or what?' Holding Lucy at arm's length, she looked into those sincere brown eyes and thought how much she would miss this young woman; with her impromptu singing and bright, happy presence, the house would be all the poorer for her not being there.

'I'm truly sorry to see ye go,' she told Lucy now, 'but I'm happy for you, so I am. You'll have your own front-door key and Jamie will have his own little room, and when me and the girls come a-calling, you'll have fresh-baked muffins ready for us, and a big pot o' tea waiting.' She gave a wink. 'Unless o' course you've a drop o' the good stuff hidden away in the cupboard for an old friend?'

With the sadness lifted, Lucy laughed out loud. 'Oi will,' she answered, mimicking Bridget's strong Irish accent. 'Sure Oi'll have a little bottle tucked away and ye can drink to your heart's content, so ye can.'

Bridget roared with laughter. 'Ye sound more like me than I do meself. Go on, ye little divil, be off wit' ye!' She gave her another hug, and craftily dropped a couple of coins into the palm of her hand. 'A little something to get ye started. Take care of yourself, m'darling,' she said softly, and before she might start blubbering herself, she sent Lucy on her way.

A few minutes later, along with her few belongings and the child on her knee, Lucy settled herself in Barney's wagon.

'Any regrets, lass?'

The young woman shook her head. 'Not a one.' The only regrets she had were old ones, and now they didn't seem to matter quite as much.

When he arrived at Bridget's house, Barney had greeted Bridget and the girls with his usual friendliness, and now he was leaving with Lucy beside him, he said his goodbyes with the same warmth, for that was his manner.

'All set, are we?' He had witnessed the emotional scene between Lucy and her friends, but like Lucy, he knew her leaving was all for the best.

'All set,' Lucy replied, a brief rush of sadness clouding her face.

'Then you'd best hold on tight because once I let this wild animal have its rein, there's no telling *where* we might end up!'

His little attempt at making her laugh worked wonders, because she laughed so hard she couldn't reply. Pleased with himself, he gave her a warming wink, gently slapped the horse's great wide rump to drive the bumbling animal forward, and told her in that quiet, no-nonsense manner, 'You did the right thing.'

And that was all he would ever again say on the matter.

As the shire ambled away down Viaduct Street, Lucy turned to look at the four women standing on the doorstep, and as they waved back, she blew a kiss. 'I'll miss you,' she murmured.

Barney glanced at her. 'There's your past and ahead is your future,' he said simply. Barney Davidson was known as a man of few words, but when he took a mind to speak, his few words said more than a vicar delivering a sermon.

As they meandered along, Lucy considered his wise words, and she knew he was right. After everything that had befallen her, this was the start of a new life, where she could put all the bad things behind her and start over again.

At long last, she had something to look forward to.

Once they were beyond the city roads and were heading towards Comberton, she watched Barney take the old briar-pipe and his baccy pouch from his waistcoat pocket; letting loose of the reins he gave the horse its head, and after carefully packing the pipe with the baccy he struck a match on the sole of his shoe and lit up. He then drew leisurely on the pipe, the twirls of smoke rising to slowly evaporate above his head.

Suddenly in the midst of his thinking, he turned to smile at Lucy in that comforting way of his. At the time, Barney's wonderful smile merely warmed her heart, though inevitably bonding her to him.

It was many years later when, looking back on that magical, intimate moment, with the child asleep and the two of them gently following the narrow country lanes, Barney contentedly smoking his pipe and the sound of the birds singing all around, Lucy realised she must have fallen hopelessly in love with him then – and she never even knew it.

Barney Davidson. A wise and kindly man who knew the earth as if it was his own; a man who had the heart of a lion and could protect the weak, that was Barney.

Just for now though, misinterpreting her deeper feelings, Lucy saw Barney only as a very dear friend. No more than that.

Yet, even though many a moon would shine before she came to realise the true depth of her feelings for him, Lucy already knew in her heart and soul, that she would never meet his like again.

CHAPTER NINE

THE WEEKS PASSED and already it was the end of July.

Lucy and Jamie had settled in well to Mr Maitland's vacant cottage. It was almost as though they had lived there forever. Lucy was happier than she had ever been; every day was like a holiday. Her life was filled with new experiences and here in the countryside where she was a part of the greater picture, what had previously seemed to her like mountainous problems, now seemed almost trivial.

She counted herself fortunate to have such friends as the Davidsons; they were a joy to be with. Working or relaxing, every minute in their company drew her more and more into their family.

Sometimes on a Sunday evening, Bridget or one of the girls from Viaduct Street would visit, and they would sit and talk, and laugh to their hearts' content. Lucy made sure to keep a measure of the 'good stuff' hidden away for when Bridget came. 'Oh, you're a darling – what are ye?' Tipping up her glass and warming the cockles of her heart, Bridget would dance and sing and go home all the merrier.

As arranged, through the week Lucy worked with the Davidsons, and on Saturday morning she went up to Leonard Maitland's house, where she did the ironing and other jobs like cleaning his silver. After midday her work was done and the weekend was her own, to enjoy the cottage and play with her child.

Each day saw Jamie grow more and more sturdy; he now was very active and the fresh air was doing him a power of good. He loved his new family and had begun to talk in his own way to them all. Everyone loved the little toddler and enjoyed having him around the farm.

On this particular Saturday, Lucy was replacing the silver in the display cabinet, just about to finish her morning's work, when she heard voices in the next room. 'Sometimes I'm not sure I'm cut out to be a farmer's wife.'

'Hmh! I wish you'd told me that before I put an engagement ring on your finger.'

There followed a girlish peal of false laughter and the light-hearted suggestion, 'Oh, Lenny! Why don't you sell everything – this house, the land and cottages. We could move down to London – or go abroad! It would be so wonder-

ful to travel. We could stay away for a whole year
. . . see the world, do something exciting.'

There was a brief silence, then the woman
demanded, 'Are you deliberately ignoring me?'
Another silence, then in sterner voice: 'Leonard!
Did you hear what I said?'

'I heard, and yes, I *am* deliberately ignoring you,
Pat. We've had this same conversation so many
times I'm beginning to tire of it.'

Only the thinness of a wall away, Lucy recognised the voices of Patricia Carstairs and Leonard
Maitland. She tried hard not to listen and even
softly sang to herself, but the voices grew louder
and angrier, and she couldn't help but overhear
every single word.

'Yes, and so am I tired of it!' Anger trembled in
her voice. 'Whenever I take the trouble to drive
over and see you, you've either got your head
buried in paperwork, or you're out with your man
discussing tractors or some such thing, or over-
seeing a delivery. Yesterday, and not for the first
time, I came here to find you ensconced in your
office with two other men, and even when you
knew I was here, you just popped your head round
the door and excused yourself. My God, Leonard!
You didn't come out for a full hour, and I was
made to hang around like a dog at its master's
heels. These days, you hardly ever have time for
me, and that is not how it should be. I should come
first in your life and I don't. And I'm really fed up!'

'Then listen to what I'm saying.' Leonard sounded weary. He *was* weary – of her demands, of her chastising, and of her misguided belief that he, like her, had nothing better to do than socialise. 'I'm a farmer, Patricia . . . a busy man. You knew that when we met and you know it now. I can't change that. I *won't* change it.'

'But you don't actually farm, do you?' Her tone was cynical.

Leonard gave a dry, angry laugh. 'You just don't understand, do you?' he said. 'I may not often sit in the tractor, or plough in the seeds, or cut the corn when it's grown. But I'm a landowner and as such have certain responsibilities. I plan which seeds go into the ground, or which tractor suits the job best. I scour the country for the best price I might get for my harvest . . . There are a multitude of things that come with working the land. I monitor every single thing. I buy and sell, and treat my part of the job with respect.'

'But you have Barney Davidson. You sing his praises so often, I'm sure if you let him, he would take a lot more responsibility from your shoulders.'

There was another moment of silence; a moment when Lucy felt uncomfortable, for she could almost taste the atmosphere.

It seemed an age before, in a cutting voice, Leonard Maitland spoke again. 'You will *never* understand, will you, Patricia? You don't even try to understand the implications of what I'm telling you. I bought this land because I needed to. If I didn't have land around me, I would simply suffocate. But land is not just for looking at, and when you take it on, you give yourself wholeheartedly to its well-being. You treat it like a living, breathing entity, because that's what it is. The land gives more than it takes, and it deserves to be cared for. But, like I say, you will never comprehend that, and I don't blame you for it.'

'I'm sorry, Lenny darling.' True or false, the voice and its owner seemed contrite. 'All I'm saying is, why not let Barney take over occasionally? After all, you've always said he knows the land as well as you do. I can't count the number of times you've remarked on how a capable man like Barney Davidson was meant to have his own farm, but that life had not treated him kindly enough.'

'Yes, Pat, and I meant it. But this is *my* land. *My* responsibility. Barney is my partner in a sense. He is my eyes and ears, and while I organise everything else, he farms, and that's all right, because he has the same love for the land that I do.'

'Oh Lenny.' The voice grew whining. 'I know how passionate you are about this place . . .'

'No, you don't.' Now he was calmer, wanting to explain. 'You live in town. You can have no idea of what it feels like to see the harvest being brought in, or to stride the fields on a winter's morning, when the snow lies deep in the ditches and the trees bend and dip with the weight.' His voice dropped. 'If you want us to marry, as I do, then you must accept that my work is important to me.'

'All right, my darling, but why can't we go away – for a month maybe?'

'We will,' he consoled her. 'Look, we're due to be married next spring, and if it suits you, we can have a much longer honeymoon than planned. How's that?'

'And can I plan where we go?' She was a spoiled child.

'If you like, yes.'

'And money's no object?'

He gave a sigh. Did his fiancée not realise that most of the world was plunged into a financial crisis? 'It is our honeymoon after all,' he said resignedly.

'Oh, Lenny, it will be so wonderful!' Excitement coloured her voice. 'Then in the winter, can we go far away – to the South of France or even further afield? My London friends spent last winter in Sydney and they said it was the best time they ever had. Oh, it would be so nice to get right away. I do get so bored visiting the same old places.'

'You're a mystery to me.' A different emotion crept into his words. 'You're infuriating and selfish, and sometimes I wonder what I see in you. But fool that I am, I can't help but love you.'

'I'll remember that when you refuse me what I ask.'

'You will have to remember something else too.'

'For instance?'

'For instance, that being a landowner, I must bow to my duties here. There will always be times when I can't just take off at your every whim and fancy.'

There came that soft trill of laughter again. 'We shall have to see, won't we? Now I think you should give me a kiss, by way of apology.'

'Don't you think the apology should come from *you*?'

'Aw, Leonard! Does it really matter who apologises? Kiss me, and we'll forget we ever quarrelled.'

Silence reigned for a moment, when Lucy imagined they were in the throes of the 'apology'. Then came the sound of a door opening and closing, and when she glanced out of the window, Lucy saw them going arm-in-arm down the driveway to the long black car, recently chosen by Patricia Carstairs, paid for by Mr Maitland, and delivered only three days ago.

'Oh darling! Won't people be envious when they see us together in this!' was Patricia's parting remark as she climbed into the car.

Lucy watched them drive off; the woman slim, beautiful, and arrogant to the quick, while the gentleman was attentive and homely, a gentle giant of a man.

Lucy thought them quite unsuited. 'That one's trouble. He should drop her like a hot potato!' Closing the curtains, she pranced across the room on tippy-toe, emulating Patricia Carstairs, one hand on her hip, the other swanking by her side, mimicking the woman's voice to perfection. *'Oh darling! Won't people be envious when they see us together in this?'* She pitied the poor wretches who had no work and no money; to see a smart car passing by, occupied by that one with her nose in the air would be like a red rag to a bull.

Breaking into song, Lucy returned to her work, gave the large silver teapot another rub with the cloth, then with the greatest of care replaced it in the cabinet, where she shifted the silverware about until the display was pleasing to the eye.

She now closed the door, took up a clean cloth from her basket and giving the door-glass a good polish, gave a sigh of relief. 'All done for another week!'

A few minutes later, she was out of the house and running across the back lawns towards the fields. Now, as she rounded the brow of the hill, she heard the laughter from Barney's house. Pausing, she took off her shoes, set off at the run and before long was at the gate of Overhill farmhouse. 'Quick, Lucy!' Vicky was beckoning her. 'Hurry!'

When the young woman ran into the garden, she saw little Jamie standing with his back to the trunk of the apple tree, arms wide and laughing as only a child can laugh. 'He's trying to walk all the way over to us unaided,' Vicky told Lucy. 'Three times he's started off and three times he's fallen. I've stood him up again, but he loves this game, and he wants to carry on playing it.'

Lucy was delighted. Jamie was a good little walker now, but his gammy leg meant he often fell over. Falling to her knees, she opened her arms wide, coaxing the boy. 'Come to your mammy, sweetheart.'

He stopped giggling and stared at her, as though he might be giving it some thought. Then he looked up to excitedly point into the skies, at a hawk hovering nearby. 'Bird!' he shouted. 'Big bird.'

Arms still wide, Lucy took a step nearer. 'Look at me, Jamie. Come on, sweetheart.'

The child would have none of it. Completely ignoring her, he scoured the skies with his big bright eyes, one finger pointing as he slowly but surely slid downwards, his back seemingly glued to the tree.

'Stay there, Lucy!' Running forward, Vicky propped him up again. 'Try, sweetheart,' she urged the little man. Slowly she backed away, one hand up flat, as though it might dissuade him from sliding down again.

Standing next to Lucy, Vicky took a cooked sausage from the picnic hamper. 'Ooh – look what

I've got.' She waved the sausage from side to side. 'If you want it, you'll have to come and get it.'

Lucy laughed. 'That's a wicked thing to do.'

Suddenly the child was interested. He licked his lips and raising his arms, made an effort to shuffle forward. 'He means it this time,' Vicky whispered. 'He'll do it now, you see if he doesn't.'

And he didn't, because when he spotted Barney appearing, he promptly sat down. 'Leave the little fella alone.' Still in his work-clothes, his cap pulled forward, Barney stood beside the two women and looking at the boy asked, 'What are they doing to you, eh?'

Lucy straightened up. 'We're trying to coax him to walk over here without falling over,' she answered. 'Vicky said he tried and failed three times.'

'Is that right?' The smile he gave Vicky spoke volumes; even when he wasn't saying he loved her, he still showed it – in his smile, in his eyes, in the way he always stood by her side – always there with her, even when he wasn't.

'Well, he looks proper fed up now, and no mistake. Poor little bugger, you've stuck him up against a tree and now he can't do nothing but sit down.' And that was exactly what Jamie had done. Sitting on the ground he was pulling the grass up and attempting to eat it.

'Go on then. Stand him up again, but this is the last attempt,' Barney insisted. 'Looks to me like he's had enough.' Tipping back his cap he stooped to one knee, and waited until Lucy had propped up the child. 'Right then, Jamie, old son.' Looking the child in the eye, he said quietly, 'You're to take no notice o' these women. They're like all women the world over – nag, nag, nag. Anybody'd think you'd only got a minute to learn the walking, when truth being, you've got all the time in the world.' He feigned a deep sigh. 'But if it's the only way you can get to sit down in peace and eat your sausage, then if I were you, I'd give it another go.'

He raised his arms and stretching them apart, he gave the boy a cheeky wink, quietly chattering to himself. 'It's up to you, son. You can either come and give Uncle Barney a cuddle, or you can refuse to budge an inch and sit down. Like I say, it's up to you. But you'd best be quick about it. I've been on the go since five o'clock this morning and every bone in my body aches. I need a cuppa tea and five minutes in the armchair to put me right, so come on . . . walk on them fat little legs o' yourn. Do it for Barney, there's a good 'un.'

Vicky gave him a playful shove. 'Stop nattering to yourself. You have to raise your voice and talk clear, or he won't hear a word you're saying!'

In that moment, Lucy gave her a dig. 'Look at him, Vicky. Look at Jamie!'

Barney's 'nattering' seemed to have worked, for the child had stood himself up straight and was now pushing against the tree, trying to get started. Arms outstretched towards Barney, he took one faltering step, then another, then a third step. When he saw Barney making faces at him, he burst out laughing and almost lost his balance again.

A few minutes later, encouraged by the big man's coaxing, Jamie completed his walk across the orchard and fell into Barney's arms. 'Who's a champion then, eh?' After giving him a kiss and a bear hug, Barney swung him round to Lucy. 'There y'are. Now that he's walking so well, you'll need eyes in the back of your head, and serves you right, the pair of you.'

With that, he gave Vicky a knowing wink and strode off, still 'nattering' to himself. 'Poor little devil never had a chance. Women and their bullying – what's a man to do, eh?' But he wouldn't want to be without his Vicky for all the treasures in the world.

Thrilled at Jamie's performance, Lucy took him by the hand and the two of them slowly followed Vicky into the house. It was another special memory that Lucy would cherish forever.

While the child slept soundly after all his efforts, the three of them sat together in the kitchen, each with a cup of tea and a generous slice of home-made fruit-cake; Vicky and Lucy at the table and Barney in the armchair. Once or twice, Lucy caught the two of them discreetly exchanging glances, as though they shared something she ought to know about.

'Where's Susie?' Lucy had grown fond of Barney and Vicky's daughter, but she was hardly ever around. She was either out with her schoolfriends, or in town learning how to make hats.

'She's gone on a picnic with a group of friends.' Vicky worried about her young daughter. Though loving and giving, she seemed unsure of what she wanted to do with her life. Whenever Vicky spoke to Barney about her fears, he would tell her, 'Leave the child be, and she'll find her way soon enough.'

'There's something I've been meaning to ask you,' Vicky told Lucy after a while. 'It's been plaguing me for some time.'

Barney looked up at her remark. 'Then you'd best get it off your chest,' he urged. 'There's no use fretting about it.' He knew exactly what concerned Vicky, because it also concerned him, though not to the same degree.

'What is it?' For the first time in their company, Lucy felt uncomfortable. 'Is it something I've done, because if it is, I can't know if you don't tell me. Or is it that you can't have Jamie any more?'

If that was the worry playing on Vicky's mind, it would only mean the problem was shifted from her to Lucy, because Lucy had no one else, other than little Tillie, and she didn't really want the child to go back to Bridget's house.

'No, of course it isn't that!' Reaching across the

table, Vicky patted the back of Lucy's hand. 'It isn't that at all. You know how much we love having the child. Good grief! I'd be lost without him now.'

Barney laughed as he remarked to Lucy, 'Now that he's walking so well, he can help Vicky peg the washing out. Give him another few months and I dare say he'll be out in that barn, chopping wood to his heart's content.'

'Shut up, you daftie!' Covering him with her smile, Vicky shook her head. 'We're talking serious here.'

Lucy was worried. 'What is it, Vicky? What's wrong?'

So, as kindly and quietly as possible, Vicky told her, 'I know it's not really my concern, and you can tell me to mind my own business if you like, only . . .' She gave a nervous little cough.

Barney intervened to save her. 'Spit it out, love. You've got Lucy thinking all sorts of terrible things.'

Taking a deep breath, Vicky said, 'It's just that . . . well, I've been wondering when you mean to have the boy baptised?' There! Now that it was said, she quickly picked up her cup of tea, took a great swig and nearly choked on it.

For a while, Lucy fell silent, and during the silence Barney and Vicky wondered anxiously whether she was angry or upset, or simply didn't want to speak about it because she considered it was none of their business.

Presently, obviously feeling emotional, Lucy told them, 'I've always meant to have Jamie baptised, only . . .' she paused to look at Barney, 'I kept waiting for his daddy to come home, hoping we might arrange for our son's christening together.' Her quick, bright smile belied the upheaval inside. 'Only when he came back and found out he had a son, he didn't want either of us.'

The humiliation was still heavy in her, and when it now showed in the threatening tears, Barney told her softly, 'You and Jamie are better off without him. It's all water under the bridge now, Lucy girl. Let it go, or it'll haunt you for life . . . you and the boy.'

Wise to the event, Vicky lifted Lucy's spirits. 'I've got an idea!' She went and stood beside Barney, from where she addressed them both. 'Why don't we have a double celebration?'

Barney laughed at her enthusiasm. 'I'm sorry, love. You can't baptise me. I'm already baptised.'

'No!' Tutting, Vicky returned to the table where she excitedly told Lucy, 'We could have Jamie baptised on his birthday. That way we'd have twice the reason to celebrate, and twice the party. What d'you say, Lucy?'

Lucy thought it was an inspired idea. 'It's long overdue and that shames me, but like you say, it's not too late, and it would be a wonderful time to have him baptised . . . on his second birthday.'

And so it was settled and the date in November

put in the diary. The two women agreed to go together to the church, to make the arrangements, then take the rest of the day off to go into Liverpool and do some shopping.

With a crafty glance at Barney, Vicky gave Lucy a wink. 'I'll need a new frock for the party,' she announced, running her hands down her thighs. 'I might go into that new shop on the corner of Victoria Street. I'm told they have some lovely stuff there.' Patting her hair, she glanced in the mantelpiece mirror. 'Oh, and I'll need a new hat for the christening – an extra stylish one, with a little brim and a big flower on the side.'

'You'd best get me one an' all,' Barney groaned. 'One with the biggest brim you can find, so I can pull it over my ears when you tell me the price of all this paraphernalia.' With that he stretched out his legs, settled himself deep in the chair and fell asleep.

∼

With the preparations and the shopping, and all the work in between, the next few weeks flew by; autumn soon arrived, and with it came a revelation concerning Leonard Maitland that surprised even Lucy.

On the Sunday afternoon, Lucy was pushing Jamie in the box-swing which Barney had slung from the big oak tree in the cottage garden.

'We'll have to find a suitable christening gown

for you,' she was telling the child as he laughed and clapped and kicked his fat little legs as he sailed through the air. 'I don't suppose I'll find a baby gown to fit you now,' she gave him another gentle push. 'You're a big boy into the bargain, so we might have to think of something else, though I want you dressed in white all the same, because when the man takes the pictures I want you to look beautiful.'

Pausing, she thought of Edward Trent and how he had abandoned his own son. 'When you're older I'll be able to tell you why I waited so long before I got you baptised.' She would tell him everything, but not with malice. After all, Edward was Jamie's father and much as she would like to, she could not change that.

Her thoughts deepened. Things could have been so different. They could have been a real family. Somehow she had known that would never be, but she had hoped, for their son's sake, that it might come about.

'Now that I know what he's really like, I never again want any part of him,' she murmured to herself. But Jamie must make up his own mind. If it's what he wanted when he was older, she would never stop him from seeing his daddy. Though she did not believe for one minute that Edward Trent would ever have the gall to show his face round these parts again.

When the swing slowed, the child began kicking

his legs and shouting, 'More!' Lucy started pushing him again. 'All right. Just a few more minutes, then we'd best get you ready for bed,' she told him. 'You've had a busy day and by rights you should be worn out.' She wagged a finger. 'Barney was right. I do need eyes in the back of my head!'

'Talking to yourself, is it?' The husky voice was pleasantly familiar. 'Sure they lock ye away for less than that.'

'BRIDGET!' Turning to see her old friend coming across the garden, Lucy ran to meet her. Flinging her arms round the woman's waist, she gave her a bear hug. 'It's so good to see you.'

'Ye little lunatic, get offa me!' Laughingly shoving Lucy away, Bridget straightened her hat – a big black flowery thing with a long white feather. 'Haven't I told ye before, you're not to hug me so hard; I'm delicate as well ye know.'

She pointed to the child who was patiently sitting in his little box-swing. 'Enough o' this nonsense. I'll get meladdo out and we'll go inside for a drop o' the good stuff.' She gave a naughty wink. 'I expect you'll be wanting all the latest news.'

Without more ado, she went to the swing, drew the wooden bar back and lifted the child out. 'And as for you, young Jamie, I'll thank ye not to pee on me!' she warned. 'You ruined my skirt the last time, ye dirty little article!'

As she carried him away, he became fascinated with the feather in her hat, and when he began tugging at it, she promptly gave him to Lucy. 'Will ye look at that? Not content with having ruined one o' me best skirts, the little divil's after ruining me hat.'

Chuckling to herself, and delighted to suffer Bridget's complaining, Lucy took the child and followed her into the cottage. The Irishwoman was striding ahead, in charge as usual, looking grand and important in the dark straight skirt, cut to just below the knee, and the smart peplum jacket that accentuated her curves. The big flowery hat was perched at an angle on top of her fiery red hair, all twirled and tamed and secured beneath it – apart from the few wispy curls that had danced their way out.

'You look really nice,' Lucy complimented her sincerely. 'Is that a new two-piece?'

Bridget sailed on. 'New *and* expensive,' she replied over the shoulder. 'So you'll understand why I don't want it peed on?'

Lucy did understand. 'Is it bought for a special occasion then?'

'It certainly is! I have a gentleman collecting me any time now, so if you've anything you need to tell me, you'll have to be quick about it.'

With an important backward glance, she went on, 'I might tell ye, I've gone to a lot of trouble to get here. I caught a bus for the first time in ages and walked half a mile down the lane ... dog's muck and horse-dung everywhere!' She glanced at her small-heeled shoes. 'I'll have you know, these were new only a few days since. This is the first time I've worn them. Now look at 'em! Whooh!' She had a whole gamut of wonderful expressions and the one she made now was priceless. 'I'll need to give 'em a shine before I leave.'

'Ah!' So this was the reason for the smart outfit and the new hat. 'You've got a new fella then?' Lucy teased. 'What's he like?'

Bridget touched the tip of her nose. 'You'll know soon enough,' she replied cagily. 'I'll tell you when I'm good and ready and not before.'

Bursting into the cottage with her usual flair, Bridget filled the room with her presence as always. She waited for Lucy to settle the child down for a nap before tea; he wriggled about for a while before falling fast and hard asleep. 'Good Lord above, will ye look at that? You've worn the child out, so ye have.' Now that he couldn't snatch at her feather, she leaned over and kissed him. 'He's such a wee, bonny thing.'

Though she loved children from a safe distance, Bridget was not cut out to be a mother and she made no secret of that. 'Making the child gives you pleasure,' she had been known to say with a twinkle in her eye. 'Raising them breaks your heart.'

Lucy went to the cupboard. 'Large or small?' she asked, the glass poised in the air.

'I'll have a large,' Bridget started, then, 'No! I'd

best have a small.' A devious little grin shaped her handsome face. 'Sure, I've got to keep me wits about me today.'

As instructed, Lucy poured out a small measure of gin and brought it to her. 'Why? What's happening today then?' She handed her the glass and watched with amazement as Bridget took a delicate sip. It wasn't like her dear friend and benefactor to drink her gin sparingly. Normally, she would down one glass and be after another, before the first was hardly swallowed.

Bridget smacked her lips and looked up, and after taking another delicate sip, she smiled at Lucy with her magic green eyes and raising her eyebrows suggestively, said in a whisper, 'I've found the fella of my dreams, so I have.' The slightly smug expression on her face told it all.

'Have you now?' Lucy sat herself down. 'So, you really think he's the one?'

'Oh, he is. I just *know* he is!'

'Well, come on then. Who is he?'

Bridget opened her mouth to answer, then changed her mind. 'Get yourself a cuppa tea first – oh, and another o' these.' She held out her glass. 'I've a thirst come on me all of a sudden.' She shrugged her broad shoulders in that apologetic manner which Lucy knew only too well.

Lucy didn't argue, because she knew it would do no good. Instead, she took the glass, half-filled it and handed it back. 'You'd best make that last.

Your fella might not approve of his woman being three sheets to the wind.'

Bridget took a ladylike sip. 'Why, ye cheeky young heathen!' She then took another sip, this time longer. 'I'll be the best judge o' that, so I will!' She leaned forward in an intimate manner. 'I'm so glad you like the two-piece,' she said. 'I bought it special. I bought these special an' all.' Clambering out of the chair, she hoisted her skirt to display vast thighs, topped by the laciest pair of knickers Lucy had ever seen. 'Pure silk, I'll have ye know!' Bridget imparted, wide-eyed. 'Cost me a small fortune, so they did. Well – what d'ye think? D'ye like them? D'ye think *he'll* like them?'

Lucy was lost for words, and told Bridget so.

'Ah, go on and make the tea,' Bridget told her, disappointed. 'Sure, if he doesn't like them, he's not the fella I thought he was.'

Smiling to herself, Lucy retreated to the kitchen where she boiled the kettle and made the tea, then came back into the parlour with a plate of little fairy cakes. 'Have one of these,' she suggested. 'It'll soak up the gin.'

Bridget laughed aloud. 'So now you're telling me what to do, is it?' she spluttered. 'Seems to me you're getting above yourself, young woman.'

Seating herself in the other chair, Lucy leaned back, cup in hand and waiting. 'Well?'

Bridget frowned. 'Well what?'

'What's the latest news then?'

All in a rush as was her way, Bridget went over all the usual items of gossip. 'Little Tillie's gone off on a week's holiday to the Lake District. She fell out with her boyfriend a few days back and says she's finished with men forever, but she says that all the time and then she's off again, seeing some other lanky, pimply, no-good thing.' Taking a breath, she proceeded at a faster pace. 'I said to her, I said, "Will ye never learn, girl? The buggers are only after what's in your drawers," but will she listen? No, of course she won't!'

Lucy thought Tillie had done the right thing. 'The change of scene will do her good. The Lakes are so beautiful. When she comes back, she can stay with me if she wants to.' Lucy had been through this all before with dear Tillie.

'What? Stay with you?' Bridget was horrified. 'She'll do no such thing! I need her back at the house, I do. While she's been gone, I've had to take on some useless woman from the other side of Liverpool.' She gave a long, agonising groan. 'I won't even tell you what a pain she is.' Rolling the palm of her hand across her forehead, she gave a trembling sigh. 'Sometimes I think I was born to be a martyr.'

'Oh Bridget, don't be so dramatic.' Wisely changing the subject, Lucy enquired, 'So tell me, what else is happening?'

Fast recovered, Bridget launched into the next snippet of news. 'I'm having a new bathroom fitted upstairs – all black marble and best cream carpet.

Going posh, I am.' She gave that naughty wink again. 'That'll cost the clients a few bob more for their pleasure, I can tell ye.'

'And what else?'

'New curtains in the sitting room, o' course. And I'm considering whether to have the old Victorian fireplace out and get a new one fitted . . .'

Lucy listened patiently while Bridget outlined all the changes she was having made to the house. 'Like I say, it'll cost a bob or two, but no matter. It'll be the clients that pay, I'll make sure o' that.'

'And what news of the girls?'

Bridget took a long gulp of her gin. 'That's what I meant to tell you,' she said. 'Mandy's only gone and got herself pregnant . . .' Drawing breath she launched into the lecture. 'Time and again I've told them, "You must never let yourself get with child," but will they listen?' She gave a long, shivering shake of the head. 'Not at all! Now I know you wouldn't be without your Jamie for all the tea in China, the darlin', but you've got to admit, it's not the easiest thing in the world, is it, having a bairn without a ring on your finger? Anyway, our Mandy has decided to marry the fella in question, and now she's gone off to meet his family, would ye believe? Of course she won't tell them about her job, nor will her fiancé, who is a nice young man, I'll give him that. Nor will she let on that she's already with child or they'll immediately think she's a trollop, and she's not.'

She drew another, longer breath. 'Mandy's a good girl, always has been. To tell you the truth, her heart's never been in her work, so it might be as well that she's gone.'

Lucy was pleased. 'I hope she remembers to write.'

'I'm sure she will,' Bridget answered. 'But I don't really expect we'll see much of her again, because the fella is French, and that's where she's been whisked off to – a place called Montpellier.' She sighed. 'And there's me, left in the lurch, so I am.'

Lucy chuckled. 'You'll have to get your fella to comfort you then, won't you?' She had wanted to ask after the 'gent', and this was her chance.

'I'm sure he'll comfort me if I ask him,' came the confident answer. 'He's a real gentleman, bless his kind heart.' Bridget dredged her glass and held it up. 'Just a wee drop more?' she suggested. 'Be a friend. Send me on my way with a smile.'

Shaking her head and thinking how Bridget would never change, Lucy poured her another drink.

'Ah, but aren't you the *lovely* woman!' Bridget said, gulping down the gin.

When she again held out her glass, Lucy was adamant. '*No.* I won't be responsible for spoiling your date. If you want another drink, you'll have to get it yourself.'

'I wish you'd stop jumping to conclusions.'

191

Bridget was suitably indignant. 'I'm only handing the glass back.'

It was just as well, because when she left half an hour later, her hat was tipsy on her head and her legs just the slightest bit wobbly. 'I'll see youse again,' she told Lucy. Then she lifted her skirt and clambered into the open-topped car.

Falling into the passenger seat, she plonked a smacker of a kiss on the man beside her; a 'gent' indeed, with his tailored moustache and cream-coloured blazer, he looked a right dapper. He also had red blood in his veins because having caught a glimpse of her knickers when she cocked a fine leg to climb into the car, he took the liberty of stroking his hand along her stockinged thigh, all the way up to the suspender, quickly removing it when he saw Lucy looking on with amusement.

She nodded a greeting to him and he nodded back. 'Hold onto your hat, my sweetie,' he told the blushing Bridget. 'We could get up to thirty miles an hour if I set my mind to it.'

He set off with a roar and a squeal, with Bridget laughing and screeching like a silly schoolgirl beside him.

Lucy held back the laughter until they were out of sight, then she collapsed in hysterics, mimicking Bridget as she was wont to do. Oh, how she hoped her friend could hold onto this one. He was an absolute treasure. Priceless!

Going inside, she wiped the tears from her eyes

and made herself another cup of tea. Thirty miles an hour indeed! she thought, then said aloud, 'I don't know about holding onto your hat. If you ask me, it's not the *hat* you're in danger of losing so much as your pretty silk *knickers*!'

The laughter bubbled up again; the sight of well-upholstered Bridget in her wonky hat, flashing her lingerie, and the dandy-man goggle-eyed at this vision of heaven, was all too much for Lucy. She laughed so much that Jamie woke up!

But if Bridget was happy, she thought, picking her son up and hugging him, then so was she, because if it hadn't been for Bridget, she would have been lost, long since.

CHAPTER TEN

THE FOLLOWING DAY, Lucy's week started all over again.

Rising early, she had her wash and got dressed; then she made her bed and collected the child from his cot.

With that done she sat him in his chair at the table, made his porridge and while he plastered his hands and face with that, she burned herself a piece of toast which she covered in Vicky's home-made strawberry jam. 'Your Auntie Vicky makes the best jam in the world,' she told the child, who was far too busy licking his chubby fingers to pay attention.

'I need you to be on your best behaviour,' she coaxed. 'There's work to be done in Long Field, harvesting the spuds, and it's a case of all hands to the deck. The crop is ready to be taken in, Barney says. The plants have died off and the soil is good and dry.'

This would be her first close experience of working on the land, and she was really looking forward to it.

She glanced at the mantelpiece clock. 'We need to be away from here by seven,' she took a great bite of her toast, 'so eat up, little fella, then I'll give you a drink and get you washed, and we'll be on our way.' Reaching over the table she tickled him under the chin, and the little boy giggled. 'Vicky said she would make up a picnic for when we stop to eat. We'll have it down by the river, that's what she said – and won't that be lovely, eh?'

In fact, life itself was so wonderful these days, she could hardly believe her good fortune.

During the next half-hour, Lucy went about her chores; she cleared and washed the breakfast things while Jamie played, then took her son and washed him, made sure she had everything they needed, then strapped him into his pram and parked him outside on the path while she secured the cottage behind her.

Taking the bridle path up to Overhill Farm, she found the going hard; one minute she was pushing the pram and the next she was pulling it, until her arms ached from shoulder to wrist. But it was such a beautiful day, she didn't mind a bit. Besides, little Jamie was in his element, laughing and chuckling, until he eventually fell asleep and all she could hear were the birds singing and the river bubbling over the boulders.

As they came through the spinney, the terrain

became easier. Well-worn by travellers and locals alike, in parts the meandering walkway was rough and bumpy underfoot, but for the most part it was easy going. From the cottage to the farm, it took exactly twenty minutes; Lucy had timed herself on the first day.

'Vicky!' Waving as she approached the house, Lucy saw Barney's wife hanging out the washing. 'I'm not too late, am I?'

Waving back, Vicky took the wooden pegs out of her mouth. 'The boys have already gone to the fields,' she replied. 'Barney's taken Susie into town for her hat-making, and he'll come back straight after. We won't be needed for a little while yet.'

She was finished with the washing. 'My! You put me to shame!' she exclaimed. 'You look lovely, Lucy. Bright and fresh as a daisy.'

It was true. Lucy did look very fetching in the long dark skirt and loose white blouse, worn to work in the fields, and something about the way she had swept her hair back into a thick plait made her seem almost childlike. 'And look at me – hands red from rubbing the sheets in the dolly-tub, and hair all over the place. I must look terrible,' Vicky laughed ruefully.

'You don't look any such thing!' Lucy would have none of it. She looked at Vicky with her sun-kissed hair and those wonderful expressive grey eyes, and all she saw was beauty and goodness. 'You always look lovely,' she said honestly. 'It's right what Barney says: you couldn't help but look pretty, even if you'd just come up from the coal-mines.'

Vicky laughed. 'That's my Barney,' she said. 'He looks at me through rose-coloured glasses and can't see the wood for the trees.'

'That's because he loves you.' Lucy wondered if she would ever find that kind of love. 'I've never known anyone love his woman, like Barney loves you.'

For a moment Vicky was silenced by Lucy's profound words. 'I love him the same way,' she quietly confessed. 'Sometimes it frightens me, the way Barney believes we'll always be together. The thing is, Lucy, when you're part of each other, like me and Barney, there can never be a happy ending. Someone is bound to be sad at the end of it all.'

When she looked up, there was a kind of desolation in her grey eyes. 'You see, when either of us is taken, the one left behind will be totally lost.'

Lucy was amazed at the depth of pain in Vicky's voice, in her eyes, in her whole demeanour. 'You're neither of you going anywhere!' she declared stoutly, in an attempt to break the moment. 'Not until you've made me enough strawberry jam to last me into old age, any road.'

The mood broke and Vicky laughed out loud. 'If you like it that much, you'd best take another jar from the pantry.' She then threw the pegs into her big basket and placing it under her arm, she put her other arm through Lucy's. 'Come on, you.' Her smile was content. 'The water's already hot in the kettle, it'll take but a minute to bring it back to the boil. We've time enough for a brew before we roll up our sleeves.'

In truth, both Vicky and Lucy had already had their sleeves rolled up these past two hours and more. All the same, it was nice to take time out for a cuppa and a chat, all girls together, and that was exactly what they did. 'Bridget came to see me yesterday,' Lucy imparted, grinning at the memory. 'You should have seen her, all done up in a new outfit and a hat like you could never imagine.'

Vicky took a gulp of her tea. 'Got herself a fancy man, has she?' Vicky was a broadminded woman who respected Bridget for her kindness, and welcomed her, when other townsfolk looked down their noses at her.

'Seems like that.'

While they drank their tea and Jamie slept on, Lucy relayed the gossip and the two of them hoped that Bridget had found a man who would take care of her, for she was a good-hearted woman and not as young as she used to be.

Twenty minutes later, with both tea and gossip done, they set about the daily chores; Lucy seeing to the bathroom upstairs and making up the beds with fresh-laundered linen while Jamie 'helped' her, and Vicky tackling the work downstairs.

Some short time later, with the house all spick and span, they made their way to the fields, where Barney and his sons were already halfway down the potato field. Armed with light forks, each of them raised up the secret treasure of the potatoes, hidden beneath the rich soil. They were beauties – no sign of rot or infestation – and Barney was delighted. A bumper crop might cheer Mr Maitland who had been looking very preoccupied of late.

'RONNIE!' Barney's voice could be heard shouting instructions to the younger of his two sons. 'Stop messing about and get on with it.' With the work piling up, Barney was in no mood for frivolous behaviour. 'We've the rest of this field to do yet!'

Unlike his father and brother Tom, Ronnie, free-spirited and happy-go-lucky, was too easily distracted. He would collect the potatoes in the barrow lined with sacking, then wheel it to the barn, where the crop was stored in the dark and cool, and on the way back, he'd lark about, talking to the horse in the next field and playing tricks on his brother.

'He's a good lad,' Vicky remarked tolerantly as she and Lucy made their way to the men. 'But he still has a lot of growing up to do yet.'

Thrilled to be here, Lucy soaked up the atmosphere. Her attention drawn every which way, she took it all in: Barney's familiar figure bent over the long trench; the sunlight bouncing off the tines of the men's forks; the seemingly endless skies, and the bright warm sunshine. Here, now, it was as though she and Jamie and Barney's family were the only people in the whole wide world.

'Fine crop of spuds this year.' Having worked many seasons alongside Barney, Vicky spoke from experience.

As Barney took his turn with the barrow, he shouted, 'Are you here to watch, or work?' He went away laughing. 'You're no good to me if all you've come to do is admire the scenery.'

'Cheeky devil!' Vicky yelled after him. 'Another remark like that and you can do the spuds on your own, 'cause we'd rather be in Liverpool, strolling round the shops!'

Vicky and Barney could bandy insults without getting offended. It was part of their deep knowledge of each other.

The hours passed too quickly and every experience was new to Lucy. Working and laughing, stumbling in the trenches and clambering up again, getting into a rhythm with the digging, with the sun on her face and the cooling breeze a welcome relief. She wanted this day never to end.

'I'll be glad when we stop for a break.' Vicky paused to wipe the sweat from her brow. 'I'm all in.' She stroked Jamie's hair as he squealed,

pointing excitedly to a worm. They were surrounded by birds, swooping down as the tubers
were revealed.

A short time later and aching through every
bone, Barney paused to stretch his limbs. Taking
out his pocket-watch he glanced at the time. 'Good
Lord! Why didn't somebody tell me it was nearly
one o'clock?'

To everyone's relief he called for a break, at the
same time taking the opportunity to slide his arm
round his wife's waist and give her a resounding
kiss. 'I'm proud of the three of you,' he told Vicky,
Lucy and Jamie. 'I might even go so far as to say
you're as good as the men . . .' At that moment he
saw Ronnie throw himself down some way off, to
lie flat under a tree. 'And maybe better than most,'
he added with a light-hearted groan.

Ronnie was the first to answer. 'Not bad,' he
said airily. 'It took Lucy a while to get the hang of
it, but she got there in the end.'

'They did well.' Thomas gave his dad a knowing
wink. 'In fact, they did so well, I reckon us men
should go home and leave them to it. Come on,
Jamie.'

'You mind we don't leave *you three* to it.' Vicky
rose to their teasing. 'Here.' She thrust a grease-
proof pack of sandwiches at each of them. 'These
should quieten you down.'

Everyone took off their sacking aprons and
quickly sluiced their hands with water from a big

enamel pitcher, before sitting down and unwrapping their lunch.

The break, though short, was a pleasure, not only because they were famished and the thick sandwiches filled with cheese, ham and pickle were delicious, but because the company was pleasant and the day glorious. 'What about you, Lucy?' Barney addressed Lucy who had fed the child and was now preparing his drink. 'Have you enjoyed your first-hand experience of market-gardening?'

'It's tiring,' Lucy admitted. 'I don't think I've ever ached so much in all my life, but oh yes, Barney, I can't tell you how much I've enjoyed it.' She cuddled the child. 'Jamie's enjoyed it too,' she said fondly. 'Though he didn't like being strapped in his pram for most of the time.'

'Well, I'm proud of you,' Barney said, and without hesitation the others echoed his sentiments.

With the food all gone, Ronnie and his brother went for a quick dip in the river, to wash the dust and grime from their backs. 'Don't be long,' Barney called after them. 'We'll need to work till dark as it is.'

Shortly afterwards, Vicky followed with the plates and cutlery. 'I'll give these a rinse in the water,' she told Lucy. 'I don't fancy the flies plaguing us all the way home.'

Left alone with Lucy and the child, who had

dozed off, Barney helped to clear the picnic things away. 'How are things,' he enquired, 'really?'

'Things are fine, thank you, Barney.' Though she had good friends in Bridget and the girls, Barney and Vicky were the only people she could really talk to; especially Barney. He had such a way with him, naturally attentive and caring, that Lucy felt she could tell him anything.

'So, did you do the right thing in moving out to the cottage?' Looking tired and worn, he leaned against the tree.

'It was the best thing I ever did, and it's all thanks to you and your family,' she answered.

Taking a rag out of his trouser pocket, Barney wiped the sweat from his face. 'And you're content, are you, working at the house with Vicky, and labouring in the fields under an Indian summer sun?' he grinned. 'Seems to me, we've thrown you in at the deep end.'

Lucy smiled. 'Oh Barney, I'm more than content. I don't know how I can ever thank you both.'

'No thanks necessary,' he answered softly. 'Just to see you smile like that, and know you're settled – that's more than enough.' Barney looked down on her and thought what a lovely woman she was.

'You and Vicky, you can't know what you've done for me,' Lucy persisted. 'I've never been so happy.'

'It's only right that you should be happy.' In a fit of coughing, he turned away, scarlet in the face.

Lucy passed him a cup of water. When the coughing fit passed, he addressed her again, his voice still a little hoarse. 'You worked well today, lass.' He didn't look round. 'I want you to know how much I appreciate that.'

'Barney, can I talk to you?'

The young woman's anxious voice caused him to swing round. 'Of course you can. What is it?'

Hesitating, she shrugged her shoulders. 'It's nothing – I'm sorry.' Suddenly it seemed foolish to voice what was in her mind.

Concerned, he came to kneel beside her. 'Come on, tell me, love. What's wrong?'

Lucy looked at him, at his strong, kind face and the endearing look in his eyes and she opened her heart to him. 'I'm afraid, Barney . . . so afraid.'

'What d'you mean? What have you to be afraid of?' His expression hardened. 'That bugger Trent isn't back again, is he, because if he's bothering you . . .'

Lucy shook her head. 'No, he's not back – at least not that I know of.' She gave a wry little smile, her heart sinking at the memory. 'After the cowardly way he ran, I shouldn't think he'll ever show his face round here again.'

'So what are you afraid of?'

In a small voice she told him, 'It might sound silly to you, Barney, but I feel I'm *too* happy, and I'm afraid because something is bound to go wrong, I just know it is.'

'Aw, Lucy girl! Come here to me.' Taking her in his arms, he held her close. 'Nothing will go wrong. I won't let it – *Vicky* won't let it. The worst is over for you now. We've got you safe with us.' He held her at arm's length. 'Promise me, Lucy, that whenever you're feeling worried you'll talk to me or Vicky. Promise me you won't ever be afraid to share what's on your mind.'

Her heart full, Lucy slowly nodded her head.

'That's my girl.' He rumpled her hair, and let her go.

~

A few minutes later, at Barney's suggestion, she left the child with him and made her way to the river. Here, she dropped to her knees and washed her grubby neck and face. Her finger-nails were grimed with mud; she'd deal with them later.

She was shaking the river-drops from her hands when she heard a noise some way further along the river. She turned her head and there, where the weir rushed down and tumbled amongst the larger boulders, she saw Thomas and Ronnie clamber out of the water, their muscular well-toned bodies magnificently naked.

Until that moment, she had seen them as merely Barney and Vicky's two young sons: Thomas, serious and deep-thinking, and Ronnie a bit crazy – a daredevil ready to have a go at anything.

Now she saw them as men in their own right, and it came as a bit of a shock to her senses.

Climbing to where they had laid their clothes, Tom and Ronnie took up their shirts and began drying themselves while, blushing to the roots of her hair, Lucy took flight and did not stop running until she was back to base.

It was the very first time she had ever seen a man stripped off; even when Edward Trent had made love to her, it was a case of undoing his trouser-buttons and lifting her skirt. A virgin when she had met him at the age of twenty-seven, in many ways Lucy was still sexually inexperienced. She had only known brief couplings with Edward, which had heated her blood and brought her a child, but the richness and depth of married physical love was unknown territory.

She knew now that what she had experienced was not lovemaking in the way it should have been; it was pure lust and nothing more, and she felt ashamed at having thought it was ever anything else.

As she neared her son, still sleeping in his pram, she was amazed to find that there was no sign of Barney. She stood a moment, eyes scouring the area. That was strange. She hadn't thought that Barney would ever go off and leave Jamie on his own.

Suddenly she could hear him, or at least she could hear something, because the harsh, rasping sounds were not human. They were more like the cries of some unfortunate animal caught in a trap.

Leaving Jamie, she cautiously followed the sounds, and there, doubled up against the side of the tractor, was Barney. Obviously in pain and fighting for breath, he looked a frightful sight. Lucy ran to him. 'Barney – what in God's name is wrong?'

Breathless and exhausted, he couldn't speak, but when he looked her in the eye, she saw the anguish there and her heart turned somersaults. 'Don't . . . tell . . . Vicky,' he gasped.

Lucy gave no answer. Instead she held him until he was fully recovered, at which point he repeated his plea. 'Lucy . . . you mustn't tell Vicky about this. She'll only worry, and it's unnecessary.'

Lucy wasn't too sure about that. 'But you're ill!' she told him gently. 'You couldn't breathe – could hardly stand up on your own two feet!' Seeing him like that had given her a scare. 'You're wrong, Barney,' she told him. 'Vicky *should* know about this.' When she saw the look of panic on his face, she assured him, 'All right, I won't tell her. But you must.'

'There's no need!' Barney was recovering his strength now. 'I'm not ill. It's something to do with handling the tubers. They don't agree with me. Summat about them gets in and clogs up my lungs, hampers my breathing and makes me feel bad. It comes on quickly and goes away the same.

Like I say, there's nothing to worry about. Right now, lass, let's get back to yon bairn. I'm sorry I left him, pet – didn't want to wake him, see?'

'All right, Barney, if you're sure.' She could see how agitated he had got when he believed she might tell the family.

'Look at me, Lucy.' Raising his arms, Barney let his hands fall to her shoulders, his smile quick and confident. 'You can see for yourself, I'm right as rain now. It was a coughing fit, that's all it was. I won't have Vicky or anyone else worrying about something and nothing.'

Lucy didn't argue. In fact, she was amazed at how quickly he had recovered. One minute he had looked so ill, she feared for his life, and the next he seemed fine. 'You're sure you're all right?'

He nodded. 'Like I said, right as rain.'

Believing she might have over-reacted, Lucy took him at his word. Besides, though his colour wasn't fully returned, he did seem fine now.

Barney called her attention to the three approaching figures; the two sons in front, obviously not aware that their mother was some distance behind. 'Remember,' he urged. 'Not a word.'

While they were looking across the field, they saw the figure of a man standing beneath the dipping boughs of a tree. 'It's the boss, come to keep an eye on us,' Barney said jokingly.

So, while Leonard Maitland watched the family,

Barney and Lucy watched him. 'What the devil's he up to?' Like Lucy, Barney was intrigued.

'I expect he's been out for a long walk and is taking a rest in the shade,' she answered.

Barney laughed. 'He may well be,' he remarked, adding tongue-in-cheek, 'He's also taking a long, leisurely look at my woman.' Thrusting his hands into his pockets he seemed a proud man. 'I should've told him,' he said casually.

'Told him what?' It had not occurred to Lucy that Leonard Maitland was watching Vicky in particular, but now she could see that while he rested from the heat, Leonard Maitland did in fact seem more preoccupied with Vicky who, unaware of his interest, walked on, the plates cradled in her arms and with eyes only for Barney.

Like the cat that got the cream, Barney wore a smile from ear to ear. 'I should have warned him,' he said. 'Every man that's ever clapped eyes on my Vicky has fallen head over heels in love with her.' His eyes shone with joy as he watched her drawing nearer. 'And all she ever wanted were *me* . . . a farmworker who owns nothing and never will.'

His eyes widened with a rush of astonishment. 'What she ever saw in me, I'll never know.' His voice dropping to a whisper, he spoke as though to himself. 'I just thank the Lord for bringing the two of us together.'

As always, whenever she witnessed the love between these two people, Lucy was humbled. She saw the adoration in Barney's eyes and the joy in Vicky's face as she waved to him.

Vicky may have been aware of Leonard Maitland or she may not. But it was Barney she was looking at. *Barney*, her man, her everything. She was one side of the coin; he was the other.

'Look! He's going now.' Lucy brought his attention to Leonard Maitland's retreating figure.

Barney made no comment just then, but he noticed how Leonard Maitland continually glanced back at Vicky. And who could blame him, Barney thought as he brought his own tender gaze to the kind, caring woman he adored.

Vicky always looked lovely, he thought, but today she was especially beautiful with the breeze playing round the hem of her skirt, lifting it and twirling it, her golden hair blown gently back from her happy face, oh and that smile. Even now after all these years, he could hardly believe that Vicky was his wife. From the moment he had first seen her, he wanted no other. And he never would, for the kind of love they shared came only once in a lifetime.

Shortly afterwards, Barney's mate Adam arrived. 'I've finished thatching Widow Mason's porch,' he told Barney, 'so I wondered if you might have use for another pair of hands?'

Barney thanked him. 'The more the merrier, matey,' he said, and his pal threw off his jacket and got to work.

Tired and sweating under the hot sun, Lucy soon forgot Leonard Maitland and his seeming infatuation with Vicky. Barney, however, for good reason kept it quietly at the back of his mind.

~

Leonard Maitland needed a drink.

Having hurried home, tired and hot, he had rushed in, closed the door to shut out the world, and was now helping himself to a small whisky. 'God knows what they must have thought!' he muttered, gulping down the drink. 'Me standing there, gawping at another man's wife like some lovesick fool!'

Deep in thought, he wandered across the room, images of Vicky filling his mind: running, tripping, laughing, she was the essence of womanhood. Yet he had other, more urgent things to think about. A few days ago, he had received a letter from America, to do with his late grandfather's estate in Boston, Massachusetts. It seemed he might have to fight to retain the old man's house and lands. Things were happening which could send it either way. If it went one particular way, it could mean him selling up in this country and making a new life over there. Leonard had spent months at a time in his youth with his maternal grandfather, Farley Kemp, on the thousand-acre farm. He loved it out there – although his English heritage meant that he loved it here, too, east of the Mersey.

He considered for a moment. If he went to America, would he take Patricia with him? And what of Barney and his family . . . and Vicky? Leonard might be well-off financially, but he didn't have endless funds. The last thing he wanted to do was put Barney out of work, but he might not be able to avoid it.

If he had to, he'd fight tooth and nail to keep it all together. But there were things happening out there which could mean he had little choice. If it went one particular way, it could mean his having to sell up in England and make a new life in Boston, America.

He considered the prospect for a moment. He would almost welcome the challenge. It would mean he could keep his grandfather's beautiful house and vast estates. He had worked his way up from a farm-labourer to create one of the most successful businesses in Boston. Besides that, it was a wonderful home, warm and welcoming, filled with happiness and contentment, the kind of which he'd never really known.

The memories still came flooding back. When he was a child, the highlight of his year was going to see his grandparents. Those amazing weeks when he was there were the happiest of his life. His grandfather would take him across the estate; sometimes on the back of his horse and later Leonard would ride alongside him on a pony, and oh, what adventures they'd get up to . . . racing each other across the headlands; climbing trees or riding to the top of a hill, so his grandfather could show him the house and lands from a distance, and even then they could never see the horizons of what belonged to him . . . lands that were loved and tended, houses and homesteads nestling in the valleys, and cattle by the hundreds; all this, all painstakingly, lovingly forged out of nothing, with only the strength of his own two hands and the heart of a lion.

He closed his eyes, his emotions in turmoil. When his grandfather lost his wife, he lost all sense of purpose, and now everything he worked so hard for was at risk.

Going to the armchair, Leonard sat down and gazed into space for what seemed an age. He gathered his thoughts and knew what he must do. He wouldn't let it be lost. He couldn't let them take it. He didn't have so much here to fight for, but he could try and save his grandfather's dream, and given the chance, that's what he'd do! Getting out of the chair, he smiled, at ease with himself. 'I think it's time I had a new life, a new direction. There is little to hold me here. I've gone as far as I can go, and now it's time to face up to a new challenge.'

Dipping into his pocket, he took out a long, official-looking envelope with an American stamp. Unfolding the letter he began to read:

Dear Mr Maitland,

I am pleased to inform you that certain matters relating to the estate of your grandfather, the late Mr Farley Kemp, are now settled. However, several important issues remain which demand your urgent attention. As you are the only surviving relative of the deceased, it is imperative that you contact me as soon as possible, with a view to visiting these offices, in order that these issues can be dealt with.

As you must be aware, time is of the essence, and the situation requires that you be here in person.

I look forward to hearing from you at your earliest opportunity.

Yours sincerely,

Justin Lovatt, Attorney-at-Law

Leonard knew the letter word for word, for hadn't he read it umpteen times since receiving it? Tomorrow, he must make arrangements to travel.

'What's that you're reading?' Patricia's voice shocked him, invading his thoughts.

'Pat! Good God – I didn't hear you come in.' He swiftly folded the letter and slid it into his pocket. He hadn't heard the taxi pull up in the driveway.

Crossing the room, she slid her arm through his. 'Is it something I should know about, darling?'

He gave a nervous laugh. 'Why would you think that?'

'Because just now when I came in, you looked so worried, and as I'm soon to be your wife, I should know what is bothering you.'

'Really?' He tested her. 'And if I were to tell you that I might have to make a difficult choice – a life-changing choice – what would you say to that?'

'It would depend.'

'Why's that?'

Growing flustered, she dislodged herself from his embrace. 'Well, for all I know it might change *my* life, and I don't know that I would be too keen on that.'

'Not even if it meant you and I would be together? Isn't that all that matters when a man and woman are in love?'

Something in his manner, in the way he was looking at her, made her nervous. 'No,' she answered defensively. 'Being in love *isn't* all that matters. What matters is that we both should be happy.'

'Yes,' he agreed, although he felt her resistance and was unnerved. 'But what if the choice I have to make is not really a choice at all, but something I feel obliged to do?'

She considered that for a moment, then like a child who wasn't sure of how to respond, she used her wiles and going to him, slid an arm round his waist. 'I think you had best tell me what you were reading, just now,' she wheedled.

'I'd rather not, Patricia. It isn't altogether settled, and it may not come to anything anyway.'

'Hmh! You're not about to do anything that would make me unhappy, are you, my darling?' she pleaded prettily. 'I mean, you will let me have my say in this choice of yours, won't you?'

Holding her at arm's length, he answered wisely, 'Of course you will have a say. But, like I said, there may not even be any choice to make. I won't know that, until I return from America.'

'*America?*' At once she was all smiles, confident that she would be going with him. 'I knew if I kept on at you long enough, you would take me away, but *America*!' She laughed excitedly. 'What an adventure that will be! When do we leave?'

Seeing her pleasure, Leonard was half-tempted to take her with him. He thought that if she saw the vast and beautiful land outside Charlestown and the sprawling house his grandfather had built over the years, she might grow to like the prospect of moving there. But commonsense prevailed, and he said merely, 'I'm sorry, Pat, but I shall be tending to important business. I can't take you with me this time. It's deuced inconvenient as it is, leaving Comberton at this time of the year.'

'Oh, come on, Leonard! What business do you need to tend that means I can't come along? We are to be married after all, aren't we?'

'Of course we are, but I simply can't take you, not this time. Look, when I get back, I promise we'll see about a weekend in Paris – would that suit you?'

'No, it would not.' Giving him a frosty look, she turned on her heel and stalked towards the door. 'I have shopping to do in Manchester. I imagine I'll be gone for at least four hours. That should give you plenty of time to decide whether I come with you or not.'

When he heard the front door slam, Leonard walked to the window, from where he could see Patricia climb into the taxi. She did not look back, but somehow that did not concern him.

Instead, he took out the letter and read it through again.

'No, Patricia,' he said aloud. 'I won't take you with me.' His mind was made up. The reason he was going to America was too important. This wasn't just about him and Patricia.

Thrusting his hands into his pockets he began to pace the room, his thoughts and loyalties all churned up. The decision was something he had to make by himself. If it turned out that there was, after all, no choice to make, then so be it. But if it came to a head, then he had to think of others who would inevitably be affected.

The people who had been loyal to him over the years, these were the people uppermost in his mind right now. He thought of Barney, that good man, and his heart was sore. Then he thought of Vicky, of maybe never seeing her again, and the prospect was unbearable. He found himself searching for a way that would allow him to take the Davidsons with him, but at the moment that seemed quite unrealistic.

His thoughts then flew ahead, and his heart sank. Whatever the outcome of his visit across the Atlantic, there was still Patricia.

And so far he had not decided what to do about her.

CHAPTER ELEVEN

'You're thirty-nine years of age and you still have the body of a young girl.' Having climbed into bed, Barney leaned on his elbow and watched his wife undress. It wasn't often she undressed in front of him; for some reason she preferred the light out, and whenever he came upon her naked, she would blush and hide, and scamper into bed. 'You need never be ashamed of your body,' he told her now. 'You should be proud.' His voice dropped to the softest whisper. 'You're very beautiful, Vicky. You always were.'

Having finished brushing her hair, she slithered into bed beside him. 'I'm not beautiful,' she protested, though with a smile. 'You only think that, because you love me . . . like I think you're handsome, because I love *you*.'

Tenderly he placed a finger over her lips. 'No,' then with his other hand he stroked a stray lock of hair from her eyes. 'You really are a lovely-looking woman, my darling. You may not see it, but I do, and so does every other man who looks on you.'

'Stop it, Barney.' She went rosy with pleasure. 'What will you say when I'm old and toothless, and bent like a willow tree?'

His answer was to take her in his arms and hold her as close as any man could hold the one he loved. 'None of that would matter,' he answered honestly, 'because you will always be beautiful to me.'

In the halo of moonlight shining in through the window, she could see in his eyes the depth of his love for her, and she was deeply moved. 'I love you so much,' she said, her voice breaking. 'I love our children and I love the life we lead, but it would not be the same without you.'

He could feel the tension in her body, and he was shocked. 'Hey!' Lifting himself up, he looked into her sad face and was afraid – not for himself, but for her. 'You mustn't talk like that. We have each other and, God willing, we'll have each other for many years to come.'

'Do you promise?' she whispered. 'Do you promise never to leave me?'

Barney saw the tears rising in her pretty eyes, and was deeply moved when one plump, watery tear spilled over her cheek. 'I can't promise,' he answered, wiping away the tear with the tip of his thumb.

'Why not?'

'You know why not,' he chided gently. 'We none of us can see what the future holds.'

She tightened her grip on him. 'You have to promise me, Barney.'

'What's wrong?' Kissing her on the mouth, he wondered why she should ask him such a thing. 'Why do you insist, when you know a promise of that kind is impossible?' Fear squeezed his heart. Had she heard him in a coughing fit? Did she know how ill he had been feeling of late? Had Lucy told her about that day in the field, when she found him gasping for breath? And now Vicky was asking him to make a promise of this kind. He couldn't do it. Nor could he voice his fears.

'Promise me, Barney,' she entreated. 'Say you will never leave me, then I'll be content.'

Gazing into her quiet eyes, in the space of a single heartbeat he saw his whole life there, and somehow suddenly, the fear he had felt began to ebb away. 'I promise,' he murmured. 'If it's in my power to be with you forever, then I will.'

'There! That wasn't so hard, was it?' She smiled, and for no reason he could fathom, he was a man at peace with himself.

Cradling her face in his hands he kissed her long and passionately, and she responded with the nakedness of her body against his, rhythmically pushing against him then pulling away, until he rolled her beneath him and placing a gentle hand round each of her legs, he drew them apart.

There was no need of words; there was nothing

to say that had not already been said a thousand times.

Wrapped around each other, they made such wonderful love; not as they had done many times before, with tenderness, but with a wild passion and a desperate, painful hunger that drove them into each other – almost as though they intended never to be separated.

And then it was over, when their bodies were aching and vibrant and the life-juices still flowing, they held onto each other. For the rest of their lives they would remember this night; when for the first and last time they made love as never before, and Vicky drew from Barney a promise which, he knew in his lonely heart, he could never keep.

~

Two days later, on a fine, breezy morning, Leonard Maitland boarded a liner for America.

'I'll be away for some time.' An hour before setting off for the docks, he had called Barney to his office at The Manse. 'I'm leaving you in charge as always, and should you encounter any problems, though I don't imagine you will, you do know who to contact?'

'Yes, I do, sir, thank you. I have his name and address.' As ever, Barney was well organised.

'Good man! As I already explained, the agent knows as much about my affairs as I do, and he's well-placed to contact me in any event. I've arranged for the house to be taken care of, so there is no need for you to concern yourself about that. On the whole, I don't envisage any problems.'

'Thank you for your trust.' Over the years Barney had come to like and respect this man who was his employer. 'Rest assured I'll do my best to keep the farm running smoothly.'

'I know you will,' Leonard declared. 'You took excellent care of my interests when I was last in Boston. And now I must get off. I have a long journey ahead of me.'

Barney walked with him to the taxi, Leonard carrying his bag and briefcase, and Barney following with his portmanteau. 'Have a safe voyage,' he said as Leonard climbed into the vehicle. 'I hope your trip goes well.'

'Oh, so do I, Barney!' Leonard declared. 'So do I!' Gesturing for the driver to move out, Leonard caught sight of Vicky as she walked towards the river. He couldn't take his eyes off her. If only Patricia was more like her, he thought, he would be a much happier man.

Seeing the taxi, Vicky waved, her face wreathed in a smile.

His heart warmed and with her face in his mind, Leonard took the smile with him, all the way to Boston, USA.

～

'Well, it seems Mr Maitland went away at the right time.' The whole family were gathered round for Sunday dinner – a grand affair with the table sagging beneath the weight of a partly-sliced beef-joint, a ham shank ready for the carving, various deep dishes of crisp-roasted and boiled potatoes, cabbage, carrots, and a pile of Yorkshire puddings the like of which Lucy had never seen before.

There were also two large boats of meat-gravy and a dish of homemade horseradish sauce, a particular favourite of Lucy's.

'What makes you say that, Dad?' That was Susie, seated next to him and already helping herself to a slice of beef.

'Because the weather's on the change,' Barney explained. 'Once the cold wind starts coming in from the north, you can expect to see winter on its tail.'

Vicky tapped the back of Susie's hand. 'Don't start eating yet.'

She gave Barney a reminding nod, and he immediately roved his gaze across each person at the table in turn; when they were suitably attentive, he folded his hands together, bowed his head and started Grace. 'We thank the good Lord for a healthy harvest, and for the food we are about to eat. God bless friends and family.' He looked up, and already the dishes and plates of food were being passed round.

'Well!' Vicky tutted. 'That was a short Grace.'

'No matter,' her husband replied, shovelling a heap of cabbage onto his plate. 'It was sincere, and we're good and ready to eat the fruits of our labour while they're still hot.'

'Why *has* Mr Maitland gone to America?' Susie was curious.

Barney passed Lucy the potatoes and gave his daughter one of his impatient looks. 'You must have asked that question a hundred times or more,' he chided. 'The answer is the same as it was before – we don't know. What's more, it's none of our business.'

Still she persisted. 'It must be something important, because that's twice he's been this year.'

Rolling her eyes, Vicky smiled at Lucy, a smile that said, 'Wait until your son starts asking questions and you don't have the answers to give, it'll drive you crazy.'

'Well?' Susie was like a dog with a bone.

'Well, *what?*' Thomas asked, his mouth full of part-chewed meat.

'Don't speak with your mouth full!' Vicky reprimanded. 'We none of us want to see what you're eating, thank you.'

Lucy loved having Sunday lunch with the Davidsons. This was a real family, with arguments and conflicting opinions, and questions without answers, and even half-chewed mouthfuls of meat. 'I think Susie's right,' she said, glancing at the girl. 'Mr Maitland must have important business to tend, or he wouldn't have gone away again so soon.' She hastily rescued a potato that was about to fall on the floor from Jamie's teaspoon. The little boy was quite good at feeding himself now, but he was staring goggle-eyed at Tom's antics and wasn't paying attention. Lucy hoisted him straight. He was sitting on the high chair they had made him, and was in his element.

'But why did he go the first time?' Susie played with her Yorkshire pudding, spinning it on the end of her fork and nibbling at the crusty bits.

'Hey!' Ronnie leaned towards her. 'If you don't want that bit of pud, I'll have it.' Having already demolished three, he still had an appetite like a lion.

'You will not pass food from plate to plate!' Vicky declared, getting out of her chair. 'There are half a dozen more in the oven. I'll fetch them.' Which she did, with Ronnie stealing one away on the prongs of his fork before she even got to the table.

As Vicky sat down to resume her meal, Barney was explaining to his daughter, 'You see, sweetheart, we didn't make a big thing of it at the time, so you probably didn't know, but Mr Maitland's old grandfather passed away earlier in the year, and he had to go out and see to things.'

Susie was indignant. 'Why didn't you tell me?' she asked petulantly. 'I'm not a baby to be protected.'

'I know that,' Barney apologised. 'But it isn't the sort of thing you like to talk about, is it?'

Susie shrugged her slim shoulders. 'It doesn't bother me.'

Ronnie intervened. 'So why did you cry your eyes out when your pet rat passed away?'

'That was different.' Susie's eyes filled with tears. 'Bobby was my friend.'

'Of course he was, and of course you cried.' Barney gave Ronnie a warning glance, before returning his attention to his daughter. 'Mr Maitland was upset about his grandfather too. Only when it's a person, there are things to be done . . . legal documents, matters o' that kind. That was why he went to America last time. As to why he's gone *this* time, I don't really know, but I suspect it might have something to do with his grandfather's estate. Y'see, Mr Maitland was brought up in Boston. He spent most of his youth there after his parents died, and from what he told me, he loved every minute.'

Having finished his first course, and patiently waiting for his pudding, Thomas addressed his father. 'From what I remember, you said his grandfather had hundreds of acres of land and a great, sprawling farmhouse?'

'That's right,' Barney replied, setting his knife and fork together and letting out a long sigh of satisfaction.

Ronnie spoke up. 'I've often wondered why he would leave the place if he loved it that much.'

'For an adventure?' That was Lucy. 'I've always wanted to see the world. Maybe Mr Maitland felt the same when he was younger, so when he got the chance, he took it?'

That sparked another question from Ronnie. 'How old is he now?' he asked Barney.

'I'm not exactly sure.' Barney cast his mind back to when Leonard Maitland had confided many things in him. 'He's not much older than me – forty-three, forty-four maybe.'

'Crumbs!' Susie groaned. 'That's ancient.'

While Lucy laughed, Vicky feigned indignation. 'Hey, young lady! I'll have you know, me and your father are still young at heart.'

Barney laughed out loud. 'We've aching limbs, a bad back and corns on our feet, but like your mammy says, we're still young at heart.'

Everyone laughed, including Jamie, which made them laugh more. The jam pudding and custard was served by Susie and her mother, and afterwards there was the luxury of a Sunday glass of homemade wine each; all except for Susie, who moaned and complained and still got only a quarter of a glass. 'Just enough to wet your whistle,' Barney advised firmly. 'Give it another year and if you're lucky, you might be allowed *half* a glass.'

When the meal was over and the women were clearing away, the men went for a tour of the farm, discussing their plans to prepare the fields for winter.

'There won't be too many more days like this,' Barney said, looking up at the cloudless skies. In a fleeting thought, he wondered how many more days *he* would have. So far he had managed to carry out his work without anyone suspecting the truth, but deep down in his soul he believed there was something badly wrong with him.

Lately, his only concern was the family. If anything happened to him, what in God's name would it do to Vicky? Dear Lord! It didn't bear thinking about, so he pushed the thoughts from his mind.

Maybe when all was said and done, there wasn't anything wrong that could not be put right, but the uncertainty was there, mainly because he still hadn't been back to the doctor.

On a different issue, yet with the bad thought ticking away in the back of his mind, he turned to his younger son, Ronnie. 'It's time you learned the farming inside out, son.'

'I already know the farming,' Ronnie argued. 'I've helped you since I were a little lad, Dad, just like our Tom. I've helped you bring in the harvest and led the sheep in for shearing, and I've walked that many times behind the haycart and made that many sheaves, I've lost count.'

Thomas intervened. 'Dad means *real* farming.'

Ronnie laughed. 'I thought that's what I'd been doing.'

'And you're right,' Barney agreed, 'but there's still much more for you both to learn.'

'Such as what?'

'Such as knowing the tractor inside out, every bit and bolt, how the engine works, how it should sound when running, and being able to put it right when it goes wrong. Then there are the implements, knowing which to use and when.' He went on, 'When the sheep are brought in for the shearing, you stay with them. You talk with the shearer and watch the job is done properly, and when he's not able to get here at the right time, you shear the blessed things yourself, or the maggots will eat them alive.'

'That's right!' Thomas exclaimed. 'The first time I saw a sheep with its back half-eaten, I didn't know what it was. I never knew maggots could get into the fleece and eat away the flesh.'

Ronnie's mouth fell open. 'God! That's awful!'

'So, that's another thing you've learned.' Barney took out his pipe and lighting up, began puffing away. 'They've to be dipped and they've to be sheared. It's a cycle and if it goes out of rhythm, something suffers somewhere along the way.'

He blew out a halo of smoke. 'You'll both make good farmers, if that's what you want. But there's still much to be learned. There's the wintering, and ordering of foodstuff, and keeping up with what's new. Then there's the paperwork, oh aye! Yon paperwork will keep you up till the early hours, and when that's done, it's time to get up for the milking.' He sighed deeply and pulled on his pipe. 'It's not like a job most other poor devils do – if they can get it – where you clock on in the morning and clock off again at night.'

He looked from one to the other. 'You work with the land and the animals; you're controlled by the seasons.' He smiled contentedly. 'It's hard work and by, it takes it out of you, but I swear to God you'll never find a better way of life.' Taking his pipe out, he paused, before saying in a serious voice, 'I can't tell either of you how to live your life and I wouldn't dream of doing that. It might be that you don't want to work for Mr Maitland and stay here in Comberton. You're both my sons and I'm proud of you, but you must spend your lives the way you see fit.'

'I've already decided what *I* want to do.' Thomas had been giving it some serious thought lately. 'At first I wasn't so sure, but now I am: I want to make farming my life. I want the kind of life you and Mother have had.'

Barney was thrilled. 'I'll not deny we've had a good life, me and your mother . . .'

Ronnie interrupted with a quiet smile. 'With many more years to come yet, eh, Dad?'

Taken aback by Ronnie's remark, Barney felt his heart turn over. 'Aye, lad, that's right . . . many more to come yet.' God willing, he thought. *God willing.*

'And I'm the same.' Like Thomas, Ronnie had missed the look of regret in his father's eye. 'I want to farm an' all. Winter or summer, it's a great way of life.'

Barney was filled with emotion, that his two sons had seen such contentment in his own life that they wanted the same for themselves. 'I'm glad,' he answered gratefully. 'It were allus my wish that the two of you would follow in my footsteps. But it had to be your decision, not mine.'

Just then, Lucy and Vicky arrived to join them, little Jamie toddling between them.

Barney grabbed hold of Vicky's free hand. 'Is there any o' that elderberry wine left over from dinner, sweetheart?'

'Half a bottle.' Vicky instinctively squeezed his hand. 'Why?'

His face beamed up at her. ' 'Cause we've summat to celebrate, that's why.' He gestured towards his sons. 'You and me have talked long and often, wondering whether the boys might take up the farming as a way of life, and tonight, they've given me their answer.'

When Barney's smile widened, Vicky gave a little squeal of excitement. 'Oh Barney! So they want to be farmers, like their dad?' With moist eyes and a smile hovering between tears and laughter, she ran to hug them. 'Oh, I'm so glad!' And now the tears came. 'We did think you might eventually decide to go out into the big, wide world and do summat different, but oh, we did hope . . .'

Ronnie held onto her a moment longer. 'If you're gonna start crying, we might have to change our minds. Stop it, Mam, you're scaring the little 'un.'

Laughing, she scooped Jamie up and said to Lucy, 'We'll go and get the kettle on, shall we, and dig out the wine again.'

'Good idea.' Lucy went up to the two young men and gave them each a kiss. 'It's wonderful news.'

Back in the big farmhouse kitchen, with everyone sitting comfortably, Barney filled the glasses and Vicky handed them round. 'A toast!' Barney raised his glass. 'To a fourth generation of the Davidson farmers.'

He thought with pride of his father and grandfather, and the ones who had gone before, all contented men who had lived well into their eighties. And now, his own two sons were to carry on the tradition.

His sense of pride was mingled with regret.

He couldn't help but wonder if he would ever see the next generation; his own grandchildren. That would be the greatest thing.

Somehow, though, his instinct told him that he was not destined to live the long life of his forefathers.

CHAPTER TWELVE

LEONARD MAITLAND HAD spent several days trudging the many fine streets of Boston, going from one office to another, placating irate creditors and dealing with problems he had never envisaged. There was no chance for him to explore the city this time. As he strode along today, he thought how he would have loved to watch the Red Sox baseball team play at Fenway Park, as he had so often done with his grandfather, but there was no time, no time! His whole future depended on putting things right. Having studied everything with the lawyer executing the terms of Farley Kemp's Will, he had been kept so busy his feet had hardly touched the ground.

And now he was on his way to the lawyer's office to tie up all the loose ends.

'Go right in, sir.' Smart and efficient, the young woman behind reception had the sweetest smile. 'Mr Lovatt is expecting you.'

'Good to see you, Lenny. Please come in.' The

big man with the horn-rimmed spectacles threw open the door of his inner office. 'I believe we're as ready as we'll ever be.'

Having been a respected lawyer in New York before the Wall Street Crash last year, Mr Lovatt's experience of matters relating to property was unsurpassed and, not surprisingly, his appointment book was invariably full.

Gesturing to the big leather armchair, he informed Leonard, 'I don't know about you, but I sure could use a cup of coffee. I'll order it while you make yourself comfortable.' With that, he pressed a button on his desk and said, 'Clara, a pot of coffee, please. Our client may also appreciate a few of those cookies your mom made – that is, if you have any left?' There was a pause, then, 'That's great!'

Returning his attention to Leonard, the lawyer took up a thick file and slid it across the desk to him. 'It's all there – names, addresses, the extent of debt and terms agreed.' He grinned smugly. 'We've covered a lot of ground, negotiated with the creditors, and now, with the meeting scheduled for tomorrow morning, the rest should be just a formality.'

Leonard nodded his appreciation. 'You've done all the back-breaking work, and it goes without saying, I'm very grateful.'

The big man settled back in his chair. 'As you know, I don't come cheap,' he said with a disarming smile. 'It's my job to know the enemy. Once you know what you're up against, you can prepare for battle.' He tapped his nose shrewdly. 'And win.'

Leonard was nervous, but he had done his homework and was ready. 'It's just unfortunate that it had to be this way.'

The big man also regretted the situation. 'Look, Lenny, with regard to your grandfather's Will, I'm real sorry it turned out like this.'

'It did come as a shock,' Leonard muttered, casting his gaze to the papers in front of him. 'I always thought that Farley was a wealthy man. He certainly always lived like one. He spoiled me rotten when my parents died, and he and Gramma Sophie came over to England to take me back with them.' A lump came into his throat. His parents had died when he was four, in an influenza epidemic in London. 'It shook me to the core when you told me he was in so much debt, he was on the brink of losing everything.'

When he looked up, his expression was pained. 'Why in God's name did he have to be so proud?' he said thickly. 'If only he had confided in me, I would have helped. Dear Lord, it must have troubled him so much!'

'I pleaded with him time and again to contact you,' the big attorney said sadly. 'I would have contacted you myself, but he absolutely forbade it.' He threw his arms out in a gesture of helplessness. 'All along, he insisted he had everything under control. I wasn't privy to all your grand-father's interests, so of course I took him at his word.'

Just then, a tap sounded on the door and in came the young woman called Clara with a tray containing a big pot of coffee, a jug of cream and a plate of delicious-looking biscuits. She poured them each a cup, and said with a smile, 'If there's anything else, you will let me know, won't you?'

The big man held out the plate. 'Cookie?'

Leonard took one. 'However could my grand-father have got so deep into gambling?' he mused aloud for the hundredth time, before drinking a sip of coffee and biting into the biscuit.

'You recall I told you about the two Irish brothers that Farley befriended?' the lawyer asked. 'How they came to work for him at the spread and turned up drunk one night, with a racehorse they'd won on the gambling. Your grandfather had been awful lonely these past few years, ever since he lost his wife. He found a welcome distrac-tion at the racetrack, and he had a few lucky strikes before it all went wrong. You see, like all gamblers, he always believed the next big win was just around the corner.' He shrugged. 'An intelligent man like that . . . He wasn't the first to get in above his head and you can bet your bottom dollar he won't be the last. It's a sad thing, Lenny – but it happens.'

Deep down, if he was honest with himself,

Leonard had not been too surprised at what the lawyer had told him. 'He always liked to place a bet on sporting events,' he admitted. 'I recall Grandmother lecturing him one time, but it was never a problem, not then anyway. And why in God's name did the banks let him get into so much debt?'

The attorney pointed to the file on his desk. 'As you've already seen, it wasn't only the banks, though they were by far the biggest creditors. Mr Kemp borrowed money from whoever would lend it, and no one refused, because they knew him as a respected and reliable man who ran one of the biggest homesteads in this part of Massachusetts. The Depression has affected everyone here in the States, as it has in your country, and these people want their loans repaying. They *need* that money, Lenny.'

'And now, if we can't agree a settlement, everything may have to be sold.' Leonard recalled the place where he had spent so many wonderful childhood years, and his face set grimly. 'I swear I'll behave honourably towards everyone who is owed money, but at the same time, I'll fight tooth and nail to keep the land.'

The other man heard the passion in his client's voice and saw how his fists instinctively clenched. 'We've done all we can,' he assured him. 'Tomorrow morning will tell us if it was enough.'

Despairing but not altogether without hope,

Leonard returned to his hotel in Beacon Hill. So preoccupied was he, he hardly noticed the pretty cobblestoned streets and grand old townhouses that characterised this famed quarter of Boston. Feverishly, he went through his notes yet again, then packed them away into his briefcase. He glanced at the clock and, seeing how he had hours before he could sleep, slipped his jacket on and went out to find the nearest bar.

Ordering a beer, he went to sit at a table in the corner, where he thought ahead to the imminent, all-important meeting with the creditors. How would they react to his offer? Would they accept it as the best course open to them? Or would they insist that the Kemp estate be sold and the monies split between them?

Gulping down his beer, he felt nervous and worried.

What if it all went wrong?

What if the estate went to auction and was lost forever? Certainly he could never afford to bid for it.

What if this . . . what if that. His mind was in a whirl.

With so much at stake, tomorrow could not come quickly enough.

~

The following morning, Leonard climbed out of bed, weary from lack of sleep and eager to be on his way. He showered and shaved and put on a clean shirt and an expensive silk tie that Patricia had bought for him. Looking at his image in the mirror he shook his head. 'God Almighty, look at the state of you!' With dark circles under his eyes and wisps of unruly hair protruding from behind his ears, he presented a sorry picture. 'Leonard Maitland, you're a damned mess.'

Slicking back the clumps of hair, he fastened his jacket, straightened his tie and turned away. He was ready to do battle. And with that he went smartly out of the room.

Farley Kemp had borrowed money from many sources, but the largest slice of debt was owed to a major bank. The meeting was scheduled to take place there.

The doorman whistled up a cab. Handing him a dime for his trouble, Leonard climbed in and gave directions to the bank. Settling himself into his seat with the all-important documents on his lap, he peered out at the Boston streets, seeing nothing.

On arriving at his destination, he paid the cabbie and watched him drive away. For a long, pensive moment he stood on the sidewalk looking up at the building; an imposing structure with dark-suited businessmen arriving and departing through its doors. This was the place where his future would be decided.

As he came out of the elevator, he could hear

them: the shuffle and bustle of many people in one room; the scraping of chairs and the pacing of footsteps; and as he opened the door to the offices, he could almost smell their anger.

Suddenly, a cloak of silence fell over the room as all eyes turned to look at him. Nervous and unsure, he nodded, his confident smile belying the turmoil inside.

'Very well, gentlemen.' Justin Lovatt took the chair. 'We're all here now, so we may as well get started.'

Everyone present made their way to the large oval table in the centre of the room. When they were seated, Leonard noted that some men were softly talking, while others sat in silence, looking angry and morose. All had but one purpose in mind: to get their money back.

When he had first entered the room, his eyes were instinctively drawn to a large, bespectacled man who, seeming to keep his distance from the others, was staring out of the window. It was he who now voiced what everyone else was thinking. 'Mr Lovatt, before you begin proceedings, can I just tell you this. All we want is to get back what we lent in good faith.' His voice was surprisingly calm and soft. 'We all have businesses to run, so let's get on with it.'

Two hours later, they were still 'getting on with it'.

An hour into the meeting, the men were on

their feet, declaring with raised voices that they wanted every cent back and would not settle for half measures. No amount of persuasion from Justin Lovatt could convince them of any other way forward.

Deeply frustrated and losing hope, Leonard asked permission to speak. He was initially greeted with a hubbub of noise from enraged men who would not be pacified, but then the big, bespectacled man called for order. 'Let Farley Kemp's grandson speak,' he said firmly. 'He is not to blame for his grandfather's mismanagement, so give him a chance. We're getting nowhere like this.'

Standing up amongst them, Leonard looked round the table at the faces of these men whom his grandfather had known well; men who had trusted him to repay what they lent in good faith – and he felt ashamed.

Clearing his throat, he began to speak. 'Firstly, I want to say how I understand your anger. You trusted my grandfather and he let you down badly, and I apologise for that. I know that, despite the Crash, some of you could well afford to lose the money if you had to . . .' when they began loudly protesting, he put up his hand . . . 'please, if you will just let me have my say.' When they were again attentive, he went on, 'I'm not saying that you will or *should* lose any money. Of course you want your money back and rightly so. And there are those amongst you who *cannot* afford to lose what you lent. I know that and I'm here today to try and settle matters one way or another.'

He looked at the documents lying on the table before him, and a great sense of bitterness overwhelmed him. His grandfather's reputation was shattered forever; there was family honour at stake, and a debt to pay, and it was up to him to pacify these men who had put their trust in a man who had betrayed them and reneged on his debts.

What could he say to appease them? How could he put things right?

He was so deep in his reverie that he had not realised how long his lapse of concentration was; until he heard them shifting impatiently in their seats, and their exchanged whispers as they grew restless.

'See here, Mr Maitland: have you got our money or not – that's all we need to know.' That was the sallow-faced, grey-suited man on the far end.

'That's right!' another voice joined in. 'Have you brought our money from England?'

'No!' he answered truthfully. Strong and clear, his stark words echoed across the room, effectively silencing everyone. 'I have money for you, yes, but it isn't what you might have hoped.'

'What in hell does *that* mean?'

The voices began to rise. 'If you're here to waste our time, we might as well leave now.'

'All we want is our money back, God dammit.'

'Gentlemen, this is the situation,' Leonard quickly explained. 'I have a farm in England, which I can sell tomorrow – and I will. But it won't make enough to clear all the debts. Since I've been here I've raised as much money as I can, but even with the sale of my own farm, it still isn't sufficient to cover the total sums owed.' Before they could start protesting again, he went swiftly on. 'I've gone through everything with Mr Lovatt here, and we've calculated that you will get back seventy per cent of what's owed —'

'Seventy per cent!' The voices began again. 'What the hell use is that?'

'We won't settle for less than what we're owed! Plus interest!'

'So, this is all a waste of our time? You got us here under false pretences. Jesus! You're no better than your grandfather!'

The rage threatened to erupt.

At this point Justin Lovatt stood up and called for quiet. 'Mr Maitland has come a long way, and gone to a lot of trouble to try and sort out his family's debts, which are not – I repeat *not* – of his making. I believe you are all men enough to appreciate what he's been trying to do. The least you can do now is give him a fair hearing.'

Something in his words seemed to calm them and with all eyes on Leonard they listened to what he had to say.

He told them how he could do no more than

he had already done, and that, 'If you wait for the Kemp estate to go to action, you may well end up with even less than I'm offering you now. You have copies in front of you, showing the proof that I am in a position to deliver seventy per cent of what you lent out. It's signed, sealed and can be delivered. With an auction, you can never be sure; it all depends on the day and how many people want the property, or can afford it. As you know to your cost, the value of the property has been badly affected by the slump in the world economy.'

'He's right.' One man who so far had remained silent spoke out. 'The farmstead is still a valuable asset, and sold to the right buyer, we may get lucky. But if there aren't enough buyers to force up the price . . .' He raised his palms in a gesture of surrender. 'Like the man said – we could end up worse off.'

Seeing how the tide might turn in their favour, Justin Lovatt intervened. 'Mr Maitland and I will leave the room for a while. You all have copies of the documents in front of you, which will verify what's been put forward: seventy per cent of what you are owed, without uncertainty, and without prejudice. Read the documents, and if you're in favour of accepting, we'll make it watertight in your favour.'

He paused, before going on in sombre voice, 'If, however, you decide to take your chances at auction, then so be it. The meeting will end right there.' With that he summoned Leonard to go with him, and together they departed the room.

In the outer hall, Leonard voiced his concern. 'There are a few in there who would rather wait and see what happens at the auction,' he said. 'And who knows, maybe the estate will bring in more than enough to pay them off.'

'All we can do is wait and see. The decision is in their hands and we have no choice but to abide by it.' As a lawyer Justin was philosophical. He had seen it all before and there was no telling which way it would go.

~

They had been waiting an hour and a half before the nondescript man in the grey suit came out to tell them, 'We've come to a decision . . . of sorts.'

As they followed him to the boardroom, Leonard looked at Justin and mouthed the words, '"Of sorts"?' Justin shook his head, meaning that he didn't quite know what that meant either.

When they entered the room, it was instantly apparent that the men were more at ease; the big man actually smiled at them as they walked to their places. 'We've looked through all the documents,' he began, and it was obvious they had elected him to be spokesman, 'and I'm afraid we still want our pound of flesh.'

Leonard's heart sank, then rose again at his next words. 'We accept your offer – but with certain conditions.' He looked around the room, making sure everyone was still of the same mind. When he received the nods, he went on, 'No one here is prepared to accept any less than the full figure they are owed.'

Leonard's heart sank again.

The big man continued, 'To that end, we *will* accept the offer, but with a legal proviso that the remaining thirty per cent is paid within a period of two years. So there you have it. That is our unanimous decision. Accept it, or we'll take our chances at the auction.'

Realising it had come as a shock to Leonard, Justin spoke on his behalf. 'You all know my part in this,' he reminded them. 'The decision does not rest with me. I can't say whether Mr Maitland can or cannot comply with what you ask. All I can say is, he and I need to talk. I request that you give us twenty-four hours to consider.'

A hush came over the room and all eyes turned to Leonard.

Head bent and heart heavy, he was lost. He frantically sought a way out and could see none. He had been prepared to sell his farm in England and borrow money on top of that, in order to keep his beloved grandfather's homestead in the family, where it belonged, but now he saw it all slipping away. To consent to this would cripple him financially.

A sense of urgency galvanised his thoughts. You

only get one precious moment which can change the course of your life forever. This was his moment. If he let it go now, he knew there would never be another.

Looking up, he saw them all anxiously waiting for his response.

A kind of madness took hold of him. Straightening his shoulders, he thanked Justin then turned to sweep his gaze across the sea of faces all intent on him; his eyes falling on the big man last. 'I accept your offer,' he said simply. 'One way or another, you will all get your money.'

There was a brief silence, then a cheer went up. The relief in the air was palpable.

The big man came over to Leonard and asked if he could shake him by the hand. 'Farley would have been proud of you,' he said quietly. 'Good luck.'

~

The next day, as he boarded the liner which would take him home to England, Leonard wondered if he had done the right thing. Even now he wasn't sure how he might repay the debt he had inherited from his grandfather. Yet he had given his word. The money was pledged and somehow, he would find a way.

Once upon a time, the Farley Kemp holdings had been a thriving, lucrative business – and it could become so again. Especially if he was to bring Barney across the Atlantic. They worked well together, he and his Farm Manager. If anyone could help him rebuild the estate and restore the place to its former glory, it was Barney Davidson. And the thought of having Vicky close at hand was wonderful. He had dreaded saying goodbye to her.

With that in mind, Leonard locked his cabin door and made his way to the nearest bar, where he ordered a large whisky. 'I've earned it,' he told the barman. 'I've just taken the biggest gamble of my life!'

CHAPTER THIRTEEN

Having informed Patricia of the date he would return, Leonard half-expected her to be waiting for him when he disembarked at Liverpool. Unfortunately, she was nowhere to be seen, even though he lingered for almost an hour, walking up and down searching every avenue in case he should miss her.

Finally he hailed a taxi and, bitterly disappointed, travelled back alone. He knew the house would be clean and tidy, thanks to his daily woman, Mrs Riley, who ran the place and used Lucy Baker on a Saturday to do any extra jobs. But it would be cold and lonely, too.

Arriving at The Manse he paid the driver and went inside; where the warm, earthy aroma of fresh bread filled his nostrils and took him straight to the kitchen. 'Why, it's young Lucy!' He was astonished to see her, sleeves rolled up, taking a crusty-baked loaf out of the oven.

'Welcome home, Mr Maitland,' she said with a

shy smile. 'Vicky offered to look after Jamie so I could nip in and make you some supper, after your long journey. There's mushroom soup to go with the bread. I didn't think you'd want anything too heavy, so late in the day. Oh, and I've lit a fire downstairs and one in your bedroom. I hope that's all right?' She looked anxious.

He smiled. 'It's more than all right – it's a wonderful welcome. Thank you, my dear, for being so very thoughtful.' More thoughtful than his so-called fiancée, he thought.

Lucy took off her pinny and went to get her coat and hat. 'Don't slice the bread while it's still warm,' she urged. 'It'll only squash up and you won't get a clean slice.'

'I'll let it cool,' he promised. 'Now go home and get some rest.' All he wanted was to be alone, put his feet up, eat from a tray and enjoy a strong drink. 'There's a chill in the air.' He held Lucy's coat open for her. 'It was cold in Boston, too.'

'Good night, Mr Maitland. It's good to see you back.' Lucy hoped she wasn't being too familiar. She was rather in awe of Leonard.

He smiled. 'It's lovely to be home,' he told her.

By ten o'clock that evening, Leonard had bathed and changed, eaten three slices of the best bread he had ever tasted, dipped into a sizeable bowl of hot, thick mushroom soup; the whole lot washed down by two cups of tea and a tot of best whisky.

God, it was good to be back by his own fireside.

Yawning, he was thinking about going to bed when a moment later, he was taken by surprise when the door opened and in walked Patricia, done up in all her finery and looking especially beautiful.

Purring like a kitten she wrapped herself round him. 'You smell delicious,' she whispered, caressing him and deeply arousing him. 'I've missed you, my darling.'

Summoning all his courage, he drew away. 'Did you now?' he asked cynically. 'So, why did you forget to meet me at the docks?'

She gave a long, impatient sigh. 'I didn't forget,' she answered rather petulantly. 'It was just . . . well, I went shopping. I wanted to look my very best when you saw me. It got late, and by the time I reached the dock, you must have already left.'

'So, you would rather go shopping than come and meet me, is that it?'

Her expression hardened. '*No* – but does it really matter? I'm here now, aren't I?'

Having moved away when she saw he was angry, she now came at him again, her avaricious eyes appraising his body and her roving hands touching him in all the right spots. 'I'm really sorry.' She put her lips to his ears and softly blew. 'I've missed you . . . I want you so much.'

He wanted her too. All the while he had been in Boston he had wondered if he should end his engagement the minute he got home. But now, when she was close like this, and his need was pressing, he had little control. He was a man, with a man's hunger, and here she was, a beautiful woman, his fiancée, freely offering herself to him.

So, he took her hand and walked her to the foot of the stairs, where he swept her into his arms and carried her up to his bedroom, lit and warmed by the fire Lucy had set earlier.

He carried her inside and closed the door behind them.

And they did not come out until morning.

～

It was eight-thirty the next morning when he took Patricia home to her parents' grand house on the other side of Liverpool. 'I'll see you later,' she told him. 'We can talk more about your trip to Boston then. I'm sure Daddy will loan you all the money you need, then there will be no need to sell Overhill Farm. Or you could still sell it and start a different business – nothing to do with farming. I think that would be a good idea, don't you?'

'I've already said, I don't want you discussing my business with your father,' Leonard said tightly.

'Why ever not?'

'For reasons you would not understand.' This woman was suffocating him.

'All right, but I think you're being selfish.'

Dear God. 'Like you said, I'll see you later.' He couldn't trust himself to say anything else at that moment.

As he watched her go inside, he thought, The more you open your mouth, the more I realise we will never be suited.

At that moment in time, Leonard was not only concerned about his relationship with Patricia. There was Barney and his entire family to think of now. How would they take the news that the farm was being sold from under them? And what would Barney's answer be, when Leonard asked him to come with him to America? And even if Barney agreed, what of Vicky and the three children? Would they be prepared to leave behind everything they knew?

Only now when he was home, did Leonard come to realise how huge a step he was taking, giving up his life here, moving back to the States, taking up his grandfather's crumbling business and starting it again from scratch, already deep in debt.

In the end, for whatever reason, he was now embarking on a lonely, daunting journey.

～

Early the following morning, Leonard drove into Liverpool. As always, the city was a busy, vibrant place, despite the serious problems of poverty and unemployment.

When he found the address he was looking for, Leonard drew into the kerb and parked. A sign hanging above the offices read:

W.H. Brewer & Son
Land Agents

Leonard had dealt before with the tall, whiskery-faced man inside, who greeted him now with: 'Ah, good morning, Mr Maitland. How can I help you, sir?' He pulled out a chair in his office for Leonard to sit on.

Mr Brewer was always very polite, particularly with a man of Mr Maitland's admirable character. Moreover, Leonard was a good customer, having piece by piece expanded his landholding until it was now some 400 acres in total.

While shaking hands he informed Leonard, 'If you've come looking for land, I'm afraid there is absolutely nothing at the moment. Investing in land is being seen as a reliable option these days; we have it one minute and it's gone the next. Oh – and the prices are on the up and up all the while.'

Leonard could hardly conceal his delight. He had been basing his own valuation of the land on rather pessimistic calculations. 'This is good news for me,' he answered, 'because I'm here to sell my entire holding.'

The other man was visibly shocked. *'Everything? Are you sure?'* he asked. 'The farm and the house and outbuildings, too?'

'Everything,' Leonard confirmed, 'although I haven't yet decided what to do about my old gardener's cottage.'

'Really?' The agent was intrigued. 'From what I can recall, it's little more than a ruin?'

Leonard nodded. 'Well yes, it is, and I've done nothing to it since he's been left these past years. It's a tiny place, with only one bedroom, and a scullery a man can hardly turn about in. I'm sorry to say it's been left to the elements; the little garden is shamefully overgrown, and the whole place is somewhat tumbledown. But I may have a mind to hang on to it so I'd appreciate it if you would exclude it from the sale.'

'What about Barney Davidson's cottage?' The agent knew how Leonard valued Barney and his sons.

'Hopefully, he won't be needing the cottage,' came the reply. 'I have other, more rewarding plans for him and his family.'

Thoughtfully, Mr Brewer stroked his finger along his beard. 'I should think we could get a substantial amount for that lot,' came the welcome answer. 'In fact, I could sell it tomorrow to a gentleman who has been searching for a property such as yours. But it would be best if we trod extra carefully on this one,' he said sagely. 'Of course I shall inform the gentleman straight away, but I will also inform some of my other clients, who might be interested in acquiring smaller parcels of land rather than the whole.'

Leonard knew only too well that buyers' ambitions were always dictated by the amount of capital they could raise. He thought of his own circumstances. If he had been able to pay off his grandfather's debts without selling his own land, he would not be in this office today.

'Sometimes, for whatever reason, a man may have more need of a smaller parcel of land,' the agent went on. 'But this can work well in our favour.'

He explained. 'We could sell off say, three hundred acres either in a single lot, or if you preferred, we could separate it into smaller units. That would leave one hundred acres with the house – which is a small farm in itself. This way, the sale will attract more money, or at the very least it will create competition, which will return a far more handsome price than if we went straight to the gentleman in question and sold him the entire holding.'

Leonard liked the idea. 'Let them fight it out between them – is that what you're saying?'

The Land Agent's smile was positively wicked. 'Of course, let them fight it out. And why not?'

So they got down to facts and figures, and when the meeting was over, Leonard dared to hope that if all went well, he might even be able to pay the US creditors every single dollar they were owed.

With that in mind, he got back into his car and drove straight to Overhill Farm, where he found Vicky standing on a box, singing to herself and cleaning the kitchen windows. When he saw her, he slowed down, his mood brightening even further at the sight of the small, familiar figure, her long silken hair gently lifted by the cool breeze. And now as she stretched on tiptoe to reach the upper part of the panes, his eyes were drawn to her slim, shapely ankles and calves. 'You're a lucky man, Barney Davidson,' he whispered, and now, as she turned to look straight at him, his heart did a dance inside his chest so he could hardly breathe.

'Morning, Vicky.' His voice gave nothing away as he climbed out of the car and went towards her. 'I wonder if I might have a word with Barney. Is he around?'

'Sorry, Mr Maitland, he's out in Top Field,' she said, preparing to clamber off the box. She was taken by surprise when Leonard reached his hands round her waist and lifted her down without effort. 'He's checking the sheep,' she said, her face flushing pink. 'I can fetch him if you like?'

'No, it's all right,' Leonard said. 'Best not disturb him at his work. What I have to say can wait until this evening.'

'Are you sure? It won't take above five minutes for me to fetch him. I can settle you with a cup of tea before I go?' Vicky's curiosity was heightened; it wasn't often the boss came down here to talk in the middle of the day.

'No, no,' he told her. 'It's fine. But will you please tell him I called by, and that I have business to discuss with him.' He paused, not wanting to alarm her. 'If you wouldn't mind, Vicky, I'd like you to be there as well. In fact, what I have to say might concern all of you.'

Seeing her expression of concern, he quickly added, 'I'd rather not discuss it now, but I'll be here at about eight. Will you have finished your evening meal by then?'

'Well, yes, but – what is it, Mr Maitland? What's wrong? It all seems very serious.'

'You're not to worry,' he said gently. 'We'll talk this evening, then. Goodbye for now.' Quickly, before she could ask any more questions, he climbed into the car and drove off, leaving Vicky in a quandary.

'Is everything all right?' Lucy had seen Leonard leave and now, with Vicky seeming deep in thought, her happy singing silenced and the window-cloth hanging forgotten in her hand, she grew alarmed.

'He told me not to worry,' Vicky answered, 'but it's odd all the same.' She raised her gaze to Lucy. 'Mr Maitland says he has business to discuss with me and Barney.' Picking up her bucket she dumped the cloth in it and walked to the kitchen door. 'It all seems very serious to me,' she told Lucy. 'He's coming back tonight, after we've had our supper.'

'Crikey!' Lucy had become as close to this family as if she was born to it, and what affected them, was bound to affect her. 'What d'you reckon it could be, to fetch him out here at this time of day? And you say he's coming back again tonight . . .'

There was something not right here, Lucy thought. Something was brewing and like Vicky she, too, was afraid.

Her friend began pacing the kitchen floor. 'I'm not sure what to do, Lucy,' she said. 'Should I go and tell Barney now, or should I simply get on with my work and tell him when he comes home?'

'Do you want my opinion?' Lucy asked.

'Of course!'

'Do what you just said – wait till Barney gets home. Let's have a cup of tea and a sandwich like we allus do at this time of day, then we'll get on with our work and leave Barney to do the same. Tell him tonight, but not until after he's had his dinner, because if you tell him before, he'll be so worried he won't eat.'

'You're right, lass,' Vicky agreed. 'That's what we'll do.'

While Lucy went to fetch Jamie from his nap, Vicky put the kettle on. Dear God, was there some sort of trouble in store? Just now, when everything was going so well, she prayed their lives were not about to be disrupted.

In the sitting room, where Lucy was lifting the child from the pram, she had that same sense of dread. 'Mr Maitland's been here,' she told little Jamie. 'It seems he's got business to discuss with

Barney and Vicky. I can't imagine what it could be, but it's important enough for him to come back and talk with them tonight.' She tutted. 'I just hope it isn't bad news.'

She kissed his head and sat him on the little enamel potty for a minute or two chiding herself for thinking the worst. For all she knew, it might even be good news. And keeping that in mind, she took the little boy to join Vicky, who was just laying the table for the three of them.

As she dragged the high chair across to the table, Lucy commented, 'Happen Mr Maitland is right and you shouldn't worry. I mean, it might be good news he's bringing tonight. There's no reason why it should be anything bad, is there?'

'No, there isn't!' Vicky's face lit in a smile. 'You could be right, lass – it might be good news.' The woman was glad of Lucy's encouraging words. 'It could be something to do with buying another tractor, mebbe, or he might even be sending in the workmen to put a new roof on this place. Lord knows, it's been leaking long enough.' She gave a comical little laugh. 'Barney's repaired it so many times it's beginning to look like a patchwork quilt.'

Going off to the scullery, she reappeared with a tray containing a pot of tea and four chunky ham-and-chutney sandwiches, together with a dish of soup for the child and an apple.

Vicky took a hearty bite out of her sandwich. She chatted and laughed with the little boy and his mother, but all the while at the back of her mind was Leonard's visit.

Lucy liked to think the best.

Vicky thought the worst.

She also thought of that unexpected moment when their employer had put his hands round her waist and lifted her effortlessly to the ground . . . 'Leonard Maitland is a kind man,' she told Lucy now, unable to leave the subject for long. 'I can't imagine he's about to bring us bad news.'

'Huh!' Lucy spooned a helping of soup into her son's mouth. 'It's that woman he's chosen to be his wife who's the bad news. The poor man came all the way back from his long journey, and there wasn't anyone with him. Don't you think she should have met him off his ship? No, if you ask me, he'll have a life of hell if he ever puts a ring on that one's finger.'

'I hope not,' Vicky answered quietly. 'He's such a lovely man, he deserves a good marriage.'

'Like you and your Barney,' Lucy said. 'But not every marriage can be as good as yours, you know.'

'I've been fortunate,' Vicky said wistfully. 'Oh Lucy, I love him so much! I don't know what I'd do without him. God did a wonderful thing, when He brought me and my Barney together.'

Not for the first time, Lucy wondered if she would ever know that same kind of love. 'I wonder what Edward Trent is doing now?' she said.

'Do you care?' Vicky was surprised to hear the girl mention that man's name.

Lucy shook her head. 'No. To tell you the truth, I don't know how I could ever have thought I loved him in the first place.'

'Well, at least he gave you little Jamie.' Vicky had come to love the child as if he was her own.

Lucy gazed fondly at her son. 'I know it's a sad thing to say, but I hope he grows up, never knowing his father.'

Vicky saw the bitterness in Lucy's face and deliberately changed the subject. 'Uh-oh – look at the time,' she said. 'Let's finish the chores, and after that, you and young James should get yourselves home before it starts getting dark. Besides, you must be bone-tired. What with cleaning all the upstairs windows and changing every bed in the house, you've done two days' work in one. I honestly don't know how I ever managed before you came to join us. Thank you, love.'

'Are you sure?' It was true – Lucy *was* exhausted and there was nothing she wanted more right now than to go home for a well-earned rest. However, seeing how worried Vicky was, she offered, 'I don't mind staying to help prepare the evening meal. I'm sure Barney or one of the boys would run me home.'

Vicky shook her head. 'Don't think I'm not grateful,' she told Lucy, 'but I'm best off working. By the time I've got the supper ready, Barney should be home. Soonever he's eaten, I'll tell him how Mr Maitland's coming by to visit.'

As she helped clear away the crockery, she added, almost to herself, 'I can't wait to know what business he has that he couldn't discuss with me – especially as he said he wants me there when he talks with Barney.'

A short time later, Lucy left, holding the little boy by his hand. It wasn't far to walk back to the cottage. She often left the pram at Overhill Farm. 'I hope everything goes all right,' she told Vicky. 'If you need me, you know where I am.'

~

At eight-thirty, Mr Maitland arrived. Welcoming him into the house, Barney took him straight through to the sitting room. 'Vicky tells me that this matter you need to talk through might affect us all.'

'That's right, Barney.' Leonard glanced round the room. 'Your children not here then?'

Barney explained, 'My sons have gone to meet friends in Liverpool and Susie is taking extra tuition on the hat-making. There is no need for them to be here. If you're bringing bad news, it's best that me and Vicky know first. That way we can talk to the young 'uns ourselves.'

'I understand.' Leonard had no way of knowing how all this might affect Barney's children. Even if Barney accepted his offer, the children might not.

'You'd best sit down.' Barney gestured to the armchair, while he and Vicky sat side-by-side on the sofa. 'I might tell you, I've been on pins since Vicky told me.'

Leonard sat down. He looked at the pair of them seated there, fine, kind-hearted people, hardworking as the day was long, and his heart sank within him. 'I have to tell you both . . .' he began. Then: 'This has not been the easiest day of my life.'

Barney looked him in the eye. 'So, it *is* bad news then?'

'I suppose it all depends on how you see it.' Leonard chose his words carefully as he went on, 'I've come here tonight, firstly to explain the outcome of my trip to Boston, and secondly, to ask something of you both.'

He took a deep invigorating breath. 'What I have to tell you has been playing on my mind these past weeks. It will be a relief to have it out in the open. I'm not like you, Barney,' he said kindly. 'I've always struggled to make friends.' He smiled shyly. 'In fact, I'd go so far as to say that you two are the nearest to friends that I've got. I have no family – no wife or children to talk things over with, so when I have problems, they often weigh heavy on my mind.'

When Barney seemed about to speak, he gestured for him to stop. 'I don't want you to say anything just yet, Barney. As you already know,

I was summoned to Boston in order to learn the terms and conditions of my grandfather's Will, and to tie up any loose ends out there.'

He looked away momentarily as though in shame, and went on in a low voice: 'It was a great shock for me to learn that my grandfather had taken up gambling and was up to his neck in debt when he died, with all his land and properties on the point of being sold from under him.'

At the gasp of disbelief from Barney and Vicky, he got swiftly to the point. 'It means two things,' he said, 'and each of them will affect you and your family, in at least one way that I can see.'

He went on in great detail, telling them how it had all come about, how he had worked every waking moment to save what he could. There had been sacrifices made, and his own future, as well as theirs, was now hanging in the balance. 'I'm sorry to tell you that I have no option but to sell both The Manse and Overhill Farm.' There was no other way to say it but straight out.

Rendered speechless by the news, Barney stood up and with haggard eyes, he looked first at Leonard, and then at Vicky. His face white as chalk, he reached out for his wife's hand. Deeply concerned, she could only leave it to the men and hope they might salvage something worthwhile from this nightmare.

Leonard would have given almost anything to remove the look of devastation on Barney's face.

'If there had been any other way, you know I would have taken it,' he said helplessly, and wondered if there had been any kinder way he could have broken the news.

He plunged on. 'I have many business contacts in the farming world, and I'm sure I can get you a place locally, if it's what you want. Oh, I know it will never be the same because you've been here all these years, but you only have to say the word and I'll find something – you know I will.'

Barney nodded. 'Thank you for that,' he said quietly, 'but you're right – it's small compensation. I've been here so long, it's as if I've lived here all my life. My children have never known anything else.'

Leonard had one more thing to say before he left. 'There is one other option . . .'

Pre-empting his words, Barney interrupted, 'If you're offering me first refusal of the farm, there is no way on God's earth I could ever buy it. I'm not a man of money, I never have been. I've lived content year to year, raising my family and tending the land—'

Leonard stopped him. 'It's not that, Barney. I know you haven't the means to buy this farm, otherwise it would be yours. What I'm asking of you now needs even more commitment from you, and your family.'

'What do you mean?' Barney was puzzled. 'What is it you're asking?'

Leonard glanced at Vicky; sad-faced and twining her fingers together in her lap, she was obviously deeply disturbed by events.

'I've managed to save my grandfather's estate,' he began. 'It took some doing and I've never been in so much debt in my entire life, but I couldn't let it go without doing my damnedest to keep it.'

'I'm pleased for you, Mr Maitland.' Barney was magnanimous in his own disappointment. 'I know how much you loved that place. You've talked about it that many times, I almost feel I know it myself.'

'That's excellent!' Barney's remarks took Leonard naturally into his proposition. 'How would you like to see it, Barney – you and your family?' He looked again at Vicky, who was intent on his every word.

While Barney was momentarily taken aback, it was she who replied. 'What exactly do you mean?'

In tender, persuasive tones he told her what he had in mind. 'It's my dearest wish for all of you to come with me. I would like Barney and your sons to help me run the farm, and for yourself to take charge of the house. As for young Susie, there are any number of milliners in Boston – it's a very smart place – who will teach her the trade, if that's what she really wants.'

With the two of them shocked into silence, he leaned forward, hands on his knees and his eyes pleading with them each in turn. 'Barney . . .

Vicky, please think about it. It would mean so much to me, if you would agree.'

When Barney spoke now, it was with a surge of emotion that trembled in his voice. 'But why?' he asked. 'Why would you want me and my family, when you could employ the best that money could buy?'

In Barney's face, Leonard could see the tiniest glimmer of hope. 'Oh Barney, don't you know that *you're* the best there is! That's why I want you – because I know the calibre of you, and I know that the homestead would be in good hands.'

He grew tremendously excited. 'Not only would I be taking the very best, but I'd be taking with me people I consider to be my friends . . . good people whom I've known for many a year.' He actually laughed out loud. 'Oh, you can't imagine what it's like over there. In Massachusetts, there's so much sky, you think it goes on forever! And the land . . . You could ride for half a day before you reach its borders. Boston itself is the capital – three hundred years old and full of history. Not everything in America is like Charlie Chaplin, you know!' He chuckled merrily.

By now he was on his feet. 'Say you'll come. Please, talk to your family. Tell them how it will be. You'll have a house twice the size of this one, and a garden to lose yourself in. There's an orchard – yes, it's overgrown now, but we'll soon get it round. Please! Say you'll accept this challenge. I won't let you down, and if after a while you're not happy there, I'll pay for you to come back, *and* I'll find you a house and work into the bargain. What d'you say? Barney . . . Vicky? Will you come?'

Suddenly Barney was laughing; the look of joy on Vicky's face urged him on. A moment later he was shaking Leonard by the hand. 'If the family are all in agreement, then our answer is yes, oh YES!' In the space of a moment his despair was replaced by a sense of joy.

In the excitement that followed, Vicky kissed Barney and then she kissed Leonard, and he was overjoyed.

'Talk to your sons and Susie,' he said. 'Tell them how wonderful a life it will be.'

Barney promised he would. 'Such an opportunity!' he declared. 'A new start – a new life. I can't thank you enough,' he told Leonard. 'It's the most amazing thing!'

A short time later, Leonard hurried away to collect Patricia. Behind him he could hear the Davidsons' old phonograph belting out some Dixieland jazz, and through the window as he drove off, he saw Barney take Vicky into his arms and wing her across the room. He smiled for them, the smile fading as he thought ahead to his meeting with his fiancée. Would it ever be like that with him and Patricia? In subdued mood, he answered his own question: no. He couldn't see it somehow.

Screeching the car to a halt, he did a three-point turn and took the lane that would lead him home.

When he arrived at The Manse, he was surprised to find Patricia already there, emerging from a taxi. Once inside the house, she turned to him and said, 'Look here, Lenny. I've decided I can't come with you to America, so if you want me for your wife, you will just have to forget your fool-hardy plan.'

'And is your mind absolutely made up?' he asked quietly.

'It is.'

'Then you don't give me any choice, Patricia.'

'What's that supposed to mean?'

'It means our engagement is over. I know now that we can never make a future together.'

'You can't say that! You're not thinking straight.'

When he continued to stand his ground, even when she nuzzled him and tried her usual wiles, she took a step back and eyed him with suspicion. 'There's another woman, isn't there?' Her eyeballs stood out like two glittering marbles. 'You've been cheating on me. American, is she? Met her over there, did you?' With every accusation her voice rose until now it was at screaming pitch.

'There is no other woman,' he answered stead-ily. 'Like I said, I can no longer see us in a future together. We want different things, Pat. That's the truth of it.'

In a swift and spiteful move that caught him

unawares, she brought her hand across his face, leaving her fingernail marks down the side of his cheek. 'YOU BASTARD!' Still spitting obscenities, she stormed down the steps and marched off at breakneck speed towards the village.

Breathing a deep sigh of relief, Leonard felt as though a great burden was lifted from his shoulders. 'I'm truly sorry it turned out this way,' he muttered after her; and he really was.

Softly, he repeated her angry words. 'There's another woman, isn't there?' He smiled. 'Yes, Patricia, there is another woman. But she isn't American. In fact, she's only an arm's reach from here.'

He knew now, without any doubt, that he was head over heels in love with Vicky. However, just as the relationship between himself and Patricia could never evolve, nor could the one between himself and Vicky – but for very different reasons.

PART THREE

~

Onset of Winter, 1930

A Choice for Barney

CHAPTER FOURTEEN

Aᴀᴛᴇʀ ᴛʜᴇɪʀ ᴘᴀʀᴇɴᴛꜱ' euphoria, the Davidson children reacted to Leonard's offer in
different ways.

'I'd rather stay here,' Susie said, in confron-
tational mood.

'Look, love, I've already told you. We *can't* stay
here,' Barney explained for the third time. 'Mr
Maitland has been forced to sell this farm to help
pay off his grandfather's debts.'

'Listen to your father, sweetheart.' Vicky despaired. 'Whether we like it or not, this farm is
being sold. It isn't Mr Maitland's fault, and it isn't
our fault. It's the circumstances we all find ourselves in. We would all love to stay here, but we
can't, and so we have to accept things the way they
are.'

Unlike Susie, Thomas was thrilled at the news.
'You're being right selfish,' he told his younger
sister now. 'The fact is, we're left with three
choices. Either we take work in the Liverpool area,

or we move away and hope something turns up that will suit everybody. Or we accept Mr Maitland's generous offer and be thankful. Think about it, Susie! AMERICA! There are many girls your age who would give their right arm for the chance we've been offered!'

'They can have it then!' Kicking the rug at her feet, Susie folded her arms and slumped into a chair. 'Because I don't want to go.'

Gesturing for the others to leave the room, Barney went and sat on the arm of her chair. 'What is it that worries you?' he asked gently. 'Is it because you'll be leaving your friends behind? If it is, you can always keep in touch. You can write to each other and later, maybe, they can even come and visit.'

'How can they?' Now the tears were falling. 'America is the other side of the world!'

'Naw . . . you've got that wrong, pet.' Sliding his arm round her shoulders, he drew her close. 'I won't deny it is a long way,' he coaxed, 'but it's not the end of the world. Look at Mr Maitland – he's gone over and come back twice this year, hasn't he?'

Susie looked up, her eyes swimming with tears. 'I'm frightened, Daddy.'

It cut him to the quick to see his daughter upset like this. 'There's nothing to be frightened of.' Barney put his hand under her chin and raised her face to his. 'Do you think me and your mammy would want to take you, if we thought you'd come to any harm?' He smiled his reassurance. 'Trust me, we'll take good care of you, my darling.'

Kissing the top of her head, he drew her closer. 'When you've seen the ships going away, how many times have you said to me that you'd love to be on one of them? Well, now you can!'

Looking up, she gave a shaky smile. 'I didn't think it could ever really happen.'

'Well, now it has. Look, we can sail off to America and try to make a new life, and if it doesn't work out, Mr Maitland has promised to pay our fare back. But we have to give it a chance, because everybody is so excited to be going, and like Thomas said, it's a wonderful, once-in-a-lifetime opportunity. And later, when we've saved enough money, we can come back for a visit. Would you like that?' With the tip of his finger he wiped away the tears that quivered on the end of her lashes.

'I think so.' At last a brighter smile. 'Yes, Daddy, I'd like that.'

Barney nodded. 'Then that's what we'll aim for – saving enough money between us to come back for a visit.'

'Do you promise?'

He hesitated, that small grain of dark instinct holding him back. 'I promise I'll do my very best.'

'So will I,' she said eagerly. 'You said Mr

Maitland told you I could get work with one of the hat-shops, and they would teach me the trade?'

'Yes. That's what the man said all right.' Barney was relieved to see a glimmer of enthusiasm. It would break his heart to force her into something that made her desperately unhappy.

'Maybe one day, I might have my own shop in Boston?'

Barney laughed. 'You might at that,' he said. 'Work hard and save, and who knows what the future holds?' For *all* of us, he added silently. He only hoped his health would hold up through the trials and thrills that lay ahead.

Having placed herself where they could not see her, Vicky watched from the doorway. Deeply moved by Barney's understanding of his daughter's fears she had wiped away a tear or two, but now that she could see how Barney had somehow managed to dispel Susie's fears, she crept quietly away.

Once Susie had run off to tell Vicky how she meant to have her own shop in America, Barney let himself slide down into the chair, where for a time he sat, lost in thought and deeply disturbed. Giving a long, shivering sigh, he instinctively placed a hand on his heart. 'No, Susie lass, none of us knows what the future holds.' A dark premonition rippled through his soul.

He was startled when his wife came rushing in. 'Barney Davidson, you could charm the birds right out of the trees!' She threw herself into his lap. 'One minute she's refusing to go, and now she's full of dreams. Somehow she's got the idea into her head that she's going to own a string of shops, right across America!'

Barney smiled contentedly. 'Let her dream,' he murmured, drawing her into his embrace. 'If we don't have dreams, how can they ever come true?' His own dream had come true, the day he met this darling woman.

Content to be silent, husband and wife sat awhile together. It was a moment of quietness in a love that was both deep and fulfilling; one of those rare and precious moments that each of them would cherish to the end of their days.

～

The following morning, when Lucy was told the news by an emotional Vicky, she didn't know whether to be thrilled for the Davidsons, or sad for herself. 'It's a wonderful opportunity,' she said, suppressing her fears. 'You must go, Vicky, you and Barney, and the family.'

While Vicky was explaining how it all came about, Barney strolled into the kitchen. 'Hello, Lucy, love. Vicky's told you then?' He had been concerned as to how the young woman might take the news.

She ran to hug him. 'I'm so excited for you!' she told him sincerely. 'But I'll miss you all so very much.' The tears were close but she would not let them be seen, not now, not when these good folk were so looking forward to their new adventure. 'Whatever will I do without you?' At the back of her mind she couldn't help but wonder where she and her boy might live.

'We'll miss you too – dreadfully.' Vicky looked at Jamie and her lips quivered. She hugged him, then opened the kitchen cupboard so he could sit and play with the saucepans and wooden spoons.

'Well, I'll tell you one thing, Lucy girl.' Barney sat her down. 'You won't need to worry about being out of work. I've just come from giving our answer to the boss, and I've spoken to him about you. He says you'll have work with whoever buys the farm, he'll make sure it's written into the contract of sale.'

It was a great relief to Lucy. 'Oh Barney, how can I ever thank you?' She felt quite weak at the knees. Without a job and a home, she and Jamie would be in dire straits.

'Don't thank me,' he protested. 'Thank the boss, and thank the fella who's buying the farm. It's good news all round. The Land Agent has already been out this morning to tell him he's got a buyer, a gent who's been looking for such a property as this, and because he means to grab this place afore anybody else, and prevent it being split up and sold off he's offered fifty guineas above the asking price.'

Vicky was amazed. 'Good Lord! And did Mr Maitland accept it?'

'He most certainly did.' He gave an aside wink to Vicky, who was thrilled to hear Lucy would not be put out of work. 'What's more . . .' Barney's smile grew wider as he looked at the two women in turn, '. . . Mr Maitland says Lucy can stay in the cottage,' he told them, '. . . it's because he's got such a good price, and I'm to tell you straight off, he's not selling the cottage with the farm. Because it's such a tiny place with so much that needs doing, it has little or no value so neither Mr Maitland nor the agent could see it as making any difference to the value of the overall holding. It's all been agreed.'

Unable to keep the news any longer, he blurted it out with a shout of triumph. 'It's *yours*, Lucy girl!' he laughed with the sheer joy of it.

He drew in a long breath and blowing it out through his nose he took hold of Lucy by the shoulders, his voice lower, more intimate. 'Now then, what have you to say to that, eh?'

For the moment Lucy could say nothing because not only had the news rocked her to the roots, but she was completely lost for words.

Instead she stared at Barney with big shocked eyes, her lips quivering, and her heart pounding ten to the dozen. 'I can't . . . believe it,' the words stumbled out. 'The cottage . . . is it really *mine?*'

'That's right, Lucy girl . . . it's yours. Mr Maitland

says to tell you he'll be along to see you shortly, and that you're not to worry, because everything will be done legal.'

'This calls for another celebration!' Rushing to the cupboard, Vicky took out the best glasses and a bottle of her homemade wine.

Barney raised his glass. 'To our new life – and to Lucy, our dear friend who, along with young Jamie here, will never again be without a roof over her head.'

It was the most bitter-sweet emotion for Lucy. She found it hard to believe her own good fortune, but while she was thanking the Good Lord, she paused again to think of how it would be when Barney and his family were gone.

Even in the midst of her joy, the thought of losing them forever was a sad, lonely thought.

~

'Are you all right, Barney?' It was two o'clock in the morning when Vicky woke to find herself alone in bed. Half-asleep and bleary-eyed she rolled sideways, looking towards the window, where Barney's shadowy figure was just visible in the dim light. 'What's wrong, pet, can't you sleep?'

Still breathless from the chest pains which had woken him, Barney sshed her. 'Go back to sleep, love.'

'I can't. Not until you come back into bed.'

In the past weeks, Barney had learned to hide

his pain and put on a brave face; it had become like second nature to him. Taking a deep breath, he painted on a smile and managing the few paces to the bed, he climbed in. 'Now will you go to sleep?' He wriggled down the bed, avoiding touching her, having stood at the window for some time, he had become chilled.

Instinctively, she turned and wrapped her arm around the girth of his belly. 'Brrr!' she shivered. 'You're freezing! How long have you been stood there at the window?'

'Not long,' he lied. 'Now go to sleep.'

Worry marbled her voice. 'Are you all right?'

'I'm fine.'

'Are you worried about moving to Boston? Is that what woke you?'

'No. I think it was a touch of indigestion.' Before she could protest, he added, 'I ate a bite from a cooking apple, and you know how sour they are.'

'You shouldn't eat them, then!'

'I know, but they looked so tempting.'

There was a groan. 'Barney Davidson, will you never learn?'

'Go to sleep now, Vicky. It's only three a.m.'

'And are you really not worried about moving to Boston?'

'No, why should I be?'

'No reason. I just wondered, that's all.'

'Are *you* worried, sweetheart? You can tell me if you are.'

There came a sigh. 'I would tell you if I was worried, but I'm not. To tell you the truth, I'm really excited! Oh, I know there are things and people here that I'll miss, but who wouldn't look forward to a brand new start? And like you said, it's not the end of the world. Oh Barney! It will be such an adventure, and the children are all looking forward to a new life there . . . even our Susie, thanks to you.' She gave him a squeeze. 'You're such an understanding father, Barney. That little chat you had with her did all the good in the world.'

In that quiet, opportune moment Barney might have confided in her; he might have confessed how he had been suffering such pain of late, and how sometimes he could hardly stand up straight for the cramp in his chest. But when he turned to her, Vicky had rolled over onto her back and was fast asleep.

Barney did not sleep though. Instead he waited a while, then he slipped out of bed again and slumped into the chair, where he remained head in hands and his heart pounding, until the sun peeped over the horizon, then he got quietly back into bed.

Even then he did not sleep, but planned his day. This morning, he had to call in on Adam. He had promised to lend his old pal a helping hand with the tractor he was working on. Afterwards, he would go and see Dr Lucas and tell him his troubles. Who knows? he thought hopefully. It might even turn out that he was worrying about nothing at all.

Finally he slipped into a shallow, unsettled slumber, where he dreamed of ships sailing away and his family always just out of reach, and when he woke with a start, Vicky was already out of bed and dressing. 'Wake up, Sleepyhead,' she teased him. 'It's time to start the day.'

As she went out of the room, she called over her shoulder, 'By the time you get downstairs, I'll have the ham and eggs on your plate ready and waiting.'

As always, Vicky was as good as her word.

Twenty minutes later, the whole family was tucking into one of Vicky's renowned and substantial cooked breakfasts.

Thankfully, the endless chatter pushed Barney's worries to the back of his mind; while enjoying a generous helping of Vicky's speciality, he took a discreet look around the table. There were Ronnie and Thomas, arguing as usual, this time about which one of them might beat the other in a horse-race. 'You're even frightened to jump the brook at the narrow end,' Ronnie tormented his brother, 'but not me! I'm not afraid to jump my horse over anything.'

'That's only because you've got the best horse,' his brother replied. 'You ride the mare, and she has the heart of a lion. You know how scared of water the stallion is.'

Ronnie sniggered. 'It's not the stallion that's scared, it's you!'

Thomas put down his knife and fork. 'Right, little brother! What about a race – across the wide end of the brook and up to the far end of Down Field?'

'What? Not likely! You've got to be out of your mind. Down Field is full of potholes.'

Whereupon Vicky cautioned them, and the subject was dropped.

Barney loved family mealtimes, when everyone sat down together and talked, when laughter and noise and arguments happened, and you felt as though you belonged to something very special.

He watched Vicky forking the two extra ham slices onto Ronnie's plate and smiled to himself. She was the bedrock of this family. She was his first reason for living.

His gaze wandered to Susie, and his smile became a burst of laughter. 'What in God's name is that on your head?'

'She thinks it's about to rain,' Ronnie teased.

'No!' Thomas had another idea. 'She's worried the ceiling might fall in, that's what it is.'

Indignant, Susie defended her new creation. 'It's my new design,' she explained. 'Miss Dandy said I should take home this material and make a hat, the like of which has never been seen before.'

'Is that so?' Trying his damnedest not to laugh, Barney looked at the hat; it was a sickly green, with a white feather sticking out of the top and a brim so wide that Susie's little face was almost hidden. He tried to think of something constructive to say, and came out with: 'Well, *I've* never seen anything like it before, and I don't suppose anyone else has.'

'So do you think she'll be pleased?'

'Well . . .' He huffed and puffed, and didn't know quite what to say. 'I just think she'll be amazed!'

'Flabbergasted, more like!' Ronnie commented.

'You've done well.' As always, Thomas was supportive. 'Not everyone could make a hat like that.'

Suddenly Vicky was rocking in her chair, helpless with laughter, tears running down her face. 'Oh, darling girl.' She couldn't speak for laughing. 'It's the most comical hat I've ever seen.'

Open-mouthed, everyone stared at her. 'MUM!' Thomas was shocked. Barney could hardly believe his eyes and Susie was close to tears. Ronnie, however, like his mammy could see the humour in what was the worst example of hat-making there could ever be. His face began to crumple and then he hooted and now he was laughing so hard he was bent double over the table.

'You're horrible!' Hurt, Susie stared from one to the other. 'It took me half the night to make this!' But in that moment when she got up to storm off, the hat fell over her eyes and she couldn't see where she was going.

In a moment the place was in uproar, with everyone shrieking with laughter; and now even Susie saw the funny side. 'I bet you lot couldn't make a hat like this!' she spluttered, and they all agreed wholeheartedly.

The meal ended as always, with good humour, and a short discussion as to what part each man would play in the day's labours. 'Right! I'll leave you to it then,' Barney said. As he went out, Lucy came in. 'Morning, lass.' Like the rest of the Davidson clan, he had a real soft spot for her.

'Morning, Barney!' Before Lucy had even got her coat off, Vicky had poured her a cup of tea and was already taking Jamie's coat and leggings off.

Barney gave Lucy a cheery parting wink and went merrily on his way, while behind him, Susie lost no time in telling Lucy how cruel they had all been about her beloved hat.

~

Taking the horse and cart, Barney went to Casey's Farm by way of the back lanes. He had arranged to meet Adam there, to help him repair the tractor. A small, nondescript place, the farm was situated some three miles away.

As they ambled along, Barney talked to the old shire-horse as usual. 'Don't you go taking off at a gallop!' he warned him, even though at thirty years old, the elderly horse did not have a gallop left in him. Content to be with his master, he pricked up his ears and listened to what Barney had to say, and understood not a single word.

On approaching the track that led to Casey's Farm, Barney spied his friend about to slide under the tractor. 'Adam, hang on a minute!' he bawled. When the little man appeared not to have heard him, he shouted again, this time louder. 'ADAM! WAIT A MINUTE!'

This time, Adam heard. Scrambling to his feet, he waited for Barney to bring the horse and cart to a halt. 'You're late,' he grumbled. 'I expected you half an hour since.'

Barney jumped down from the cart. 'What the devil d'you think you're doing! You know how dangerous it is to be getting underneath a tractor without anyone else about.'

'Old Casey needs this oil leak plugged before he can use the tractor,' Adam explained. 'And being as he's got mountains o' stuff to shift before the weather turns, he needs it right now.'

'In that case, first we'll get it jacked up proper, afore somebody gets hurt. If we get a move on, it shouldn't take above an hour. Besides, I've an appointment this morning and I don't want to be late.'

They completed the task within the hour and now, all that was left was for Adam to tidy away the tools and such. 'Leave it to me now, Barney. I'll finish up later, after you've gone off to your appointment,' Adam told him. 'The old fella's left the kitchen open for us to get a drink and a wash, so we'll away in, eh?' He led the way. 'I appreciate you helping me out on this one,' he said as they went along. 'I'd never have done it on my own.'

'It's no trouble.' These two were always there for each other, and it had been that way for many years. 'That's what friends are for.'

Washed and thirsty, Barney sat himself at the table while Adam mashed the tea.

'You look tired, matey.' Adam put the teapot on the table, together with a plate of sandwiches. 'Mrs Casey made these afore she went to the shops,' he explained. 'The Caseys are not a bad old couple, but if you ask me, it's time he called it a day. He doesn't walk so good these days, and his sight isn't what it was, but he still refuses to retire gracefully.' Seating himself in the chair, he passed the bowl of sugar to Barney. 'He's much like you – work is his life. I dare say he'll not stop till he drops!'

When Barney seemed to be deep in thought, his friend delivered a torrent of questions. 'What's wrong? Didn't you sleep well? Are you worrying about the move – is that it?'

Curious, he studied Barney's face and thought he had never seen him so worried. 'You've changed your mind about going and you don't know how to tell them. I'm right, aren't I? You don't want to go after all?'

Barney smiled. 'You're so wrong, Adam.' Unbeknownst to anyone, Barney had a drastic plan, and though it would shatter his life, Barney believed in his heart that it was the best option for his family. 'Think about it,' he urged. 'I have the most wonderful wife a man could ever hope for, a daughter who already has ambitions, and two fine sons with farming in their blood, but what is there here for them?'

'The same as what there's allus been.' Adam was a simple man with simple means. It didn't take much to make him happy; a good friend, a day's honest work, his own little place to come home to, and a warm smile from Lucy . . . though there wasn't a waking minute, when he didn't wish it could be more.

Unlike Barney, he had no family to rely on him, and so he did not have the same responsibilities, whereas Barney's family was his entire world. There was no doubt in anyone's mind but that he would lay down his life for them.

'It's a hard cruel world out there,' Barney replied. 'England is beautiful. It's our home and we love it, we always will. But everybody knows the bigger opportunities are out there in America.' Barney's instincts told him that his children would make it big in America.

He smiled, a painful, wistful smile that betrayed his own regret at not being able to share in his beloved family's once-in-a-lifetime adventure. 'I can see it all now,' he murmured. 'My two boys, riding across their own land ... with my Vicky watching from the house ...' He looked up, the pride alive in his face. 'Oh, Adam! I know they can do it. Given the opportunity, I just know they'll grasp it with both hands.' His excitement heightened. 'I can see it! I can feel it in my bones!'

'I know you want the best for them, Barney, and so you should ...' Adam had a gut feeling there was something going on in Barney's mind, something other than what he was telling. 'But, don't you think it's a big step to take? Uprooting yourselves to sail away to a strange land when there's always a chance they might make it good here?'

Barney slowly shook his head. 'I've worked hard all my life,' he answered sombrely. 'I've brought scrubland back to life, I've toiled every godsent hour until my hands bled and my knuckles were raw. I've sown the seeds and reaped the harvest, but nothing was mine. I did everything a man could be asked, but I never made enough money to buy even a square foot of land to call my own ... to look out across the fields and say this is mine, this is what I've given my life for.'

He paused, his mind going back over the years. 'It's allus been the man in the big house who's been able to do that.'

He gave a long heartfelt sigh. 'Nothing's changed. There's no magic formula that says my boys will do any better than me, even though they'll work the same hours and give the same blood and sweat.'

'But, Barney, don't you think they'll be content just to work the land alongside their dad?'

Even though he could see Barney's reasoning for going away to make a new life, he so much wanted him to stay. But that was selfish, and he felt ashamed.

Barney tried to explain. 'You might well be right, old friend,' he conceded. 'They *are* content to be working alongside me, but for how long, eh? There'll come a day when they'll need to strike out on their own. That's when they'll realise like me, that nothing is for nothing. All they have is the wages I pay them, and Lord knows that's poor enough. What chance have they got of owning their own farm? The way things are, they'll be old and grey and still working somebody else's land. What kind of a future is that for two strapping lads who have it in them to do better?'

In the face of Barney's explanation, Adam was convinced but saddened. 'All I can see is the way the three of you work . . . a well-balanced team, strong together, all pulling the same way, and all the while seeming to know what the other is thinking.' He nodded his head. 'Happen I don't see the true picture after all.'

Barney corrected him. 'NO! You do see the true picture, and it's a wonderful way of life. But can't you hear what I'm telling you? None of it belongs to us and it never will . . . not the land nor the cattle, not even the roof over our heads. There have been many times when I've dreamed of going to America . . . who hasn't? And now, we've been given an opportunity that may never come again.'

He went on quietly, 'I have little money . . . certainly not enough to buy my own land. So if we stayed, I'd be forever a tenant farmer, with no chance of ever owning my own farm, and that being the case there will be nothing for my sons to build on. Oh, yes, I accept that they might move on and somehow, sometime in the far distant future they just might get as far as owning something or another. But I can never be certain of that, and neither can they. As for Susie, if she's ever to fulfil her ambitions, she'll need all the help she can get because sometimes talent and skill isn't enough. She needs opportunities to show what she can do; money to put her through the right kind of college, and then the means to ease her into her own little business.'

He paused, thinking of Vicky and their children, and his heart swelled with pride. 'I want them to have every chance,' he murmured. 'I want them to see something of this beautiful world we live in. I want them to have every opportunity to make a wonderful life, and because of the generosity of one man, they've been offered the best chance they'll ever have . . . a new life, a bigger sky, new horizons and the way forward to make something of themselves.' His eyes shone with love. 'They're so excited. They want the challenge.' His voice dropped to a whisper. 'Who am I to deny them that?'

Adam's tone changed to one of admiration. 'You're right, old friend, but it's a big step for anybody to be taking, and I'll tell you this . . . I'll miss you all like the very devil, but I do envy you. You're a brave man, Barney, I'll say that. There's many of us who would love the same challenge, but some of us are forever dreamers while others, like yourself, have the courage to give it a go.' He saw the sadness in Barney's eyes. 'All the same, it's worrying you, isn't it?'

Barney shook his head. 'No, Adam.' He took a sip of his tea. 'It's not *that* that's been worrying me, well, not for the reasons you might think anyway.'

'Hmh! If's not that, what is it then?'

Barney paused, his expression serious as he caught Adam's curious glance. 'What I'm about to tell you now, Adam . . . you're not to repeat it to a living soul, d'you understand?'

Concerned, Adam replaced his biscuit onto the plate. 'I've never been one to spread folks' business,' he chided, 'especially when it's an old friend confiding in me. You should know that by now, Barney.'

Barney was mortified. 'I'm sorry, Adam. It's just that, I've not told anybody else, and I won't. When I leave here, I'm seeing the doctor. I've not told

Vicky, and I don't want her to know . . . whatever the outcome.'

Now, as Adam began to grasp the seriousness of the situation, he gulped so hard, his Adam's apple felt like a brick in his throat. 'I think you'd best explain what you mean by that,' he said.

Barney felt such relief that he had been able to confide in someone, and as it was Adam, he knew his secret would go no further. 'I'm sorry to put you in this situation,' he said, 'only I had to talk to somebody.'

Deeply worried, the other man brushed aside his apology. 'What is it, Barney old mate? What's wrong?'

Barney didn't want to frighten Adam unnecessarily, but on the other hand, should anything untoward come of his visit to the doctor, he needed someone outside the family to be in full possession of the facts. 'I reckon as how there's summat wrong wi' me,' he began quietly. 'Summat the doctors can't put right.'

Adam was visibly shocked. 'God Almighty, Barney, whatever makes you say a thing like that?'

Barney explained. 'For some months now, I've been getting these crippling pains in my chest. Sometimes I can hardly breathe, and other times I'm as sick as a dog at the slightest thing. I'm allus tired, but I can't ever get a good night's sleep. It's summat serious, Adam, I know it is.'

'And why are you so sure about that?' His pal

would have none of it. 'You're no doctor, to say it's summat serious that they can't put right. Good God, Barney, it could be any number o' things.'

A glimmer of hope fluttered through Barney. 'What could it be then?'

'Well, *I* don't know, do I?' Adam replied irritably. 'Like yourself, I'm no doctor. All I know is, you shouldn't go jumping to conclusions. It could be a simple little thing that can easily be dealt with.'

'Such as what?'

'Well, such as a bad bout of indigestion. I get it all the time – it nigh doubles me up, but it's nothing to worry about. Then there's the nature of your work; you're out all hours in all weathers, and how many times have I seen you lying on the damp ground, under a machine, or hanging on the edge of a ladder reaching for this or that, then another time you'll be stacking hay up to the ceiling in the barn. Jesus! You're allus up to summat, stretching your body to its limit and not giving a thought to the consequences.'

He wagged a finger. 'You know as well as I do, there's many a farmer gone crippled because of his work and the changing weather.'

'I know that, but it's not the same thing at all.'

'Like as not you've overstretched a chest-muscle, or you might even have fractured a rib. That's been known to happen afore now and not been discovered for many a week – by which time it's got worse.'

Barney's hopes rose. 'You're right. I didn't think of all that.'

'No, you didn't,' Adam confirmed. 'You were too busy thinking the worst instead.'

'So, do you reckon I should still see the doctor?'

'It wouldn't hurt, not now that you've made the appointment.'

Barney nodded. 'I'm glad I told you, Adam.'

'So am I.' The other man, though, was secretly worried. 'You'd best mek tracks, lad. Soonest done is soonest mended.'

A few minutes later, Barney was ready to set off. 'I'll call in and see you at home on my way back,' he told Adam. 'Let you know what Dr Lucas says.'

His old friend waved him off. 'You do that,' he advised. 'And stop your worriting!'

Long after Barney was out of sight, Adam stood at the door, mulling over what Barney had told him: pains in his chest, being sick, sleeping badly and at times hardly able to breathe. He had assured Barney it could be any number of minor things, but deep down he had to consider that it could be really serious – far more serious than he had led the other man to believe. He was frightened for his pal.

So frightened for him that he downed tools there and then and made his way home, intending to wait for Barney to let him know what Dr Lucas had to say.

~

Expecting his appointment to last some fifteen minutes or less, Barney was in Dr Lucas's surgery for a whole hour and a half.

Having been pummelled about and then quizzed for what seemed an age, Barney dressed behind the screens and came out to stand before the man's desk. 'What's the verdict then, Doctor?' he asked. He needed to know, but was dreading the answer. Not for nothing had Raymond Lucas called in his colleague from the other consulting room, and each in turn had examined Barney yet again; in quiet tones discussing his condition while he quickly dressed.

The doctor smiled. 'Sit down, Mr Davidson.' His quick smile was not a reassuring one; instead, to Barney it seemed more of a consoling smile, and sure enough with his next words he confirmed Barney's suspicions. 'I'm afraid it's not good news.'

Suppressing the fear inside him, Barney asked tremulously, 'It's my heart, isn't it?'

Dr Lucas slowly nodded. 'I'm sorry.' Quickly adding, 'But it's not all bad news. With proper medication and rest, you could go on for years yet.'

Shocked to the soul, Barney interrupted him. 'What you're saying is, if I stop work and spend

299

the rest of my life doing nothing, then I might live a few years more?'

'Well, I'm not suggesting you should do *nothing*. I'm saying you will have to take things a lot easier. No more building haystacks, or driving in the sheep on a frosty winter's morning. You have a damaged heart. It isn't functioning as it should and that's a dangerous thing, especially for an active man such as yourself, whose very livelihood depends on him using his strength to carry out his work.'

A note of impatience marbled his advice. 'From now on, you must be sensible in everything you do, and I cannot emphasise that strongly enough.'

Barney wasn't listening. By now he was seeing the future in his own mind, and what he saw was more crippling than anything he had so far endured. 'Tell me, Dr Lucas . . .' he paused, hoping against hope that he might receive the answer he needed. 'Is there anything you can do to repair the damage?'

The doctor shook his head. 'I'm afraid the damage seems to be quite considerable. The breathlessness, the pain and sickness . . . it all has to do with the heart not doing its work. As far as we can tell, there is little that can be done, except to give you the advice I've just given, and for you to follow it to the letter.' He bent his head to his desk and taking out a notepad, began scribbling furiously. 'I can carry out any number of tests and no doubt get a fuller picture. But the heart is a complex organ and often it can be more dangerous to interfere with it, than to leave it alone.'

Looking up, he added in a serious voice, 'My opinion and that of my colleague is for us to treat the symptoms, and for you to do your part ... follow my advice, and take the medicine prescribed. That way, it's certainly possible that you may enjoy a few more good years.'

Handing Barney the folded paper, he told him, 'I've made an appointment for you to be admitted into the Infirmary first thing in the morning.' His smile was sympathetic. 'I'm sorry the news was not what you might have expected, Mr Davidson, but we'll do the best we can – as indeed *you* must.'

Barney was devastated.

In a kind of half-drunken stupor he left the surgery and made his way to the horse and cart, which he had tethered outside. Without his usual greeting to the old horse, he climbed aboard, took up the reins and clicking the horse away, sat back on his slatted wooden bench and turned his thoughts to Vicky and the family.

As he left the village behind and came into the open countryside, he stopped the horse in its tracks, and climbing down off the bench, stood at the top of the valley, from where he could see the whole world.

He stood for a long time, his mind numbed and his heart sore, and when the doctor's words flooded back . . . *It's possible you may enjoy a few good years* . . . he lifted his face to the skies and with the tears streaming down his face, he accused that Great Master somewhere in the heavens: 'Every step of my life I've always trusted You, and now when my life seems to be taking a turn for the better, You snatch it away.' Anger roared through him. 'WHAT TERRIBLE THING DID I DO TO DESERVE THIS?' Sobbing, he fell to the ground.

In his mind's eye he could see Vicky, and his children. He saw the joy in their eyes and the excitement in their voices as they spoke of their imminent new life in Boston, and it was as though a knife was twisting his soul.

Sobered by the prospect of telling them, he climbed back onto the cart, but he did not take up the reins. Instead he sat hunched and desolate, without hope; without a future.

～

Adam was sitting on the doorstep smoking his pipe when he saw Barney coming up the lane. 'At last!' He had almost given him up. Knocking out his pipe on the porch column, he laid it beside his empty beer mug and ran out to meet his old friend. 'Where've you been? You've been gone an age,' he told him as Barney wearily climbed down. 'I thought you were never coming back.'

Half an hour later, the dreadful news imparted and shared, tears shed and dried, and a pint pot of beer swallowed, Barney turned to Adam and confided his chief worry.

'How on earth can I go off to farm in Boston when I'm in this state, fit for nowt? I can't see myself sitting about like an old-timer, gazing across the land, watching while the others work their fingers to the bone.'

When his voice broke, it took a moment to compose himself before he could go on. 'I couldn't do that to them, Adam, and I won't do it to myself. I think I've known these past few months that my time on earth is short, but it's so hard to think of leaving Vicky and our children. But I'll have to! Dear Lord, somehow I'll have to.'

When he now turned to look at Adam, the latter saw the sorrow in his eyes and the bitterness in the hard edge of his mouth. 'You above all people know I can't do it,' Barney confided. 'I can't *not* bring in the harvest or go out in the tractor when the earth is just waking, seeing the dew sparkle like jewels on the ground and the night creatures running before me as I plough the furrows.'

As he spoke his eyes lit up. 'The joy of my life is bringing in the sheep, collecting the apples from the branches where Vicky can't reach, tending the land from first light to darkness. It's in my nature, it's in my blood, Adam – you know that! If I can't do it, my life might just as well be over.'

As he stood up to leave, Barney placed a hand on Adam's shoulder. 'This is just between you and me, old friend,' he said quietly. 'No one else need ever know.'

Slumped forward, shocked by Barney's news, Adam was lost for words. There was no man on this earth could change Barney's mind once it was made up.

He knew Barney better than most, apart from Vicky who knew him like she knew herself. And he was aware that, whatever Barney decided to do, he would not embark on it without a great deal of thought and much agonising.

Fixing his gaze on the clumps of mud he had earlier walked onto the path, Adam nodded. 'I shall be here if you need me,' he said simply.

It was little enough, he thought. But at a time like this, God help him, what else could he do?

CHAPTER FIFTEEN

Throughout the following week, Barney carried on as usual, though sometimes when he was out in the fields alone, he would take time to rest, not because he wanted to, but because he was tired, and ill, and stubborn as he had ever been.

He had always loved the onset of winter, with the crisp clean air coming up the valley to pinch his face and make him feel alive, but on this particular day he found it all too much. His whole body ached, and for the first time in an age, he had felt the need to wear an overcoat.

'Things aren't the same, are they, old fella?' He wrapped his arms round the thick hairy neck of his four-legged pal. 'I thought I had years to go yet. I'm not old, only in my mid-forties, and I still have ambition in me. I thought I might be going on the greatest adventure of my life, taking the whole family to America and starting all over again. But I'm useless now, and growing more useless by the day.'

His voice carried a sense of irony. 'In horse years, you must be as old as the hills.' He gave a wry little laugh. 'But summat tells me you'll still be here, long after I've gone.'

Drawing away, he went to the back of the cart and took down a nosebag of hay. After he'd tied it round the horse's ears, he walked to the top of the hill, where he stood and gazed around him, imprinting that familiar, magnificent panorama in his mind, in case he might never see it again.

Lost in memories and regret, he did not hear the footsteps drawing closer. 'Hello, Barney. Vicky told me where I might find you.'

Startled, Barney swung round to find Dr Lucas there. 'I was out walking,' he told Barney. 'Being that it was on my way, I thought I'd call in at Overhill Farm and have a little chat with you, but you'd already gone.' He glanced at the cart, which was loaded down with branches, half-trees and all manner of debris, and wagging a finger at Barney, he said, 'I sincerely hope someone helped you on with that load?'

Barney didn't answer. His mind was still with the doctor's greeting, and he was horrified. 'You say you've been to the house?'

'I called in, yes.'

'You haven't told Vicky anything, have you? She doesn't know yet.'

'No, Barney. I haven't told anyone. You specifically asked me not to betray your confidence, and

I won't. I can't.' Raymond Lucas knew how badly Barney had taken the news – and who could blame him? 'It's you I'm concerned about. Twice now, over the course of the past week, I've seen you from a distance, standing up here, on the edge of this very hill.' He frowned. 'Today, I thought I might come and chat awhile.'

Barney couldn't help but chuckle. 'You thought I might throw myself over the edge, is that it?'

Dr Lucas shook his head. 'I would never think that of you, Barney. Whatever obstacle life puts in your way, I know you'll face it head on.' He smiled. 'Given the same disturbing news, some people might well throw themselves over the edge. But not you.'

Looking down, Barney nodded. 'Don't think I haven't considered it,' he said truthfully, kicking the ground. 'Because I have.'

The other man said nothing. Instead, he walked back to the cart with Barney, and listened to what he had to say.

'It's the family I fear for,' Barney confided. 'I don't know how to prepare them. I know I should tell them, but I don't want them to know. We've allus been close – too close, mebbe, because that makes it all the more painful. As for my Vicky . . .' He sighed heavily. 'She's been my reason for living ever since the day I first saw her.'

When his voice began to waver, he stopped, composed himself and when he was ready he looked up at Dr Lucas. 'I've searched my heart and I've turned every which way, to think of how I might break the news. Then I imagine what it will do to them, and I can't . . . I just can't do it!'

They walked on in silence for a moment, the doctor filled with sadness, and Barney hurting like he had never hurt before. 'I'm not sure yet how to deal with it all, but I will,' he said softly, as though talking to himself. *I'll find a way!*

Not for the first time, Raymond Lucas felt helpless. In latter years, there had been significant strides forward in medicine, but as yet, there was no way to renew a heart that was damaged beyond repair. 'I'm sorry, Barney. I hope you know that.'

Barney slowly nodded his head. 'So am I,' he said, and then he had a question. 'If I had come into the Infirmary like you wanted, could you have made me healthy again? Would I have come home, being able to do all the things I've allus done?'

The other man shook his head decisively. 'No.'

Barney smiled. 'Thank you. That's what I thought.'

Dr Lucas had heard the exciting news, about how the Davidson family were off to America. 'Have you decided what to do about Mr Maitland, and his offer of taking you all to Boston?'

'I'm working on it.' Barney climbed onto the cart, took up the reins and reminded the other man about his promise. 'Don't you worry your head about that,' he said firmly, but not disrespectfully. 'It's my business and I'll deal with it my way. Your part is to say nothing. That's our agreement as I understand it. Am I right, Dr Lucas?'

'Yes, you are, Barney. But you mustn't leave it too late before you tell them. It would not be fair – not to you, or to them.'

That said, he waved goodbye and took the path to the forest, while Barney went the long way round, through the valley and down by the river.

He wasn't ready to go home just yet.

He had a lot to think about.

~

By the time he got back to the farmhouse, Barney was his usual self. 'What's all this then?' The dining-table was piled high with all manner of things – clothes and papers and odds and ends he had never seen before; even a leather football he had bought years back to teach his young sons the game.

'I'm clearing out what we won't be taking to Boston with us.' Flicking the dust from her hair, Vicky gave a muffled sneeze. 'You would not believe the things that have turned up,' she chuckled. 'I even found that cowboy hat you wore to the first barn-dance we ever gave.'

Grabbing the hat from the table, Lucy plopped it on Barney's head. 'It suits you,' she laughed. 'You should wear it when you're bringing in the sheep.'

'Why don't I wear it to the celebrations?' he suggested cheerfully.

'Great idea!' Smiling, she turned to Lucy. 'I'm glad you decided to have the child christened the day *before* his second birthday.' Having both celebrations on the same day would have been too much.

Lucy was looking forward to it all. 'There you are, Barney,' she cried. 'Two parties in one. You'll never have a better excuse to wear that hat.'

Barney took it off and placed it on the pile. 'Look at this!' Certain articles had slid to the floor and there wasn't a single spare inch on the table. 'It looks like a rag-shop in here,' he said jokingly. He picked up a pair of trousers some two sizes too big for him now. 'I hope you're not expecting me to wear these an' all,' he said, making a face.

'I might, if you don't stop complaining,' Vicky answered with a click of the tongue.

Seeing the garments and artefacts piled high on the table was like the remnants of their lives together, and it shook him deeply. 'Why you felt the need to clear out wardrobes and such just yet, I'll never know,' he declared. 'The ship doesn't sail until the sixth of November . . . that's still well over two weeks away.' If things had been different he might have been helping but now, it was too frightening how fast the days were rushing by.

'That's not long,' Vicky argued. 'Not when I need to sort every drawer and cupboard, throw

310

some stuff away, give some to the church for the needy, and get the rest washed and ironed to come with us. It can't all be done in five minutes.'

'Vicky's right.' Lucy had been helping all morning and still they had hardly started. 'Then there's the whole house to be gone over – floors so well-scrubbed you could eat your bacon and eggs off them, cupboards washed and lined with fresh newspaper, and every window-pane polished to a brilliant shine . . .'

'And that's only the *inside*!' Vicky was beginning to panic. 'You men haven't got a clue, have you?'

'I've got a thirst though.' Barney made his way to the kettle. 'I expect you could both do with a cuppa?'

'You two sit yourselves down.' Bringing him back, Lucy sat him in the chair. 'I'll mash the tea.'

Tired and weary, Barney didn't argue. 'I wouldn't mind a piece o' that fruit-cake, if there's any left?'

There was, and when Lucy brought it in along with the tea, Barney wolfed it down. 'By!' He washed it down with a gulp of hot tea. 'I reckon my girl is the best cook in the whole world,' he said, smacking Vicky's bottom as she walked by.

'Enough o' that, Barney Davidson,' she reprimanded. But there was a twinkle in her eye, and the twitch of a smile on her lips as she turned away.

'I wouldn't mind another piece o' cake if you're going to the kitchen?' he called out hopefully.

'I am going to the kitchen,' she called back, 'but it's no cake for you.'

'Aw – why's that?'

' 'Cause your dinner will soon be on the table, that's why.'

For the next few moments while Vicky was clattering about in the kitchen, Barney and Lucy sat together as they often did, talking and planning and wondering what the future held.

'I'll really miss you, Barney,' Lucy told him shyly. 'I know I shouldn't say it, not when you're all so excited and looking forward to it, but sometimes I wish Mr Maitland had never asked you.' She was instantly mortified. 'Oh, that's a terrible thing to say! I'm sorry, Barney, really I am.' She almost hero-worshipped this man, and didn't want him to think badly of her.

Instead, he said kindly, 'I wish you were coming too, you and young Jamie. You're part of the family now. As you know, I even asked Mr Maitland if there might be a place for you, but he's already altered the contract of sale on your account.'

Lucy understood. 'He's done a generous thing in leaving me secure with a job and a home. You're not to concern yourself about me,' she said. 'I'll be fine. I've got Bridget, and I've got little Jamie, and to tell you the truth, I've never been happier – though it will take some getting used to, not having you Davidsons just up the road.'

Reaching forward, she slid her hands over his.

'I'm really glad for you, Barney ... all of you. It's wonderful what's happening!' She allowed herself a little daydream. 'I don't know anybody who's gone to start a new life in America.' Feeling the warmth of his hands through hers, she drew away.

It was strange, the way she sometimes felt a thrill when he looked at her; and unforgivable, how she had come to think of Barney as more than a friend.

Just then, Barney felt the pain beginning in his chest. When he tried to take a deep breath it sounded like a strangled cough, and now the pain was spreading, like two mighty hands squeezing the life from him. Bending forward, he got out of the chair, his face drained and his mouth half-open as though he was having difficulty breathing.

'My God, what's wrong?' Lucy was quickly on her feet and helping him. She would have shouted for Vicky, but Barney gave her a warning glance.

As quickly as he could before Vicky came back into the room, he brushed past Lucy and stumbled outside. Frightened by what she had witnessed, Lucy ran after him; thankfully, Vicky neither heard nor saw them as they went out through the front door.

Lucy found Barney in the wood-shed; leaning over the pile of stripped saplings, he was still gasping for breath, but seemed to be recovering by the minute. 'I'm sorry, lass.' He afforded her a smile as she came rushing in. 'It were a raisin or summat out o' the fruit-cake. Went down the wrong way, I reckon.'

'Don't lie to me, Barney,' she warned him. 'I've seen you like this before. You're ill, aren't you? Tell me, Barney . . . what's wrong? What's happening to you?' Fear struck at her heart. She could just about cope with the idea of him going to America, but if anything bad should happen to him . . . no! The prospect was unthinkable.

'It's summat and nowt,' he wheezed, trying to sound casual. 'It's just an upset. It comes and goes.' Another spasm gripped him and he gasped.

'Have you seen the doctor?'

'I have, yes. And if you don't believe me, ask Adam Chives.' A thought occurred to him; he must remember to warn his pal not to let Lucy know the truth. 'You mustn't mention any of this to Vicky,' he wheezed. 'She's got enough on her plate at the minute, without worrying about me.'

Lucy came closer. 'You're not lying to me, are you?'

Barney appeared shocked. 'Good God, woman! Why would I do that, eh?' He stretched his arms out either side, inviting her to, 'Look at me, Lucy. I'm fit and strong, and like I said, it were summat and nowt.' Taking her by the arm he turned her round and walked her back to the house. 'Any minute now there'll be a houseful. Happen you'd best give Vicky a helping hand with the dinner, eh?'

Over dinner, Lucy watched Barney closely; he laughed and chatted and played with young Jamie and she began to wonder whether she'd imagined it all. In the end she gave up the worrying and joined in the excited chatter about the forthcoming adventure.

'I mean to be a millionaire before I'm thirty,' Thomas declared.

'Not before me,' Susie butted in. 'Miss Dandy showed me a map. She thinks I could have at least ten shops in Boston, before I start on New York.'

'Lucy, will you dance with me at the party?' Ronnie asked. 'I've been let down and now I've nobody to partner me.'

'Well, thank you, I'd be honoured, sir.' Lucy laughed. She was thrilled. It was a long time since anyone had whisked her round the dance-floor. She thought of Edward Trent with a familiar flash of anger. All along she had loved him, and all along he had told her how much he loved her back. Like a fool she had believed him, and he let her down badly.

Now, though, because of what he had done when she lay injured, she could walk by him in the street and not even turn a hair. Gently, unconsciously, she fingered the scar by her hairline where she had smashed her head against a rock.

'That reminds me!' Barney had completely forgotten. 'First thing tomorrow, I need the pair of you lads to help me set out that wooden floor in the barn. It hasn't been used since me and your mam had our twentieth wedding anniversary. With all the invites that have gone out, I've an idea we might need to make a couple or more extra squares.'

The excitement mounted. 'Christenings, birthdays and sailing off to a new land . . . whatever next!' Vicky raised her wine-glass for the umpteenth time. 'To the future!' And everyone drank heartily.

Everyone except Barney, who touched the wine against his lips and pretended to drink; Lucy, who saw him do it, wondered if he was hiding something after all.

In that worrying moment he glanced up and smiled at her; and the smile was so beautiful and easy, it took her breath away. She smiled back and raised her glass. 'All right, Barney?' She mouthed the words. He nodded, raised his glass and took a sip. Soon he was laughing, and all seemed well.

~

The christening went even better than planned.

The sun came out to brighten the day and the service was simple, yet awe-inspiring. Even when the sacred water was poured over his forehead, Jamie did not flinch. He seemed to enjoy the whole thing.

Barney picked him up and held him; Bridget

and Adam swore to be godparents, and the child was blessed.

'Now, how d'you feel about it?' Barney asked afterwards, and Lucy told him she felt it had been the right thing to do.

Vicky said he was now a child of God, and they drank to his future.

Then, in all the excitement, Jamie wet his pants. Lucy changed him and he promptly fell asleep, exhausted from being the centre of attention, while family and friends held a simple little lunch. 'We've still got the birthday party tomorrow to look forward to,' Ronnie said, and Susie ran upstairs to check that nothing had happened to the pretty dress Vicky had bought her for the occasion.

Later that afternoon, Adam was tidying up his porch when he caught sight of someone going across the headland. Convinced it was Barney, he put on his coat and climbed the hill towards him.

When he got to the spot where he thought he had seen Barney, there was nothing there, not a bird or a rabbit, or anything, save for the winter-chill that swept across the land when evening came.

'That's funny!' Adam was sure he'd seen some-one up there. Cupping his mouth, he called against the wind. 'BARNEY! Where the devil are you!' but there was no answer.

Puzzled, he made his way back to Casey's Farm.

'I could have sworn . . .' He shook his head. 'Adam Chives, you must be losing your marbles.' But then, he chided himself, was it surprising he'd begun to imagine things, when his best and only real friend in the world had told him he would probably not live to see another Christmas?

Further down the hill, the figure remained hidden until Adam had gone on his way, then furtively it emerged, to continue along the path in the direction of Overhill Farm.

~

The two Davidson boys were in the barn and had been for the past hour. 'No, no!' Barney rushed forward, just in time to stop Ronnie from laying the section too close to the corner. 'You need to leave room for the dancing,' he said. 'If you take it too far into the corner, there'll be no space for folks to swing about.'

Ronnie laughed at that. 'Oh, so you do intend we'll all be swinging about, do you?'

'I hope so!' Thomas brought forward another two sections. 'I'm bringing the prettiest girl ever, and I'd be real disappointed if we weren't able to dance!' He winked at Ronnie who told him he was fortunate, because so far, he himself didn't have a partner.

'You've got Lucy,' Barney reminded him. 'And if you think she can't dance then you'd best think again, because from what me and your mammy have seen, she can cut a rug along wi' the best of 'em!'

In fact, he had often caught Lucy when she was playing the gramophone and dancing on her own across the parlour. 'What's more,' he added, 'she's a fine-looking young woman. You should be proud she's agreed to dance the evening away with you, my lad.'

'How many more sections do you think I need to make?' Thomas had been making wooden-slatted squares all morning, and now it seemed his father was right and there wouldn't be enough of a dance-floor to cope with all the folks that were invited.

Barney walked the area with him. 'We'll need it right up to there,' he said, pointing to the barn wall. 'That's where the food will be. Then it needs taking to within three feet of the far end. That's where the benches will be set out, and folks can sit if they're not dancing.' He scratched his chin and mentally calculated. 'I reckon if you could make another two, that should do it.'

As Thomas went back outside, Barney informed Ronnie, 'That's your job when once you've finished laying the floor. We'll need at least four long benches for folks to sit on.'

'I like the way you say "we",' Ronnie quipped. 'I haven't seen you lift a single thing yet, Dad!'

'Cheeky young divil!' Barney wagged a friendly finger. 'Some of us have more to do than prepare for a barn-dance. There's plenty of other work wants seeing to.'

Just lately, Barney had found it increasingly necessary to delegate the work he was physically incapable of doing. Thankfully, so far he had managed to hoodwink everybody. 'Stop your moaning and get on with it, you young scoundrel. And be quick about it. Afore we know where we are, tomorrow will be here and so will all the folks.'

By the time evening came the barn was ready, with colourful trimmings hanging from the rafters, a long table set up to hold the food and a whole wall of benches to accommodate weary bottoms. Much to Barney's delight, the makeshift dance-floor was not only a job to be proud of, but large enough for the dancing of many partygoers. 'You've done a grand job,' he told his sons. 'I couldn't have done better myself.'

Ronnie reminded him that the tables for the guests to eat at were not yet put up. 'There'll be time enough to root them out tomorrow,' his father said. 'If I remember rightly, the fold-up tables are buried under all kinds of rubbish at the back end of the wood-shed.'

It was gone nine by the time Barney and his sons returned to the house. 'That's us done for the night,' he told Vicky who, together with Lucy, was still taking trays of pork pies out of the oven. 'It's over to you now, girls.' He was concerned at the late hour. 'It might be best if Lucy and the child stayed the night,' he suggested to Vicky. 'She looks fair worn out – you both do. Leave it all now, and get up early in the morning. The party doesn't start till evening. There'll be plenty of time to finish off whatever needs doing.'

'I've already asked Lucy to stay.' With the back of her flour-speckled hand, Vicky wiped away a wisp of hair. 'Bless him, little Jamie's fell asleep hours ago . . . Lucy's just about to go up.'

Bone-tired and ready for her bed, Lucy washed her hands at the pot sink, said her good nights and climbed the stairs to be with her child.

After checking little Jamie she stood for a while at the window, looking at the night sky and thinking how strange life could be. One minute she was footloose and fancy free; then along came Edward Trent, who promised her the world, made her with child then cleared off; then back he strolled into her life, fooled her into thinking he'd mended his ways and was ready to make her his wife and give his son a name, when he ran away again – in the most cowardly fashion yet.

Somewhere along the way, her life had gone very wrong, and now here she was, without a husband and Jamie without a daddy, and in a couple of weeks' time, her dear friends would sail away and she would be left here alone.

She worried about Barney. No matter how hard he tried to reassure her that things were fine with him, Lucy could not rid herself of a niggling doubt. Was he ill? Or was it, as he said, 'summat and nowt'?

Too weary and weighed down with regrets to make sense of it all, she undressed and, climbing into bed, drew the child to her. It was only a matter of minutes before she, too, fell asleep.

CHAPTER SIXTEEN

WHEN, AFTER A fitful few hours Lucy woke, it was to hear the stairs creak as someone crept down them. Darting to the door, she inched it open and saw Vicky on her way down to the kitchen. She turned to see Lucy and hissed, 'Go back to bed! It's only half past five. I'll call you in an hour.' With that she continued on tiptoe down the stairs.

Lucy went into the bathroom, had a wash at the basin and quickly got herself dressed. A look to make sure that Jamie was still deep asleep, and then she was down the stairs and after Vicky.

'I thought I told you to go back to bed?' Vicky already had the mixing bowl out and the flour jar in her hand. 'You could have had another hour's sleep.'

Grabbing a pinafore, Lucy wrapped it round her. 'While you're doing the scones, I'll make the apple-pies,' she said, and before Vicky could answer, she was inside the pantry, collecting together all the ingredients.

Over an hour later the men came downstairs, followed by a very sleepy Susie; the pleasant aroma of baking filled the air and Barney commented on the array of goodies covering the dresser. 'By! There's a table fit for a king,' he said, licking his lips at the pies, cakes, scones and joints of meat ready for the slicing.

Vicky scrutinised him. 'Are you all right, love?'

''Course I'm all right.' Barney's heart turned somersaults. 'Why wouldn't I be?' He had suffered another bad night, pacing the floor half the time or propped up against the pillow, massaging the ache in his chest.

'No reason.' Vicky shrugged her shoulders. 'You seemed restless, that's all.'

'How d'you mean?'

'Well, you shifted about a lot, turning this way and that.'

'So, did I disturb you?' He was afraid she might have seen him pacing the floor.

Vicky chuckled. 'You know me,' she answered. 'Once I'm out, it would take an earthquake to wake me. No, you didn't disturb me,' she assured him. 'It's just that when I got out of bed to visit the bathroom, you seemed a bit unsettled.'

'I expect I was dreaming of all the things that could go wrong with this party.' He looked round. 'Where's the birthday boy?'

'Still fast asleep.' Lucy poked her head out from the pantry. 'So don't you go waking him.'

'And don't you go worrying about things going wrong with the party!' Vicky advised. 'Because everything is in hand. It's all been checked and double-checked; Jamie's presents are all wrapped and ready, the birthday cake is setting and will be perfect for cutting tonight, the trimmings are up and the barn is all ready . . . or so you say!'

'It is!' Ronnie grumbled, falling into the room. 'Apart from a few finishing touches which'll only take a few minutes.' Hunched in his chair, unshaven, unwashed and with his hair standing on end, he looked like he'd been fished out of the river.

'Right!' Clapping her hands together to release a flurry of flour, Vicky went to the tap and filled the kettle which she then put on the stove. 'Lucy! A dozen rashers of bacon and a bowl of eggs, if you please. We've a hungry mob waiting to be fed.'

'I'll have three eggs if they're going.' That was Thomas, bleary-eyed and yawning.

'God Almighty! Look at the state of the pair of you!' Vicky laughed. 'I hope you can both manage to recover for tonight.' She did a little jig on the spot. ' 'Cause your mammy's expecting you to give her a dance or two!'

Lucy saw how Barney's strained face lit in a smile at his wife's antics. 'There you go, Vicky.' Placing the eggs and bacon on the side, she peeped again at Barney, and suddenly in that one precious moment, there was not another soul in the room but herself, and him.

~

At 6.30 p.m. the first partygoer arrived. 'I'm a bit early,' Adam apologised. 'Only I thought there might be summat I could do to help.' In truth he had wanted a quiet talk with Barney.

'You'd best come wi' me.'

Barney guessed the reason for his early arrival. 'We'll check the barn and see if I've forgotten anything.' In his grey corduroy trousers, best blue shirt, and with his unruly hair tamed to a shine, Barney looked good.

'The ladies are upstairs titivating theirselves and the boys are in the kitchen picking at the food.' He chuckled. 'If Vicky catches them, they'll wish they'd never been born.'

As they strolled to the barn, Adam asked, 'How are you feeling, matey?'

'If you mean am I looking forward to the party,' Barney replied, 'the answer's yes. If you mean have I accepted what's gone on with me . . .' He shrugged his shoulders. 'What choice have I got, old friend?'

Saddened to his heart, Adam nodded. 'And what will you do about America?' He was reluctant to interfere but knew the dilemma Barney faced. 'There'll come a point when you have to tell the family.'

'I'm dealing with it.'

Adam sighed. 'Remember, you're not on your own, Barney,' he said softly. 'I'm here for you. Any time you want me, I'll be here.' When the tears filled his eyes he blinked them away.

'I know.' Throwing an arm round the little man's shoulders, Barney walked him to the barn, where he threw open the door. 'Well, what d'you think?'

Adam was mesmerised. The barn was festooned with colour from one end to the other: paper chains and streamers hung across the roof and down the walls, and in between, strategically hung so as to be safe, were a dozen long lanterns, all lit and twinkling. The benches were set out; the food table was dressed in a long pink cloth, and the dance-floor stretched away as far as the eye could see.

'It's like Wonderland!' Adam marvelled and Barney laughed. They went inside and walked round the floor. Then Susie came running in. 'Mam says you're to come and help carry the food,' she said, and ran out again.

For the next half-hour it was mayhem, with everyone trotting backwards and forwards with plates and dishes of food, cutlery and jugs, dodging each other and making a second and third trip, and when the long table was filled to bursting, the guests started arriving: the butcher and his wife; Doris Dandy from Everton, various villagers and others who had known the Davidsons for many years.

Jamie was getting very over-excited; dressed in his best clothes and overwhelmed by all the noises and strange faces. Lucy let him enjoy himself for a half-hour or so, then she popped back to the farmhouse with him and put him to bed, waiting until he had fallen asleep before returning to the festivities.

Leonard Maitland arrived alone, his attention instantly drawn to Vicky, who looked very fetching in her new cream-coloured skirt and pink lace blouse, with her hair loosely looped up on top of her head, and long wispy strands curling round her face. She was a picture of loveliness.

There were two neighbouring farmers and their entire families, and finally, arriving in a flurry of excitement with one of her new girls trailing in her wake, Bridget came waltzing through the doors. 'Jaysus, Mary and Joseph, will ye look at this! It's like heaven come to earth!' she screeched with excitement.

A moment later, taking the young woman aside, she reminded her, 'You're not here to enjoy yourself.' She kept her voice low. 'Sure, haven't I suffered the bad atmosphere in the house these past few days, the pair of youse, fighting and arguing like two alley cats! I've only brought you here tonight so I can keep an eye on you, while the other one calms down.'

She wagged a warning finger. 'Watch your tongue and keep yourself to yourself, Brenda. I don't want ye messing with the men tonight.' She edged closer until they were eyeball to eyeball. 'I swear, if I so much as see you look at a fella, I'll thrash the arse off ye, so I will!'

Wisely, the young woman backed off. 'What am I supposed to say if anybody comes talking to me?'

'Oh, you'll think o' something, I'm sure.' Bridget gave her a gentle shove. 'Now be off and fetch me a glass o' that wine they're handing out.'

With everybody safe inside and a glass of best homemade wine in their hand, Barney stood on the chair and welcomed them all. 'This is really a triple celebration,' he said, winking at his wife. 'Not only is it to mark little Jamie's birthday and christening although the little chap in question has gone to his bed, but as most of you will already know, the Davidson family are away to start a new life in America.'

Pausing for breath, he thought about the imminent journey, and his secret heart was heavy. 'It's good to see you all here,' he finished. 'And now let's have a toast – to Jamie . . . and America!' There was an almighty cheer. 'To Jamie and America!'

'God bless you and your family, Barney, and all the luck in the world. It's no more than you deserve.' The glasses were raised again, and when they were empty, Vicky and Lucy and Susie were on hand to fill them up again.

While the toasts were given, Dr Lucas stood at the back of the barn and raised his glass along with everyone else. But, with the exception of Barney and Adam, he was the only one who knew that Barney might never be going to America. And if that was the case, then his family would not be going either.

It wasn't long before the music started, in the form of old Victor and his accordion and beside him, the blacksmith, who could not only shoe a horse in record time but could also play a mean flute. Between the two of them, they played a merry tune and soonever the music struck up, the party-goers flocked to the dance-floor and let themselves go.

'Would you look there!' Barney nudged Lucy, gesturing across the dance-floor to where the butcher was swinging his wife round on the edge of his podgy arm. 'I reckon he must think she's a side o' beef,' Barney joked, 'the way he's chucking her about!'

Lucy's attention was caught elsewhere. 'It didn't take Leonard long to get Vicky on the dance-floor,' she remarked, and when Barney looked across he was taken by the manner in which his boss held Vicky, close and tight, as though he did not want to let her go.

The smallest surge of jealousy rippled through him. 'Come on, lass, let's show 'em how to do it!' Grabbing her by the arm he ran her onto the dance-floor, and when the music suddenly changed to a waltz, he slid his arm round her waist and bent her to him. 'You look lovely,' he whispered in her ear. 'I meant to tell you that soonever I saw you, all dressed up like a princess, with your pretty eyes shining.'

Lucy laughed. 'Why, thank you, sir, and you don't look bad yourself either.'

Secretly, she was thrilled to be in his arms, and as he moved her slowly round the dance-floor, she closed her eyes and imagined he was her real partner; having brought her to the dance, later, when it was over, he would take her home again. On the doorstep he would kiss her good night, and she would go to bed and dream of him.

She laughed as Barney swung her round again. She knew it would end, but it didn't matter. Tomorrow was reality. But tonight was a memory she would keep forever.

While dancing with Lucy, Barney kept an eye on Vicky. Looking up at Leonard, she was talking, seemingly unaware that he might be holding her too close, or that he wasn't listening to a word she was saying. Instead he was looking into her eyes, discreetly content to be holding the woman he loved.

Barney saw all this and now, as Vicky turned to

smile at him, he smiled back and winked; pleased when his wife blew him a conspiratorial kiss.

Barney laughed with Lucy, and swung her round like a young man with his sweetheart, yet all the while he was thinking of the future, and his lovely Vicky. He knew how devastating the news of his illness would be to the family, and to her, and he would have done anything on God's earth not to have to tell her. If only there was a way, he thought. If only he could somehow save his family from the pain and anguish they were bound to suffer.

In the darkness of his mind, an idea was growing; an idea which, in the fullness of time, would come to fruition and shape their destiny.

~

During the evening, Lucy would return to the farmhouse every so often; an old dear from the village was there, keeping an eye on little Jamie. 'He's the same as he was when you came in half an hour since.' A widow these many years, old Meg now filled her life with looking after other people's children. 'He's sleeping,' she told Lucy with a toothless grin. 'You go and enjoy the party, dear, and leave me to my knitting. Your little lad is safe enough with me.'

After going upstairs to check Jamie, Lucy gave the old woman a grateful kiss and returned to the party.

Outside in the shadows, Edward Trent emerged

from his hiding-place and crept stealthily towards the barn. Placing himself where he would not be seen, he peered in through the window.

He saw Barney's son, Ronnie, hand-in-hand with Lucy as he led her onto the floor. The two of them danced wildly to the rhythmic sound of the accordion, Ronnie playing the fool and Lucy laughing at his antics while he flirted outrageously with her.

When the music stopped and Lucy was making her way back to the table with Ronnie, his brother Tom came on the scene and grabbing Lucy, he led her back onto the dance-floor. The music changed to a slower tempo, and soon she was moving effortlessly round in his arms, chatting and smiling, and seeming at peace with herself.

Edward saw all this and the rage inside him knew no bounds. Thrusting his fists against the window it seemed for one moment that he might smash it from its frame. Then the music stopped and everyone was clapping, and when in that moment a woman turned towards him, he ducked down and disappeared into the shadows again.

'What d'you think you're doing?' Ronnie demanded light-heartedly of his brother. 'Stealing my woman from under my very nose?'

'I rescued her,' Thomas answered, stuffing a piece of pork pie into his mouth. 'I could see she was fed up dancing with a four-footed idiot, so I thought I'd show her what a real partner could do.'

Lucy giggled. 'Stop it, you two,' she said. 'I'm having a wonderful evening. You're both good dancers and you know it!'

'Ah, you're just saying that.' Ronnie searched the table for another chunk of fruit-cake. 'I bet you're really in agony from the number of times he's trodden on your toes.'

At half past midnight the evening came to an end.

As they left, everyone said what a wonderful time they'd had, and how good the food was, and how they would be so sorry to see the Davidson family leaving.

Standing side-by-side at the door as they saw everyone out, Barney and Vicky thanked them all in turn.

'I'll see youse out and about before you sail away, so I will!' Having downed more booze than she was capable of holding, Bridget was four sheets to the wind. 'Oops!' Laughing raucously, she hobbled out to the waiting car, clutching hold of her companion, her jacket stained with wine and her hitherto beautifully coiffured hair looking as if it had been through a wind-tunnel.

Behind her, Barney and Vicky walked arm-in-arm back to the house with Lucy and Susie, who had danced with her friends until her feet ached.

'Leave all that till the morrow,' Barney told his sons, who had a mind to start clearing away the furniture. As it was, he left them sitting on the barn floor, finishing off their drink and deep in conversation. 'D'you think they're worried about going to America?' Barney asked Vicky.

'Not a bit of it!' she declared. 'They're very excited, like the rest of us. In fact, Thomas said he would be brokenhearted if Leonard Maitland suddenly changed his mind and said we couldn't go after all.'

Her words did not help Barney. Instead he felt as though his own heart might break, because very soon he would have no choice but to confess the truth of his illness. And the more he thought of it, the more he dreaded the day.

Inside the house, they found old Meg fast asleep in her chair, with the knitting on her lap and snoring like a good 'un. Barney chuckled. 'We'll have to wake her,' he said. 'The old dear needs her bed.'

Vicky gently shook her, and when she woke it was with a start that frightened them all and sent her knitting clattering to the floor. 'What's up? What d'you want?' With big eyes she stared at them. 'Oh, it's you.' Her mouth opened in a tooth-less grin. 'I thought for a minute it was me old man come back to haunt me.'

'Come on, my old darling, it's time you were tucked up in bed.' Barney helped her out of the chair, Vicky went to fetch her hat and coat and Lucy paid her for the night.

Ronnie came rushing in. 'Your son's here,' he told her, and her old face lit from ear to ear. 'He's a good lad,' she said. 'He does look after his old mammy.'

No sooner had she been helped into the car than she was fast asleep. 'Salt of the earth,' her son told Barney with a proud smile. 'Never stops . . . allus on the go. She's in her seventies now, but I reckon I'll be worn out long afore she is.'

After Meg had gone, Jamie woke up and started crying. Lucy ran upstairs and came down with him in her arms. 'Oh dear, he's wet the bed. I am sorry. I've put the sheets in the pail to soak and I'll rinse them through tomorrow. The mattress is still dry – thanks to your old rubber sheet. Look – I think we'd best go home.'

'If you want to stay I'm sure we'll find something suitable to wrap his little bottom in,' Vicky said. 'And there's plenty o' clean sheets – you know where they are.'

Lucy thanked her but thought it might be best if she took Jamie home and saw to him there. 'It's been a very long couple of days and he'll rest easier tucked up in his own cot.'

'We'll see you tomorrow then,' Vicky told her, while Barney went to fetch his big coat.

Ten minutes later, wrapped against the cold night air, she and Barney set off with the child, who by now had nodded off again. 'I don't know how to thank you,' Lucy told Barney.

'Thank me? What for?' He hoisted Jamie higher in his arms.

'For giving Jamie the party.'

'It was a pleasure,' Barney answered. 'And don't forget, it was also to mark our going to America.'

Something in his tone caused Lucy to ask, 'And is that what you really want, Barney, to go to America?'

The man chose his words carefully, not least because Lucy had already voiced her concern about his health. 'O' course I want to go! Why wouldn't I?'

Lucy gave him a sideways glance; in the moonlight he looked incredibly pale, and there was a quietness about him that wasn't natural. Twice during the evening she had seen a kind of sorrow in his face that worried her.

'What's wrong with you, Barney?' she asked quietly. 'And don't fob me off with untruths. I've come to know you fairly well, and I've a feeling there's something up. What is it? You can trust me – you know that, don't you?'

Barney didn't answer, nor did he look at her. Instead he kicked irritably at the roadway. 'It's high time somebody did summat about these damned ruts in the lane,' he grumbled. 'Last week, old Ted Foggarty's horse caught its fetlock in one and had to be put down!'

Lucy persisted. 'Talk to me, Barney.'

'I *am* talking.' He gave her a cursory glance.

'I haven't said anything to Vicky and I won't, but I know there's something wrong,' Lucy repeated. 'Bridget told me she saw you going into the doctor's surgery some time back.'

Turning to look at her, he said, 'I won't hear any more of this nonsense, Lucy. Yes, I won't deny I went to see the doctor, but only because I was feeling run down. I've been under the weather recently and I thought it might be a good idea to go and get some tonic.'

'And did he prescribe some?' Lucy was slightly relieved but still left with the feeling that he was not telling all.

'He did, and I've been taking it religiously.'

'And is it working?'

Barney was feeling trapped. 'Well, you've not seen me being other than fine, have you?'

Lucy shook her head. 'No.' Enough was enough. Barney was getting grouchy. 'But I'm not always looking in your direction, am I?'

Barney laughed it off. 'I should hope not!'

When they reached Lucy's cottage, he helped her inside with her bag and the child. A few minutes later, he and Lucy emerged from the front door. 'Good night, Lucy girl,' Barney said, and yawned long and hard. As always, he kissed her on the cheek. 'See you the morrow.'

'Good night, Barney.' She waved him off down

the lane, and afterwards went back inside, her face still burning from the touch of his lips. It was a sad thing, she thought, to love a man who belonged to your best friend. But love him she did, and try as she might, she could not change that.

Neither Barney nor Lucy had seen Edward Trent hiding in the shadows, watching and waiting. When Lucy was kissed good night, he was shaken by the look of love on her face as she waved Barney off. And his heart was black with jealousy.

Having had a run of bad luck of late, he had heard through the grapevine how Lucy had been given a cottage to live in and regular work. With no sailings available and with nowhere to live, Trent had thought to foist himself onto Lucy by persuading her that he loved her and the child. Once he'd got his feet under the table, he'd plan his next move, while Lucy worked to bring in the wages and he worked to spend them.

The thing that shocked him now was that, having come back with purely selfish motives, he had seen Lucy in other men's arms and realised he still had deep feelings for her. She belonged to him, by God. He'd taken her virginity, and by rights she was his, and the mother of his son – not that he could even remember the brat's name.

Inside the cottage, Lucy quickly washed the child with a drop of warm water, talking to him as she did so. 'This is our home, Jamie. It might be small and cramped, but now that Barney's mended

339

the roof and fitted new doors, and me and Vicky have polished the entire place till it shines, it might not be the poshest place in the world, but it's cosy enough for me and you.' In fact she loved its every nook and cranny.

'It was a good party,' she said, slipping on his pyjamas. 'Barney and Vicky gave it just for you.' She recalled what Barney had said. 'And it was to say goodbye to their friends as well, because soon they will be off to a new life across the water.'

Pushing the heartache to the back of her mind, she told the child, 'You're christened now, sweetheart.' She kissed his sleepy face. 'It's wonderful, isn't it? You have your name written down in the book for everyone to see.'

When she tickled him he chuckled and squealed, and she took him in her arms, hugging him as if she would never let him go. 'You're Mammy's big boy,' she said. 'We'll soon be losing the best friends we've ever had, so we'll need to look after each other, you and me, eh?'

'Not when I'm around to take care of you.'

'EDWARD!' Even before she turned, Lucy knew the voice, she knew the man, and could hardly believe he was standing right here in her house.

'You should always lock your door at night.' His slow, dangerous smile enveloped her. 'You never know *who's* lurking about.'

'What do you want?' Instinctively, she held the

child closer. When he took a step nearer, Lucy stepped back.

'I want *you*, Lucy.'

She had been afraid, but now she was over the first shock, she was angry. 'You didn't want me when you ran off, leaving me unconscious, like the coward you are!'

Cunning as a fox, he momentarily bowed his head as though with shame. 'That's why I'm back,' he lied, his eyes sad with regret. 'I did behave like a coward, and I want to make it up to you.'

'I don't believe you!' Standing tall and defiant, Lucy looked him in the eye. 'I've made a life for myself, Edward, and I'm happier than I've been in years. There is no place here for you now.'

'Please, Lucy, don't say that,' he whined. 'It took a lot of courage for me to come here after what I did.' He glanced around the room, thinking it warm and cosy; a far cry from the dives where he'd been holed up of late. 'We could have a good life together,' he went on. 'You've already got work up at the farmhouse, and I'll find a job, I promise. We've got to give it a go.'

When he saw her expression he grabbed her roughly by the arm. 'Aw, look, Lucy. We were always good together, you know that!'

'You used me!' Shaking him off, she told him in a quiet, trembling voice, 'You lied to me all along, and when I needed you more than ever, you ran off.' She stared at him, wondering what she had ever seen in him. 'We don't need you, Edward. We don't want you here. Please go. Leave us alone.'

He was desperate now. 'I love you, Lucy, it's why I keep coming back. I've always loved you. I didn't realise it until now.' Darting forward, he grabbed her by the arm. 'I had you, and I threw you away,' he said angrily. 'But I've got you back now and I don't intend to let you go.' Cupping her face in the palms of his hands, he whispered earnestly, 'I know I did wrong, but I do love you, Lucy. You've got to believe me.' And he did love her, as much as a man like him could ever love anyone.

'Get off me!' Lucy's instincts told her that at long last he might be telling the truth, but it was too late. Edward Trent no longer meant anything to her. Thankfully she was over him now, and could see him for the selfish, vicious man he had always been. 'I don't want you here, now get out!' She put Jamie down and tried to distract him with a toy while she hissed, 'Go on! Get out of my house!'

Realising she meant every word, Edward shook his head and smiled. 'I'm not going anywhere,' he said softly. 'Not without you.'

Afraid now, Lucy had to think hard. She had to be rid of him, but how? Suddenly an idea came to her. 'For a long time I hoped and prayed you might come back,' she lied, 'but you didn't. So I had to make a life for me and little Jamie, and now I'm going away to America. We're leaving soon, Edward – it's all arranged.' She added as an afterthought to appease him, 'I'll write to you. Give me an address, and I promise I'll write as soon as we get there.'

Visibly shocked, he took a step back. *'America!'* Looking into her eyes he gave her a shaky smile. 'I don't believe you.'

'It's true.' She was desperate to make him believe. 'Why would I lie? If you were hanging about outside, you must have seen Barney Davidson bring me home. There's been a big party up at Overhill Farm to say goodbye to all the friends and neighbours. Mr Maitland has sold up here, and we're all going with him to help run his farm in Boston, Massachusetts. If you don't believe me, ask anyone. It's common knowledge round here!'

'You little bitch!' Without warning he tore the child from her, and over the sound of his terrified cries, he said calmly: 'You're not going anywhere, with Mr Maitland or anyone else. You're coming with me. We're getting right away from here. I'll find us lodgings in London. Somehow we'll manage. We'll be all right together, you and me ... and him.' Though he had acknowledged his love for Lucy, he had little feeling for the child; so far he had not spoken to Jamie, or even looked at him.

'No, Edward! There was a time when I would have walked to the ends of the earth for you, but not any more. You see, I don't love you.' The calmness in her voice belied the turmoil inside. 'Now give me my son.' Reaching to collect little Jamie, who by now was screaming hysterically, she did not expect what happened next. Raising his hand, Trent brought it down hard against her temple and sent her reeling across the room.

'I must be out of my mind to want you back,' he snapped. 'Dancing and laughing, and flirting with every man in sight. You're nothing but a trollop!'

Hurt and dazed, she dragged herself up by the chair; somewhere in the chaos of her mind she heard Jamie crying. 'Give me back my son!' she said hoarsely.

'Want the brat back, do you?' He gave a low, grating laugh that sent shivers through her. 'You can have him . . . but you'll have to take me as well.'

Lucy was frantic. 'Please, Edward, it wouldn't work between us. All I want is to be left in peace.'

Clambering up against the chair, she went sprawling again when he thrust his booted foot into her side. 'You don't seem to understand what I'm saying,' he growled. 'You either come with me now, or I'm taking him with me, and you'll never see him again. So, what's it to be?'

Terrified that he might carry out his threat, Lucy was tempted to give in and let him stay – anything to have little Jamie safely back in her arms. But what then? He might rape her – get her with child again! Her flesh shuddered at the thought of his touch. He was repulsive to her. Anyway, he would soon discover that it was a trick on her part, and then his rage would know no bounds. What would happen to her and Jamie then?

'*Well?*' He stood over her, his face dark with loathing.

Lucy looked at her son, still sobbing with fear. She turned her gaze on Edward and begged, 'Don't hurt him, please. If you want to stay, you can stay, and we'll talk again in the morning.'

When she saw the look in his eyes she knew it wasn't enough. 'Please, Edward, you're asking me to give up everything I know and love, to go away with you. I'm not saying no, but I'm not saying yes either. Give me time to think about it; you owe me that much.' She held out her arms. 'And now . . . *give me the child.*'

~

As he cut across towards the river on his way back home, Barney thought his world was a beautiful place, when the moon was full and round and the skies speckled with a myriad of twinkling stars. All along the chilly hedgerows he could hear the night animals scurrying about, and in the distance, the unique sound of a barn owl. 'You made something wonderful when You made this earth,' he murmured, his gaze roving the heavens. There was such peace and beauty on God's earth, and he felt deeply privileged to be a part of it.

Then, suddenly, Barney was made to stop in his tracks. 'What's that?' From somewhere close he could hear the sounds of human voices raised in anger. Turning this way and that, he tried to pinpoint where the voices were coming from, but it was difficult; the tumbling of water from the weir diverted his senses.

There it was again! His attention was drawn back, towards the high bend in the river, not too far from Lucy's cottage. It sounded as if somebody was in trouble! Quickly now, he made his way back, pausing every now and then to catch his breath, and taking off again when a child's wail shattered the night air.

As he came round by way of the spinney, he saw a figure running in the moonlight; he was carrying something – what was it? A sack . . . a child? Dear Lord, it was a child! And coming up behind him was a woman, running and stumbling, and all the while calling out for the man to stop.

When he recognised her, he was horrified. 'Lucy?' He couldn't believe his eyes. The woman was Lucy, and the child must be little Jamie . . . but the man – who was he? His name appeared in Barney's mind like a lit beacon. EDWARD TRENT! It had to be!

'Lucy!'

Quickening his steps to a run, time and again Barney called out her name, but Lucy didn't hear. They were too close to that part of the river where the water tumbled over the rise and thundered down into the basin beneath.

Gasping for breath, his chest afire, Barney took off again to gradually close the gap between them. He saw how, on reaching the river, Lucy launched herself at Trent. There was a struggle during which, with one backward swipe of his burly arm, Trent knocked her down.

At the top of the rise, Barney had to stop again. He bent his head low, and with his hands on his knees, he took some long deep breaths, and after a moment or two, slowly regained his composure. When he set off again, he could see Edward Trent. With the child under his arm, he was using the moonlight to illuminate his way across the most dangerous part of the river – a line of big boulders straddling the water. Doggedly pursuing him, out of her mind with fear, Lucy was yelling for him to give her the child. Jamie was frantically struggling in the man's arms, making the situation even more dangerous.

When Trent ignored her pleas, she followed, slipping and sliding across the slimy boulders towards the far bank.

'No, Lucy, come back!'

When Barney yelled out, in a part of this nightmare Lucy heard, but she kept on going, because

Edward Trent had her baby, and she would follow him to Hell if needs be.

By the time Barney came to the river, Lucy and Edward Trent were locked in a fierce struggle on the rocks above the weir, with the terrorised child screaming hysterically.

Desperate to get Lucy and her son out of there and with no thought for his own safety, Barney ran slithering over the boulders. Taking hold of her, he tried to get her to safety, but she wouldn't listen; all she knew was that her baby was in terrible danger. When driven by desperation she foolishly made a grab for the child, Trent lost his footing, and to her horror Lucy went with him.

Wading through the water to get to them, Barney saw Trent scrambling towards the shore and when, with the saturated clothes clinging to her body, Lucy went after him, Barney warned her to stay back. 'Leave him to me, Lucy!' He bellowed a warning. 'You're putting the child in more danger!' But with reason long gone, she took no heed.

Everything happened so quickly there was nothing Barney or anyone else could have done. Going against Barney's advice, Lucy made another grab for the child. As she caught him safely in her arms, Trent missed his footing and fell into Lucy, who then lost her balance – and in seconds the fast-flowing river snatched Jamie from her arms and whirled him away in its embrace.

Lucy made a brave effort to rescue her son, but not being a strong swimmer she was buffeted against every obstacle, as her son got washed further away.

Ahead of her, Barney got to the child first, but it was already too late. The force of water that had snatched him away and carried him downriver, had wedged him between two half-submerged rocks.

When Barney found him, the water was swirling over his face, and there was nothing he could do.

Desolate and bedraggled, he took the drowned child into his arms and waded upriver, to where Lucy was making her way towards them.

At first she began shouting for joy. 'You've got him!' She laughed out loud. 'Oh Barney, you've got him!' Her heart soared at the sight of her boy, safe in Barney's arms.

With tears streaming down his solemn face, Barney looked into her eyes and slowly shook his head.

When Lucy saw the expression on his face, it was as if the world had come to an end; there were no words to describe the horror that tore through her. For the longest, deepest moment, the silence in that place was awesome.

As she tenderly took her baby from him, Lucy thought she would never again in her life know such pain.

Half-blinded by her tears, she gazed on that

small, still face and her heart-wrenching cry echoed across the valley, shaking the night and striking fear into the cowardly heart of Edward Trent, who by now was already some distance away.

CHAPTER SEVENTEEN

Like everyone else in Comberton-by-Weir and far beyond, Leonard Maitland was deeply shocked by the events of that night.

When Jamie Baker was laid to his rest, Leonard had been there for Lucy, along with her friends and neighbours; for with her parents split up and out of touch, with no thought or care for their little grandson, since he had been born – and died – out of wedlock, poor little mite, Lucy had no real family to help her through.

The service was very emotional, and afterwards, when everyone gathered at Overhill Farm, the air was thick with disbelief. No one there could recall anything of such a tragic nature happening in their lifetime.

In the dark days that followed, Lucy withdrew into herself; by day she wandered restlessly over the fields and hills, as though searching for her lost child, and at night she headed blindly for Barney's house, where he and Vicky and the children were waiting to give support and comfort. They, too, missed the little boy and were heart-broken.

On this chilly day, with the date of departure fast approaching, Lucy and Barney prepared to visit Leonard Maitland. 'Lucy, love, are you sure you know what you're doing?' Barney had worried about Lucy's decision and had done all he could to change her mind, without success.

He tried again to dissuade her, but she was adamant. 'You and your family have been kindness itself,' Lucy told him, 'but soon you'll all be gone away. I have to take charge of my own life now.' Her voice broke. 'You know how much I love the cottage, Barney, but I could never go back there, not without my little angel.' Taking a moment to compose herself, she said in a whisper, 'How can I ever forgive myself, Barney?'

'Whatever d'you mean?' But he knew well enough what she meant, for hadn't he told her time and again that she was wrong?

'I know you will never admit it, Barney, but it *was* all my fault.' Gulping back the tears, she went over that awful night in her mind. 'If I'd only listened to you and kept back, you would have saved Jamie, I know you would . . .' When emotion overtook her, she crumpled into him and he held her close against his heart, his two arms keeping her safe while she sobbed helplessly.

After a time, when she was quiet, they walked

on, with Barney keeping his arm around her shoulders. 'Listen to me, Lucy love,' he said tenderly. 'What happened that night was no fault of yours. Evil took your baby, and the way things were, there was nothing more you or I could have done to prevent that terrible thing. We both tried our level best to save little Jamie, but it wasn't enough.'

He sighed from deep within. 'Sometimes, sweetheart, there are greater powers in force than we could ever hope to understand.'

Gently bringing her to a halt, he turned her round to face him. Looking into her reddened stricken eyes, he said emotionally, 'I'm so proud of you, Lucy. We all are. You've come through what will probably be the worst time of your entire life, and you've already begun to make decisions.' He smiled wryly. 'I don't agree with the decision about moving back to Bridget's, but it's your life, and you have to do what you feel is right.'

Lucy gave a little gulp. 'The truth is, I don't know what's right any more,' she confessed tearfully. 'All I know is that I have to make a new start, and before I can go forwards, I need to go backwards.'

Even in her sorrow, she noted the change in Barney; the trauma of that night had made him look so terribly ill. Raising her hand, she laid it on the side of his dear face as though comforting *him*. 'You mustn't upset yourself on my account,' she pleaded. 'You look so worn and tired, and I don't want to be a burden on you.'

Afraid that she might see how truly ill he was, he laid his hand over hers and, moving it from his face, held it tightly as they walked on. 'You could never be a burden to us,' he said gruffly. 'We love you like family, you know that.'

Lucy smiled wistfully. 'I know, and I love you for it, but I won't always have you to lean on. I have to try and get my life together, if I can.'

'You will.' He was sure of it. 'But I'm not happy about this business today.'

'It will be all right,' Lucy assured him.

But he was far from satisfied.

~

Some twenty minutes later, in Leonard Maitland's study, the pair of them explained what Lucy had decided, and like Barney, Leonard disagreed with her. 'Of course it's your decision, my dear, but is it wise to return to your friend Bridget's house? Don't get me wrong, she's charming and kind, and I know she's been the best of friends to you, but she runs a bad house, Lucy. If you want my opinion, I don't think that's the right place for you to be.'

'It's the *only* place for me to be,' Lucy answered. 'Since she took me in, and right up until I moved into your cottage, she was like a mother to me. We understand each other, and I know that when

Barney and his family leave, she will be my rock. She's been kind enough to ask me if I want to stay with her, and I've accepted.'

'Well then, if your mind is made up, I have to ask if you will do something for me?'

'If I can, I will,' Lucy readily agreed.

On arriving, she had placed the keys to the cottage on his table. He now took them up and held them out to her. 'Please take these back. I gave you the cottage to live in, with a secured tenancy, and though you may not want it at this moment in time, you may be glad of it later, when you're able to think more clearly about your future and security.'

When she hesitated, he lifted her hand and placed the keys on her palm. 'Take them, Lucy. If you can't go in yet, that's fine, but there may come a day when you find comfort there. Whether you like it or not, the cottage is yours to live in, legal and binding.'

With her hand still stretched out, Lucy remained unsure until, taking a step forward, Barney closed her fingers around the keys and pressed her arm to her side. 'Mr Maitland's right,' he told her gruffly. 'There might come a time when you need that cottage.'

It was a moment before Lucy responded, and then she threw her arms round a startled but delighted Leonard Maitland. 'Thank you,' she whispered, her eyes bright and sad, and her heart so sore she could hardly bear it. She had come dangerously close to being lost forever, but these kind, caring folks had brought her back from the brink of despair. Maybe after all, there was a future for her. Time alone would tell.

On the way back, feeling unwell, Barney stopped several times on the pretence of watching a hare or seeing 'summat running through the spinney'. Lucy saw nothing of what he pointed out, so deep in thought, she took him at his word.

'I'm so glad Mr Maitland managed to delay our voyage and the signing of the sale for another two weeks.' Having recovered for a while, Barney strolled beside her. 'He's a thoughtful sort, don't you think?'

Lucy agreed. 'You've all done more than enough for me, and now I've prepared myself for you all to be leaving soon. An extra two weeks won't change that, will it?'

'Mebbe not, Lucy love, but Mr Maitland is a real gentleman. He explained the circumstances to his solicitor, and out of respect for you, they've managed to hold it back, but only for the short term.' He had other reasons for being grateful that the leaving would be delayed. 'Vicky will be pleased when I tell her. She's been that worried about you.'

When a short time later they relayed the news to Vicky, she was thrilled. 'At least now we'll have a little more time together and it will help you get used to the idea of us going. What's more, I can satisfy myself that you're properly settled before we leave.'

While they carried on talking, Barney excused himself. 'I've a few things to tend to,' he said, hurrying away before Vicky could question him too closely.

Dodging anyone who knew him, Barney made his way to the village and Dr Lucas's afternoon surgery. There was no one else there, and he was quickly shown in. 'I trust you're here to tell me you're now ready to admit yourself for the tests?' Having asked Barney several times to agree to go into the Infirmary, Dr Lucas never gave up hope that his patient would at last change his mind.

Barney, however, soon shattered the man's expectations. 'If I came in for the tests, would it improve matters in any way?'

'I can't promise that.' He was the kind of doctor who answered straightforward questions with straightforward answers. 'As I've already explained, your heart is badly diseased, but we can't tell how badly until we investigate further.' Having already observed Barney's laboured breathing and the grey pallor of his skin, he was deeply concerned. 'I hope you realise how serious your condition is?'

'I'm beginning to.' Barney was truthful. 'I've noticed how quickly I get tired of late, and sometimes it hurts to breathe.' He gave a bright smile.

'But I'm still here and I'm still fighting, so it can't be all that bad, can it?'

Giving no answer, but taking the stethoscope from around his neck, the doctor asked Barney to go behind the screen and take off his shirt. A moment later, he gave Barney a thorough examination.

'Right! You can put your shirt back on now,' he said, walking away and perching himself on the edge of his desk. There was a look of apprehension on his face.

'Well?' Barney, too, was apprehensive. 'Is it worse?'

'Bad enough.' Looking directly at Barney he told him flatly, 'You're playing with fire, man.'

'In what way?'

'You haven't followed my instructions at all, have you?'

'Yes, I have,' Barney blustered. 'I'm taking the medication, just as you advised.'

'That's only part of it, and even that is only a short-term precaution until we know the extent of the damage. You haven't slowed up much in your work, and I've seen with my own eyes how you still slave away on the farm, even after I warned you not to exert yourself.'

Anger thickened his voice as he reprimanded his patient. 'Good God, man! Are you intent on killing yourself? Keep on the way you are, and I can't promise you'll be alive a year from now, or even less!'

Barney had known he was ill, but to have it spelled out like that, shocked him to the core. 'I'm a working man, Doctor,' he said quietly. 'I can't stop doing what I do; the cows won't milk themselves if I can't do it. My sons are a boon, but they need me with them a while yet.'

The doctor did not mince his words. 'If you continue to ignore my advice, they won't have you at all.'

'Then tell me this.' Barney was torn all ways. 'If I stopped working right now, and sat about like a cabbage in a patch, would that prolong my life by any great measure?'

The doctor carefully considered Barney's question before giving an honest if vague answer. 'As I told you before, we don't really know with these things. Your heart is in bad shape, and if you agreed to slow right down, that could well improve matters. I can't be more specific than that.'

Barney's courage was never as low as it was in that moment; he was afraid for himself, but more so for his beloved family. When he spoke now, his words were sure and final. 'There will be no hospital, and no tests,' he said gruffly. 'If I have a year, or less, then so be it.' Standing to leave, he smiled wearily. 'Thank you for all you've done.'

Dr Lucas had known Barney well, and it pained him to see his spirit so low. 'I'm very sorry,' he said. 'I only wish there was something more I could do.'

'There is.'

'Then name it.'

'Without me to drag them down, my family have the chance to start a new life, and nothing must spoil that.'

The doctor was astonished. 'What are you saying? Surely you don't still intend taking such a long and arduous journey?'

'That's for me to decide,' Barney replied firmly. 'All I'm asking of you is that what transpired between you and me goes no further.'

Dr Lucas nodded. 'I believe we've already agreed on that.'

'And do I have your word, as a gentleman?'

'As a gentleman and a doctor, yes.'

Barney shook him by the hand. 'Goodbye. I won't be coming to see you again.'

He left then, a wiser, sadder man. A man who knew what must be done, and had to find the courage to see it through.

CHAPTER EIGHTEEN

'Excuse me, miss ... I believe this is your stop.'

The bus conductor had noticed how Lucy was not watching the landmarks. Instead, she was sat deep in thought, in the far corner, sometimes looking out of the window, sometimes with her eyes closed. Now, staring ahead, she appeared to have no idea of her surroundings.

Startled by his concerned tap on the shoulder, Lucy thanked him and made her way to the platform. When the bus came to a halt, she quickly clambered off.

It had been comfortingly quiet on the bus, but now as she set off in the direction of the church, the noise and bustle of Liverpool was all around her; the clatter of horse and cart, the smell and sound of petrol-driven vehicles; the sight of rich women in furs, poor women in thin coats and men in suits, all going about their business. This was Friday, a day when people looked forward to their weekend and couldn't wait for the day to end. But for Lucy, since losing her child, every day seemed the same.

Leaving the mayhem behind, she came up the rise towards the church. The further from the centre she got, the more the wind seemed to swirl and blow. Beginning to shiver, Lucy drew her coat more tightly about her.

Taking the side path, she went along by the hedge and into the churchyard; little Jamie's resting-place was to the right of the gate under the oak-tree. Lucy had chosen St Saviour's as she had come to Sunday school here as a child, and had happy memories of it. The church at Comberton now seemed tainted, somehow, with the evil of Edward Trent.

Removing a handkerchief from her coat-pocket she wiped it over the small cross, which was temporarily erected until a marble heart could be set there. After laying down the posy of pretty leaves, together with a small toy, she knelt down to tell Jamie how much she missed and loved him. As always, she imagined him in her mind; toddling in the garden and chuckling as she chased him, and the tears were never far away.

After a while, when the cold seemed to penetrate her bones, she said a heartfelt goodbye. 'I'll see you again soon, my darling.'

In the church, she lit a candle to guide her child on his way to Heaven, and when the flame flickered and danced to life, she remained there for some long time, asking questions of the Lord. What had she done that was so wicked He had to take her baby? What would she do now without him? Why had the police not caught Edward Trent and brought him to a harsh punishment? And finally, would He please take care of Barney and the Davidson family on their long journey to a new life?

A short time later, spent of emotion, Lucy made her way back to the bus-stop. As she clambered on the bus, she caught sight of Barney. Emerging from a public-house and somewhat unsteady on his feet, he had a woman clinging to his arm.

Laughing together, they set off down the street and were soon gone.

Falling into her seat, Lucy was riveted with shock. She had recognised the woman as being a close friend and colleague of Bridget's, and knowing the nature of her business, Lucy found it hard to understand what Barney was doing in her company. She suspected also, if his unsteady gait was anything to go by, that he had been drinking. That in itself was astonishing, because as far as Lucy knew, Barney enjoyed the occasional glass of something only when the occasion demanded.

Convincing herself that there must be an innocent explanation, she vowed to ask him next time they met.

On arriving home, she went into the kitchen to make herself a cup of tea. 'Make one for me while you're at it.' Bridget almost fell into the room. 'I've been trudging round the shops for hours and I've got a throat like sandpaper.'

She threw down a heap of bags and sitting herself at the table, she told Lucy, 'I've left the girls searching for new outfits. They've bagged a lucrative job for next week, escorting some London businessmen about town. Lord knows, if we're to put the business on a more respectable footing, they'll need to look their best.'

With her mind still on Barney and the woman, Lucy heard not a word. 'Three sugars, isn't it?' she asked, beginning to spoon it out of the bag.

'Best make it four,' the woman advised. 'I'm shattered, so I am!'

When Lucy placed her cup and saucer before her, Bridget noticed how preoccupied she seemed. 'What's wrong wit' you? You've got a face like a wet weekend.'

'Nothing.' Lucy sat down with her tea and took a sip of it.

'Aw now, don't give me that.' The big Irishwoman wagged a finger. 'I've known you long enough to spot when something is wrong, so out with it! What's on your mind?'

Hesitating for a second or two, Lucy told her, 'I've just seen Barney Davidson coming out of a pub, and he was drunk . . . or near as dammit.'

'I see.' Bridget raised her cup to her mouth and took a long slurp. 'And ye are sure it was Barney ye saw?'

'I'm certain.'

Bridget peered at her over the rim of her cup. 'Was he alone?'

'No. He was with a woman.' She hesitated to say it was one of Bridget's friends.

'I see.'

When Bridget next spoke, it was to give Lucy a warning. 'Don't get mixed up in what you don't understand,' she cautioned. 'What Barney does or doesn't do is none of our business.'

From Bridget's reaction, Lucy suspected she knew more than she was saying. As the realisation dawned, she confronted her. 'You knew all about it, didn't you?' she demanded. 'You knew Barney was drinking and womanising. Don't deny it, because I can see it in your face!'

'All right, yes, I did. In fact, I'm told it's been going on for some time, and now it seems he doesn't give a bugger who sees him! But I didn't think it was my place to tittle-tattle. If Barney Davidson has a problem, he'll deal with it. Doesn't he always?' Not wishing to be drawn onto danger-ous ground, Bridget quickly drank up her tea, took her shopping and went upstairs with it. 'I'll see youse later,' she called back.

Unable to get Barney out of her mind, Lucy vowed to visit the Davidsons that evening. 'I've got to go and see him,' she muttered as she helped Tillie to peel the potatoes for dinner. 'I need to ask him outright.' She knew him well enough to do that.

Barney had been preying on her mind a great deal of late; behaving strangely, going away for hours on his own, and now this. In the beginning, she had thought it might be the trauma of what had happened that night, but drinking in a public-house with such a woman; arm-in-arm in the street and laughing as if he didn't give a damn who saw him . . . this was not the Barney she knew and loved. In the wake of Jamie's death, her embarrass-ingly romantic feelings towards him had vanished; but now they had resurfaced and she couldn't help it, he was never out of her thoughts. It was getting to the stage where she was afraid to look Vicky in the eye, in case her friend read the truth on her face.

Later that evening, when dinner was over and the kitchen at 23, Viaduct Street was spick and span, Lucy put on her hat and coat and set off for Overhill Farm.

As she went up the path to the front door she heard raised voices and the sound of a door slam-ming. Suddenly, the front door was flung open and Susie came rushing out, straight into Lucy's arms. 'Oh Lucy! Ronnie and Daddy are saying bad things to each other, and they won't stop . . .' She began to sob uncontrollably.

Lucy held her close. 'Ssh, don't worry, it'll be all right,' but she could still hear the two men inside, and now Thomas's voice, pleading with them to stop arguing. A moment later, the door opened and Vicky emerged, looking distraught as she searched for Susie. On seeing Lucy she was visibly relieved. 'Oh, dear God, Lucy, I don't know what to do. It's like my whole world's falling apart.'

Trembling and distressed, she took Susie by the shoulders. 'Run inside, sweetheart, and fetch our coats.' Calming herself for the girl's sake, she suggested with a shaky smile, 'We'll go for a little walk, eh, you, me and Lucy? When we come back, happen it'll all have sorted itself out, eh?'

Relieved to see her mammy smiling and comforted by her words, Susie ran to get their coats. 'What's happening?' Lucy asked worriedly. 'Is it Barney?' In her troubled mind she could still see him and the woman.

'Yes.' Vicky shook her head. 'There's something very wrong,' she said. 'Barney's been so odd of late – wandering off and not coming back till all hours. He's not been sleeping easy, and sometimes when I wake in the middle of the night, I look out of the window and he's pacing the yard like a trapped animal. He's suddenly got the devil of a temper on him, too, snapping and snarling and jumping down our throats at the slightest thing; he even smacked Susie last night because she came downstairs crying after having a bad dream. It's not like him, Lucy. He's always been such a loving man.'

She took a long, weary breath. 'And now, Ronnie swears he saw Barney in Liverpool today ... "arm-in-arm with a trollop", he says, and he swears that the pair of 'em were drunk.'

With raw eyes she looked into Lucy's face as though searching for some kind of reassurance. 'I didn't believe it of him, Lucy. "It couldn't have been your father" – that's what I told Ronnie. "He would never do such a thing".' Her voice broke. 'But to be honest, Lucy, somewhere in the back of my mind, God forgive me, because of the way Barney's been behaving, I'm half-inclined to believe what Ronnie saw.'

When Susie returned and they had on their coats and scarves, the three of them wandered away to the spinney; these days they were reluctant to go near the river, because of the bad memories.

Lucy made no mention of the fact that, like Ronnie, she too had seen Barney on the streets drunk and laughing with a woman. Instead she told Vicky, 'I've an idea Barney might still be suffering the effects of that night. It was a terrible thing for him to witness. Grief and shock can affect us all in different ways,' she said in a low voice. God knows, she herself was half-demented with it. 'Maybe Barney is not able to deal with the horror of what happened?'

Vicky had already considered that. 'Of course he suffers from remembering, as we all do.' She reached out to squeeze Lucy's hand. 'But it's more than that,' she went on sombrely. 'Now I think about it, I've seen a few changes happening in Barney, long before that night. He's been getting more preoccupied and distant, as though he's always got something on his mind, and none of us are a part of it.'

She shrugged. 'He's been working so hard – pushing himself until he hurts. It's as if he's trying to prove something. He's changed, Lucy, and now it's got so I can hardly recognise him as the man I married.'

In spite of her determination not to let young Susie see her upset, Vicky began to cry, softly at first, and when she could no longer hold it back, the crying became wrenching sobs that tore her apart. 'I'm sorry,' she kept saying. 'I'm so, so sorry.' For the first time in her married life, she did not know how to deal with Barney.

Running to her, Susie threw her arms round Vicky's waist; in a choked voice she told her, 'Don't cry, Mammy, it's all right. Please don't cry.' The normal roles of mother and child were reversed, and Vicky was ashamed.

After a time they walked on; Lucy lost in her own thoughts, Vicky also quiet now, and Susie with her hand clutched in her mammy's.

All three were thinking of Barney. Lucy was

determined to get him alone and have a heart-to-heart with him; Vicky wondered how she could win back the man she loved; and her frightened daughter silently brooded over the night's event, her heart alive with all manner of emotion – and shockingly, even the smallest beginnings of hatred towards the father she adored.

When they got back to the house, despite the cold, Ronnie was seated on the garden bench. With his head down and his hands over the back of his neck, he did not hear them approach.

'Ronnie?' Going immediately to him, Vicky put her arm around his shoulders. 'What are you doing out here in the cold?'

Ronnie looked up. In the half-light from the windows she could see that he'd been crying. 'What is it, love?' She sat beside him. 'What's happened?'

For a long anxious moment, Ronnie gave no answer. Instead he glanced back at the house, then he looked at his mother and the tears ran down his face. 'That man in there,' he whispered brokenly. 'I don't even know who he is any more.'

Rising to Barney's defence, Vicky told him firmly, 'Whatever he says or does, and whatever you may think of him just now, he is still your father!'

Ronnie shook his head. 'No, he's not. I know my father like I know myself, and that man in there is a stranger.'

Vicky understood but was horrified all the same. 'Your father is ill,' she said lamely. 'He doesn't seem to understand how he's hurting us. Barney is a good man. He's stood by all of us at one time or another, and now it's our turn to stand by him.'

Scrambling to his feet, Ronnie looked down on her in amazement. 'How can you say that?' he demanded. 'I saw him with my own eyes! He was drunk in the street, in the company of a woman like *that* . . . They went away laughing – laughing at *you*, Mother! He's not only cheating on you, but he's doing it openly. He gets himself drunk and then he comes home arguing and causing trouble in the family.'

His voice shook with rage. 'You can stand by him if you like, but I won't! I can't forgive him.'

Seeing her brother stride off angrily into the night, Susie wailed, 'Stop him, Mammy. STOP HIM!'

Grabbing her close, Vicky held her tight. 'I can't,' she said, 'but he'll be back. You'll see, sweetheart, Ronnie will be back.' In her heart though, she could not be certain of that.

'Do you want me to go?' Having witnessed the distress in this close-knit family, Lucy was afraid for them all, including Barney. She wanted to stay but sensed that Vicky needed to be alone with her family.

Vicky nodded. 'I'm sorry, Lucy,' she apologised. 'I'll get Thomas to see you home.' Because the night was cold and because she had great affection for Lucy, she invited her to come inside first.

She led the way, with Susie at her side and Lucy following.

When she walked into the sitting room, Lucy was shocked at the sight of Barney. Unkempt and unshaven, he sat in the armchair, his shirt undone to the chest and his head lolling sideways. Lucy thought he looked ill and quietly said so to Vicky.

Thomas had been standing before the fire, his eyes alive with anger as he stared at his father. 'He's not ill.' He spat out the words. 'He's drunk!'

'I'll deal with your father.' Taking hold of him by the arm, Vicky led him away. 'I need you to take Lucy home in the trap.'

Thomas nodded. 'Will you be all right?'

'I'll be fine,' she answered with a smile. 'Oh, and take Susie with you.' When the girl protested, she told her gently, 'Lucy would like that, wouldn't you, lass?'

Realising Vicky's intent, Lucy nodded. 'Yes, I would.' Addressing Susie she told her, 'I need to know all about the new clothes you and Mammy have bought for the journey to America.'

At Lucy's remark, Thomas gave a grunt. 'That's if we ever go!'

Susie gave a cry. 'We *are* going, aren't we, Mammy?'

Vicky nodded. 'That's the plan, sweetheart.' Though her heart was breaking, she smiled her brightest. 'In just over a week's time we'll be boarding the ship for America.' She gave Barney a sideways glance. *'All of us!'*

On the way back to Viaduct Street, Thomas sat hunched on the driving seat, quiet and morose. He had only ever seen his father drunk once, and that was when his friend Adam had brought back some strong homemade cider to mark his birthday. It was a memorable night, which ended in laughter and good humour. This time it was different. And in all his life, Thomas had never felt so helpless.

～

Over the next few days, Barney's hitherto good name deteriorated further. 'Cheating on his good wife,' people tutted. 'Carrying on wi' all kinds, and drinking himself into a stupor every chance he gets.'

'I hear he stayed out all night a while back.' Even on the bus they tittle-tattled about him. 'Lord knows what that family's going through, and them supposed to be leaving for America any day now.'

Seated behind the two gossiping women, Lucy could not wait to get off at her stop; though as she passed them she commented loudly on 'folks who can't help but gossip, even when they don't have a clue what they're talking about'!

As she hurried home, she wondered where it would all end.

Bridget was alone. 'The girls have gone on another one of these "business" appointments,' she said proudly. 'Sure, haven't we gone up in the world, don't you think?'

'Mmm.' Seating herself at the table, Lucy recalled what the women on the bus had said. 'I hear that Barney stayed out all night a while back. How on earth do folks find out so much so soon?'

Bridget plonked a cup of tea down on the table. 'What exactly are we talking about?'

Lucy told her about the two women and the conversation they were having. 'What on earth are we going to do about Barney?' she asked. 'I'm at my wit's end.' She gave Bridget a wary look. 'What if Vicky ever finds out he was here the night he went missing?'

'I won't tell if you won't,' Bridget replied. 'What was I supposed to do when he turned up, soaking wet and looking to come inside? He only slept the drink off while I dried his clothes, that's all.' With big eyes she chided Lucy. 'Should I have turned him away – is that what you're saying?'

Lucy shook her head. 'No, of course it's not.' All the same, she felt as though she was betraying Vicky by not telling her, and she told that to Bridget now.

Bridget was angry with her. 'Now look here, young lady! Sure the man himself pleaded with you not to tell where he was for most of the night. You did right not to say anything, and besides, didn't they have the holiest of rows and didn't she get angry and lock the door against him?'

'So I'm told, yes.'

'There y'are, then! Even if he'd gone home, he wouldn't have been able to get in. He'd have had to sleep on the garden bench, so he would!'

Once Bridget was in full sail there was no stopping her. 'I gave him a bed for the night and there's nothing to be ashamed of in that. You and I both know how hard I'm trying to get this house respectable. It may well have been a house of pleasure a while back, but things are changing.'

She bristled with pride. 'You'll notice I'm more of a businesswoman now, so ye will. What's more, little Tillie has taken to her new job of bookkeeper like a duck to water.' She gave a short whistle. 'I never knew she was so good at keeping proper accounts! And she's delighted with the shorter hours and the bigger wage-packet.'

Lucy had to smile. 'You always were ambitious,' she said fondly. 'And happen you're right about giving Barney a bed for the night. If he had upset Vicky so much that she locked the door against him, she might have done worse if he'd gone banging on the door in the middle of the night.'

Bridget beamed. 'Well, there y'are then. Sure, isn't that what I've been saying all along?' She had a question. 'Did ye manage to have a quiet word with him ... about the womanising and the drinking?'

Lucy shook her head. 'I've tried time and again to get him on his own, but he always manages to dodge me.' This time she was determined. 'I've spoken with Adam. He's worried sick about Barney, but even he hasn't been able to talk any sense into him. Vicky and the boys will be up at Leonard Maitland's tonight. Apparently he's concerned about Barney and unsure about what's happening. He's asked the family to come and talk it through, so tonight, Barney will be on his own.'

Bridget was doubtful. 'Will Barney stay in, d'ye think? Or will he be off out with his floozy?'

Lucy tapped her nose by way of a confidence. 'It's all been arranged. Barney's agreed to see Adam, and being as he's let Adam down twice before, we're hoping that this time he'll keep his word and be at home when his old pal arrives.'

Bridget got the picture. 'But it won't be Adam who turns up, will it? It'll be you, is that right?'

Lucy confirmed that was the idea. 'Seeing as he keeps avoiding me, this seems to be the only way.'

'Well, I hope it works, because somebody needs to talk some sense into that foolhardy head of his,' Bridget declared. 'Sure, if anybody can do it, you can.'

Just then the girls came in, dressed in their new outfits and looking like a million dollars. 'I've just spent a whole afternoon in one of the best hotels in Manchester.' Brenda's tall, willowy figure was wrapped in the most expensive coat with fur collar and deep fur-trimmed pockets.

'And I've been to the races.' Shorter and perfectly formed, Lynette was better suited to the small-brimmed hat and brown silk two-piece.

'I hope you both behaved like ladies?' Raising her eyebrows, Bridget gave them a warning glance.

On hearing how they had been paid handsomely for their escort duties, Bridget congratulated them. 'Sure if we keep on like this, we'll have to move to posher premises,' she joked. 'Now off upstairs wit' ye, and out of those expensive clothes. You'll need them again, I hope, so make sure you hang them up nice and neatly.'

Shortly after the girls had departed, Lucy excused herself. 'I'd best get ready,' she told Bridget.

'Off ye go then, and I wish ye well.' Her friend was concerned. 'It's a crying shame to see how Barney's hurting that poor family of his. If he doesn't come to his senses soon, there'll be no America for him, and no family to speak of neither.'

With all that preying on her mind, Lucy got washed and changed and made herself ready to meet Adam. Having lately acquired a little black Ford, he was to run her up to the end of the lane and wait there until she came out again.

She didn't have to wait long before the little car drew up outside number 23. 'What d'you think to it?' he asked proudly. 'Cost me an arm and a leg, but it was worth it.'

Lucy told him she thought it was handsome, and smiling from ear to ear he helped her climb on the running board and then get inside, before taking the starting handle and thrusting it into the front of the car. Perspiring from the effort, Adam drove up the street erratically, with the car lurching and bumping. 'I'm not quite used to it yet,' he apologised sheepishly. 'But I'll get us there – don't you worry about that.'

When they reached the end of the lane leading to Overhill Farm, they sat awhile. 'Have the family gone out yet, d'you think?' Adam was on pins.

'I'm not sure.' Lucy, too, was nervous. If she did get to see Barney on his own, what would she say? How could she convince him that what he was doing was tearing the family apart? What about the future? What about America, and the family so looking forward to it now? *And why was he doing this?* That was the main thing.

While they waited and watched, Lucy spoke her mind to Adam. 'I don't understand why Barney's suddenly started behaving like this,' she said. 'He's an intelligent man, compassionate and caring, and yet here he is, wantonly throwing away everything he cherishes.'

Adam had an idea, but he could not give her the answer. 'It's the strangest thing,' he said thoughtfully. 'I've known him a very long time, but I can never recall him acting the way he is now, hurting the ones he loves and seemingly hell-bent on destroying himself. One minute he's all fired up at going to America, and now it's as though he has to destroy every chance they've got of starting a new life. I've tried to reason with him, but he just walks away. He won't listen to me.'

Reaching out, he took Lucy's hand into his. 'Happen he'll talk to you,' he said, patting the back of her hand. 'Happen *you'll* get through to him where I can't.' In the half-light he smiled on her, trying not to show the love he felt. She was his good friend, and he was not prepared to spoil that by speaking his heart.

Suspecting nothing of his true feelings, Lucy gave him a nudge. 'Here they are now,' she said. The family emerged from the house; Vicky and Susie first, then the two sons. Huddled together, they set off on foot in the other direction, along the lane and on towards Leonard Maitland's house, The Manse. 'We'll give it another minute or so and then you'd best go in,' Adam said. 'D'you think he'll open the door to you?'

Lucy smiled secretly. Reaching into her handbag, she drew out the key to Overhill Farmhouse. 'I never thought to give this back after I stayed there once,' she told him. 'I knew it would be more polite to knock, but like you say, he might see me out of the window and be gone through the back door. So I shall just let myself in.' She did not like the idea of doing it, but saw no other way.

Climbing out of the car, Lucy softly closed the door and approached the house. She could see Barney through the window; slouched in his chair he was leaning forward, deep in thought and looking lost.

Concentrating on what she was doing, she slipped the key into the lock, opened the door and went inside; and because she did not want to alarm him, she deliberately made a noise as she came towards the sitting room.

'Who's there?' Barney's voice sailed through the house. 'Vicky! Is that you?'

When suddenly he was standing before her, his face fell with astonishment. 'Lucy! What the devil are you doing here? How did you get in?'

'Sorry if I frightened you.' When Lucy now took a step forward, Barney took a step back. 'Please, Barney. We need to talk.'

'I don't want to talk. Go away, and leave me be.' Seeing her there and knowing how, like the rest of his beloved family, she was worried out of her mind, he so much wanted to take her in his arms and open his heart to her. But if he did, then all of this would have been for nothing. 'How did you get in? Did Vicky let you in, is that it? Did she think you might get me to tell you things I can't tell her?' His eyes bright with tears, he lowered his sorry gaze to the floor.

'Vicky doesn't know I'm here,' she told him. 'Look! I still have my key.' She laid it on the coat-stand. 'There. I've returned it now.'

As she walked towards him, he barred her path, his shoulders squared tall and his face blank, with no expression. 'I don't need you here. I want you to go.'

Now, as Lucy stared him in the eye, he looked away, as though he could not bear to see the pain and anxiety in her face. 'I said I want you to leave. Now!'

Lucy refused. 'You'll have to throw me out, Barney.'

The man was in anguish; he wanted to tell her the truth, but he daren't. He *couldn't.*

'Talk to me, Barney.' Laying her hand on his arm, she thrilled at his nearness, but for now all she wanted was to make him at peace, to let him know that he was not on his own. 'Why are you doing all of this?' Her voice was like silk to his ears. 'You were always such a kind and loving man, concerned about other people's feelings. You're not a drunk, or a bad man. You're a worker and a fighter. You risked your own life to save my baby and you were my strength afterwards. Was it that night, Barney? Was it because of what happened to little Jamie?' Her voice broke. 'You said it your-self – there was nothing we could have done. It was too late, Barney . . . all too late.'

When she paused, choking back the pain of

remembering, Barney looked up. He was so ashamed. 'How are you now, Lucy?' His voice was merely a whisper, but it came from the heart.

Looking up with bright eyes and a sorry smile, she told him, 'I'm coping, Barney. But I'm so worried about you . . . we all are. What is it? What's wrong? You have to let me help. You have to let *us all* help.'

She could sense that he was weakening, when suddenly the front door was pushed open and in walked a woman, tall and attractive, with wild hair and a ruddy complexion, and the smell of booze about her. 'You shouldn't leave your door open of a night-time,' she quipped. 'And who might this be, Barney? I know it's not your wife because you told me she'd be out with the family.'

'Jesus!' Thrusting Lucy aside he took hold of the woman by the arm. 'What the hell are you doing here, and drunk into the bargain!'

She smiled. 'I remembered you saying your family were going out and that I should come and pay a call on you if ever I was passing. Well, I might not have been passing, but I'm here now, and I've brought us some cheer.' Holding up a bottle of sherry, she taunted him with it. 'If you don't want to stay here, we can always go to my place. I've got a car outside.' Staggering sideways, she almost lost her balance. 'The driver is an old friend of mine . . .' she gave a wink '. . . if you know what I mean?'

About to throw her out into the night, Barney stopped himself. No! This might be his best chance. Just now, Lucy had almost got him to confide in her, and if his unwelcome visitor hadn't turned up, he might well had said things he regretted. And that would have been a disaster.

'She's the woman I saw you with in Liverpool.' Lucy was shocked and angry. 'Ask her to leave, Barney. She's tainting Vicky's lovely home.'

Enraged, the woman made a grab for her. Barney stepped between them. Turning on Lucy he sounded like a stranger. 'Good night, Lucy. I don't want to see you again. You can leave now.'

Lucy was taken aback. 'You don't mean that?'

He gave a slow, affirmative nod. 'Thank you for coming here tonight, but I don't need your help.'

Lucy could have argued with him, but there would have been no point. Instead she reached up and, placing her hands on his shoulders, she kissed him on the cheek. 'Think what you're doing, Barney,' she pleaded quietly. 'We all love you so much.'

For what seemed an age he looked at her, and just for the briefest moment she really believed he was listening. Then he took her by the arm and led her to the door, where he pushed her unceremoniously onto the outer step. One hard, appealing stare, and then he closed the door.

As she walked down the path, Lucy could hear

their laughter. 'May God forgive you, Barney Davidson,' she whispered.

Climbing into the car she sat for a moment, unsure what to do.

'I saw the woman.' Adam's voice interrupted her thoughts. 'I wondered if I should come in, and then I thought it best not to.'

'If you'd come in, it would only have made matters worse.'

'What about the woman?'

Lucy shook her head. 'She's the one he's been seeing. He's got her in there now, and he's not in the mood for talking.' She turned to him, a sad little smile on her face. 'He almost confided in me,' she revealed. 'If that woman hadn't arrived, he would have talked, I know he would.'

They sat a moment longer; Adam feeling as though he should go in there and throw her out, and Lucy thinking how low Barney had sunk.

'What's wrong with him, Adam?' she asked now. 'Why is he doing this?'

Adam didn't know any more than she did, although a suspicion lurked at the back of his head. 'Maybe we didn't know him as well as we thought we did,' he answered thoughtfully. 'Or maybe he's pushed himself so hard, and then . . . your awful tragedy . . .' He paused, making sure he had not upset her. 'Who knows what it takes to turn a man like Barney?'

Lucy had to agree. 'We've tried,' she murmured.

'We couldn't have tried any harder. Maybe there'll be an opportunity later on.' She gave a deep sigh. 'I don't know any more.'

'Home then?'

When Lucy nodded, he started the engine, turned the car about, and went down the lane at a leisurely pace. They did not talk. For now, there was too much on their minds.

CHAPTER NINETEEN

Leonard Maitland had welcomed the family into his home, and for a time they had enjoyed his hospitality. When the discussion turned serious, he asked Vicky outright, 'So, with the way things are at home, will you and the family still be able to come with me to Boston?'

Vicky looked at her sons, and her heart was breaking. 'I'm sure you know what's happened with Barney?'

Leonard nodded. 'I'm sorry.' He was more sorry than she would ever know, he thought, because if he was going to Boston without Barney, he would be going without Vicky. He knew that, even before she told him.

'I'm not sure if we'll be able to come or not,' Vicky said solemnly. 'We so much want to – in fact, we've all been so excited about it . . .'

She would have explained, but Ronnie blurted out: 'Tell him the truth, Mother! Tell him how we might have to give up the greatest adventure we're ever likely to have, and all because my father's turned into a drunk and a laughing stock.'

'That's enough!' Now, when Thomas put his hand over his brother's arm, Ronnie bent his head in shame. 'It's true though, isn't it?' Getting out of his chair, he strode across the room and ran out of The Manse into the night.

'Go after him, Tom. Take care of him.' Vicky was desolate. As Thomas went to look for his brother, she addressed Leonard with a degree of pride. 'I'm sorry we've caused you so much concern,' she said. 'If you have to look for someone else to help you with the farm in Boston, we will understand.'

Leonard stopped her there. 'Vicky, listen to me.' Coming to sit beside her, he spoke with real compassion. 'I fully understand what you must all be going through at this time, and I wouldn't dream of rushing into looking for anyone else.'

'Do you mean that?'

'Of course. We still have a little time. Until then, I'll assume that Barney is going through some sort of crisis; probably stemming from the idea that he should have saved the child and couldn't. He's a good man, and he did his best, that's all any of us can do.'

'Pray it will turn out all right,' Vicky said. Deep down she feared that Barney had gone so low he might never come back to her. 'All I'm saying is, I don't want you to be hampered in your plans, especially when you've been so good to us.'

Outside, Thomas had managed to calm his brother, and when Vicky came out with Susie, the four of them began their way back down the lane. 'It's all gone, hasn't it?' Ronnie was broken. 'Our happy family, our dream . . . all of us wanting to go to America and start over – all gone.'

Quickening his steps he walked on in front. Thomas kept a close eye on him, while Vicky walked between him and Susie, wondering why her happy, safe little world had been so cruelly shattered.

~

Inside the house the woman was all over Barney. 'You're not very friendly tonight, are you?' Seated on his knee, she nibbled at his ear. 'C'mon. Want to make love, do you?'

Barney didn't answer. The touch of her skin against his was repugnant to him, and he could smell her boozy breath on his face. 'Best not,' he said. 'There's no telling what time the family will be back.' In his mind he could still see Lucy's downcast face. She had come here to help him, and he had turned her away. What kind of monster was he becoming?

Yet what choice did he have? This was the worst time of his life and he desperately needed his family by him. Instead, for their own sakes, he was deliberately alienating them.

When the door suddenly opened to admit his two sons, Barney was flustered; for a split second he wasn't sure what to do, but then he knew and with a sore heart he played his part well. 'Oh look!' Kissing the woman soundly on the mouth, he pointed to his family who, shocked and disgusted, were now gathered at the door. 'It's my precious family,' he laughed. 'Shall we ask them to leave? What d'you think?'

Brazen, the woman sniggered. 'A minute later and they might have caught you with your trousers off,' she said.

'Get out of my house!' White-faced, her fists clenched with rage, Vicky rushed towards the woman. 'Get out, or I swear to God, I won't be responsible for my actions!'

Realising he had tipped Vicky over the edge, Barney clambered to his feet. Taking hold of the woman he told her, 'You'd best go.'

'I want you to go with her.' Vicky spoke quietly, but the rage trembled in her voice. She did not look at Barney. She had seen enough. 'You've gone too far this time,' she told him. 'I don't want you near me any more.' The tears were rising, but she would not let them see.

He hesitated, hating himself, loving her so much it hurt. He wanted to take her in his arms and tell her it was all an act, that he had never stopped wanting her, that he would always love her.

But he couldn't do that. Instead, he looked at her and drank in her beauty, knowing he might never again hold her in his arms.

'You heard what she said. GET OUT!' Giving Barney a shove, Ronnie sent him sprawling towards the door.

Before Barney could recover, his sons took one arm each and bundled him out of the door; the woman with him.

'What kind of man are you?' Thomas was shocked to his soul by Barney's inexplicable behaviour. 'You must know what you're doing to us all. But it's done now! You can't hurt us any more. As far as we're concerned, the Barney Davidson we knew is gone forever.'

Outside in the cold, with the door to his own house closed against him, Barney was made to realise that at long last, he had earned the cold hatred of the family he adored. *Dear God, what had he done?* Not for the first time he questioned the wisdom of his own behaviour.

'Come on, handsome!' The woman grabbed hold of his arm. 'Never mind them. Let's find somewhere to bed down for the night.'

Angry with himself, angry with her, he thrust her away. 'Get out of my sight!'

'Well, yer miserable bugger, all I'm doing is trying to cheer yer up!'

Realising it wasn't her fault, Barney softened. 'You said you have a car waiting?'

'That's right.' She pointed to the small vehicle tucked into the lane. 'There it is.'

Barney took her by the arm and leading her to the car, told the driver, 'See she gets home safely, will you?'

The driver, a burly fellow wearing a trilby, gave him a nod. 'I got her here, and I'll get her back,' he said.

Barney helped her into the front seat, and watched them drive away. For a long time, he stood hidden by the window, watching as his sons comforted Vicky. Seeing her sob like that wrenched him apart.

Suddenly, Susie saw him there and running out, she grabbed up a handful of mud and threw it at him, catching him hard on the neck. 'I hate you!' Sobbing uncontrollably, she kept saying it over and over, throwing the mud and telling him, 'I hate you, I hate you . . .'

A moment later, Vicky appeared to put her arm round the girl's shoulders. 'Come away, sweetheart.' She looked at Barney, covered in mud, forlorn and haggard, and for a while it seemed she might go to him. But then she said brokenly, 'I don't know who you are any more.' Head bowed and with her daughter close, she walked away, and never once looked back.

Barney was a finished man. He saw the curtains close against him, and he remained there until he felt the cold reach right into his bones. Broken, he turned away, and walked on through the night, not knowing where he was going, not caring.

~

Having talked with Barney's family, Leonard Maitland set out for a walk across the heath, as he always did at this time of night. It was a sorry affair, he thought. Barney had a new life just for the taking, and now it all seemed to be thrown by the wayside. He couldn't know how fortunate he was, to have a lovely family and a wife like Vicky – so beautiful, hardworking and totally devoted. Leonard would have given anything for such a woman, and here was Barney, casting her aside, like the bloody fool he was!

He walked on; his usual route was to turn at the spinney and come back by the river. Just then, he saw a figure sitting on the ground. Leonard could hardly believe his eyes. 'Barney Davidson! What in God's name d'you think you're doing, man?' Coming forward, he leaned down. 'Are you all right? Are you ill?' Sitting, arms folded with his back to a tree trunk, Barney was shivering uncontrollably.

Leonard went to help him up, visibly startled when Barney took hold of him. 'You have to listen,' Barney pleaded. 'You have to help me.'

'Of course I'll help you. What on earth are you doing out here? Come home with me. We'll soon get you warmed up and then I'll run you back to the farm. Heavens above, man, you're like ice!' Taking off his jacket he wrapped it round Barney's shoulders.

But Barney would not budge. 'You don't understand,' he mumbled. 'None of them understand.' Suddenly he was sobbing. 'I had to do it, y'see? I had to turn them against me, it was the only way. The booze, the women, the fighting – it was all an act. *I had to do it . . .*'

When the sobbing took hold and he could no longer speak, Leonard took him gently away.

'Come home with me,' he said compassionately. 'Whatever it is, we'll make it right. I promise.'

Half-supporting, half-carrying him, Leonard took Barney through the night, and when they reached The Manse he settled him on the sofa in front of a roaring fire. 'I'll get a blanket . . . keep you warm. Then I'll let your wife and family know that you're safe,' he told him.

Panicking, Barney stumbled from the sofa and taking hold of Leonard by the collar, he begged him not to tell them. 'I can never go with you, but the family can. They mustn't know about me. Nobody knows, except for Adam and the doctor, and they are duty bound not to tell.'

When he began fighting for breath and pleading with Leonard not to tell, the older man calmed him. 'Very well, Barney, your secret is safe with me, but let me get the blanket, and a hot drink, then we'll sit and talk, you and me, with no one else to bother us. All right?' He was shocked and saddened by Barney's situation. Grey-faced and with his eyes all but sunk into his head, Barney looked more ill than Leonard could ever have imagined.

Barney nodded feverishly. 'All right, yes, but I need to ask you something . . .'

'You can ask anything you like,' Leonard promised. 'But not until I have you settled and warm.' Lifting Barney's legs he laid him back onto the cushions before going off to the kitchen. 'I'll be as quick as I can.'

He returned within minutes, carrying a tray with hot milk with whisky and biscuits, and under his arm a blanket. 'Here we are!' Setting the tray on the side table, he wrapped Barney in the blanket. 'Good! You've stopped shivering.' He was relieved to see that the man's colour was already returning.

Handing the mug to Barney, he warned him, 'Be careful, now . . . it's very hot.' But it was exactly what Barney needed. 'Now then.' Leonard sat in the armchair facing him. 'Are you ready to talk?'

Barney gave him a wary look. 'Can I trust you?'

Leonard assured him, 'I'm not one to betray a trust.'

Setting his mug of milk on the hearth, Barney threw back the blanket and edging his legs round so as to be sitting opposite Leonard, he sat quiet for a while, with the only sound the ticking of the clock. When he finally spoke it was to say in a low, secretive voice, 'I want you to take my wife and family to America.'

Leonard was curious. 'But isn't that what we have already decided? You and the boys are to help me run the farm, and Vicky is to run the house. I thought it was all agreed.' He paused. 'You've changed your mind – that's it, isn't it, Barney?' There was disgust in his voice. 'That's why you've been behaving in such a shocking way – because you've changed your mind and didn't have the guts to tell me. So you thought if you behaved badly enough, I wouldn't want you with me anyway?'

'I wish to God that was the way of things,' Barney said sadly. 'You asked me a moment ago if I was ill. Well, yes, I am ill . . . *very ill.* In fact, there isn't much time. The thing is, I'm concerned about Vicky, and my children. If they knew how desperately ill I am, they would never leave me, and I'm so afraid for them. I want you to take them with you, Mr Maitland. Make a good life for them, and I'll be forever in your debt.'

Leonard was shaking his head in disbelief. 'I don't understand. Are you asking me to take them, *without you?*'

'That's exactly what I'm asking.'

'For God's sake, man, what's going on in your head? Have you lost your mind altogether? For one thing, if you're so ill, you need your family more than ever. Vicky would never go without you.

And there's another thing: I need *you*, Barney. No other man could help me put the farm back on its feet like you can.'

There was a long moment when Barney laid back on the sofa, eyes closed and wishing he was not having this conversation. However, he had no choice, not if his family were to have the chance of a new life in America.

Leaning forward he told Leonard, 'You're not listening to me. I want you to understand why I've been behaving the way I have. More than that, I need you to help me, or it will all have been for nothing.'

Realising how serious Barney was, Leonard remained silent, attentive to his Farm Manager's every word.

Barney told him everything: that his heart was fading and that he could never recover. He had agonised over and again about how he might still give his family the chance of starting a new life without him, aware that if they were to suspect that he was seriously ill, they would never abandon him. He told Leonard of their great excitement and of his own despair because, 'Through no fault of my own, that wonderful opportunity you gave us has been snatched from me. But it must not be snatched from my wife and children. That's why I've behaved the way I have – to turn them against me – to make them hate me as they have never hated anyone.'

He paused again, unable for a moment to go on, and when he did, the tears spilled over. 'I know you love my Vicky,' he said. When Leonard made to protest, Barney put up a staying hand. 'Please don't deny it. I've known for some long time that you love her. I've seen the way you watch her when she's in the field. I saw how you danced with her at our party, with love in your eyes and the tender touch of a man with the woman he loves. She has the children, but she will need you more than you know. You're a good man, Mr Maitland. Take her, and look after her, I beg you. I will ask Adam to write to you and let you know when it's all over, so you can marry my lovely Vicky in the fullness of time.'

He had one more thing to say, because now his strength was depleted. 'I'm not strong any more, but my sons are. I can't help you bring the farm back to life, but they can. I've taught them everything I know. Give them their dream, I beg you! Take them away, and never in your life tell them about our conversation this night.'

Exhausted, he lay back on the cushions. 'You have to promise me this, or the bad things I've done will all have been for nothing.'

Leonard had been devastated by Barney's terrible news, and now this request had him in turmoil. 'You're asking too much of me, Barney.' With his head bowed low, he searched for the right words. 'How can I take a man's family across the Atlantic and leave him behind to . . .' He couldn't even bring himself to say it. 'How can I possibly do that?'

'You can do it, Mr Maitland, because if you don't, they'll remain here, with no home and no one to guide them. God knows, I'll be gone soon enough, and it's more than I can bear. I'm asking you to help me. Who else can I turn to? You offered them a new life, a journey the like of which they will never know again. It's up to you.' His voice weak, he pleaded for the last time: 'Surely you won't refuse me? Think of Vicky. Think of her, alone and unprotected. No, Mr Maitland, you can't refuse me this.'

For a time, Leonard paced the floor, back and forth, up and down, occasionally stopping to shake his head and turn the matter over and over in his mind.

Presently, he came to sit in the armchair. 'What will happen to you, Barney?' he asked worriedly. 'Who will take care of you?'

The sick man did not hesitate. 'Lucy will be there when I need her, I'm sure.'

Leonard gave a long, deep sigh. 'I don't know, Barney, I just don't know. You're ill, you need your family about you. *You need Vicky* . . . What would she say if she ever found out that I had taken her away when you needed her most?'

Barney looked at him then, a world of understanding in his eyes. 'Vicky must *never* know. None of them must know.'

Leonard was humbled. 'Do you really trust me that much?'

'I do, yes. I trust you never to tell, for as long as you live. I trust you to promise me and keep your promise. Will you do that for me, Mr Maitland? Will you promise to take them and look after them, and never betray me?'

Amazed at Barney's calm manner, Leonard observed him as never before; that ordinary man, with an extraordinary courage, and he was deeply humbled. 'I'm sorry, Barney,' he said harshly. 'I'm sorry for what's happened to you, and I'm sorry that your family will be losing the bravest man it's ever been my privilege to meet.'

'But will you promise all those things? *Will you?*'

Leonard got out of his chair and began pacing the floor again, his hand cupping his chin as he thought deeply about this unique situation. It was true that he loved Vicky, and it was true that he desperately needed men he could trust, like the Davidson youths, to help him restore his grandfather's farm to its former glory. Barney was the Farm Manager here, but his two fine sons were made in the same mould.

The promise weighed on his mind. How could he promise never to tell Vicky about Barney, to say that she ought to be worshipping the ground he walked on instead of rejecting him? Everything Barney had done – the bad things and the angry things, making them despise him while he was suffering so terribly – all of it had been done deliberately, so as to save his family a world of further pain and suffering.

Could he play his part in it, as Barney pleaded with him to do? And if he did, could he live his life, seeing Vicky and her sons every day; working alongside and getting to know them and keeping secret the amazing truth about their father? Was he that strong?

It seemed a wicked, deceitful thing, and yet it was what Barney wanted, what he craved: to see his family settled and safe – the only thing that could give him peace of mind and heart.

While Barney patiently waited, Leonard continued to pace, and when at last he came to rest, his mind was made up. 'All right, Barney, if it's in my power to grant you the peace of mind you seek, I promise to do as you ask.'

Visibly overwhelmed, Barney leaned back and closed his eyes. After a moment, his eyes shining with tears, he looked up at this man, and in a strong, quiet voice he told him, 'You can't know what you've done for me, my friend. You have my deepest gratitude. Whatever happens from now on, I know I can rest easy.'

On the pretext that his milk had gone cold, Barney asked Leonard if he wouldn't mind bringing him another glass. The man readily obliged, and while he was gone but a few minutes, he returned to find the front door open and Barney loping slowly along the lane, making his way through the darkness like a wounded animal.

At first, Leonard started out after him. But then he thought better of it. 'No doubt you have things to think about,' he whispered, closing the door. 'We *all* have much to think about now.'

CHAPTER TWENTY

I T WAS THE day before the Davidson family were
due to sail. The mood in the farmhouse was
one of excitement, though it was tempered with a
sombre atmosphere. 'I never thought I'd see the
day when your father turned his back on all of us.'
Vicky had suffered sleepless nights since Barney's
departure from their lives.

Ronnie was unrepentant. 'I don't have a father
any more,' he declared angrily and, though his
heart was sore at the thought, Thomas also agreed.
Too much had happened. There had been too
many tears and too much soul-searching, and now
it was time to call an end to it.

'He's chosen his way, and now we have to choose
ours.' Going to his mother, Tom put his arms
round her shoulders and held her close. 'We'll
look after you, Mother, me and Ronnie and our
Susie.'

Having gathered the last of her things to be laid
out for packing, Susie looked up at her brother's

words. 'That's right,' she said. 'We won't let you down, not like *he's* done!' Shutting her father out of her life was the hardest thing Susie had ever had to do, but now it was done, and though there were regrets, there could be no turning back.

Ronnie looked on, morose and bitter. He had said all he wanted to say on the matter of Barney Davidson, and now he was concentrating on the exciting prospect of a long sea-journey, and at the end of it, a new life; a life in which there was no place for the man who had once been their beloved and respected father.

Although their mother assured them that everything was going to be all right and that they must not worry about her, inside she was broken up. Her love for Barney had never wavered, even through the terrible times when he had humiliated her, flaunted his women and driven her to the edge of sanity.

'Mr Maitland is coming for us early in the morning,' she reminded them. 'Make sure you pack everything you want to take. There'll be no coming back once we've gone.' The words stuck in her throat – *once we've gone.* How casual it sounded, when all the time this remarkable journey to America would be the most frightening step she would ever take, especially without her beloved Barney by her side.

'I need to get a few things in town,' she lied now. 'I won't be long. You all carry on with what you're doing and we'll go through everything when I get back.'

Ronnie walked with her to the door. 'It'll be all right, you know,' he said quietly. 'We will manage without him.'

Displaying a bright smile, she nodded. 'I know, son.'

'You still love him, don't you?'

The smile slid away and in its place came a bitter-sweet look of regret. 'Yes, I'll always love him,' she answered softly. 'And so will you . . . we all will.'

Feeling her pain, he took her in his arms.

Neither of them spoke again, and when Vicky drew away, he helped her on with her coat and opened the door for her. And when she went down the lane he stood there for what seemed an age. 'It's just the four of us now,' he murmured. 'We'll have to take care of each other.'

Vicky had already done all her shopping and was ready to leave Liverpool forever. But she had to make one last desperate attempt to recover the Barney she knew, and rebuild the marriage in which she had found such great joy all these years.

With that in mind, she made her way to Bridget's house.

~

Lucy was in the sitting room talking with Barney when she heard the knock on the door. 'I bet that's Bridget, forgotten her keys again,' she told him. Having taken Lucy's advice these past few days, Barney was rested and feeling much better.

When she opened the door, Lucy was astonished and delighted to see Vicky standing there. 'Oh, Vicky! I'm so glad you came,' she told her. 'I was going to come and see you later on, to wish you well.' She stood aside. 'Come in. Please, come in.'

Vicky made no move. 'I wondered if you might be thinking of coming out to the house again.' Her tone was unfriendly. 'But you would not have been welcome today, any more than you were yesterday. You know how we feel about Barney staying here.' Her expression hardened. 'You're the last person I would have thought to keep my husband away from us.'

Lucy was about to reply, when Barney himself appeared. 'Lucy has nothing to do with it,' he told Vicky. 'I'm staying here with a woman friend.'

Vicky looked at him, at this stranger, unshaven and thinner than she remembered, and in his eyes there was a look she did not recognise. 'It's not too late,' she told him. 'You can still make amends.'

Now, as Barney gazed down on her tired face, he realised the pain she had suffered, and all because of him. His head swelled with love and he wanted so much to take her in his arms and tell her that he adored her still, and that his family meant more to him than anything else in the world.

Instead, his expression stiffened. 'Why would I want to make amends?' he asked cruelly. 'These days I have no worries or responsibility. I'm free to do what I want, go where I want, and I don't have to break my back working to keep a family.' His smile was wicked. 'I'm shot of all that rubbish. Yes!' He even managed to swagger a bit. 'I consider myself to be a fortunate man!'

For a moment, Vicky was at a loss as to what she could say. In the end she said nothing.

Instead she walked away and Barney fell back into the hallway, his hands covering his face. 'God help me!' he cried. 'How can I do it to her? How can I be so cruel?'

Lucy took him back into the sitting room. 'It's a terrible thing you're doing,' she said shakily, 'but you've gone so far down the road and now that you've told me the truth about how ill you are, I can see how it might be the only way to protect and secure your family, even if it means sending them away, hating you.'

She held him in her arms while he sobbed. 'But you're right, Barney. Even though what you're doing is terrible, not only for them, but for you as well, I do understand.'

He turned to her then, his eyes scarred with pain. 'So am I right, Lucy?' he asked. 'Am I right to do what I'm doing?'

It was some small compensation when she smiled on him, a smile that was filled with love and sorrow, and hope. 'Yes, Barney,' she said honestly. 'You're putting yourself through the worst nightmare, and at the end of it, you'll be left without family or peace. But yes, I do believe you're doing the right thing . . . *for them.*'

Not for himself, she thought. Not for this darling man, who was making a sacrifice, the enormity of which she could not even begin to imagine.

'Thank you, Lucy, you're a good friend,' he murmured. 'So, you do think I'm doing the right thing.' His smile was content. 'That's all I needed to know.'

~

Early the following morning, Lucy walked with him to the quayside. From their vantage-point they watched as Barney's beloved family clambered aboard that great ship. To see them go without him was more crippling than anything he had ever endured. What he felt now, in that terrible moment, was the most desolate feeling in the world.

Aware that Barney must be watching them from some secret, lonely place, Leonard Maitland looked repeatedly over his shoulder for a glimpse of him. He did not spot him because, reluctant to let his family see him there, Barney was well hidden from view.

It was only when the ship began to move out, that Barney shifted his position, the better to watch as the big liner took his family further away from him. He gave a futile wave, but they didn't wave back. How could they?

From the deck, Vicky stretched her neck to see if he was there. When she could see no sign of him, she returned to her cabin and there she sobbed until she thought her heart would break.

A moment later, Susie came running into the cabin, excited about everything and, for the moment at least, seeming to forget about the man they were leaving behind.

'Come quick, come and see!' she cried. 'Mr Maitland's taking us all to the bridge!' Taking Vicky by the hand, she rushed her away.

As they ran, Vicky discreetly wiped her eyes. She was all they had now. And unlike Barney, she would not let them down.

~

Later that day, when Barney was sleeping, Lucy asked Bridget to keep an eye on him. 'I'm going up to the cottage,' she said. 'I think Barney would be more comfortable there. It's been shut up since . . . Edward Trent came back.' She still could not bring herself to say what had actually happened. Even though most days she visited the churchyard, it still seemed like some kind of a nightmare to her – not real, not possible.

Bridget agreed with her, not least because she could see for herself how desperately ill Barney was and she imagined the kind of care he might need before he was back to strength. Yet she did not know the truth, that Barney had so little time left to live.

'I expect the cottage will want airing,' she told Lucy now. 'You'll need to light a fire, and there must be an inch of dust all over. Take what you want from the cleaning cupboard, and if there's anything else you need, let me know and I'll send one of the girls up with it.'

Lucy thanked her and as an afterthought she added, 'If it's all right with you, I'd like to keep the cleaning work; I will still need the wages.'

Bridget groaned. 'Ah, sure, who else would do it if you didn't? Tillie's gone above herself with the bookkeeping, and the girls think they're God's gift, so they wouldn't dream of spoiling their delicate hands. No, the work is yours, Lucy girl, for as long as you need it. Who else would I want in me house, tell me that?'

On leaving 23, Viaduct Street, every step Lucy took reminded her of Jamie, and Edward Trent. 'I won't let that monster ruin my life any more,' she muttered, nearing the cottage. 'I'll make a new life here, with Barney, and I'll care for him as long as he needs me.'

Opening the door to the cottage, she stood looking into the tiny sitting room. Her very first and only home of her own, it had been a bright, happy place, with its chintz curtains and pretty rugs, and the little seascapes hanging on the walls.

Swallowing a sob, she flung open the curtains and let the afternoon light flood in. Bridget was right, the whole place was covered in dust. It was covered in memories too. Memories of Vicky and her family; memories of Barney when he was fit and strong and life was wonderful, and Jamie was everywhere . . . toddling around the house, holding her hand, so full of love and trust.

She wallowed in nostalgia and then she cried, and then she got on with the work. Within two hours there was a cheery fire in the grate, the furniture was shining and the place felt like home again. It was not the same as before – it could never be the same – but it was alive with memories she did not want ever to lose.

'We'll be happy here, Barney and me.' A sense of belonging came over her as she thought of that wonderful man.

'I'll look after you,' she murmured. 'We'll make use of every moment we have left. We'll walk and talk; we'll sit by the river and watch the birds come to drink, and in the evening we'll laze in the garden and watch the sunset. Such plans. Such love.'

A great sense of peace entered her soul. 'We'll be good for each other,' she told the walls. 'And maybe, even after all that's happened, life won't be so bad after all.'

Later that evening, however, Barney was not so

easily persuaded. With his heart and soul dented by the savage hand Fate had dealt him, he wanted only to curl up in a corner and die, for he could see little future without his loved ones.

'No, Lucy.' The two of them had been given the privacy of Bridget's parlour. 'I can't move into the cottage with you. What would people say? Your reputation would be in tatters.'

'I don't care about my "reputation"!' Lucy argued. 'I only care about you.'

'Lucy, sweetheart, don't think I'm not grateful because I am, but the answer has to be no. I won't do that to you.'

Lucy was persistent. 'Please, Barney.'

Barney shook his head and said not another word. Lucy knew he would not be persuaded.

When she departed some half an hour later, he went to his bed to rest, while Lucy made her sorry way home. 'I want you to need me,' she murmured as she walked away. 'I need to care for you, Barney.'

But Barney was already sleeping. He was heart-weary, and for the moment there was only one thing on his fevered mind, and that was his family. 'God help me!' he cried. 'I'll never see them again . . . oh, dear God! Dear God!' When he slept he dreamed, and his dreams were soul-destroying.

~

Over the following weeks, Lucy visited every day. She and Barney sat in Bridget's parlour and talked.

Occasionally she made him laugh and when he did, she knew it was the thinnest veneer over his hurting, but it was good to hear it all the same, and her heart soared with hope.

Maybe the doctors were wrong and Barney would get better. Maybe there was a future for the two of them – oh, not in the same way it had been with his Vicky, but in a warm, dependent way, with each filling a need for the other, because now they each knew what loneliness was.

All too soon, though, her hopes were shattered.

More and more Barney took to his bed, and though Bridget was a wonderful friend, she found it all too much. 'Much as I would like to, I can't run a business and take care of him,' she told Lucy. 'And there is no room for you here, you know that.' In a soft, caring voice she urged Lucy, 'He really needs to be where he'll get proper medical help.'

Lucy was at her wit's end. 'I won't let them take him away!' she protested. 'I couldn't bear it.'

With a plan forming in her mind, she went to Barney. 'Let me take you home with me?' she pleaded. 'Bridget has been wonderful, but now it's my turn.'

Weak though he was, Barney was still adamant. 'I know she's been wonderful, and I know she's finding things difficult just now. But I'm not totally bedridden,' he smiled, that old cheeky, mischievous smile. 'So don't write me off yet, my girl!'

'Come home with me, Barney. Let me take care of you . . . please.'

'So that's your plan, is it?' he asked. 'To "take care of me"?'

'Yes.'

'And you think I can't take care of myself?'

'I know you can, but for how long, Barney?'

Barney thought about that, because of late he had been growing weaker. 'And are you prepared to risk your reputation just to keep me from ending my days in a hospital bed?'

'You know I am!'

Barney gave that same wonderful smile. 'Then how can I refuse?'

'Oh, Barney!' Thrilled that they would be together at last, even though she did not fool herself it would be for long, Lucy threw her arms round his neck. 'You won't regret it, I promise.'

Barney laughed. 'If you don't stop suffocating me, I won't be around long enough to regret it,' he said.

Lucy let go with a look of horror. 'You mustn't say things like that,' she chided.

In serious voice he told her, 'And you mustn't pretend I'll be around forever, because I won't.'

Subdued, she nodded, the joy gone from her eyes. 'I know,' she whispered. 'But it will be so good to have you near for now.'

And so it was arranged, and surprisingly no one saw the move as anything other than Lucy looking after an old friend. Indeed, they admired her for it.

Over the coming months, Barney and Lucy spent almost every minute in each other's company. 'I'm so glad you persuaded me to come here,' he told her one night when they were seated by the fire. 'Being here with you has been a joy. I watch you sometimes when you're hanging out the washing, and I think of Vicky. I'm deeply humbled by the way you've become part of my life . . .' he smiled wryly, 'what's left of it. The doctor told me a year at the outset, maybe less, but lately I've found a new strength and it's all thanks to you, Lucy.'

'I'm glad.' Lucy had seen the way he had rallied since coming out to the countryside. 'But it's not me,' she said. 'It's the country air that suits you.'

Barney corrected her. 'It's not only that, Lucy,' he said softly. 'It's the peace and comfort I feel, just being here, with you.'

'I wish I could be Vicky,' Lucy answered. 'I wish I could get your family back for you.' If only she could restore his happiness and the family he adored, she would have given up every minute spent with him.

'You can't bring them back,' he murmured, 'and even if you could, I would not want you to. I hope they never know the way things are with me. That's why I sent them away . . . so they would find the new life they so looked forward to, and not be made to watch me suffer, or feel the anguish I feel.'

He reached out to take hold of her hand. 'You can't know how grateful I am to you,' he said. 'You've been the best friend anyone could ever have.'

'I wish you could . . .' Lucy's voice broke. 'I wish . . .'

She was about to say she wished he could love her as she loved him, but instead the tears began to fall, and before she realised, he was holding her in his arms, and when he kissed her, she could hardly believe it. 'I know what you wish for,' he soothed. 'I've seen it in your eyes and somehow I just know . . .' He cradled her face. 'You are the sweetest person, Lucy . . .'

The kiss was gentle. The lovemaking that followed was fumbled and tender, and Lucy gave herself to him with all her heart.

Afterwards, they held each other, and Lucy cried, and he comforted her. 'We belong together now, you and me,' he whispered. 'We could never be as Vicky and I were, but we're together, and that must mean something.' He smiled into her eyes. 'Do you understand what I'm saying?'

Lucy nodded. 'I think I've always loved you,' she said.

'And I've come to love you, but it's a very different love from what I feel for Vicky. Ours is a quiet, gentle love. But is it enough for you? Is it, Lucy?'

'Yes.' Lucy's heart was at peace. 'It's enough,' she whispered, nestling contentedly in his arms.

~

Over the coming weeks, Barney confounded the doctors by finding a new strength. Life was good; they took gentle strolls through the countryside; they sat long in the garden, and once a week they would go to the churchyard and lay a posy on little Jamie's resting place. But in the back of their minds there was always the fear of Barney's relapse, and the growing weakness in his limbs.

When Lucy found to her immense joy that she was carrying Barney's child, their happiness knew no bounds. But Barney was adamant. 'We can't let it be known that you're with child,' he said. 'That would only set tongues wagging. God knows they've already been busy enough, what with me being here and the two of us living under the same roof.'

It was true, Lucy thought. At first everyone had accepted that she was merely caring for Barney. But now, after months passing and the two of them being seen out together, the gossip knew no end, and it was not pleasant.

'Look, Lucy, I have a small amount of money put by. Let's move away . . . rent a place somewhere far off, where folks won't point the finger at you or the child.'

It was just an idea, but Lucy was reluctant to

leave the area. 'You need to be near the doctors, you know,' she told him. 'You don't want to be starting over with someone new who doesn't know you like Dr Lucas. You're doing all right for now. Please, Barney. don't take any risks.'

'But you will think about it, won't you, Lucy?' he urged.

And the more Lucy thought about it, the less she liked the idea of moving Barney out of the area. He had Dr Lucas, who knew him like an old friend, and the hospital close enough to have him in quickly should it be needed. He had his old friend Adam, who came to visit regularly, and others who were concerned for his health.

But none of this bothered Barney. All he wanted was that the child should not grow up where people pointed the finger.

Lucy's immediate concern, however, was for Barney, and so, for the moment she tactfully let the matter slide.

When she told Bridget about the coming baby, and Barney's wish to move away, Bridget was thrilled and horrified at the same time. 'Oh, Lucy! I think it's wonderful that you and Barney have found each other. Even though he'll always pine for Vicky, at least he's found a measure of peace and happiness with you, and as for you, well, you're positively blooming!'

She observed Lucy's bright eyes and the spring in her step when she walked and her heart went out to her. 'I've always known you loved him,' she confided. 'Anyone with half an eye could see it.'

~

Some months later, the child, a girl, was born to Lucy and Barney. They called her Mary, after Barney's late mother. 'She's beautiful,' he said, the joy written on his face. 'I know I will never see her grow to a woman but, God willing, I might be here long enough to see her as a real little person.'

And he did, for though his illness was a terrible threat hanging over all of them, he saw little Mary when she began toddling, and when she gurgled her first word it was for him alone. 'LUCY! . . .' One fine morning, Barney greeted Lucy from the garden with tears in his eyes. 'She called me . . . "Daddy".' It was one of the most beautiful moments in his life, and Lucy thanked the good Lord for His mercy in letting Barney live long enough to experience the joy of it all.

But on Mary's second birthday, Barney took a turn for the worse. Confined to his bed for a week, he had time to consider his future, and that of his daughter and Lucy. 'It's time to leave here,' he told Lucy one evening when they sat by the fire. 'I don't want Mary to know what happened to Vicky and the family. I don't want her to think me some kind of monster to have sent them away without me. I made them hate me, Lucy, I made them think I was a drunk and a womaniser. What kind of thing is that for our daughter to hear? And hear it she will, because I'm certain everyone round here must know the truth. As soon as she can understand, Mary will hear it, and I don't want that. D'you hear me, sweetheart? I don't want her to know until she's old enough to understand the tittle-tattle and to be able to forgive me for it!'

Lucy gently replied, 'I'll tell her when the time is right. I'll tell her what a courageous and wonderful thing you did for love of your family. She'll understand.'

'But I want us to move, Lucy,' he pleaded. 'I know it's the right thing for Mary.' Barney could not be dissuaded, and when she gave it more thought, Lucy could see the wisdom of his reasoning. So, she spoke to agents and even wrote away as far as Bedfordshire.

Before Mary's third birthday, the cottage was sold. The same businessman who bought Leonard's farm wanted it to extend and then sell on with a minimum of five acres of pasture-land. He had competition from another source, and between them they sent the price up, enough for Barney and Lucy to secure a sizeable property further afield.

It wasn't long before her efforts paid off. She got news of a house some two hundred miles away in a small hamlet near the town of Bedford.

The house was of some substance, a 'proud and beautiful woman past her best' was how it had been described to her. Apparently the house had stood empty for many years and had gradually fallen into disrepair. Consequently it was going cheap for anyone who had the heart to bring it back to its former glory, and if not, then it was still habitable, with no apparent structural defects.

Because the journey would be too arduous for Barney, Lucy went with Adam to view the house. She fell instantly in love with it. There was also a small house in the grounds, that too brought to its knees by neglect and the elements. 'If I move with you and Barney, I could set up a business in the village.' Adam grew excited. 'Meantime, I could work on the house. I'm not a builder, but I do know how to use my hands.' The truth was, he could not bear the thought of being so far away from Lucy in her hour of need, especially when Barney's health seemed to be failing fast.

In truth, Lucy had seen Barney's health deteriorate so much of late, that even though he fervently assured her to the contrary, she feared he might not be strong enough for the move.

On Lucy's return, she thanked Bridget who had kindly stayed at the cottage with Barney while Lucy travelled south to view the house. 'So, what did you think of it?' Bridget was excited, though she would miss her dear friend. 'Was it as grand as they said?'

Lucy described the house in detail, its strong Edwardian features, the high ceilings and panelled walls, the long windows with panoramic views across open countryside. 'It could be beautiful,' Lucy told her. 'But it does need a lot of work, though Adam has come up with an idea.'

When Adam explained it to Barney, he was thrilled. 'That would be good,' he told him. 'I've been so concerned about Lucy and the child. I could rest easy if I knew you'd be around to keep an eye on things.'

So the deal was done and plans were quickly underway.

In a few weeks' time Barney, Lucy, Adam and Mary were away to pastures new; though for Barney it would never be a long adventure; they all knew that.

PART FOUR

~

Back to January, 1952

Mary and Ben

CHAPTER TWENTY-ONE

WHILE LUCY SLEPT upstairs, Adam Chives sat by the fire in Knudsden House, his mind going back over the years, and his heart both proud and sad. 'Barney and your mother lived in that cottage together for more than two years,' he told Mary, while Ben listened. 'The doctors had given him a year at the most, but Lucy brought him a degree of peace, and after a time they made a life together.' He smiled wistfully at the memory, for he had loved Lucy as much as she loved Barney. 'To this day, she has never stopped loving him.'

'*You were born out of that love, Mary.*' Lucy's quiet voice filled the room. 'You're so much like your father. You have the same beautiful eyes and the same gentle ways.'

'Lucy!' Adam was horrified. 'Dr Nolan said you were to stay in bed.'

'Nonsense, I'm perfectly all right,' she argued. 'There is nothing wrong with me, and I'm far from in my dotage, for heaven's sake! Doctors don't know everything. I've simply been overdoing it, that's all.'

Hobbling but determined, she came into the room where she stood beside Adam, her hand resting on his shoulder and her gaze bathing every inch of her daughter's face. 'Every time I look at you, I see Barney.'

Adam looked at Mary and he, too, saw Barney in her every feature – softer and more feminine, yes – but strong and handsome too.

'I was there when you were born,' Adam said fondly. 'I waited in the sitting room with your father, while Dr Lucas was upstairs bringing you into the world. When he heard your first cry, Barney went up those stairs like he was born all over again. He took you in his arms and oh, he was such a proud, happy man.'

When Adam laid his hand over Lucy's, she hardly noticed, though deep down she derived a measure of comfort from his touch.

Deeply moved by everything she had heard, Mary went to Lucy and taking her mother gently over to the armchair, she sat her down. 'I never knew,' she said. 'I never dreamed that was the secret you kept from me all these years.' She had learned more about her father and her own background in one evening, than in all the years she was growing up. There was so much to think about. The revelation that she had three half-siblings in America, plus the sorrowful knowledge that her half-brother Jamie had died before her, was a huge shock to her system, and she knew that it would take a long, long time to come to terms with everything she had learned tonight.

Lucy was glad that Adam had chosen to tell the truth. 'It's been such a burden all this time,' she admitted now. 'But I gave my promise, d'you see? I gave my promise and I could never break it.'

Adam reassured her. 'You didn't break it,' he reminded her. 'It was me who thought Mary should be told. I've always thought it was her right to know.'

Lucy smiled. 'So you thought you'd tittle-tattle while I was laid up, did you?'

'I'm not sorry the truth is out,' he said stoutly. 'I'm only sorry if I've upset you.'

Lucy sighed. 'You did right, my old friend. You did right.' She turned to address Ben, who had been mesmerised by the whole story. 'What do you think of my darling Barney?' she asked. 'Do you think *he* was right in what he did?'

Lucy was testing him. In Ben she had seen something akin to Barney, but she needed reassuring.

Ben considered her question, and when he gave his answer, he gave it with a sense of wonder. 'In all my life, I've never heard of such a man,' he said. 'What he did was incredible. For the sake of his loved ones, he belittled and punished himself beyond endurance. I understand now what the inscription means. "He made the greatest sacrifice of all."'

Lucy asked him another question. 'In those circumstances, would you have done the same?'

Ben smiled inwardly. Already, because of what Adam had told of Lucy's strength of character, and because he had witnessed it for himself from the moment they met, Ben knew he was being tested, and he suspected her view of him would hinge on the kind of answer he gave.

'Well, young man?' As was her way, Lucy grew impatient.

Ben considered the question again, and when he answered it was as straight an answer as he could give. 'Any man would be prepared to do whatever was in his power to protect his loved ones,' he told her, 'but like a grain of sand or a drop of rain, each man is different. A man will be judged on his merit. Barney Davidson is the kind of man every other man would want to be, but I'm not Barney, nor could I ever be. All the same, I would hope that, given the same circumstances, I might find the courage and fortitude to do what he did. Other than that, I can't say.'

There was a moment while they reflected on his words, before Mary asked of her mother, 'What happened to my father? How did it end?'

Lucy gave a whimsical smile. 'It ended the way we always thought it might end,' she said. 'It was the most beautiful summer's evening. We were sitting in the garden watching the sun go down, when Barney turned to me and told me how much he had come to love me . . . but that he could never love me in the same way that he loved Vicky. She had been his life, while I had *become* his life, that's what he said.'

Lucy thought about Barney's words, just as she had done on that memorable night. 'I often wondered about that,' she said. 'I thought it a strange thing for him to say, and for a time I couldn't understand his meaning.'

Looking up at Mary, she took hold of her hand. 'After a while, I did understand. What he meant was that he and Vicky had grown together, learned together and knew each other's very thoughts . . .'

She paused. 'With me it was different. When Barney and I met, I simply became part of the family that was already Barney's; I was an outsider coming in. But then suddenly it was just the two of us, and we learned to know and love each other. Like Ben said just now, he could not be Barney . . . any more than I could be Vicky. We're all different and we touch each other's lives in different ways. But love is love, no matter which way you look at it.

'Thank you,' she said gravely, and he knew he had passed the test. 'Love *is* love, and that's what we had, me and Barney. We had such love to share, just talking and laughing and simply being together. And if I never have another day of contentment, I had more happiness in those years with Barney, than most women have in a lifetime.'

Suddenly, Lucy shivered. 'I'm tired now, my darling,' she told her daughter. 'Take me back to my bed?'

Mary took her upstairs and when Lucy was made comfortable, the young woman asked, 'Did you ever hear from Vicky, or the family?'

Lucy shook her head. 'No, never.' Fearing that Mary had too many questions to which she might not have the answers, Lucy told her, 'For reasons I hope you now understand, Barney did not want them to know about you.'

'So I have two brothers and a sister I may never see?' Though Mary had been deeply touched by the story of her father, she felt cheated somehow, filled with all kinds of regrets, regrets that she had never known him, and regrets that she was never told the truth. But now she knew it all, and it was as though a cloud was lifted from over her head. But what of the rest of her family?

'Will I ever meet them – Thomas and Ronnie, and my sister Susie?'

Lucy was not ready for this. 'Leave me now, love,' she said. 'Let me sleep.'

Quietly, Mary left. Tomorrow, when her mother was rested, she would ask again. And she would keep on asking, until Lucy agreed to reunite her with the family she had never known.

~

It was much later that Adam tapped on Lucy's bedroom door to check on her. Ben had gone home and Mary was in bed. Lucy herself was sitting up in bed, awake but at peace with herself.

'Ben is so much like Barney,' Lucy murmured. She had Barney strong in her mind tonight.

'Tell me something,' Adam asked. 'Do you think you will ever contact Vicky?'

'I made a promise never to tell them,' she sighed. 'You made that same promise.'

'I know, and I've always regretted it. I kept it when Barney was alive, and I've kept it all these years. I didn't even mention it when informing Mr Maitland of his death, as Barney requested in his last hours. But I've never felt comfortable about it, Lucy. I think they have a right to know why he did what he did, the same as Mary had a right to know. God only knows how they have suffered all these years.'

When she remained silent, he asked her again. '*Will* you tell them, Lucy? *Will* you contact Vicky?'

Unable to answer such a momentous question, Lucy thought fleetingly of her daughter and Ben, and her heart was glad. There was magic happening between those two.

'I love you, Lucy.' Adam's voice was so close to her ear, she felt his warm breath against her skin.

'I know.' She turned to smile on him. 'I've always known.'

'You never said.'

'Because there would have been no point and I might have hurt your feelings. You see, I didn't love you back.'

'Do you love me back now?'

'I think so.' She turned away. 'You realise I could never love you in the same way I loved Barney?'

'Will you marry me?'

'We're too long in the tooth for that nonsense,' she laughed. But secretly she felt quite excited. She had had two children by two very different men – one full of darkness and one full of light – and yet had never been married. Maybe that was the next experience that Fate had in store for her.

For now, the moment passed and they were quiet again.

'When you get in touch with Vicky,' Adam persisted, 'will you tell her what Barney did for them?' Taking Lucy by the shoulders, he turned her round to face him. 'I know Leonard Maitland gave you his address. You can get in touch if you want to,' he said. 'They won't have moved from the farm.'

Lucy patted the tip of her nose in a gesture of secrecy. 'I might – and I might not.' Her smile grew mischievous. 'But that's another story altogether, don't you think?'

Adam knew that when Lucy was in this strange mood of hers, there was no reasoning with her. He kissed her then – not the kiss of a lover, but the kiss of someone who knew her well. 'Good night, Lucy.' Smiling resignedly, he shook his head. 'Sleep tight.'

For a while after he'd gone, she continued to gaze at the little photograph still lying on the eiderdown. It was the only picture she had of Barney, and it was her treasure. Taken on the day he took delivery of his new tractor, Barney stood beside it, a proud man, while Leonard Maitland recorded the moment forever.

Taking the photograph into her hands and looking down, she let herself be drawn back over the years, to summertimes and harvests, and picnics and laughter, when Jamie was always at her side and in her heart. Moving pictures in her mind; warm and real in her heart. They were glorious times with the Davidson family, all together and not a cloud in their sky.

'Happy days,' she murmured. 'But it's not the end, my darlings.'

Replacing the photograph, she glanced again towards the window, where outside, new love was beginning.

~

'Your father's story is the most remarkable I've ever heard.' Ben had been deeply shaken by the turn of this night's events, and if he lived to be a hundred, he would never forget this night nor the man who was Barney Davidson.

'I never knew,' Mary answered thoughtfully. 'All these years and I never knew.'

'Your mother said you looked like him.' Ben observed her small pretty face, and he had an urge to take her in his arms. 'You have such a calmness about you, I can imagine you must also have inherited some of his character traits as well.'

Mary smiled. 'I hope so.'

'I'm glad we met.' Reaching out he took hold of her hand, and to his delight she did not draw it away. 'Do you think we might have a future together, you and me?'

Thrilled by his remark, her answer was to lean forward and kiss him. She looked into those dark, sincere eyes and at the strong set of his jaw and that air of confidence about him, and she thought of all that had passed long ago.

But that was not her life. This was her life, hers and Ben's, and suddenly, when she felt his loving arms about her, she knew it was where she belonged, with this man whom she hardly knew, and yet she felt as though she had known him forever.

'You still haven't answered me, Mary.' His voice was soft in her ear. 'You haven't said if you think we might have a future together?'

Turning her head, she looked up at him. 'Yes,' her smile was content, 'I really believe we might.'

Lucy saw it all. She saw them kiss, and she saw the tenderness in his embrace, and it made her think of Barney. 'I hope you find happiness together,' she whispered.

Wearied and content, Lucy climbed into bed. For a while she lay awake, her mind back there where it all took place. It had been an amazing adventure. But it was not yet over.

For now, though, it was time to reflect, and be thankful.

Read on for an exclusive peek of Josephine Cox's new novel *Journey's End*, which follows the fortunes of the characters from *The Journey*, and is available in hardback in February 2006.

~

Late March 1954

The Telling

SHE WOKE WITH a cry. It was the same as before, the same place, the same faces, the same jolt of terror; real in her dream, real in her life. Would it never leave her be?

The sweat dripping down her temples and her whole body trembling, she clambered out of bed and went to the window, where for a moment she stood, regaining her composure and collecting her senses.

Drawing back the curtains, she peered into the darkness, thick and impenetrable, like the deepest recesses of her mind.

'Dear God, give me the courage to do what's right.' Her quiet whisper betrayed the fear she had borne for almost a lifetime. The questions never went away. Should she tell? Would it destroy lives and minds? Would they hate her or, as she desperately hoped, would they thank her? But then, why would they thank her when the news she had to tell was so unbearably cruel?

Maybe it would be better if the truth was never told. Yet that would be the coward's way out, and though she might be many things, Lucy Baker was no coward.

She glanced at the clock. It was five minutes past three; another day beginning. Taking her robe from the back of the chair, she slipped into it and sat on the edge of the bed where she remained for a time. She sighed, a long, broken sigh that betrayed the torment inside her. 'Oh my dearest Barney, my joy, my life.' There was a murmuring of guilt but never regret. 'I loved you then . . .' she smiled a bittersweet smile '. . . I love you still.'

Barney had been her only love but it was a love all-consuming, all powerful. There was no way to describe how much she missed him. No words. Only memories.

The smile slipped away. While Barney had brought her joy, Edward Trent had brought her torment.

'Edward Trent – monster!' Her mouth curled with loathing, she spat out his name as though it was tainted with poison. His wickedness had caused such pain. She would carry the burden of it for the rest of her days.

Lucy was no stranger to nightmares. There were times when she when she would wake, terrified and sobbing, reliving the night when Edward Trent had taken away her only reason for living.

In the years that followed, he had haunted her every waking and sleeping hour. In the daytime she would be in the middle of a mundane task, like washing the dishes or drawing the curtains, and suddenly he was gnawing at her mind until she could hardly think straight. Then at night came the dreams which left her breathless and shaking. She had grown used to them. Like the hatred, they had become part of her life.

In the dreams it was always the same; the darkness, the water, and the chase . . . that haunting, unforgettable chase, ending in such tragedy.

This time though, the dream was different. There was no frantic chase, no sound of tumbling water as it forced and fought its way downstream, lapping at her ankles and tugging at her balance; there wasn't even the soul-destroying sound of her child crying. This dream was different, like nothing she had ever experienced.

She had seen only his face, that swarthy, oddly handsome face, the curve of his mouth frozen in a cold, easy smile. Unlike before, he was not threatening her nor was he reaching out. There was only the smile. And those eyes, mesmerising, chilling to the soul. The silence, meanwhile, eerie and pervading.

'Take a hold of yourself, Lucy!' Grabbing the crumpled corner of the bed-sheet, she wiped the sweat from her face. 'It was just a dream. He can't hurt you any more.' So many times she had tried to convince herself of that. Even so, the fear never went away.

~

In the adjoining room, in that lazy space between sleeping and waking, Mary lay in her bed and listened. She heard her mother open her curtains, and she heard the soft, muffled footsteps as they paced the floor. She did not think about going in. She knew her mother would not want that. Instead, for the next hour, she lay in her bed and waited, the only sound the ticking of the clock.

This was not the first time she had heard her mother agitated, unable to sleep. The first time was many years ago, when she was just a child. The sound of her mother sobbing had disturbed her deeply. Mary had gone to comfort her but her mother sent her away. Since then, whenever she heard her mother fretful and heartbroken in the night, Mary would lie in her bed, desperately hoping it would not be too long before her mother went back to sleep – as she always did.

Mary had known there was something disturbing in her mother's past; some fearful thing that tormented and touched all of their lives in some way – herself, her mother and Adam, that dear kind man who had always been there to protect them.

Only recently, Adam had taken it upon himself

to tell the truth of what had happened all those years ago. In the telling, he had misguidedly betrayed Lucy's trust and broken his vow to his old friend Barney. At the time he believed it was for the best. Now, however, he was not so sure.

Mary was shaken to the roots by the story he had told. Even now it was not ended. There were others who had to know the truth. The ones who had got away; the ones who had never known the truth of Barney's sacrifice.

In Mary's far-off memories, she recalled her father, a special kind of man, a man frail in body but powerful in spirit. She recalled how he would sit her on his knee and create magic through his vivid fairytale. He made her laugh with his comical mimickry, and sometimes when she might wake crying, he would hold her up to the window and show her the stars and describe the beauty and wonder of a world they lived in. He told her she must never be afraid because there would always be someone looking over her.

She loved him so much, and then he was gone and their lives would never be the same again.

~

A while later, when she was satisfied that her mother was sleeping, Mary turned over and relaxed. Tomorrow, there would be no mention of this night. They would smile and chat and talk of everything else and it would be as though the nightmares had never happened. Because that was how Lucy wanted it.

~

By half past eight, Lucy was out of her bed, washed and dressed and sprucing herself up in the mirror. 'Not bad for an old woman if I say so myself!' Laying down the hairbrush, she ran her hands through her short cap of greying hair, teased out a few stray curls and thought how if it wasn't for the occasional moment of forgetfulness and the odd, embarrassing stumble, she could maybe pass for a much younger woman.

Sighing wistfully, she shook her head. 'Wish all you like, Lucy Baker,' she chided herself, 'it won't change the fact that you're past your prime so stop fancying yourself in the mirror. Before you know it, the doctor will be here . . .' She frowned. '. . . not that you need him because you don't. But it makes him feel wanted, so shift yourself and be quick about it.'

'Still, you look more human now,' she chuckled. 'At least you won't frighten the doctor when he eventually comes.' She observed her image in the mirror. Still willowy and upright, she did her best to keep what was left of her looks, but had not yet regained her strength since stumbling in the churchyard over a year ago.

The skin was not alive as it used to be and there appeared to be more of in which hung in little loose swathes around her neck and there were deep wrinkles round her eyes and mouth. But the features were still there: that small, straight nose and heart-shaped face, and the blue eyes were still bright as ever. 'You were never a beauty,' she murmured. 'But you're better off than most women because even though it was for a cruelly short time you had the love of a man like Barney.'

Thoughts of Barney overwhelmed her again. 'He never loved you like he loved her but you always knew that. In the end you may have filled his heart but it was Vicki who filled his soul.'

Reaching down to lift the photo frame from the dresser, she gazed down on herself and Barney and the infant girl in his arms. It was a cherished picture, taken only a few months before Barney was lost to her and, even then, when the illness ravaged him, and his pain was frequently unbearable, the goodness of the man and his absolute joy of life shone out of his face, a still handsome face for all that.

Lucy choked back a sob. 'We had so little time together, you and me, Barney. And yet I thank God for every second we had.' They had shared everything: the anguish of seeing his wife and children leave for America; the guilt and tears afterwards; the companionship that followed which grew into a kind of uneasy contentment; the sheer joy and pride when Mary was born to them.

Through all the ups and downs of every passing

day they never forgot the others: Leonard, a man who crossed continents knowing the truth but for ever forsaking peace of mind, while Vicki and the children had sailed with him, never knowing the price Barney had paid for their new lives in America.

The loud sputtering of a car engine brought her hurrying to the window as well as back to the present. The brightness of the spring day was startling, the skies above blue and cloudless. For late March, it was unusually warm.

'Adam, what's going on?'

Covered in muck and oil, Adam was standing before the car. He had the bonnet up and the starter handle lodged into position.

'Adam, what's wrong?' Lucy had been considering changing the old car but had not got round to it yet.

'The damned thing's been playing up again,' he groaned, 'and now it's completely given up the ghost.' He gave a long weary sigh. 'I've done what can but I reckon she'll need a new engine.' Diving his head under the bonnet, he fiddled with a few nuts and bolts before returning to swing the handle for the umpteenth time. There was a violent shuddering and sputtering and then a shout of victory when he thought he'd done the trick. But then after a curious little dance, the engine fell silent. 'It's no good.' Defeated, he gave a shake of the head and sighed. 'There's no spark at all now.'

Lucy called him, 'Leave it! Come inside. Come on!'

His heart warmed by the invitation, Adam waved up to her, 'I'll be there in a minute.'

Closing the window, Lucy smiled to herself. 'No spark 'eh? Let's hope the day never comes when they say that about Lucy Baker!' She went down the stairs, chuckling to herself. Life might be a bit more of a challenge these days and her health was not as robust as she would have liked but, by God, she wasn't done yet. Not by any means!

By the time Adam showed his face at the kitchen door, both Lucy and Mary were seated at the table, Lucy enjoying her fried eggs and bacon and Mary toying with her scrambled eggs.

'Look at the state of you!' she said, pointing to Adam's mucky hands and face. 'Have you had your breakfast yet?'

'Not yet, no.' Because the car had been playing up the previous day, he'd got out of bed early this morning to work on the engine. 'There was no time for breakfast,' he explained. 'Two hours I messed about with that blessed machine this morning.' He groaned. 'I honestly thought I'd fixed it.'

'Never mind that now. Get cleaned up while I cook you some breakfast.'

Lucy felt as though she had known him for ever.

A loyal friend, Adam had been part of her life with Barney and, after Barney was gone, he had seen her through a bad time and remained ever close. Lucy had often wondered why he had never married until some time ago he had confessed to her that she had always been the only woman he had ever truly loved.

Time and again, Adam had asked her to be his wife and time and again she had gently refused. But knowing how persistent he was, Lucy was in no doubt that some time in the not too distant future he was bound to try again.

~

Later, after the doctor had left, Adam came in through the back door.

'Is the car alright?' Lucy asked.

'Running like silk now.'

'So you'll be away on your errands now, will you?'

'That was the plan,' he answered quietly. 'Go into Bedford and collect the curtains you ordered, then the post office and the bakers on the way back.'

'How long will you be?'

'I can't say for certain.' Sensing her loneliness, he asked, 'Do you want to come with me?'

Lucy shook her head. 'No.'

He knew Lucy's every mood, every regret, and he knew at this moment he should not leave her alone with her memories.

'Look, Lucy, there's nothing so urgent it can't

wait till later,' he said softly. 'I'll keep you company for a while, if you want me to, that is?'

The tears moist in her eyes, Lucy looked up at him with a smile. 'Thank you, Adam, I'd like that.' No one alive knew her better than Adam, she thought fondly.

Relief flooded through him. When Lucy was sad, he was sad. 'Tea then?'

Lucy nodded and away he went, content to be with her, even if only as a friend though, one day, God willing, she might come to see him through more loving eyes.

A short time later he returned with two piping hot cups of tea. 'Now then . . .' He settled himself in the chair opposite. 'What's wrong? And don't say there's nothing wrong because I know you too well. You're thinking of Barney, aren't you?'

Drawing a deep sigh, Lucy place her cup on the side table. 'I can't stop wondering about Barney's family – his other family, I mean . . . Vicki and the children. Lately I can't seem to get them out of my mind, wondering where they are, if they're safe, if they're happy.' She gave a nervous smile. 'I won't always be here, Adam – I'm getting old. How could I go to my maker with such a weight of secrets on my heart?'

'I understand how you feel, because I, too, often think about them. To tell you the truth though, Lucy, I'm not sure if it would be kinder for them to know how it all came about or whether the truth would ruin what small contentment they may have found.'

Adam's concerns echoed in Lucy's heart. 'Like I said, I'm getting old and time is rushing by. I must soon decide one way or the other.'

The very thought of not having her around filled him with dread. 'Don't talk as though you're old and decrepit because you're not,' he urged. 'God willing, you and I have many more years to enjoy before our time comes.'

For a moment, Lucy reflected on his words; as always Adam had brought a kind of calmness to her heart. 'I hope so,' she whispered. 'But I can't shut out the past and I can't see a way forward.'

'All I'm saying is don't torment yourself. For all our sakes, try and let it rest. For now at least. But there's one thing I would like you to do . . . Lucy, will you let me take you back?'

'Back?' She knew what he meant but could not bring herself to acknowledge it. 'What do you mean?'

He hesitated. 'Back there . . . to Jamie.' Before she could protest he went on, 'For your own peace of mind, you must go back. Do you think I don't know how it haunts you? Sometimes, when your mind wanders, I know you're thinking of him . . . reliving that night, remembering every little detail. I feel your pain, Lucy. You need to go there.'

Pausing a moment he then went on in a softer tone, 'I know how, deep down, you long to go back. Let me take you, Lucy. Please! Let me do that much for you at least?'

'I can't!'

'Why not?'

For a long moment, Lucy lapsed into silence, her mind alive with the past. Then, in a fearful voice, she asked, 'What do you think happened to Edward Trent?'

Adam snorted with disgust. 'We can only hope and pray he's already got his comeuppance. A man like that must incur enemies and hatred wherever he goes.'

'Why do you think they never caught him after . . . after he . . .' Her voice broke.

'Because like all rats he know the dark places where he can scurry away and hide.'

'Do you think he's still alive?'

Adam shook his head. 'Who knows? If there's any justice, he'll be rotting in the fires of Hell where he belongs.'

'You're right, Adam.' Suddenly she knew what she must do. 'It's the only thing. I will go back.' She looked up to the skies, a deep yearning for peace flooding her heart. 'I'll face the demons.'

It would not be easy, she knew that. It had been a lifetime since she had travelled that particular road. When she left that familiar and much-loved place, she left behind a wealth of laughter, sun-filled days and happiness. The pain she took with her; it had never gone far away.

Her train of thought turned back to the monster who had snuffed out her baby boy's life.

Even now, after all these years, she could not think of him without loathing. She had no idea where he was. After the tragedy he fled and had not been heard of again. Many times over the years, Lucy prayed that somehow he had been made to pay for the evil thing he had done. In the beginning, the hatred had eaten in to her very soul but now, as the years caught up with her, she had learned to live with it, albeit not very far under the surface.

Now she needed to put things right before it was too late – for herself, for Jamie, for Barney and for Vicki and the children.

'I need to tell it all, to try and bring a measure of peace to everyone. First, though, there is someone I need to see.'

CHATTERBOX
The Josephine Cox Newsletter

If you would like to know more about Josephine Cox, and receive regular updates, just send a postcard to the address below and automatically register to receive Chatterbox, Josephine's free newsletter. The newsletter is packed with competitions and exclusive Josephine Cox gifts, plus news and views from other fans.

Chatterbox
Freepost
PAM 6429
HarperCollins Publishers
77–85 Fulham Palace Road
Hammersmith
London
W6 8BR

Alternatively, you can e-mail chatterbox@ harpercollins.co.uk to register for the newsletter.

Also visit Josephine's website – www.josephine cox.co.uk – for more news.